Praise for *All Things*

'**Haunting** . . . Brundage exposes the mind of the killer in slow and forensic detail' Joan Smith, *Sunday Times*

'A portrait of a dysfunctional marriage with supernatural shadowing . . . so **beautifully written**, so full of neat observations and telling details' John O'Connell *Guardian*

'What, at first, seems to be a crime novel is much more, working on several levels. It's the painful story of a marriage that should never have happened . . . Furthermore, it's a chilling portrait of a pyschopathic killer. **Not so much a whodunnit as a whydunnit,** this richly imagined, sprawling novel contains scalpel-sharp dissections of the characters and their increasingly complex relationships' Fanny Blake, *Daily Mail*

'A book as lyrically written, frequently shocking and immensely moving as Elizabeth Brundage's *All Things Cease to Appear* transcends categorization . . . Reading this book is **at once wrenching and exhilarating** thanks to Ms. Brundage's prose, which can make you gasp in astonishment or break your heart with a single line' *Wall Street Journal*

'A marriage, a sociopath, a family destroyed by the economy, the things we do for love – all finely drawn . . . In the end, justice is done and redemption found though not as one might expect, which makes the book **all

'**Exquisitely gut-churning** . . . Brundage's elegant exploration of motive—in all its directions—sets this book apart . . . Paranormal activity hangs in the atmosphere [and] Brundage takes us compellingly inside the perverse machinations of a violently narcissistic mind [that] recalls Patricia Highsmith's talented Mr. Ripley . . . **Brundage's language is the real draw**, with her vivid portraits of spouses on opposite sides of a brutal abyss' *Time*

'Superb . . . think **a more literary, and feminist,** *Gone Girl*. As the seemingly perfect marriage at its core reminds us, the most lethal deceptions are the stories we tell ourselves' *Vogue*

'A **beautifully written treat** . . . as much a disturbing portrait of family and town life as it is a provocative mystery' *Elle*

'Ghosts, murder, a terrifying psychotic who seems normal, and **beautiful writing. Loved it**' Stephen King

'At once **high art and a spellbinding thriller**, this is a book of many wonders, including **a character as creepily sinister as any created by Patricia Highsmith**' Beverly Lowry

'I bloody loved this. I could have taken weeks over it, lingering on the harmony and beauty of her language and the creeping delicacy of what was going on—but the plot and the people pull you in. **It's an iceberg in disguise.** Beneath the daisies and farmhouses, the drinks parties and local dramas something **grand, tense and terrifying** is shifting, between men and women, between townies and newcomers, between adults and children. And then a crack shoots through – unexpected light, the clarity of hatred, inevitability . . . **A lot of people will be getting this for their birthdays this year**' Louisa Young

'Brundage's brilliant new novel is as terrifyingly unsettling—and as beautiful—as cracking ice over a raging river. Part murder mystery, part ghost story, it's also a profound look at how past guilt informs the present, how what we yearn for is not always what we get, and how it's not only houses that can be haunted, but people as well. **One of the most ambitious, original and gorgeously written novels that I've ever read—and been unable to forget**' Caroline Leavitt

'**A riveting ghost story, psychological thriller, and literary page turner**. It's also the story of four women: Ella, Catherine, Justine, and Willis. With masterful skill and brilliant empathy, Brundage brings each of them to vivid and remarkable life. At its heart, this is a story about women's grit and courage, will and intelligence. It's a powerful and beautiful novel' Kate Christensen

'Brundage's **searing, intricate novel epitomizes the best of the literary thriller,** marrying gripping drama with impeccably crafted prose, characterizations, and imagery . . . **Succeeding as murder mystery, ghost tale, family drama, and love story,** her novel is both tragic and transcendent' *Publisher's Weekly*

'A dynamic portrait of a young woman coming into her own [and] of a marriage in free fall. . . . **It rises to great literary heights** and promises a soaring mix of mysticism' *Booklist*

'Mesmerising . . . This isn't a whodunit—the mystery's easy enough to solve. Instead, it's a psychological portrait of a whole community . . . [the] novel is **compelling, as coldly beautiful as it is unsettling**. It's haunting, in the best possibly way'
Crime Scene

Elizabeth Brundage graduated from Hampshire College, attended the NYU film school, was a screenwriting fellow at the American Film Institute in Los Angeles, and received an M.F.A. as well as a James Michener Award from the University of Iowa's Writers' Workshop. She has taught at a variety of colleges and universities, most recently at Skidmore College as a visiting writer in residence. She lives near Albany in upstate New York.

All Things Cease
to Appear

✳

Elizabeth Brundage

riverrun

First published in USA in 2016 by Knopf.
First published in Great Britain in 2016 by riverrun.
This paperback edition published in 2017 by

riverrun

A imprint of

Quercus Editions Limited
Carmelite House
50 Victoria Embankment
London EC4Y 0DZ

An Hachette UK company

A CIP catalogue record for this book is available
from the British Library

Paperback ISBN 978 1 78429 689 6
Ebook ISBN 978 1 78429 688 9

10 9 8 7 6 5 4 3 2 1

Printed and bound in Great Britain by Clays Ltd, St Ives plc *for Joan and Dorothy*

... she who burns with youth and knows no fixed lot, is bound
In spells of law to one she loathes.

—WILLIAM BLAKE, *Visions of the Daughters of Albion*

Beauty is finite; the sublime is infinite.

—IMMANUEL KANT

Beneath those stars is a universe of gliding monsters.

—HERMAN MELVILLE

All Things Cease to Appear

The Hale Farm

THIS IS the Hale farm.

Here is the old milking barn, the dark opening that says, *Find me*.

This is the weathervane, the woodpile.

Here is the house, noisy with stories.

It is early. The hawk winds down through the open sky. A thin blue feather turns through the air. The air is cold, bright. The house is silent, the kitchen, the blue velvet couch, the small white teacup.

Always the farm sings for us, its lost families, its soldiers and wives. During the war, when they came with their bayonets, forcing their way in, their muddy boots on the stairs. Patriots. Gangsters. Husbands. Fathers. They slept in the cold beds. They raided the cellar for jars of canned peaches and sugar beets. They made great fires in the field, the flames twisting, snapping up to the heavens. Fires that laughed. Their warm faces glowing and their hands warm in their pockets. They roasted pig and pulled the sweet pink meat from the bone. After, they sucked the fat from their fingers, the taste familiar, strange.

Then there were others—there have been many—who have taken, who have stripped and pillaged. Even the copper pipes, the delft tiles. Whatever they could, they took. Leaving just the walls, the bare floors. The beating heart in the cellar.

We wait. We are patient. We wait for news. We wait to be told. The wind is trying to tell us. The trees shift. It is the end of something; we can sense it. Soon we will know.

Part 1

February 23, 1979

AGAIN, it was snowing. Half past five in the afternoon. Almost dark. She had just laid out their plates when the dogs started barking.

Her husband set down his fork and knife, none too pleased to have his supper interrupted. What's that now?

June Pratt pulled aside the curtain and saw their neighbor. He was standing there in the snow, holding the child, her feet bare, neither of them in coats. From the looks of it, the little girl was in her pajamas. It's George Clare, she said.

What's he selling?

I wonder. I don't see a car. They must've come on foot.

Awful cold out. You better see what he wants.

She let them in with the cold. He stood before her, holding the child out like an offering.

It's my wife. She's—

Momma hurt, the child cried.

June didn't have children of her own, but she had raised dogs her whole life and saw the same dark knowing in the child's eyes that confirmed what all animals understood, that the world was full of evil and beyond comprehension.

You'd better call the police, she told her husband. Something's happened to his wife.

Joe pulled off his napkin and went to the phone.

Let's go find you some socks, she said, and took the child from her father and carried her down the hall to the bedroom where she set her on the bed. Earlier that afternoon, she had laid her freshly laundered socks over the radiator, and she took a pair now and pushed the warm wool over the child's feet, thinking that if the child were hers she'd love her better.

They were the Clares. They had bought the Hale place that summer, and now winter had come and there were just the two houses on the road and she hadn't seen them much. Sometimes in the morning she would. Either when he raced past in his little car to the college. Or when the wife took the child out of doors. Sometimes, at night, when June walked the dogs, you could see inside their house. She could see them having supper, the little girl between them at the table, the woman getting up and sitting down and getting up again.

With the snow, it took over a half-hour for the sheriff to arrive. June was vaguely aware, as women often are of men who desire them, that Travis Lawton, who had been her classmate in high school, found her attractive. That was of no consequence now, but you don't easily forget the people you grew up with, and she made a point of listening carefully to him, and acknowledged his kindness to George, even though there was the possibility, in her own mind at least, that the bad thing that had happened to his wife might have been his own doing.

HE WAS THINKING of Emerson, *the terrible aristocracy that is in Nature.* Because there were things in this world you couldn't control. And because even now he was thinking of her. Even now, with his wife lying dead in that house.

He could hear Joe Pratt on the phone.

George waited on the green couch, shaking a little. Their house smelled like dogs and he could hear them barking out back in their pens. He wondered how they could stand it. He stared at the wide boards, a funk of mildew coming up from the cellar. He could feel it in the back of his throat. He coughed.

They're on their way, Pratt said from the kitchen.

George nodded.

Down the hall, June Pratt was talking to his daughter with the sweet tone people use on children and he was grateful for it, so much so that his eyes teared a little. She was known for taking in strays. He'd see her walking the road with the motley pack at her side, a middle-aged woman in a red kerchief, frowning at the ground.

After a while, he couldn't say how long, a car pulled up.

Here they are now, Pratt said.

It was Travis Lawton who came in. George, he said, but didn't shake his hand.

Hello, Travis.

Chosen was a small town and they were acquaintances of a sort. He knew Lawton had gone to RPI and had come back out here to be sheriff, and it always struck George that for an educated man he was pretty shallow. But then George wasn't the best judge of character and, as he was continually reminded by a coterie of concerned individuals, his opinion didn't amount to much. George and his wife were newcomers. The locals took at least a hundred years to accept the fact that somebody else was living in a house that had, for generations, belonged to a single family whose sob stories were now part of the local mythology. He didn't know these people and they certainly didn't know him, but in those few minutes, as he stood there in the Pratts' living room in his wrinkled khakis and crooked tie, with a distant, watery look in his eyes that could easily be construed as madness, all their suspicions were confirmed.

Let's go take a look, Lawton said.

They left Franny with the Pratts and went up the road, him and Lawton and Lawton's undersheriff, Wiley Burke. It was dark now. They walked with grave purpose, a brutal chill under their feet.

The house sat there grinning.

They stood a minute looking up at it and then went in through the screened porch, a clutter of snowshoes and tennis rackets and wayward leaves, to the kitchen door. He showed Lawton the broken glass. They climbed the stairs in their dirty boots. The door to their bedroom was shut; he couldn't remember shutting it. He guessed that he had.

I can't go in there, he told the sheriff.

All right. Lawton touched his shoulder in a fatherly way. You stay right here.

Lawton and his partner pushed through the door. Faintly, he heard sirens. Their shrill cries made him weak.

He waited in the hall, trying not to move. Then Lawton came out, bracing himself against the doorjamb. He looked at George warily. That your ax?

George nodded. From the barn.

In Lawton's unmarked car they drove into town on dark, slippery roads, the chains on the tires grinding through the snow. He sat with his daughter behind the mesh divider. It was a satellite office across from the old railroad depot, set up in a building that might have once been a school. The walls were a soiled yellow, framed out in mahogany trim, and the old iron radiators hissed with heat. A woman from the department brought Franny over to the snack machine and gave her some quarters from a plastic bag and lifted her up to put them in the slot, then put her down again. Now watch, the woman said. She pulled the lever and a package of cookies tumbled out. Go ahead, those are for you.

Franny looked up at George for approval. It's okay, honey. You can have the cookies.

The woman held open the plastic flap at the bottom of the machine. Go on and reach in there, it don't bite. Franny reached into the darkness of the machine to retrieve the cookies and smiled, proud of herself.

Lawton crouched down in front of her. Here, let me help you, sweetheart. He took the package and opened it and handed it back to her, and they all watched her fish out a cookie and eat it. Lawton said, I bet those are good.

Franny chewed.

I bet you're hungry, too.

She put another cookie in her mouth.

Did you get any breakfast this morning? I had a bowl of cornflakes. What'd you have?

Crackers.

Is that so?

With jelly.

What your momma have for breakfast, Franny?

She looked at Lawton with surprise. Momma sick.

What's wrong with your momma?

Momma *sick*.

It's hard when your momma's sick, isn't it?

She turned the cellophane package over, and a dusting of brown crumbs spilled out through her fingers.

Did anybody come to the house today?

Franny ignored him and crinkled the wrapper, occupied by the sound it made between her fingers.

Franny? The sheriff is talking to you.

She looked up at George.

Did Cole come?

She nodded.

Lawton said, Cole Hale?

He sits for us sometimes, George said.

Was it Cole? Are you sure?

Franny's lower lip began to tremble and tears ran down her cheeks.

She just told you it was, George said. He picked her up, annoyed, and held her tightly. I think that's enough questions for now.

Do you want to try this again, Franny? The woman held up the bag of quarters.

Franny blinked her wet eyes and wriggled out of his arms. I want to do it.

We'll be fine. I've got a whole lot of change here. And we've got a TV in there.

They let him call his parents. He used a pay phone in the hall and called collect. His mother made him repeat the news. He stood there under the green lights with the words marching out.

They're driving up, he told Lawton.

All right. We can go in here.

Lawton ushered him into a small room with tall black windows; he could see his reflection in the glass and noted his hunched posture, his wrinkled clothes. The room smelled of dirt and cigarettes and something else, maybe misery.

Take a seat, George, I'll be right back.

He sat down at the table. With the door shut he felt cut off from every-thing, waiting there with his own reflection. He could hear the train clat-tering through town, slow and loud. He looked at the clock; it was just after seven.

The door opened, and Lawton backed into the room with two cups of coffee, a file pinched under his arm. Thought you could use some of this. He set the coffee down and tossed out some sugar packets. You take milk?

George shook his head. This is fine. Thanks.

The sheriff sat down, opened the file and took a sip of the hot coffee, holding the rim of the cup carefully between his fingers. He pulled a pair of bifocals out of his shirt pocket and wiped the lenses with a napkin, then held them up to the light and wiped them again and slipped them on. I want you to know how sorry I am about Catherine.

George only nodded.

The phone rang, and Lawton took the call and made some notes on his pad. George put his mind to just sitting there in the chair, resting one hand over the other in his lap. In a vague sort of reverie he thought of Rembrandt. Again, he looked at his reflection in the window and decided that, for someone in his situation, he didn't look too bad. He pushed the hair off his forehead and sat back in the chair and glanced around the small room. The walls were gray, the color of gruel. At one time he had prided himself on his instinct for color. One summer, back in college, he'd interned at the Clark with Walt Jennings, a color specialist. He'd rented a house on the Knolls and had fallen in love with a girl who lived in the old Victorian across the street, although they'd never once spoken. All that summer she was reading *Ulysses,* and he remembered now how she'd come out on her terrace in her bikini and lie on the chaise. She'd read for five minutes, then lay the fat book on her stomach and lift her face to the sun.

Lawton hung up. We don't get many robberies out there. Usually just bored teenagers looking for booze. You have any enemies, George?

None that I know of.

What about your wife?

No. Everyone loved my wife.

Somebody didn't.

He thought of the girl, her sad, dark eyes. I don't know anyone who would do this.

Lawton looked at him but said nothing, and a long minute passed.

I need to go soon. Franny needs her supper.

There's lots of stuff in that machine.

George picked up the paper cup and could feel the heat in his fingers. The coffee was bitter and still hot enough to burn his tongue. Lawton took out a pack of Chesterfields. You want one of these?

Quit.

So did I. He lit a cigarette with a brass lighter, dragged on it deeply and blew out the smoke. You still over at the college?

George nodded.

What time you get home this afternoon?

Around five, a few minutes before.

Lawton made another note. So you pull up to your house, and then what?

George described how he'd parked in the garage and gone into the house. I knew something was wrong when I saw the glass. Then I went upstairs and found her. She was—he coughed. Just lying there in her nightgown. With that—he stopped. He couldn't say it.

Lawton dropped the cigarette in his coffee cup and tossed it into the wastebasket. Let's go back a minute. Walk me through the kitchen to the stairs—did you notice anything? Anything unusual?

Her pocketbook was sort of dumped out, her wallet. I don't know what was in it. There were coins everywhere. They might've gotten some of it.

How much cash would she keep in her wallet?

It's hard to say. Grocery money, not much more.

Not enough, likely. That's what my wife tells me. But you know how women are. They never know what they have. He gazed at George over his bifocals.

Like I said, it was probably just grocery money.

All right. Then what?

I went upstairs. It was cold. There was a window open.

Did you shut it?

What?

The window.

No. No, I didn't want to—

Touch anything? The sheriff looked at him.

Right, George said.

Then what?

Then I found her and she—

A sound erupted from his belly, a kind of guttural hiccup, and he let the words gush out like puke. She had that . . . thing in her head . . . and there was all . . . the blood.

He grabbed the wastebasket and retched into it while Lawton sat there and watched. Deputy Burke came in and took it away. It was one of those gray metal things they used in grammar schools.

You all right, George?

He was nothing close to all right. Burke came back into the room with another wastebasket and set it down. He stood there a minute looking at him, then went out again and shut the door.

What time did you leave the house this morning?

The question seemed impossible to answer. Six-thirty, he managed. He'd had an eight o'clock class. He could remember the sky, the thick clouds. The drive to work. The usual traffic. People in their cars behind fogged windows. My wife, he said. They were sleeping.

What time she usually get up?

I don't know. I guess around seven.

Your wife work?

He shook his head. Not up here. She'd worked in the city.

What as?

She was a painter—she did murals, restoration.

Lawton made another note. What you all do last night?

Nothing, he said.

Nothing?

We had dinner and went to bed.

Any alcohol with dinner?

A little wine.

What time you go to bed?

George tried to think. I guess around eleven.

Let me ask you this. Your wife—she a heavy sleeper?

No. Not especially.

How 'bout your daughter? She sleep pretty good?

George shrugged. I guess.

Lawton shook his head and smiled. We had a heck of a time with ours. I don't think even one of 'em slept through. Not the whole night. Then they're up again at the crack of dawn. Lawton looked at him evenly, and a whole minute seemed to pass before he went on. Small kids can be rough on a marriage, he said. I don't think people give themselves enough credit. But I think it's harder on the women, don't you?

George looked at him and waited.

Women got such a keen *sense,* don't they? The tiniest little whimper and they're *up.*

His brain was beginning to hurt. The overhead lights, buzzing tubes of fluorescence. He tried to look the sheriff in the eye.

See, that's the thing I can't get my head around here, George. You go to work, right? Your wife's sleeping, your daughter's sleeping. The house is quiet. And sometime after that—that's what you said, right?—when they're still asleep, this incident occurs. You agree with that?

I don't know what else to think.

Let's assume this happened sometime after you left the house, after six-thirty and before your wife and daughter woke up—say, between seven and eight. Would that be fair? We do need to narrow this down.

All right.

So let's say it's around quarter to seven. This individual's outside some-place, maybe he even sees you drive off. He finds the ax in your barn, right? He walks a hundred or so feet to the house and breaks in through the kitchen door. We don't know why. Maybe a robbery, that's possible, we don't understand the motive yet, but that's the setup, am I right?

George thought it through. He nodded.

By now it's around seven. You're still in your car, driving to work. You get to campus, park your car, go up to the office. Meanwhile, back at home, somebody's murdering your wife? Lawton waited a minute. Do you accept that scenario, George?

What choice do I have?

That's what you said, isn't it? It's what you told us.

George just looked at him.

Somebody broke that window. Somebody came up those stairs. Somebody came into your room. And your wife didn't wake up?

So?

That doesn't strike you as odd—a young mother like her?

She was sleeping, George said. The pain in his head sharpened. He feared it might make him blind.

Somebody brought an ax into your home, Lawton said, slowly rising from his chair. They carried it up the stairs. They entered your room. They stood over the bed, looking down at your dreaming wife. They raised the ax like this—he raised his arms over his head—then brought it down, and *bam!* He slammed his hand down on the table. One blow. That's all it took.

George began to weep. Can't you see? I'm sick over this. Can't you see?

Just when he thought he'd secured Lawton's sympathy, the sheriff walked out.

It occurred to him that he needed a lawyer.

WHAT THE SHERIFF PROMISED would be a brief interview had turned into five hours. Lawton and Burke took turns asking him the same questions over and over again, hoping George would break down and confess to murdering his wife.

We'd like to interview your daughter, Burke said.

We've got people who know how to talk to kids in these sorts of situations, his partner added gently.

And get the answers they want, George thought. I don't think so, he said.

Burke scoffed. She was in the house. She might've seen something. I'd think you'd want to know.

George didn't like the look on his face. It's not happening, he said. I won't allow it.

The cops exchanged a look. Burke shook his head and got up and walked out. A moment later, the phone rang.

Yell-o, Lawton said a bit too happily. He listened and replaced the receiver. Your parents are here. Apparently, your daughter's tired. He looked at George carefully. She wants to go home.

Yeah, George said. Me, too. And he meant those words with all his heart. But neither of them had a home now. That was over.

Your folks got you all a room at the Garden Inn.

He nodded with relief. He couldn't imagine going back to that house tonight—or ever.

Lawton walked him out. In the anteroom, his parents were waiting on plastic chairs. At first glance, he hardly recognized them. They looked old. Franny was squatting on the floor, playing with a rubber stamp that declared *Official Business* across a piece of scrap paper.

She's getting ink all over her hands, his mother said, displeased, her

French accent more pronounced than usual. Frances, come up from that dirty floor.

She pulled Franny onto her lap. It was only then, with the child between them, that she looked at him directly.

Mother, he said, and bent to kiss her. Her face was cold. His father stood up, grim, and shook his hand. They looked at him; they would not look.

Daddy, Franny cried, reaching out, her little fingers straining, and he suddenly remembered who he was. He pulled her up into his arms, grateful for her affection, and when she clung to him it somehow gave him the strength to say good night to Lawton, to be a gentleman.

We'd like to see you here first thing in the morning, he said.

What for?

We need to finish this.

I don't have much else to say, Travis.

You could think of something else. We'll expect you at eight-thirty. If you want, I'll send a patrol car around to pick you up.

That's all right. I'll be here.

They crossed the parking lot in silence and got into his father's brown Mercedes, an older model that smelled of cigars. His mother had brought a bag for Franny, clementines and Lulu biscuits and a couple bottles of milk. Catherine had gotten her onto a cup, but she still took a bottle at night. Thinking about it now made his eyes water. He didn't think he had the courage to raise her alone.

As they drove to the hotel, Franny fell asleep. No one spoke. He put her on his shoulder when they walked into the silent lobby and rode up in the elevator. His mother had arranged for two rooms. Why don't you let Franny stay with us? she said. We'll be right next door. I'm sure you need the rest.

No, he said. She'll be with me.

His voice was cold, he knew, but he couldn't help it. Their faces bleached and cautious. Wanting to know. Wanting a reason this had happened *in their family*. The potential embarrassment. They wanted the facts. Intimate details that were nobody's business. They couldn't help being suspicious—he guessed it was only natural. Maybe he should even forgive them.

No. He hated them for it.

Suddenly his parents looked like strangers, refugees who'd been thrown together with him until whatever end awaited them all. They turned into their room and closed the door. Through the wall he could hear their muted conversation, though he couldn't imagine what they were saying to each other. When he was a boy, his bedroom had been next to theirs, and they often talked late into the night. George would fall asleep trying to decipher the conversation. His father would sit on the bench at the end of the bed, pulling off his shoes and socks, while his mother sat up in her nightgown, her face greasy with wrinkle cream, the newspaper open on her lap. As parents they'd been strict, rigorous. His father, the disciplinarian, occasionally used his belt. George could remember the shame of it.

The room was clean, innocuous, with two double beds. He set Franny down as gently as he could, but she woke, slightly alarmed. Daddy?

I'm right here.

For several minutes the room intrigued her, the paisley bedspread, the wine-colored drapes, the matching shag carpet. She stood up on the bed and started jumping. For a second, while she was suspended in midair, a smile lit her face; then she dropped to all fours like a puppy and rolled up in a ball. Come here, you big lump of sugar. He pulled her into his arms and held her.

You cry, Daddy?

He couldn't answer her. He cried raw, lonely tears.

She turned away from him, hugging her stuffed rabbit, and shuddered a little. Her eyes were open, fixed on some spot across the room, and it occurred to him that she hadn't asked for Catherine since they'd left the Pratts', not once. He found it strange. Maybe somewhere inside her little head she understood her mother wasn't coming back.

He pulled the blankets up and kissed her cheek. Mercifully, she fell asleep.

He sat down on the other bed, watching her. It was just the two of them now. He tried to think. The curtains swam, ghostlike, in some unexplained breeze. It was the heater beneath them, he realized, not without relief. He went to the window and adjusted the temperature and looked out into the night, the dim parking lot, the distant lights of the interstate. It had been a long, cruel winter. Again, it was beginning to snow. He pulled the heavy drapes across the cold glass, making the world out there disappear, and turned on the TV, muting the volume. A commercial ended and the nightly news came on. He was both surprised and not that his wife's murder was their lead story: footage of the farm, the empty barns, an ominous shot of the unutilized milking contraptions, a dreary photograph of the house from the assessor's office with the word *Foreclosure* stretched across it like a police banner. Then a picture of his wife that had been in the local paper, taken at the Chosen Fair, an annual tradition in which everybody came together to eat corn dogs and fried dough—one of the few levelers in a town of extreme wealth and poverty with little in between. Catherine, in overalls, a moon and a star painted on her cheek, looking angelic, almost childlike. Finally, a photo of him—his ID picture from the college, which made him look like an inmate. He could see what they were doing; it didn't take much.

He switched it off and went into the bathroom. The light was overly bright, the fan roaring. He turned it off and peed in the dark. He washed his hands and face. Unwittingly, he looked at his new reflection—the whites of his eyes, the curve of his lips, his vague outline—and it occurred to him that he was beginning to disappear.

He removed his shoes and put them on the carpet and lay down on the bed fully clothed, pulling up the bedspread. What would they do next, arrest him? They wanted to question him again; what more could he tell them? He'd come home, found her, grabbed Franny and run out. Obviously, they were hoping for a confession. He had seen it happen often enough in movies, and the next thing he knew he'd be shipped off to some prison in chains. It could actually happen, he realized. Shockingly within the realm of possibility, it terrified the hell out of him. He didn't think he could bear it.

Just before six the next morning, he heard someone knocking. His mother stood in the doorway in her robe, drawn, withered. His father wanted to talk. He'd been up all night and had concluded that they should ignore Sheriff Lawton's request and return to Connecticut immediately. Since George knew nothing, his mother emphasized, another meeting with the sheriff's office would not be productive. Once they got to Stonington, they'd arrange for a lawyer. It was still early. They had time to stop at the farm to get a few things. George could take his own car and then they could drive in tandem to Connecticut. They'd be out of the state before Lawton even got to his office.

It was cold, the sky white, the landscape drained of color. Evergreens, distant fields and barns, unmoving cows, sunless horizon. The house on Old Farm Road seemed defiant, dressed in police tape. A notice had been pinned to the door. Look, he said to his parents. I'm sorry about all this. I'm really very sorry.

George's father nodded. We understand, son. It's a terrible thing that's happened. A terrible thing.

They waited in the car with Franny while George went in through the porch, just like he'd done the day before. He kept his gloves on. He knew not to touch anything. The surfaces had been dusted for prints, and a fine silt remained. This was a crime scene now, and even the most ordinary objects seemed to pulse with collusion: a plastic doll ruined with ink, candlesticks ornate with wax, one of his wife's blue pumps sticking out from under the couch. These things he saw in flashes as he crossed the floor to the stairs, trying not to make a sound, as if someone else were already here, as if he were the intruder. He stood for a moment, just listening. He could hear the trees blowing around in the wind, Catherine's wrangling chimes. He was sweating, his face, the back of his neck. Overcome with a sudden nausea, he wondered if he'd be sick.

Again, he looked up the staircase.

He had to go up. He had to.

Clutching the banister, he climbed to the second floor and briefly stopped in the hall. It was cold, the air practically shaking with it. His daughter's room was a bastion of innocence, the pink walls and stuffed animals flaunting their betrayal, and he could sense an awful strangeness, some lingering malevolence. He wanted very badly to leave. It was as if this house, this strange farm, wasn't even his. It belonged to those people, the Hales. He knew it always would.

In Franny's closet, he found a small suitcase and filled it with whatever he could—clothes, toys, stuffed animals—and stepped back into the hall. The door to the master bedroom was ajar, an invitation that he didn't think he could answer. Instead, he started for the stairs, hearing voices outside. On the landing, he saw they'd gotten out of the car. His mother was bouncing her granddaughter from hip to hip, singing a song. Franny had her head back, laughing. It didn't seem right, he thought, annoyed. It wasn't right for anyone to be happy, including his daughter, and he knew Catherine would admonish such behavior *at a time like this.*

When the phone rang, it seemed incredibly loud. Who could possibly be calling? He looked at his watch: ten to seven. The phone drilled through the empty rooms. After ten rings it stopped.

The silence seemed to be listening.

Then something stirred at the end of the hallway. Wind, sunlight, a vicious shimmering—and he thought, wildly, *It's her.* Yes, *yes,* it's *her*! Standing there in her nightgown by the bedroom door, her delicate hand on the knob, a halo of light around her head. *Let me show you,* he almost heard. Her hand reaching out. *Come.*

In that moment the world went silent. Again he looked out at his parents, his daughter, and saw them all fiercely animated, but could no longer hear them and knew they existed in separate worlds. And understood, too, what was required of him now, what she wanted, his dead wife, and he fumbled down to the room they had shared. He would end his own life, he thought, if she wanted him to. It was what he deserved. For not protecting her, for his misguided impression that she'd be happy here and for all of the other things he'd done to make sure she never would be. And then he felt something, like a cold hand on his chin, making him look. There it was, the bed. They'd taken the bloody sheets, the blanket. Now it was just the mattress, the outline of the stain, an uneven circle like a lake on a map. Again he heard the wind, the bare branches of the trees. Again that distraction of sunlight. *Cathy,* he whispered. *Is that you?*

THEY DROVE one car after the other. Franny lay across the back seat sleeping, breathing heavily. It was four hours through sleet. He had to concentrate, to focus. How could he go on? All that blood. Her pale, lovely arms, her delicate wrists.

They'd had dinner; she hadn't eaten. She'd been cold, distant. Shoving the plates into the sink. Her shoulders raised. I know about you, George.

What?

I know what you did.

Ruined, he thought. A wasted life.

I can't stay here, George. I can't stay here with you. I have to go.

He wanted to hit her but instead said, If that's what you want.

You don't have a fucking clue what I want.

He had washed his hands over and over.

He had pressed his ear to the door and opened it silently. She looked up in her white nightgown, her skin already so pale, and lowered her brush.

THE SOUND APPEARED, stretched long and black across the horizon. There was no sleet here at the shore. He pulled over at an overlook and stumbled out onto sand that nearly swallowed him. He got to his feet and ran across the cold beach like a man in the desert who has at last found water, vaguely aware that his parents were screaming at him. He felt almost as though it was the very end of the world, and there was nothing left, neither day nor night, heat nor cold, laughter nor joy. And he belonged here. He belonged in nothing.

He wanted to feel something, the water in his hands, the smell of it, of life, the salt, the cold sunlight. Distantly, he felt the water rising up his legs, his hips. Make me clean, he thought. Baptize me.

They had to coax him out. Blankets, then hot soup at some roadside place after he'd changed his clothes in the men's room.

What were you thinking, his mother said, going into the water like that? She's going to need you, George. Your own life comes second now. *You don't matter anymore,* she might've said. *You don't deserve to.*

They waited in the parking lot while his father bought an ice-cream cone for Franny. His mother's eyes were as watery and gray as the Sound. Looking shrunken in her outsized coat, she reached out to take his hand and he could feel something breaking inside of him.

They think I did it, he said.

Well, they won't get far with that.

The wind blew hard. He wondered what she was thinking. She looked up into the suddenly bright sun and closed her eyes.

They lived in an old saltbox on a cove, overlooking the water. As a boy, he'd owned a series of sailboats. When they got out of the car, he wondered vaguely if his old Vagabond was still in the shed. He had to remind himself that this was no ordinary visit.

They left him alone. He stayed in his childhood room, lying on the twin bed, and the afternoon brought the thick gloom of a winter storm. In the kitchen downstairs, the radio repeated its grinding emergency warning: more snow predicted, travel advisories, etc. He could hear Franny's staccato footsteps all over the house. At least she was all right, he thought.

Even though he couldn't begin to predict what she'd experienced; he doubted he could ever know.

He nodded off for a while and woke to the ringing telephone. He assumed that it was Catherine's mother, or perhaps her sister. Later, his father knocked and leaned into the room in his cardigan sweater, tentatively, as if George had some contagious illness he didn't want to catch.

They called here, looking for you.

Lawton?

His father nodded. They want to talk to Franny.

George shook his head. I won't allow it.

All right. That's your decision.

His father stood there, watching him.

She wasn't happy, George said. With me, I mean.

His father waited.

We were having problems.

This information made no difference, and his father was suddenly all business. I've been in touch with that lawyer you suggested. He's on retainer now and has already done some good. Nothing you said last night can be used against you in a criminal case. As it turns out, you didn't have to submit to an interview. Of course, they didn't tell you that. If the police want to talk to you again, your lawyer will have to be present. Those are the stipulations now.

I didn't know that was possible, George said.

Anything's possible with the right attorney. His father looked at him briefly, definitively, and closed the door.

THE HOURS slowly passed. He was like a tenant in their house. He sensed their uncertainty, their judgment. He thought of this time, this schism of abeyance, as his own realized version of hell.

Your in-laws are on their way, his mother told him, a warning. They've agreed to have the funeral here.

She was making pancakes and had burned a few—not a new tendency. The kitchen had the same smell he remembered from childhood, the ever-present salvages of burnt toast left on the Formica like fossils, evidence of her good motherly intentions. She poured him a cup of coffee.

How soon?

A couple hours.

Okay, he said, sipping the coffee, not tasting it, his mouth tasting of rubber or some other toxic residue, fear. Seeing Catherine's parents would be difficult, witnessing their grief. Suddenly ill, he pushed the cup away and got up.

I made these for you, his mother said, holding the plate of pancakes, standing there, her face pale, her hair as wiry and brittle as pine needles. It was nearly noon and she was still in her nightgown, and in a cluttered corner of the countertop he spotted her glass of gin. Don't you want to know where Franny is?

He asked her with his eyes.

Your father took her to the carwash. You used to love that.

Yes, he said—but that was a lie. He had always been a little terrified of the dark cement tunnel on Liberty Street, the long arcade of equipment, the vicious yellow tubes of the vacuums, the deep-black skin of the employees.

I need some air, he said.

Of course. His mother looked ravaged, there was no other word for it. Go for a walk.

He found one of his old jackets in the closet. Bracing himself for the cold, he walked down the narrow lane to the empty, desolate beach. All the neighbors were gone for winter, and the flat sand stretched down to water that was dark, almost black. Walking along the shore, he shoved his hands into his pockets and discovered a crushed pack of Camels, the unfiltered brand he'd smoked in graduate school. He lit one, dragged deeply. The tobacco was stale, but he didn't care. He wanted the burn in his chest; he'd smoke a whole pack if he could. He watched a low-flying gull surveying the water, the beach. It flew up into the white sky and disappeared.

AN HOUR LATER, maybe two, he heard a car and his mother-in-law's high-pitched voice: Frances Clare, look how you've grown!

He stood in front of the mirror and buttoned his collar, then tucked in his shirt, trying not to look at his face.

He went downstairs. His mother had Franny at the kitchen table, coloring. She was watching the child intently, as if some telling revelation would appear on the paper, when in fact all Franny had drawn were flowers. He kissed the top of her head. That's a nice picture, Franny.

I'm making daisies. She was pressing hard, making thick waxy stripes of grass.

Isn't that nice, his mother said. She looked up at him, appraising or admiring him, he couldn't tell which, and he knew it didn't matter. His mother was on his side, no matter what. They're in there with your father, she said.

When he entered the living room, the room went quiet. Rose and Keith were sitting on the couch and looked up at him without recognition, like strangers waiting for a bus. Without a word, George leaned over and kissed his mother-in-law, then shook her husband's hand.

Rose stood to embrace him, shaking in his arms. What happened, George? What happened to our Cathy?

I wish I knew.

Her eyes filled with tears. Who could do such a thing?

Of course they're trying to pin it on me, George said.

Rose blinked, looked away. Her whole body seemed to contract, and he took his hands away as she sank back into the couch.

I don't know what happened, he told them. I don't know any more than you do.

It's just an awful thing, she said to the room. Just awful.

Can I get you anything?

No, thank you. I just want to sit here.

To his relief, Franny ran into the room with her picture. Look at my picture, Grandma Rose.

Well, now, you're quite the artist, aren't you? Come onto Grandma's lap. She pulled the child into her arms. Now, where'd my kiss go? Did you take my kiss?

Franny shook her head and held up her empty palms. I don't have it.

Is it in your pocket?

I don't have any pockets!

Is it in your shoe? I'll bet it is.

Franny scrambled onto the floor, pulled off a shoe and shook it hard. Here it is, she cried. It fell out like a little rock. She held out her hand for her grandmother to see.

Oh! I knew it.

You take it, Franny said.

Put it right here, Rose told her, leaning forward.

Franny touched her grandmother's cheek and Rose hugged her tight. Lord our God, that's the best darned kiss in the whole world.

THE SNOW TURNED to rain. They sat there together with the cold light pouring in through the picture window. His father was watching a game, college basketball. Intermittently, bursts of wild cheer filled the room. George drank a little gin. Just after halftime, a car pulled into the gravel driveway.

There's Agnes now, his mother-in-law said.

I'll go. George went to the door, glad for something to do, and watched his sister-in-law and her husband get out of the car. Agnes, newly pregnant, had already put on weight. Paul was carrying a platter of food wrapped in plastic and held his wife's arm as they came up the walk.

Agnes, George said, and kissed her cheek.

Her eyes seemed to prickle. How is this possible?

I don't have an answer for that.

He held her a minute, loosely, and without affection. She was shorter than Catherine, round-shouldered, substantial. She broke their embrace and wiped her eyes as her husband came inside.

Hello, Paul, he said, shaking his hand.

I'm sorry for your loss.

Here, let me take that. You all go inside.

They all drank too much. Now and again, Rose was overcome. Water and pills were fetched. They tried to remain composed for Franny's sake, but their stagy enthusiasm confused her, and she fussed and cried and twisted in their arms.

Time for a nap, little puppy. When he scooped her into his arms, she giggled and shrieked and kicked her legs.

No, Daddy, not yet.

He laid her down in the guest room, on one of the twin beds, and pulled the blankets up under her chin. Are you warm enough?

Where's Momma?

The question alarmed him, and he tried to mask it. She's up in heaven with God, sweetheart. Remember what Mommy told you?

God lives in the sky.

That's right.

But I want her, Daddy.

You can whisper to her. Just whisper and she'll hear you.

She looked up at the ceiling. Up there?

Yes, right up there. He kissed her forehead. She looked at him and he hugged her. She held him very tightly.

Mommy is with you, Franny. She's with you every minute. Okay?

Franny turned away and closed her eyes. He sat there a moment, watching her. He sensed someone in the doorway and turned and met his mother's eyes. At once he felt supervised, self-conscious. She was his warden now, he thought, joining her in the hall.

Has she said anything?

No.

She looked at him sharply. I just can't stop wondering. She was all day in that house.

I know.

Unsatisfied, she shook her head. She must have seen something.

We may never know.

That's not good enough. What about that boy? I wonder if he had something to do with it.

He's just a kid, Mother.

You never know. Kids these days. It's a different world.

He sighed. What could he possibly say? I'm sorry, Mother, he finally said.

She looked at him strangely, as if trying to determine his meaning. I know you are, son. I know.

LATE IN THE AFTERNOON, Agnes wanted to walk. He took his mother's cigarettes and went with her, pushing an umbrella over their heads. Briefly, after college, she'd lived with them in the city. He'd gotten to know her, and the one thing he understood about Agnes was that she was prone to compromise. Easily accepted things just as they were, whether in her work or in her relationships. Her husband, he thought, was a drip. He sensed that she'd admired Catherine, but never told her so, which maybe wasn't so unusual. Perhaps that was how sisters were.

Winter on the Sound offered a bleak dissolution of color. They stood looking out at the water. He lit a cigarette.

I want you to know, she said, that you can trust me.

Okay, he said. That's good. I appreciate that.

I mean with anything.

He nodded.

I know you had nothing to do with this.

I don't know what to say, Agnes.

I can't imagine what you must be going through.

It's very difficult.

She put her hand on his arm and kissed him on the cheek and he could smell the perfume she'd put on that morning, Chanel N° 5, the same scent his wife had been wearing since college, and he wondered if it had been deliberate. Agnes seemed, in that moment, a complete and total stranger. It came to him that he hardly knew these people. And they certainly didn't know him. They'd already come to their own conclusions about his wife's murder. And, like a good son-in-law, he'd acquiesced, assuming the stoic resignation of the accused.

ON MONDAY MORNING, hours before the funeral, the police came poking around. His father had seen them in town, blatant outsiders. A couple camera crews parked at the end of their road, waiting to get a shot of him. They were at the cemetery, too; George and the others watched it later that night on the local news, the two families standing over her grave. Their faces. The distortion of grief.

The next afternoon, two of Lawton's lackeys knocked on the door. George was up in his room, trying to rest. He could hear his mother letting them in, their voices filling the living room as if they wanted him to hear every word.

He won't be interviewed without his lawyer, his mother told them.

All right, one of them said. We understand that. But tell your son we've got an investigation to run. It would be helpful to talk to him. He knew his wife better than any of us. We could certainly use his help.

His mother said something he couldn't make out and they left. From the window in his bedroom George watched them walk down to the beach, their jackets filling with wind as they stood at the shore. One of them scooped some sand into his hand and jiggled it around like pocket change. The partner said something and he laughed, and they glanced up at his window. Caught, George backed away, letting the curtain fall into place over the glass.

A WEEK OR SO LATER, he drove back to Chosen to pick up some things—his bank book, checks, his wife's jewelry. The trick to hiding something, she'd told him once, is to put it right out in plain sight. His father had offered to go along, but he needed to do this on his own. He needed to be alone in that house, with her.

He took the three-hour drive in silence. In the freedom of his car he allowed himself to think of the girl, and how she'd looked at him that last time.

At last he turned down their road, where he feared some unseen surveyor might be watching him. He scanned the trees, the outlying fields, but saw no one. The house looked abandoned. As he stepped out of the car, it occurred to him that he was frightened. His mouth was dry and his head ached. He had history here, he reminded himself, and some of it had been good.

The police had come and gone. The house felt used, trampled by strangers. Their old room looked bare. Someone had come in to clean up the blood. You couldn't see any on the walls. He wondered who had done it, if it was a specialized job. He stood over the bed, looking down at the space his wife had filled. On impulse, he grabbed the mattress and jerked it upright and jostled it into the hallway and down the stairs and out the front door, sweating and cursing. He dragged it into the field over ice and snow and left it there on the hard ground. Then he went to the barn to look for gasoline. The can wasn't full, but there was enough, and he poured it out over the mattress. It only took one match.

And he stood there and watched it burn.

Chosen, New York, 1978

I

JUST BEFORE WINTER they took the cows. Their mother had sent them upstairs, but the boy and his brothers watched from their window. There were two trucks with slatted sides and he could see the cows all pushed together and he could hear them moaning, for this old farm was the only home they'd ever had. Then the boss, a carton-shaped man in a plaid shirt and gloves, whirled his arm around like he was working a lasso and the first truck pulled out and a thick brown dust rose up in the air. Their father waited, his arms crossed on his chest like someone about to be hit. The man shuffled over in his untied boots, kicking up the dirt, and handed him a slip of paper and said something, the words turning to smoke in the cold air, and he touched the brim of his hat like he was sorry and climbed up into his cab and jerked the gears and rolled out. Again dust filled the air, and the sun went away. For a minute or so they couldn't see their father, and the boy thought it was like a trick, how one minute you have everything, the next you don't. It went quiet for a little while, and then the sky opened like it was cut, and the rain fell into the dirt and yammered on the old tin buckets.

Ignoring his brothers, he ran down the staircase hung with crooked pictures of dead relatives, the banister black with filth, and across the scuffed floors, vaguely aware of his mother in the kitchen, and pushed open the storm door and ran out into the rain, past the barns with their empty stanchions, into the field of broken grass, and kept on running. Up the hill, over the hard ground, along the ridge with its mangled dandelions, and finally, when he could run no farther, he stopped with his hands on his knees, gulping the cold air, knowing he had finished crying and also that he was too old for it now. He looked down at the farm where his mother had first çarried him and then bore him and held him as an infant in her arms, and now he cried some more, this time like a man cries, when he knows what is to come.

HIS NAME WAS Cole Harold Hale. He'd been named after his great-grandpa, who had bought the farm in 1908 and turned it into a dairy. Cole's father, Calvin, had grown up here and had taught Cole and his brothers how to do things just like his own father had taught him. He hadn't gone past high school, but if you asked him anything he always came up with some answer. Didn't matter what it was about, he knew a whole lot of things. He was tall and stoop-shouldered and walked around in an old blood-colored coat, and he had a tight, sewn-up look on his face, like he'd swallowed glass. His hands were big as Frisbees and they'd fly at you when you didn't expect it. He spoke in a code. Not even Eddy understood it. He could hurt their mother. Doors would close. He'd drive off in his truck.

On that night, though, he didn't go anywhere. He stayed out in the barn with his whiskey. Finally, their mother went out to check. She stood in the doorway, holding a blanket like a sleeping child, but he wouldn't take it. She came back to the house and lay on the couch with her back to the room. Cole covered her with the same blanket and waited for her to say something, to tell him he was a good, thoughtful boy like she often did, but she said nothing, and he went up to find his brothers.

The room was cold without much heat and they all three of them got into one bed with all their clothes on and lay with their arms and legs touching and their eyes on the ceiling. Wade fell asleep first, as he always did. He wasn't a worrier like their older brother, Eddy. Worrying kept Eddy up at night. He'd open the window and climb out on the roof and sit there and smoke, and when he came back he brought the cold in with him and the stink of cigarettes.

In the morning, Mrs. Lawton came over with her boy, Travis Jr. Cole's mother had washed her face and brushed her hair and put on lipstick. She stood at the mirror buttoning her sweater. She had yellow hair and little baby teeth, and people smiled at her like they do at babies or cupcakes or butterflies. Even with nothing she'd made cookies, and the whole house smelled good and sweet, like it always used to when he was little.

Why don't you boys go for a walk, Mrs. Lawton said. Your mother and I want to talk.

Travis was a year younger than Cole and went to St. Anthony's and had to wear a uniform. St. Anthony's was around the corner from the middle school, and sometimes Cole would walk over and watch the St. Anthony's kids behind the fence in their blue shirts and gray trousers, the girls in plaid skirts. He knew one of those girls, Patrice, and was in love with her.

They went down to the creek, getting their sneakers wet, and started throwing rocks. Cole's went the farthest, which was no surprise. He was tall for his age and had big hands and feet like his father and would grow up to be as big and tall as him, that's what everybody always said. People always compared him to his father, but they didn't know anything. For one thing, he didn't plan on being poor, and he'd never hurt a woman or use a belt on his children, and when he thought about these things his chest went on fire and his eyes prickled, but he wouldn't say a word. How he really felt about his father was nobody's business.

Travis Jr.'s father was the county sheriff. One time Wade got caught stealing something in Hack's and Sheriff Lawton walked him into the parking lot and put his hand on his back to talk some sense into him. They stood there with their heads bowed like two men praying, but it made no impact on Cole's brother, who was always figuring a scheme.

He fished one of his mother's butts out of his pocket and lit it, aware of Travis Jr.'s eyes on him. His mother smoked Pall Malls. He dragged on it hard and it hurt a little bit and an ugly taste covered his tongue. How many guns your father got?

Couple.

He let you hold 'em?

One time I did.

They threw some more rocks, and Travis said, Sorry about your farm.

Cole threw a rock and it made an arc through the sky and disappeared, almost like a shooting star.

You can't tell, Travis said ominously. In life. One minute to the next. You don't know, you just can't predict it.

Cole looked off at the hills, waiting for them to blur. If you looked at anything long enough it would start to become something else, or even completely undefined, and no matter what it was, you thought about it differently than you had before, and usually it was less important. This was a philosophy he'd been developing in his own mind. He had an interest in philosophy, about how people thought. And physics, too, how one thing influenced another, and he was a good student and really good at science. But there were mysteries in life that could not be explained.

Travis touched his arm. You okay?

He shrugged him off.

They walked through the woods, the cold darkness of the trees. When they got back from the creek his mother put out cookies and they ate them and drank the milk of their lost cows on the steps outside in the bitter sun. The air still smelled of the cows, of the sweet manure-smell that he'd known all his life and that always made him happy, but when he remembered the long white barns and empty stanchions, the milk suddenly tasted sour. He used to complain about his chores—his father's hand on his back to wake him, being pulled from the warm bed, shuffling half dressed out into the pitch-black to milk and feed the cows and clean the barn before school. Too lazy to put on socks, his feet always freezing in his old boots, and his brothers shoving him across the dirt yard into the warm light of the barn, where the cows yearned for him and stamped their feet. He had hated every minute of it, but now missed it so much his guts hurt.

The women came outside. His mother buttoned her coat, sniffling, her eyes watery in the bright sunlight. She was clutching a yellow tissue like a trapped warbler, and in his mind's eye he saw the crumpled wad unfold itself and fly away.

You okay, hon? Mrs. Lawton asked. I know you're worried.

He looked at her wormy forehead, her wide orange mouth.

You just go about your business, she said.

I will.

Thanks for coming, Mary, his mother said. Goodbye, Travis.

Bye.

Travis climbed into the car. His cheeks looked clammy and pink, and when the car pulled slowly down the road, he pushed his face against the window like a retard, and just before they turned the corner he waved. Cole raised his hand and kept it up even after the car had disappeared out of sight.

He stood there a minute, listening to the sounds moving through the air. They were familiar to him. He could hear the train; it came loud at first, then went on through the woods and grew quiet. He could hear Mrs. Pratt's dogs. Inside, his mother was sitting at the table with a ledger book and a pile of bills. He could tell she'd been crying even though she smiled at him like a girl who'd just won something. He made her tea and brought it to her on a saucer, spilling it a little, the spoon tinkling. Then he took her hand tenderly, sheltering it in his own, closing his eyes very tight and trying to send something from himself into her that would keep her going, because he sensed her distance, that she was fading out, becoming some quiet figure in the background who nobody noticed. In her old pink sweater, she stared at the tabletop where the bills were laid out like a game of solitaire. He would watch his mother very closely, noting the changes in her face. She was like a warning sound in the distance. You knew something was coming, something bad, and it would hurt.

Then she got up and brought the empty teacup and saucer to the sink and washed them and set them each in the dish rack, and watching her do this made him feel a little better. His father came in with mud on his boots and shuffled across the floor and lay on the couch, and she stood there looking at him, her face so pale. She went and untied his boots and pulled them off, and like a small child he let her do it. She covered him with the blanket and put her hand on his forehead like she did to Cole when he had a fever, and she looked into his eyes and his father looked back. She told Cole to go outside and make good use of the day, but he said he didn't feel like it and she didn't make him. While his father slept and some stupid thing played on TV, she pushed the mop across the wrecked boards, her eyes fierce. She cleaned the bedrooms and the bathrooms and then pulled the twisted sheets from the wash and took them outside in the wood basket to hang on the line. It was cold and Cole helped, and the wet sheets slapped against their bodies and made him think of the chill of death and of the shadows he sometimes saw out in the fields, the men who rose out of the dirt in their cavalry uniforms. They had done the Revolutionary

War in school and he knew about how the battles had played out on the fields behind their house. His grandpa used to say you could dig up their brass buttons and claimed to have a jar full of them somewhere. When they came back inside she started collecting all the junk nobody ever used, piling it up on an old horse blanket—a half-busted toaster, roller skates that didn't fit, an old music toy from when he was a baby—and when the blanket was full she pulled the corners taut like Santa's bundle and hauled it out to the truck, and they brought it into town and gave it all to the church. Cole waited in the truck while she talked to Father Geary in the courtyard. The morning had gotten cloudy but now sunlight poured out of the sky and splashed on their backs. Father Geary put his hand on her shoulder and she nodded as he spoke to her, her hand over her eyes like a salute, and it came to Cole that his mother wasn't used to being touched so gently and maybe didn't like it.

Driving home, they stopped at Tasty Treat and she bought him an ice-cream cone with all the change she'd found around the house, and they sat there while he ate it with the sun bright on the windshield. His mother watched him closely and smoothed his hair with her cold fingers. You need a haircut, she said.

His father was up eating toast when they got home. Cole could see his brothers out back trying to fix the tractor. There were parts strewn on the ground and a mess of greasy rags. His father swallowed his tea and put on his coat and went out. Cole watched him as he stood on the step, lighting a cigarette. He said something to Wade and Eddy, his voice sharp. His mother wiped off the table, glancing up through the smudged glass of the door, and when his father got into the truck a look came over her face, like she was glad.

Later, after dark, they went to get him. It was a bar called Blake's. She made Cole go in. Walls like pea soup, and a smell you didn't find anyplace else. He stepped over the sleeping dogs. The bartender said, You got company, Cal. You better get on.

What for? his father muttered.

Cole pulled on the greasy rim of his coat sleeve. Come on, Pop.

She out there?

Yes, sir.

Well, goddamn her.

They left him there and drove home. His mother didn't look at him. It was just the dark road, her cigarette, the wind through his butterfly window. Don't turn into someone like him, she told Cole.

While his brothers slept, Cole lay there thinking about how to save the farm, but he couldn't come up with anything good. He fell asleep, and a little while later he heard her downstairs, the clatter of plates and silver, and he got up and went down the cold hall and looked over the banister. He could see her setting the table with her good china, one plate after another, as if for a party, and then she sat down at the end of it and looked out at her imaginary company with a dull fire in her eyes.

He was woken later by the rattling diesel of his father's truck, then the kitchen door banging open, his keys hitting the old china plate and his staggering footsteps up the stairs. Cole faked sleep as his father shuffled down the hall to their room and shut the door; he could vaguely hear them talking, but he was drowsy and glad they were talking at least, and he thought maybe things would be all right.

HIS MOTHER WOKE HIM the next morning before church to cut his hair. Even in the cold she made him sit outside on the stepstool with a dish towel across his shoulders and as she moved around behind him he could feel the itchy wool of her coat brushing against his neck. Wade was making a wreath out of sticks. His brother wasn't much good at school but he had a knack for making one thing out of another. He could make a rose out of hay, twisting the strands into a pretty knot, and he could cane a chair.

Not too short, Cole said.

She didn't answer, but she'd do what she wanted anyway. When she finished she looked at him with her hands on his shoulders. He was taller than her now, and she gave him a funny smile and went inside. Cole looked in the hand mirror. His hair was far too short. His face had thinned down and his eyes were hard and blue. His shoulders had gone rigid. He could hear them inside, fighting about the piano she'd inherited, his father threatening to sell it, his mother crying and a disruption of chairs. Then his mother left the house, climbing up to the ridge in her church dress and muck boots and baggy old coat. In her fist a hunk of wild daisies. She walked in the way of a pony, her bony knees, her long neck, her hair hanging down, and he wished she would just turn around and come home.

SMALL FARMS LIKE THEIRS were going broke. You'd hear sad stories about this family or that one. His father organized a rally and people came from all over the state. Cole and his brothers set up picnic tables in a row and covered them with oilcloths. They butchered a pig and roasted it in a barrel, and the air smelled of it and he was hungry all day, waiting for it to cook. His mother made baked beans and cornbread and coleslaw and everybody ate their fill. After they finished they tossed their paper plates into the fire. The women handed out coffee in paper cups while the men stood in the field, hunkering in their plaid coats, their faces smacked red by the cold. His father stood on an upside-down barrel with a megaphone. You couldn't see his mouth but words came out the other end and carried across the yard. They made a banner out of a white sheet and broom handles that said THIS IS AG PROFIT! and stuck it in a manure spreader heaped with dung and drove it down to City Hall. Eddy and Wade got to go and the next morning they had their picture in the paper. They showed the truck down in Albany with all the men standing around it. The headline read: NY FARMS IN CRISIS: DAIRY FARMERS UNITE. For a couple weeks everyone was a little happier, but then they saw it was a trick. Not a thing had changed.

She had to sell her pretty things. They packed the good china and the special porcelain figures from his grandmother that she kept in a glass-front cabinet in the living room that trembled a little whenever anyone walked into the room. His favorite was of a blond-haired girl with a pony-tail, holding apples in her apron. His second-favorite was a boy in coveralls with a puppy in his arms. When he was younger he used to try to make up stories about them. His mother had explained they were from Spain and were very fine. She told Cole that he took after her father, who had died when Cole was a baby, and she described him as a self-made man and said that's what she expected from Cole, to be the kind of man who makes up his own mind and does things his own way. She said he was the most careful of her children and the smartest, and that's why she let him handle her nice things.

They loaded the boxes into her car, an old green Cadillac that had been her mother's, and drove to the pawnshop in Troy. He guessed she didn't want anyone knowing she was a farmer's wife, and when he gazed over at her across the seat in her butter-yellow dress and camel-hair coat, he saw the life she could have had, away from the farm, someplace easier, married to somebody else, someone who was nicer than his father and gave her special things.

It was a long drive on back roads. The countryside dropped away, replaced by neighborhoods with curlicue streets and houses lined up one after another. They got on the highway and went along the river, past the old shirt factory, and then over the bridge into Troy, with its narrow cobblestone streets and red brick buildings. You could hear the church bells ringing. He saw a one-legged man in a wheelchair with a little American flag stuck to it. He saw a huddle of nurses outside the hospital, their sweaters like capes over their shoulders. Slowly, they drove past the ladies' college behind its high black fence, the marble buildings lined up around a square like the pieces on a chessboard.

I went there, she said so softly he almost couldn't hear. I was going to be a nurse.

The pawnshop was on River Street, the word spelled out in gold letters on the window. Cole helped his mother with the boxes, but she wouldn't let him go in and made him wait outside. For a while he sat on the bench under the window. A group of girls in school uniforms came up the sidewalk, noisy as ducks, followed by two nuns. Cole got back into the car and played the radio and smoked one of his mother's butts, and a little while later she came out, clutching her purse. The man from the shop stepped out as well and lit a cigar. He had a napkin tucked into his collar, like he'd just finished lunch and had forgotten all about it, and he was big and fat. He squinted hard at Cole as they pulled away.

After that the days went into each other and they wore him down. He couldn't count on anything like he used to, not even supper, and he was always a little relieved when she came into their room to get them up for school.

That Friday morning she even made breakfast, her back keeping a secret as she worked the frying pan. His father sat at the table in his one church suit and a bolo tie he'd carved himself in the shape of a horse head. In his hand was the bank ledger where he wrote down his numbers. Cole heard him tell her, I'll get on my knees if that's what it takes.

There's your bus, boys, she said.

It was just him and Wade. Eddy had been out for two years. He'd wanted to go to music school but their father said no. Eddy filled out the application anyway, putting in twenty bucks he'd stolen from their mother's wallet, but the old man found it and ripped the papers to pieces. Now it didn't even matter, since they wouldn't need him on the farm anymore. The stupid fight had been for nothing.

The bus came to a stop and they climbed up into the noise. Their mother stood watching from the doorway, her pale hand like a flag of surrender. He thought about the word *surrender* and didn't like it. The bus rocked over the pitted road. Rain on the windows like spit. He looked out at horses, sheep. They passed the plastics factory and the park nobody ever went to and the electrical substation with the chain-link fence. The sign on the fence said *High Voltage* and had a skull and crossbones on it, which got him thinking how the world was set up and how your life could depend on other people's mistakes.

The bus turned into Chosen, past the crummy houses on Main Street, with their *Beware of Dog* signs and Holy Virgin statues, before stopping at the light. Out his window he saw Patrice standing on the curb, clutching her notebook. Last year, at the town fair, they rode the roller coaster together. It was just how the line worked out, the two of them ushered up together and strapped in. The whole time, they held hands in the screaming dark. Seeing her now, standing there in her uniform and baggy knee socks, made his insides go sharp. As the bus turned into the parking lot she looked up for a second and met his eyes. He put his hand up on the window as if to secure some imaginary pact, but she had already looked away and was crossing the street.

The last thing he could remember about that week was on Saturday, when their father took down the kites. All winter they stayed in the barn, stretched across the old beams next to the skis and fishing poles. He could remember his father's face as he worked the string, winding it around his elbow to the crook of his hand, a dreamy light in his eyes. They carried their kites like rifles up to the ridge, where the wind was fast. You could hear the wind rattling the thin paper, which was adorned with snakes. The kites were from Tokyo, from when their father was stationed with the air force, back before he'd had kids. He said he'd gotten to know the city pretty well and had liked it. He'd been there a whole year. One time they found some pictures in a cardboard box. There was one of his father in his uniform and a canoe-shaped hat, and another of a strange woman in her undergarments, her skin marshmallow-white, her smile pointy in the shadow-filled room.

Let her go, their father said, as the wind shook their kites—that sound they made, like a thousand birds, as they shot into the sky, free at last.

2

THEN, when they had nothing left, he found them. It was morning, before school. People said it was an accident. She left her car running. Their room was over the garage, and fumes had drifted up through the uneven boards. There they were in the bed, pressed close like lovers or maybe children, holding hands. Lined against the wall were baskets of folded laundry, and the thought occurred to him that, even dead, she didn't want anyone getting stuck with her chores.

An accident, people said. A mistake. But Cole knew, they all did.

They had a wake, people drifting by their coffins, afraid to get too close. After it was over Father Geary came to the house in his black Beetle. Their uncle, Rainer, brought his girlfriend, Vida, and stood around in his cheap suit, smoking. The boys carried their ashes up to the ridge. Eddy held their father's, Wade their mother's. The muddy field swallowed Vida's shoes. She took them off and walked across the soft earth in her stockings. Up on top, they stood in a tight circle, the sun full and bright. They spilled out the ashes and the wind blew them away. Father Geary said a prayer, and Cole wondered if his mother was with Jesus now and hoped she was. He pictured her up there taking His hand, and that made him feel a little better. He pictured her in a white gown, standing on a cloud, the yellow rays streaming out like they did on the cover of his catechism book.

We're all you boys have now, his uncle apologized, his hand heavy on Cole's shoulder as they walked back down to the house.

In the afternoon, people came to pay their respects. Mrs. Lawton and her husband came with Travis. Why don't you boys get some fresh air, the sheriff said.

Cole put on his father's coat and it swam around him like a shadow. He pushed his hands into the pockets, curled his fingers around a bag of

Drum and some papers. Cole could smell him, tobacco and gasoline and sweat. He thought maybe it was the smell of bad luck.

They crossed the wet field and walked back up to the ridge, the wind in their ears. Travis watched him roll a cigarette and they stood close so he could light it. Cole could smell the fried chicken Travis had eaten for lunch and it made him hungry. Travis dragged on the cigarette like somebody playing a kazoo and looked at Cole mournfully. I'm real sorry about your folks. He held out his hand like a grown man and Cole shook it. They stood there a while longer, looking down at the house, the brown fields, the cars parked haphazardly in the dead grass.

After everyone left, Father Geary tucked a dish towel into his trousers and made them a dinner of pork chops and peas and potatoes. When they were done, Eddy rolled cigarettes while Wade made tea and then they sat there, drinking tea and smoking. Father Geary liked to drink his out of a glass and taught Wade how to pour the boiling water over the blade of a knife so the glass wouldn't break. Drinking tea like this seemed exotic to Cole, and it gave him the idea that there might be life beyond the farm, although he could hardly imagine it.

He had come to know the priest through observation and his mother said he was a man of the world, but Cole didn't know what she meant by that. Maybe that he'd been places, important places, and knew things ordinary people had never heard about. His mother had been fond of Father Geary and sometimes Cole imagined she was a little in love with him, even though priests aren't supposed to fall in love. He wondered how much she'd told Father Geary about his father and how meanly he'd treated her, the things he sometimes did to her.

They walked Father Geary to the door, where he put on his coat and wrapped a scarf around his neck. He pulled Cole close and patted him on the back, and Cole could smell his hair cream and the shrill lozenge in his mouth as he whispered, Your mother's with God now. Cole watched him cross the front yard in his black clothes to his car and could see the heavy clouds collecting on his windshield. As he drove away, Cole wondered where this man lived and what he'd do when he got there.

THAT DAY, after the pawnshop. The last time he'd been with her alone, she hurried into the car, her cheeks painted with shame. Going home, they passed some girls selling kittens and pulled over to have a look. His mother scooped an orange kitty into her hands. Cole picked a black one. How much? his mother asked.

Pop's gonna be mad.

Oh, they're free, the older girl said.

He thought he saw his mother smile. They put the kittens in the car and she sat there for a minute without starting it and then tears rolled down her cheeks again. The same girl came over and said, Is she all right? Like his mother couldn't answer for herself, like she wasn't even there.

She pulled back onto the road, and for a long time they were quiet, with just the wind blasting through the windows and the kittens mewing. He finally said, You'll be okay, Ma, and she nodded like he was right and said, I'll be fine, like she needed to say it out loud and confirm it in her own mind. He smiled at her even though he wasn't happy, then turned on the radio, and it was a Woody Guthrie tune and they sang it together, heading home: *Hey, boys, I've come a long ways / Well, boys, I've come a long ways / Oh boys, I've come a long lonesome ways, / Along in the sun and the rain.*

She was dead now and he had begun to hate her for it. He would try very hard to remember her, how pretty she looked in her church clothes or the hard face she made when she smoked, but the pictures in his mind only made him sad.

He never knew what happened to those kittens, because the next day they were gone. He searched the house and the barns and the fields, but there was no trace at all, and he thought maybe his father had dumped them someplace, and sometimes, when he thought back on that last day with her, the orange sky, or singing together so loud, he wondered if it was just something he'd dreamed up.

That whole week Cole didn't go to school and no one came looking for him. Everything kind of stopped. His brothers roaming around, doing nothing. Dishes piled up on the counters, old cans full of butts. For half a day he watched things in the house. The curtains barely moving. Stink bugs climbing up the window frame, then falling back to the floor right before reaching the top; he'd throw his ball, trying to hit one. You could hear things, the wind. Time passed, he guessed. Time had become something else, something strange. You couldn't see the beginning or the end of things. There was only this middle part.

Strangers bringing food, neighbors. Climbing onto the porch, their arms outstretched, holding platters of fried chicken, meatloaf, stuffed peppers. One night, Mrs. Pratt cooked them dinner. Roast beef and green beans. Her name was June, her husband called her Juniper. She had hands that crept softly, like frightened animals. For some reason they didn't have any kids. Mr. Pratt worked for General Electric. He wore clean shoes and had clean fingernails and smelled like limes, and Eddy said he had a desk job. They ate in silence, their forks clanking, like they were waiting for something. After they left, Eddy sat in their father's chair and rolled cigarettes and drank their father's whiskey, and his fingertips had gone yellow and his hands were big and square. Smoke drifted lazily through the room, mixing with the flashing blue light of the TV, and Cole got scared, and thought about all the things around the farm that needed fixing and how nobody had ever bothered to repair them or even notice they were broken.

Eddy was the boss now. He took after their father, ornery and skeptical, but also had their mother's patience. Like all of the Hales, he was tall and had blue eyes, though Eddy's were meaner and the girls liked that. In his dark farm clothes he offered them a dare. They thought they could save him.

Wade shuffled around the house, his clothes baggy and not fastened or buttoned. That was just Wade. He wasn't a stickler for details. He said he planned to join up with the army the minute he turned eighteen and nobody could stop him.

I made up my mind.

You got to finish school first.

Long as they don't throw me out.

Long as you don't cause any trouble.

You don't have to get mad.

I'm not mad.

I made up my mind. You can't talk me out of it.

Eddy handed Cole a toolbox. Here, he said. Make yourself useful.

The greasy metal toolbox had been their father's. It held a bunch of rusty screwdrivers and a hammer and a whole array of nails. With satisfaction, he nailed down some loose boards. When that was done he figured out how to replace a broken windowpane in the cellar with a fresh square of glass and only cut his finger a little bit and it didn't even hurt. He tried to screw the banister back onto the wall, but the screw was stripped and he didn't have another one that fit just right and the wood was too soft to hold it anyway. It was beyond his expertise, he told Eddy.

After a few days he got to thinking things would be all right, that they could go on just the three of them, but then these two men in suits showed up. They stood on the porch like they were selling something. After they made their introductions, the skinny one said, You all's got a default on your loan. I'm here to tell you that the bank's repossessing this farm. He presented the letter like they'd won something.

Eddy said, Our mother had plans to sell it.

The man put his hand on Eddy's shoulder. Too late for that now, son. It'll go up for auction in a couple of weeks.

The other man gave them each a box. Put your stuff in it.

After the men left, Eddy said, Go get in her car.

The garage was dark, the car just sitting there. Eddy swung the doors open with a kind of grace, like a magician about to do a trick. Since Cole was youngest, Eddy made him sit in the back. Cole thought he could still smell exhaust and tried to hold his breath. Where we going, Eddy? Wade said. Eddy didn't answer. He started the engine and backed out fast and drove into the field. The car dipped and lurched. One of her lipsticks rolled around on the floor. The sun was sinking down behind the ridge. It was halfway to dark, and the locust trees were ready to fight with their curled black fists. The wind slammed up against the windows. In the middle of the field Eddy fishtailed and cut the engine.

For a couple of minutes they just sat there, watching the sky go pink like it was hurt. Then Eddy got out, stretching tall with an air of ceremony. Get out.

They stood there waiting. Eddy opened the trunk and took out a bat and held it up over his head. This is for her, he said, and brought it down onto the hood. He raised it up again and brought it back down and went on like that over and over again, and you could hear him heaving with the effort, his face full of menace. Cole cried, he couldn't help it, and Eddy said he'd better quit it or he'd give him something to cry about. Go on, he said, handing him the bat.

I can't.

Eddy gripped his shoulder. Do it for your mother.

The bat was heavier than he could remember from his days in Little

League. He raised it up and closed his eyes briefly, as if in prayer, then brought it down on the car. It scarcely made a dent, but Eddy nodded that he'd done good and rested his hand on the back of his neck, just like his father had.

They took turns. The hood jutting up in a heap of triangles. The windshield splintered. His brothers beat that car so hard Cole almost felt sorry for it. He watched and cried. Tears rolled down his cheeks into his mouth and tasted of dirt. It was their dirt. It was their father's and their grandpa's dirt and all the men who had come before who were ghosts now and guarded the land in their church suits and stocking feet, their pockets full of worms. When he was little, his grandpa took him out on the big orange tractor with wheels as tall as a full-grown man. Cole sat on his lap, surveying the pasture that would one day be his; then his grandpa cut the motor and you could hear all the little creatures scrambling in the dirt and you could hear the grass and the wind. You're a Hale, son, his grandpa told him. Around here that counts for something.

They believed in things—the good Lord. His grandma was always saying the good Lord this and the good Lord that. She said most people were good on the inside, where it mattered. You have to give them a chance to show their goodness, she used to say. Some people need more time, that's all. She liked to make stained-glass cookies and let him do the hammering, crushing the hard candy into tiny bits. He'd climb up on the kitchen stool at the counter and she'd do some design, usually a cross, and tell him how to arrange the pieces. Once it was done, she'd hold it up to the window, and splotches of color shone on the walls. We got church right here, she'd say. Don't even have to leave the house. His grandma could cook. She had big hands for a woman. In her apron, she'd kneel in the garden, tugging weeds, cradling fat tomatoes. Snapdragons up to his elbows. A whole parade of flowers. He had a tire swing. Summers, his mother gave him lunch out of doors. She'd cut the sandwiches in triangles, cream cheese and jelly, her pretty hair full of sun, wind. He'd come through the screen door at the end of the day with dirt on his skin.

They left the car there in the field. They dug a hole and buried the keys like something dead. That car ain't goin' nowhere, Wade said, his shirt soaked through with sweat. We made sure of that, right, Eddy?

Eddy didn't answer him. He was breathing hard, hugging himself.

Cole saw that he was crying. The wind came up behind them, and it was a cold wind. Their shirts filled with it. His brothers stared at the car and what they'd done to it.

The house was dark. The windows pushed back the sunset. The cold wind came up again and he almost felt like running.

What we gonna do now? Wade said. What we gonna do without Mother?

I wish I knew, Eddy said.

They watched TV for a while, and Eddy and Wade got drunk on their father's Jim Beam. Cole left them sleeping on the couch with the television on. He liked the sound of it as he went to bed, and for a minute he could pretend that his parents were out somewhere. He slept in, and when he finally woke it was afternoon. The house was quiet, waiting. He didn't know where his brothers were.

He stepped into the hall and stood outside his parents' door. Since that morning when they'd taken them away on stretchers and covered them with blankets, Eddy said he couldn't go in. Sometimes Cole would put his hand on the wood as if feeling for a heartbeat. Now he turned the knob and stepped inside.

The room was dark; the shades pulled. He tugged on one and it snapped up and flapped around like it was angry, and the room filled up with so much light he had to squint. It was still windy out, and you could see all the trees moving around like a chorus of blind people. His ears filled with the sound they made, and the shadows of branches stretched across the floor and mingled against one another. He tried to open a window, but it was painted shut and he remembered his parents arguing about it, his mother accusing his father of being careless, and this brought their voices back to him and he looked at the unmade bed, half expecting them to be there. He could still see where their heads had been on their pillows. He was crying a little and couldn't remember why he was here, or even who he was. He was like a spirit, feeling the whirl of some other place, the place his mother had gone to.

He climbed onto her side of the bed and pulled the satin hem of the blanket under his chin. He could smell his mother. He shut his eyes very tight and tried not to be afraid, but he was. He tried to talk to God, hoping to feel His presence. He sensed that something was there but didn't know if it was God or not. He had no proof; there were no signs. Gradually, the room came back to him, and he was no longer afraid. He could see the white mountain of his father's pillow and the nightstand beyond it, where the hands of the clock twitched as they moved, and the glass of water his mother had drunk from—three-quarters full. He reached out for it and held it up and the sun filled the glass and then he drank the water and it was warm and tasted like nothing. Maybe he fell asleep, and after a while he heard footsteps and knew it was Wade, because he was slower and stockier than Eddy, and he was glad it was him and then he felt his brother's thick hand pulling him out of the bed, his heavy arm wrapping around him. Wade got him into the hall and down the stairs and out onto the porch, where the sky was a crazy purple and you could see the top of the ridge, the jagged trees. And that's when he saw her. She was up there on the ridge, waving at them. And he waved back. And the sun was behind her and it was red and bright, so very bright. And he shut his eyes, knowing that when he opened them she'd be gone.

3

THEY SLEPT in their uncle's attic on narrow army cots lined up like piano keys. Rainer was his mother's only sibling. His father and his uncle hadn't spoken in years, nobody remembered why. Cole wondered if Rainer even knew. He ran a halfway house full of used-up crooks and put them to work in his window-washing business. It was what he called a satisfactory arrangement. He was skanky as a ferret with his greasy ponytail and coyote face. People said the war had done something to him. He liked to show off his tattoos. Did this one here with ink and a guitar string, he'd announce with pride, twisting his arm back and forth. Every day he wore the same black leather vest with studs on the back like tooth fillings. Eddy called him a burnout, but Cole knew better. You could tell he'd seen things. Sometimes he'd call out in the middle of the night, like he was scared. He told Cole he'd lost his best buddy on a patrol boat. The guy had been blown to pieces. I held him in my arms till the blood ran out, his uncle said. Now he wore his friend's earring, a tiny silver star.

Rainer's woman, Vida, was from Mexico City. Her name, Cole knew, meant *life*. She had a tight mouth, like she was holding pins between her lips. Then she'd smile all of a sudden like someone on a merry-go-round.

Rainer had found her someplace, saved her. It's what their uncle did, save people. Now he was saving them. You could see she'd lived hard. In her eyes you could see her quiet past. After she cut onions and cried or rolled out tortillas, she'd rub her hands like they were sore. Her cooking tasted good, and she was nice to him. Sometimes she pushed his hair off his forehead with her damp, onion-smelling hands and said, *Tan bonitos ojos.* Just wait till the *chicas* find you. They no let you alone.

His uncle warned them to stay away from the ex-cons, who lived in a cinder-block addition off the back porch, but this one named Virgil did card tricks and one time pulled a blue feather out of Cole's ear. He had a face like a mess of old wires. See here, he said. I got the devil in my pocket. He turned his pockets inside out, black dust running through his fingers. You ever seen somethin' like that?

No, sir.

I already been to hell and back, can't go twice.

What was it like?

Let me show you somethin'. He sat down and untied his shoes and took them off and set them aside. Then he rolled off one of his socks. The bottom of his foot was charred black, like he'd walked through fire. See what they done? That's what you get in hell.

How'd you get out?

Virgil glanced up at the sky. The man upstairs got me out. That's the only explanation for it. But I know somethin' 'bout you.

What's that?

Virgil took a pencil from behind his ear and drew an oval on a piece of paper and gave it to Cole. Hold that there, over your head.

What for?

Go on.

Cole did what he said.

Hallelujah! I'm in the presence of an angel.

You're crazy. Cole crumpled up the paper and threw it away. I ain't no angel.

They would talk about their crimes: what they did, what they should've done, what they would've done different if they'd had the chance. By the time some of them had gotten caught they were ready and went willingly. Others put up a fight. It seemed to Cole that their prison memories kept them company, like old friends.

Their uncle's business gave them hope. To his assembled infantry he would declare, Here's your chance at redemption. Make it count.

Solemn as pallbearers, they'd line up to receive their ammunition: a squeegee, a sponge and Rainer's marvelous window-cleaning solution, the recipe for which he would take to his grave. Everybody jammed into Bertha, a boxy copper van that said *Truly-Clear* on either side of it, and, like warriors, they set out to wash windows all over the county, from Hudson all the way to Saratoga.

On weekends, Rainer let the boys work off the books. Even Cole got paid, and he absorbed the experience like an education, peering into the fancy houses in Loudonville or the crooked old row houses down in Albany or the factories on the river, the dirty windows blinking in the sunlight like the sleepy eyes of gangsters and thieves. They did the old house where Herman Melville had lived as a boy, and his uncle gave him a rumpled copy of *Moby-Dick*. Read this, he said.

Cole did. He stayed up turning its pages, the book heavy on his chest. Wade fussed, yanking the blankets up over his head, but Cole kept reading until his eyes drooped. Then he set it down on the nightstand and closed his eyes, thinking about the sea and the smell of it and the sound of the wind and what it would be like out there in the middle of the ocean, and he wished he could go. He wanted to be free, to be on his own. When he worked for his uncle he felt good and he enjoyed it. He liked to use his hands. To go out in the truck. You saw things on the road, people doing stuff you never thought of. Ordinary things. You'd catch people doing this and that.

You see all kinds of things in this business, his uncle told him. Rich and poor, we see it all.

One time they did the college, named after some Indian chief. The campus was high on a grassy hill. You could see the river in the distance, bright as a switchblade, and it gave him the feeling of a miraculous recollection, a memory that comes to you so sudden and true, like the smell of his mother's coffee, how it always woke him before light, or her perfume at the end of the day, hardly noticeable, when she'd lean down to kiss him good night.

They set their ladders up against the library and went to work. The men tried not to be noticed, like they'd get kicked out for being stupid, and it occurred to Cole that being smart was another reason people could be afraid of you. On the drive home, his uncle asked if he wanted to go to college, and the men started whistling and making jokes, so he shrugged as if he didn't care, but Rainer reached across the seat and gripped his shoulder like he knew better. I got a feeling about you, boy, he said. You may just make it out of this town.

RAINER SAID he knew what people were made of. The war had taught him. I could tell you stories, he'd say, make your hairs stand on end. Speculating about one person or another, he'd say, Well, I wouldn't put it past him. If you messed with him he'd never forget it. Same thing if you did something nice. He'd read the newspapers with a magnifying glass, like someone searching for clues. Taking an interest, he called it. You had to look out at the world. You had to open your eyes.

He knew things about his customers, what cars they drove and when they went on vacation. Once, they did some banker's house in Loudonville. Rainer tiptoed all around the place, like someone walking through a minefield. He told Cole to do the garage windows. You won't find no trouble out there. Cole set up his ladder and got started. He had a view of the pool. It was still cold and the pool was covered. He could see a boy around his age in the yard, playing catch with a friend. Must be nice, he thought, rolling out of bed on a summer morning and jumping into that pool. He wondered what it was like to be rich. It didn't seem right that some people got to live like kings and others lived in shit-boxes like the old farm.

After he finished his windows he told his uncle he had to use the bathroom.

Make it quick.

The housekeeper was a black lady with tough eggplant skin, wrangling the hose of the vacuum like an alligator wrestler. She pointed him down the hall. He wandered up a back stairway and found the boy's room, his name, Charles, spelled out in red letters on the door. Soccer trophies lined a shelf, along with other things the boy had collected. Cole had begun to perspire. He went to the window and saw the boy and his friend in the yard, tossing the football. The men were loading the ladders into the truck. He could hear the housekeeper running the vacuum. He was about to leave when something caught his eye on the shelf, a snow globe.

On impulse, he took it down and got some dust on his fingertips. Inside the globe was a trolley car. Cole wondered where he'd gotten it. He knew there had once been trolley cars in Albany and he remembered seeing one on a box of rice in the cupboard, but since the boy had put it on his shelf he concluded that it was a souvenir from some special place. Cole didn't have any souvenirs of his own; he'd never gone anywhere. He shook the snow globe and watched the little flakes dance. Then he put it in his pocket and went back downstairs.

He muttered his thanks to the housekeeper and climbed into the van, his hand curled around the warm glass. Everybody piled in and they got back on the road and a few minutes later they were on the interstate. He felt strangely light, weightless, a little dizzy. Almost like he'd left a piece of himself in that room, some clue to who he was, the real person inside that nobody else knew, not even him.

Later that night, he took out the snow globe and held it in his hands. He shook it once. Taking it had been wrong, but he didn't care. He was glad he had. It was his souvenir now. Again he shook it, watching the flakes swirl, and wondered if the boy would even realize it was gone.

4

THEIR UNCLE KEPT a used 1967 Cadillac hearse in his barn that he'd take out now and again for what he called State Occasions. It still had the white curtains in the windows and he kept a good shine on it. Sometimes he'd go out and sit in it and Vida would leave him be. Death is closer than you think, he told Cole. You can wake up one day not even knowing it's your last. By sundown it's all over.

His other prized possession was an old Harley-Davidson with hornet-green fenders. He'd tinker around with it sometimes, but he never took it out. How come you never ride it? Cole asked him one afternoon.

Rainer looked over at the bike longingly. Someday I'll tell you a story, he said, and wandered off, scratching his head.

Cole decided it was a sad story that had to do with a woman. He had found a dusty old Polaroid in his uncle's desk of this woman who looked like Pocahontas, sitting on the bike with her arms crossed, smirking at whoever was taking the picture. Cole had a feeling that his uncle had missed out on some things. But there were a lot of people like that. This thing or that had happened, or they'd done something stupid. And suddenly their lives weren't what they'd thought. Cole wondered what had happened to this woman, and if his uncle even knew.

At school, people kept their distance, as if the bad thing that had happened to his family was a smell on his clothes, like skunk spray. But there was this one kid, Eugene. Free period, they'd go down the street to Windowbox for burgers. Or they'd walk around the corner to St. Anthony's to see Patrice. She was always hanging around the doors without her coat, shivering. She'd wander over to the fence at the last minute, after the nun blew her whistle. They'd only have a second, her eyes roaming over his face as if she was looking for something. Their hands touching on the fence, her fingertips like raindrops. She had stopped wearing baggy knee socks. Now they hugged her scrawny calves, and her hair was coiled up on the back of her head like a doughnut. Blue powder dusted her eyelids like sky dust, if that even existed. They had something between them, something quiet, true.

Eugene's grandmother lived above Hack's Grocery. His father was in prison for running drugs off the trains. He never spoke of his mother, but one time a picture of her fell out of his pocket when he took out some change and Cole picked it up off the sidewalk. She's dead, Eugene told him. It was something they shared, dead mothers. His grandma worked at the plastics factory. She was a sorter and had the biggest hands he'd ever seen on a woman, like scooped-out tortoise shells. She would rest them on her lap and weave her fingers together. Eugene was serious about school. They did homework together at the library. People would always look at Eugene on account he was black and stood out. The library was in an old house, and when it was cold out they'd light a fire, and the fireplace was so big you could walk into it, with an old black kettle hanging there like the kind witches use. The books sat on their shelves like spectators and smelled of all the dirty hands that had turned their pages. The regulars sat in the green leather chairs, geezers with sharp red faces, or ladies who looked like teachers, sourpusses, Eugene called them, snapping their pages, pursing their lips. Old people were always ready to condemn you for something. Even his own grandfather used to beat him with a rolled-up newspaper when he hadn't even done anything. There was this one guy who sat up in the stacks at his own personal table, with papers all over the place. He'd made an impressive chain out of gum wrappers, the length of his arm. Once, he offered Cole a piece of Wrigley's Spearmint. A day or so later, Cole remembered the stick of gum in his pocket, now warm, and took it out and split it with Eugene, thinking fondly of the man up in the stacks as he chewed it.

In Chosen, there was a man who walked backwards. He was nearly seven feet tall, stooped over a little, with legs like an ostrich's. He made it look easy, his neck twisted over his shoulder so he could see where he was going. Nobody had a clue why he did it. One day they followed him home, zigzagging across the street like spies. The man lived with his mother in a trailer park behind the Chinese restaurant that was rumored to cook dogs and cats. People said they drove around in a van at night, picking up strays. When you walked past the kitchen door you could hear the steaming pots and hissing woks and the cooks arguing in Chinese with cigarettes hanging out of their mouths or sometimes shooting dice. Cole didn't know how the man who walked backwards could even fit inside the trailer. He'd heard his mother was a gypsy, that you could go to her if you wanted your fortune told. They saw her poke her head out to see if anyone was watching, then she slammed the door and dropped the little shade.

He and Eugene left the trailer park walking backwards. It felt kind of good. You saw things differently. When they got back to Eugene's, his grandmother was sitting out on the stoop in a lawn chair. What you boys doing walking like that? she said. For some reason it was the funniest thing they'd ever heard and they couldn't stop laughing. The old woman shook her head. Lord, you a pair. I just don't know what to do wit you.

His uncle dug up a bike for him, a rusty blue Raleigh, and set it up with a crate on the back tire and had him do errands when he needed something, lightbulbs at the hardware store, a carton of smokes, and Cole didn't like how people always looked at him in town, like he had the words Dead Parents stamped on his forehead. He found he could get away with things. He could lift a candy bar in plain sight, and even if somebody noticed they never said anything.

On Sundays, Rainer made them go to church. They slicked down their hair with Brylcreem and buttoned up their shirts and polished their shoes, and he'd hand out ties. They walked there, passing the front porches on

Division Street, inviting the sympathetic admiration of the neighbors. Impromptu fatherhood had elevated their uncle's status in the neighborhood, and he walked with the sweep and grace of a dignitary.

In church, Rainer would sit in the last pew with his long legs stretched out in the aisle and his arms crossed over his chest, rolling a toothpick around in his mouth. Usually he'd do the crossword puzzle. A look of enlightenment would cross his face and then he'd fill in a word. After church he bought them doughnuts and the other customers would nod and smile too much, like they felt sorry for them and were trying hard not to show it.

Everybody knew the Hales. You'd see it register on their faces. Even his teachers. They knew the dirt farm he'd been raised on. They knew his parents were freaks who'd killed themselves. They knew his brother Wade got in fights, and that Eddy was a lowlife hood who'd end up fixing cars. They didn't like Rainer and his ratty ponytail and his Mexican girlfriend and his halfway house and his crooked window-washing outfit. And even when Cole knew the answers and raised his hand they never called on him.

But his uncle thought he was a genius.

One Sunday, late in the afternoon, this salesman came to the door, hawking encyclopedias. They were in the middle of supper, but Rainer let the man in. You won't be needing no sales pitch in this house, he told him. I got a real intelligent boy on my hands.

Is that so?

Rainer came around behind Cole's chair and put his hands on his shoulders. The weight of his uncle's hands reassured him that he was all right, that he would grow up and become a man just like anybody else. In that same moment he knew that he loved his uncle better than his own father and that he hated his father for hurting his mother and taking her with him.

I always say you can't go no place in this world without an education. Just look at me if you don't believe it.

How's that? the salesman asked.

I guess I got sidetracked.

What by?

A little something called Vietnam.

The salesman nodded and took his money. Well, you won't find no better source than them books.

They figured out how to make shelves out of cement blocks and wood planks and stacked the books while Rainer stood there with his hands on his hips. Not half bad, boys, not half bad. His eyes twinkled with happiness and pride, and Cole was proud, too. From then on, every night before bed, his uncle asked him to read something out loud. Cole would pick one of the volumes at random and close his eyes as the pages flipped back and forth, then stick a finger down to mark a spot, any spot, it didn't matter. He read about ancient civilizations, aerodynamics, medieval castles, India, taxidermy. You can never know too much in this life, Rainer said. Don't be ignorant like your uncle.

SOMETIMES, they missed her so bad they had to go home. They ran through the woods like wolves, jumped over logs, spun out of thickets. With the moon on their backs they ran.

They stood at the top of the ridge.

Wade said, It's still ours.

Always will be, Eddy said.

They ran down through wet grass, knocking crickets to the ground. They climbed onto the porch, noisy in their muddy boots. They peered through the black windows. You could see the empty living room where they used to watch TV, and the couch where their father slept away half the day. They found the spare key where their mother kept it, in the spigot of the water pump, and went in like thieves and dug around in the old cupboards. Up in the very back of one, Eddy discovered a bottle of Jack Daniel's and saltines and baker's chocolate, and they handed the whiskey to Cole and he swallowed some, and Wade said it was about time he got drunk, and Cole wanted to. They all three of them drank the whiskey and ate the crackers and the bitter chocolate, and pretty soon the world looked soft and warm instead of cold and sharp, and it was a good feeling and he liked it. They ran into the field and howled at the moon, riling up the coyotes, whose cries rose up over the trees like fire, and then they appeared on the ridge with their tails up like the tips of bayonets and went on yelping, too scared to come down. Wade did his monster walk and the whole pack ran away. They found a horse blanket in the barn and lay in the cold darkness under the stars and slept all rolled together, as they'd done as small children, until the sun came bright and sudden, like a fist.

THE HOUSE WAS cursed. That's what people said. No one wanted it. The bank owned it now. They'd already sold off the land on the other side of the ridge and somebody was putting up houses. You could see the frames going up, one next to another around a horseshoe, and bulldozers slumped in the field like strange clumsy animals. During the day you could hear the hammers and the radio and the laughter of the men, who always pissed in the woods. They had taken away their mother's car on a flatbed. The car was in the junkyard, waiting with all the other ruined cars to be crushed for scrap. After hours, they'd go to see it, knowing it was never getting out of there in one piece. Eddy had a thing for this girl, Willis, who sometimes came along. They would climb up on the old cars and Eddy would play his horn. Some of the cars looked pretty good and Cole liked to pretend to drive them. One time Eddy got one started and showed him how to drive it. He steered around in the field with the tires squealing and the girl laughing in the back seat and fireflies all over the place. Willis had the prettiest laugh he'd ever heard and she always smelled nice. When they found a car that worked, he'd play chauffeur and Eddy would act like a big-deal trumpet player, sitting with his woman in the back. If they started kissing, Cole got out and wandered around. He'd climb up the hill near the wires. From up there you could see the little houses in town and the big houses here and there on the outskirts. You could see their old farm with its empty barns. And you could see the long silver trains, the moonlight gleaming on the rails, and you could hear their sad songs all through the night.

A couple weeks later, a big brown dumpster appeared at the farm, up on the lawn. A man in coveralls was down there, throwing stuff out. At night the boys went through it all, the artifacts that defined the Hales. They opened his mother's old canning jars and ate the fat, sweet peaches and oily red peppers, the juice dripping down their wrists. They found their father's fishing gear and wading boots, Wade's football trophies, Cole's old crayon drawings from kindergarten, Eddy's boutonniere from the prom, and there were birthday cards and Halloween masks and marbles everywhere. It was all stuff that had no meaning to anyone else, but to him and his brothers it was evidence that their family had existed, that they'd lived a happy life here once, that they'd raised cows whose sweet milk was put in bottles and hand-delivered all over the county. All because of them, people had milk in the morning and ate corn in summertime with lots of butter and salt and pepper on it. If that wasn't something to be proud of, he didn't know what was.

Winter ended finally and you'd see colors here and there and people came out of their houses, yanking at their gardens, hammering nails into fences. You'd see horses kicking out their hind legs like they were figuring out how to use them again. Cole was busy with school. He'd fold his tests up in his pocket and present them later to his uncle, ironing out the creases in the paper with the heel of his hand, his grade, usually an A, chicken-scratched in red pen as if based on some tentative conclusion and bestowed with regret. Still, he got along all right, but the farm, the house, was always in his mind, the idea of his mother wandering past the windows, fluid as water.

In May their father's birds returned, landing on the barn up near the cupola, the same three falcons that came back every year when the weather started to warm. His father had raised them from birth. He'd kept rats in the cellar to feed the baby birds, and sometimes the rats would escape and their mother would stand on a chair and scream while everybody ran through the house trying to catch them. You can't count on much in this world, his father told him once, but those birds come back every year.

Always in spring, when the apple trees got their pink buds and you could go outside without your coat and the air smelled like his mother's perfume, his father would walk out into the field like a soldier in his *F Troop* gloves and stretch out his arms like a crucified man. A bird would drop down on his arm for a moment, flutter its wings a little and then fly away again.

They were majestic creatures, he thought, perched up there on the roof. They lifted their brown wings ever so slightly, as if in greeting, their claws clicking on the rusty sheet metal. Cole wondered if they'd seen his father up in heaven. Maybe they'd brought a message from him. Hey, you birds, he called. They fluttered their wings again and he knew what they wanted, so he lifted up his arms into a *T* and stood there waiting, rigid as a scarecrow. The birds teetered on the ledge like they were trying to decide, and then the biggest one flew down and landed on his forearm. He wasn't prepared for its weight and staggered back a step. The sharp yellow claws tore through his shirtsleeve and cut his skin.

Easy, now, Eddy said, coming up behind him.

The falcon fluttered prettily. Cole's arm shook under its weight and it hurt, but he refused to cry. He thought maybe it was a test. The bird looked at him and he looked at the bird and in that moment something was decided, something important that Cole could not name, and then it opened its wings and flew off. It made a wide arc across the sky like a sigh of music, then joined the others and disappeared behind the trees.

5

THE NEWS ABOUT the farm started down at the café over hash and eggs and went home with a variety of strangers, who exchanged it with deliberation, like a foreign currency. They were city people. He was a professor, she a homemaker. They had one little girl.

Bank practically gave it to 'em, their uncle reported over supper.

But the house stayed empty for a few months and then one day in August they saw a car parked on the lawn. It was a sports car—a shiny green convertible. Then they saw her, and everything slowed down. She was like the delicate porcelain figures his mother had collected, with pale skin, blond hair. She was carrying a cardboard box and talking to someone over her shoulder, and then a man came around behind her and they climbed up the porch steps and went inside, the door closing with a slap that echoed through the air.

It's theirs now, Eddy said.

They were up on the ridge, their pockets jammed with raspberries, and Wade and Eddy were getting high. They watched the lights come on one by one. They could hear the little girl laughing. Soon it was dark and the whole place was all lit up, big yellow squares of light, and Cole remembered how their father would holler about burning electricity for no good reason and how money was running down the drain every goddamn second. Well, that was all right with him, because it didn't matter anymore, there was no money anyway. And then he'd scoop up whatever change he could find and drive off in his truck. But these people didn't seem worried about their money running out. They opened the windows and their voices drifted out, and it occurred to Cole that they sounded happy and he found himself feeling happy, too, like he did when he watched happy people on TV shows. Then somebody started playing their old piano, the first song his mother ever taught him, the *Moonlight* Sonata, and it came back to him how she'd told him to play it slow and explained that when Beethoven wrote it he was full of longing, and how she longed for things, too, and how longing was a private thing, it was a part of life you eventually got used to, and he remembered that she'd looked up at the window for a moment, at the willows scratching against the glass, and he could see the woman she was, underneath the one he knew as his mother, and it scared him.

The music stopped, and he realized they'd all three been listening.

How could she do it? Cole said.

Eddy smoked his cigarette down to the filter and flicked it into the dark. I don't know, Cole. Some things you can't explain.

They didn't want us no more, Wade said.

Hey. Eddy yanked Wade's arm. Quit that. She didn't mean nothing. It was Pop. He made her do it.

Wade shoved him away and Eddy looked mad and suddenly they were on the ground, pushing and pulling and smacking each other. Cole tried to pull them apart, but once they got going you couldn't stop them, and he started to cry a little, and it felt stupid and good so he cried some more and it made them stop, and they got up off the ground and came over to him and tried to steady him and waited for him to calm down.

Eddy said, Hold on, now, Cole. Take it easy.

She loved you best, Wade said.

Come on. Let's get you home.

Cole glanced back at the house and saw somebody pulling down a shade and then another, and before long all the shades had been pulled, and this signified to him that it was over, this part of his life, this place. Everything would be different now. Everything would change.

They walked back to Rainer's in silence. Vida had kept supper for them and they sat down and ate with the TV on, some John Wayne movie, and nobody said anything and they brought their dishes to the sink and went up to bed. Cole got into bed and Eddy came and sat on the edge and pulled the covers up and smoothed his forehead with the cold, rough palm of his hand. I'll be back later.

Where you going?

I got a date.

With Willis?

Yeah. You okay?

He nodded and turned away so Eddy would leave, but he wasn't okay. He could feel a darkness filling up his legs and arms and hands and feet, like the blackest, coldest water. As he lay in the dark the idea occurred to him to run away. He let himself picture life on the road, hitchhiking from place to place, sleeping in yards and churches, cooking hot dogs on sticks like he'd done in Boy Scouts, but the interstate with its screaming trucks and doting strangers terrified him.

One of the ex-cons started playing harmonica on the back porch, and he liked the cowboy sound of it. It was a comfort to him. And he knew that whoever was playing it had been through something, too, something bad, and had survived it. When you thought about it, a lot of people did things. It wasn't like you could just jump off the side of the earth and disappear. You had to figure out how to go on. That's all you could do.

All these men had done things, been through things. They didn't want to be there, either. Maybe they wanted to live someplace warm, where the sun was hot and bright, where nobody knew them. He felt kin to them now. Men who'd been in prison had dulled-down faces like the dented hubcaps his uncle sold to the poor suckers on Baker Avenue. Rainer would set up a lawn chair and lay out all the hubcaps like expensive jewelry and then bring home pork chops for Vida. You could see in their eyes they had broken hearts. They were heartbroken men who couldn't do much, couldn't even love. It was the simplest thing to do, loving someone, only it was the hardest thing, too, because it hurt.

The next morning, his uncle took him to buy shoes. These are going in the trash, he said, holding up Cole's old pair. For one thing, they stink. And for another, they don't tie good.

He'd always worn his brother's shoes, third time around.

You can't walk around in another man's shoes, his uncle told him. That's enough of that.

They went to Browne's and looked over the selection. Now, style's important, but comfort matters most. You can't mess around when it comes to your feet.

What about these? He showed his uncle a pair of Converse sneakers, the same ones Eugene had.

All right. Let's see if they have your size.

The woman measured his feet and then squeezed his bones. You're a thirteen, she said.

You got them tall genes from your father.

She disappeared into the back and they sat there, waiting, in the vinyl chairs. Finally, she brought out a box. We have them in white. It was like opening a present—taking off the lid, pulling the paper away, holding the brand-new sneakers. They had the good smell of fresh rubber.

You won't get struck by lightning in those, his uncle said. Them things are sharp.

They fit, Cole said.

You're your own man now, son.

Yes, sir. He walked around the store, back and forth and in a circle.

Can he wear them out?

Of course, the lady said.

Sold! his uncle proclaimed, taking a wad of cash from his pocket.

He felt good in his new All-Stars and he wondered what Eddy would think. He touched his uncle's shoulder. Thanks, Uncle Rainer.

That's my pleasure, son. Wear them well.

Disappear

DISAPPEAR, she thinks. And he does.

Now she is alone.

And the world is gray.

She won't miss him. She refuses to.

Before, well, there was a whole life inside that word. Before he lost all their money. Before that woman. Had he convinced himself she didn't know?

The last time, she sent Cole in and sat out in the car, watching the empty streets, thinking maybe he'd come out and apologize and they could go back to being normal. The minutes went by and she watched the trains rolling in, rolling out. People going and coming. Not her, she'd never gone anywhere. All of a sudden a whole hour had gone by, so she had to go in. She didn't like bars, and especially not Blake's, which smelled dirty, and she inevitably saw people she could do without, men at the bar or shooting pool in the back, men she'd gone to high school with who had wanted to date her, men who'd fixed things around the farm or did business with her husband. Her boy wasn't there, and the bartender nodded that he'd gone upstairs. She stood there, trying to look indifferent, and he poured her a coffee, but she pushed it back for something stronger. I'll take some of that Wild Turkey. She drank it down. She wasn't a drinker, this was only medicinal. He didn't charge her.

She stepped into the narrow vestibule and saw her son waiting for his father at the top of the stairs, the door shut, their drunken laughter pushing through. Come on, she said, and waved him down. He can walk home for all I care.

Relieved, Cole hurried down. She heard the door open, but she didn't look back to see her half-dressed husband. Instead, she took her son's warm hand, a hand already callused beyond its years, and they went out to the car and drove back to the farm. She'd glanced in the rearview mirror and saw Cal running into the street, his shirt buttons undone, his shoes and socks in his hand. He could go to hell.

For her, it was over right then. *They* were over. Nothing much mattered after that, not really it didn't. But she knew he'd never let her leave him on her own two feet.

Still, she entertained a variety of fragmented dreams. For many years she'd done so and had a whole collection of possibilities that sang to her like the silver bars of a tree chime. She'd always wanted to go back to school, to become a nurse. Medicine intrigued her. Maybe because she'd grown up with sick adults and tended to them. Her mother first, then her father. She'd done right by them; she had nothing to apologize for. Like many women, she'd dreamed of marrying somebody rich. She'd had the looks for it. But she'd fallen for Cal and that was all there was to it. How he'd loped around in that big coat of his with eyes that could stop your heart at a glance. Even how hard he'd hold her; she was not fragile.

Somewhere around three in the morning, she heard the truck. She'd fallen asleep on the couch, a little afraid about what she'd done, guilt pinching her nerves. He came in heavily, stomping through the house in his big boots. Maybe he saw her, maybe he didn't, she couldn't tell with her eyes shut tight, and then he yanked on the banister and hauled himself upstairs, where the door closed behind him. They were apart all right. They were done.

In the morning, she got the boys up to milk and feed the cows, then fixed them eggs and pancakes and sat there drinking coffee while they ate. The younger two caught the bus, and Eddy took her car and drove out to the community college, where he was taking a business course, even though he had no interest in it; he wanted to be a musician. It was his father pushing him to go, but of course he wouldn't pay for it. Eddy paid his own fees.

That's all right, Ma, he told her. I don't want nothing from him.

She'd heard him play in the school band, going to all the football games just so she could. Same bleachers as when she was a girl, to watch Cal play. With his broad back and big hands, he'd been a good quarterback. Once she first saw him she knew she'd have his babies. His pretty eyes, his good-smelling red coat, how warm he was underneath, the sting of tobacco on his tongue, the moon later in the field. But she was terrified of love. She did what he told her to.

That morning, she did the breakfast dishes, then washed the floor and went up to make the boys' beds and clean their bathroom, and when she had finished that she went back down to the kitchen and made a pot roast with potatoes and carrots and onions so they'd have a decent meal when they came home. Finally, she did the ironing, taking care to get Cal's collars just so, the way he liked them. He was a farmer through and through, but had certain vanities when it came to special occasions. After church he always went to the track and lost more money, and she'd scream at him and flail away at him, but he'd always give her some little gift, saltwater taffy or licorice drops or just a sweet gesture, and she always ended up forgiving him. And they'd go on again till the next time. He could be gentle with her when they'd cuddle up at night, and sometimes she was so amazed that such a rough man could show such sweetness that she'd cry over it.

SHE'D BEEN a good mother. This is what she has, the one thing she knows for sure. It was best when they were babies. Those little T-shirts with the snaps. The smell of the baby detergent. Their little puffy hands, perfect little feet. She and Cal made pretty babies—everybody said so. They'd grown up to be strong, good-looking boys and they'd be good men, too, she'd put money on it. Even Wade, who liked his food. He was the child who made her feel safe. Her protector. Anything happened, Wade could take care of it. But people thought he was slow. Dumb, even. He just took his time, that was all! The teachers didn't have the patience to teach him right, only she did, and she'd taught him to read as well as anyone else. And he had the same lovely disposition as their cows. Sometimes he'd get sent home from school for beating somebody up, but when he told her about what happened with such earnestness, his blue eyes so wide and true, she always believed he'd been in the right. Sometimes it's innocent people who get punished the most, she'd tell him, and he'd cry in her arms.

She'd spend the next few days just being around him, working side by side doing chores, or watching him build something, as he so often liked to do. Her oldest, Eddy, didn't fight but still had an edge to him. He'd give you a look and that's all it took. He was something like Cal, with the same ego, the same showy confidence. Her youngest took after her in how he thought and saw things. A diplomat. They had long, detailed conversations even when he was a small child. He could work things out in his head so they made sense. He could put things together and take them apart. At the age of ten he could wire a lamp and fix a radio. She could talk to him like an adult and sometimes told him private things that she knew she shouldn't. He didn't need to hear about her problems, but he'd listen. And she needed somebody to talk to. Considering all the aspects of a problem, he'd finally say, You'll be all right, Ma.

Other women were always complaining, but she loved being a housewife and mother. Tending the children. Going outside come morning with the dogs. Climbing up the ridge through the high grass, her apron dappled with burrs. The fresh sun, the cold air. The feeling in her body of being used. The heaviness in her womb and breasts. Her thighs. God had given her a capable pair of hands. And she used them. She used her whole body.

She loved the house, too. If she had to pick, it would be her kitchen she missed the most. That big old porcelain sink she never could get the stains out of. The pies and cookies she'd make—a quince pie sometimes, with apples and honey. The quince tree outside the kitchen door had been in the ground for a century, and in spring the boys tracked in the red petals on their shoes. The satisfaction she felt putting a meal on the table. It was in the small things, she knew, where life made sense. When she had a meal served and the boys would sit down, polite as nuns, and nod their heads with pleasure, the warm food filling them up, making them grow, making them happy. Well, there was nothing more satisfying in her mind than that.

How do you evaluate a life? He had taken her with him; he'd made her. Lie down here next to me, he said. You'll be all right. Stroking her hair, her damp head. Just start dreaming, that's all you gotta do. Just let yourself go.

And he'd touched her. Even as the fumes grew thick. I've loved you my whole life, he said.

And that's all she remembers. It was her last gift to him. Because in her life she was someone who gave. Gave, not took, and never asked for anything.

THE SHERIFF COMES first. Her boys stand outside, wearing blankets like cloaks. Her youngest crying, slapping his tears so nobody sees. They watch the men bring them out—first Cal, then her—and push them into the truck like bread in an oven. Sheriff Lawton with his clipboard, his eyes prickling—he's not a man to show his feelings. He sets his big hand on Cole's shoulder. Anything you need? he says, and her boy just looks at him. Who could answer that question? Even now she doesn't have a clue. Death brings no revelations.

Her boys wait, watching the truck pull out, the patrol car. The air fills with dust. Always there was dust in her house, no matter how much she scrubbed, and she scrubbed plenty. Dust on the surfaces, on her boys' handsome faces, in their fingernails when she'd pull the covers up, on their cheeks as she bent to kiss them good night. They worked this farm. They worked this land. It gave them something in return. It gave you your strength, your will. You can never wash it off. You never should.

MARY LAWTON'S STATION WAGON pulls onto the grass. She gets out and stands there, shaped like a club chair in her big coat, round in the middle with skinny legs. Then she gets her bucket, mop and jug of ammonia and marches inside the house like a suffragette, ready to speak her mind. While she works, scouring the kitchen, tearing the sheets from the beds, she scolds the empty rooms. She doesn't rush, relishing the clean smell, her accomplishment. Mary: her best true friend, her confidante. The only person she told things to. Because Mary knows this life, how it can cross you.

When her work is done Mary sits on the steps and smokes and cries a little and shakes her head. Then she grinds her cigarette into the dirt, locks the place up and goes home.

TOWARD THE END, she'd had to find work. Any work, doing whatever. She wasn't proud. The manager at Hack's took pity on her and hired her for the graveyard shift, stocking shelves. When the rodents came out, that's when she did, too. All the creatures of the night—skunks, opossum, Ella Hale. Cal didn't like her working, of course, though only for selfish reasons. He said it wasn't right, her going out late at night. As if he gave a damn. She should be home with her children, he argued. It's money, she told him, knowing full well it was Cal who didn't want to be at home.

She remembers the drive into town on those long black roads. The feeling of it, the feeling in her. A kind of freedom. How she'd smoke two or three cigarettes one after another. Roll down the window, the wind like a shout, the whole world alive with cold. Then, in the parking lot, just sit for a minute, thinking. Put her hair back in a barrette, slide some gloss on her lips. Pull her flannel shirt down, smooth her jeans. She wore Cole's roller-skating knee pads so it wouldn't hurt when she stocked the low shelves. She could kneel down there for a long time, pushing in boxes of laundry soap, kitty litter, big bags of kibble.

They let her have a break, and usually she'd get something from the machine. Sit there in the plastic chair. Unwrapping the candy bar, taking her time to eat it. Then out into the cold night to smoke. Freight trains wailing. Nothing like a cigarette on a cold night. When she drove home it was just getting light, the fog an eerie tide rolling in over the fields. Like a woman returning from a secret assignation, she'd wearily climb the stairs, looking in on her sleeping boys. She'd undress in the bathroom, relishing the privacy, scrubbing herself with cold water, then climb into bed naked beside her husband, lulled by the cadence of his breathing, the stink of bourbon, and fall asleep as the room filled with sunshine.

SHE VISITS the boys at her brother's place. Rainer and the Mexican woman. They will have to do what they can. The boys around the table, their fingers clasped in prayer, like men playing poker, hiding their hands and muttering the words they can no longer trust, *Our Father, who art in heaven* . . . Their uncle smiling with quiet pride, not wanting to let on how much he's missing her, his only sister. They hadn't spoken in five years, a quarrel between Cal and him over nothing important, just two grown men slobbering over their convictions. Her blue-eyed babies grown up so big, silently passing bowls of food, sneaking scraps to the dogs at their feet.

She cannot cry now. Tears are not allowed. Only the strange gray light pressing down, a gray warmth like the fur of a new skin.

HER HUSBAND HAD STRAYED, but not her, she'd been loyal to a fault. She had run her soft hands across his lean frame, his long torso, ribs that reminded her of the hull of a ship.

He had a physical grace, a kind of distinction that her boys now have. Maybe not Wade, who is stout and slow-moving, but Eddy and Cole certainly, with agile hands and long limbs like their father.

You have this life and what you make of it. And what had she done? Wife and mother. Her life in the kitchen and other disorderly rooms, folding and shoving and ironing and scrubbing, and her one indulgence, the fine lemon-verbena cream she rubbed on her feet. She was a country-woman, large-boned yet slim, strong yet aching—lonesome, neglected. She had loved him so hard and gotten her heart broke. Her mother had said not to marry him. He was coarse, lacking emotional fluency, an eloquence of the soul. He was rough with her, could make her feel small, vulnerable. But also protected. *Alive.*

Life History

I

THEY WERE chroniclers of art. Historians, they admired authenticity. They responded to beauty, to the elegant mathematics of composition, the moody pulp that was color, the spectacle of light. To George, line was the narrative; to Catherine, it was an artery to the soul.

She was a painter, a muralist. Mostly she worked in churches, broken cathedrals in remote corners of the city. The work had come to her by accident through an old professor from graduate school. Over time she'd developed a following and was well known among a particular few.

They paid her little, but she didn't mind. The pay was irrelevant.

Her work was meticulous, ornate. Sacred. She had the hands of a nurse, careful and sure. She was a Catholic. She painted her love for God, her fear. At the end of the day her arms ached. She cleaned brushes, folded rags, the smell of pigments and linseed oil in her nostrils.

She went to work in overalls, her hair pinned up in tortoiseshell combs. It was a cathedral off Columbus on West 112th Street with goblins and cherubs tucked in the corners. The smoke of burning candles. In the transept chapel, a wall painting of the crucifixion had been damaged during a storm. The roof had leaked and rain had run down over the face of Jesus like tears. Was it an ironic accident, she wondered, or some portent of imminent sorrow? Often superstitious, she believed a divine subtext could be found under the meaningless shimmer of ordinary events.

Late one afternoon, several weeks into her restoration, an elderly couple came into the church. They were an odd pair. He appeared to be the woman's attendant, a black man in a plaid wool cap and an overcoat, holding the woman's arm. She was white and perhaps a good deal older, dressed in an outfit with a high ruffled collar, her shoes echoing across the terrazzo floors. He shuffled her along, their voices amplified in the emptiness. Together, with the man's hand over the woman's, they lit a candle, the wick igniting with the rasp of a secret.

Catherine stood back, evaluating her work. She had addressed the detrimental changes caused by the rain and had matched the pigments precisely. The vibrancy of the original painting shone through. It might've been odd to think that she'd become intimate with her subject, but she had. She found herself wondering what He thought of her, His attaché to the living world.

It was almost five, already dark. She hated the unyielding darkness of winter. Franny and the nanny would be back from the playground by now, and Mrs. Malloy eager to catch her train. A cold draft summoned her from the doorway as she pulled on her coat and scarf. Behind her, she could hear the old couple's clattering approach through the empty sanctuary. They were mumbling to each other, words she couldn't make out, and then the woman clutched ahold of Catherine's arm. Alarmed, she turned around.

She's just saying hello, the old man said.

But the woman offered only a troubling stare, her eyes fluttering like moths, and Catherine discerned that she was blind.

Now, you know it ain't polite to stare, the man told the woman. Let's leave this nice young lady alone. He unclenched her grasp from Catherine's coat and, in an awkward sort of dance, maneuvered her toward the door. The woman twisted around again, looking back at Catherine, and held her unseeing, terrified gaze.

Catherine buttoned her coat. She needed to get home.

Through the clerestory windows she could see the moonless sky. Leaving the balmy darkness of the cathedral for the swift cold air of the city she felt overcome, troubled by the interchange with the strange couple, the woman's blindness. She walked home quickly, wrapping her scarf around her head, the people on the street hiding their faces, bracing themselves against the bitter wind.

• • •

IT WAS THE WINTER of 1978. They were living in a gloomy apartment on Riverside Drive, a short walk from the university where George was completing his doctorate and teaching two sections of Western Art Survey. Often, he'd told her, at the end of a slide presentation, he'd find the students asleep. This didn't surprise her. Her husband could be dull. Since their marriage, it would be four years in August, his life, and hers by extension, had been controlled by his dissertation and the temperamental declarations of his adviser, Warren Shelby. George would come home from their meetings in a state. Pale, beleaguered, he'd retreat to the bedroom with a juice glass full of Canadian Club and watch reruns of *M*A*S*H*. In Catherine's mind, the dissertation was an existential malfeasance, a relative from some foreign place, a hoarder of conundrums and neurotic tics, who'd moved into their lives and refused to leave. His subject was the painter George Inness, a disciple of the Hudson River School, whom she had come to know through an esoteric collection of evidence, the walls of the apartment shingled with index cards, scraps of insight and cryptic notations, postcards of Inness's landscapes taped here and there (even one over the toilet) and an Inness quote that had been gone over so many times with a blue pen that the paper had ripped. Folding laundry or doing some mundane task, she'd read the quote again and again. *Beauty depends on the unseen, the visible upon the invisible.*

On George's small fellowship, the apartment was barely affordable. They had few possessions: the wingchair they'd found at an estate sale, prickly with horsehair, its spent legs splayed like a drunk's; the Persian rug that had belonged to his parents; the camelback sofa from her distant aunt, covered in faded celadon damask, that served to accommodate the rare visitor, usually her sister, Agnes, who'd stay a few days until the crowded apartment drove her crazy. The building had no elevator. She'd drag the stroller up five flights, holding her daughter's little hand, and it could take half an hour to get upstairs. Finally, she'd twist open the locks and enter their cluttered, diminutive haven, every scrap of its splintery floors devoted to some indispensable child-rearing apparatus. Their bedroom was the size of a sandbox, the lumpy double bed jammed between the walls. Frances, who was three, slept in the alcove, the foot of her little bed piled with coats, hats and mittens that wouldn't fit in the closet. The apartment's only redeeming feature was the view, which reminded her almost exactly of George Bellows's *Winter Afternoon,* the heartless blue of the river, the rusty milkweed on its banks, the white snow and banners of shadow, the ordinary mystery of a woman bundled up against the cold in a red coat. The river made her pensive and a little melancholy, and as she gazed through the dirty windows she would try to remember her original self—the girl she'd been before she met George and they'd married to save themselves, his name like a stranger's dress you slip on and walk around in, before she'd become Mrs. George Clare, like her rapacious, chain-smoking mother-in-law. Before she'd assumed her alias as devoted wife and mother. Before she'd left Cathy Margaret behind—that heron-boned, spider-legged, ponytailed girl, now abandoned for more important tasks, like changing diapers, ironing shirts, cleaning the oven. Not that she was complaining or even unhappy; for all intents and purposes she was content. But she sensed there must be something more to life, some deeper reason for being, some dramatic purpose, if only she could find out what it was.

LIKE MANY UNSUSPECTING COUPLES, they'd met in college. She was a sophomore; George was graduating that May. With mannered indifference, they'd pass each other on the sidewalks of Williamstown, she in her bulky Irish sweaters and hand-me-down kilts, he in his ratty tweed blazer, smoking Camels. He lived in the mustard Victorian on Hoxsey Street, with a group of art-history majors who had already cultivated a stuffy, curatorial arrogance that, with just a glance, reduced her to the chubby girl from Grafton with gravel dust in her shoes. Unlike George and his tony friends, Catherine was here on a scholarship; her father managed a quarry just across the border. She lived in the dorms, in a suite with three monastic biology majors. This was 1972, she was nineteen years old, and in those days, the unspoken hierarchy in the Art History Department ensured that the few female students were decidedly underappreciated.

Their first conversation occurred at a lecture on the great sixteenth-century painter Caravaggio. It had rained that morning and she was late, the auditorium a sea of brightly colored rain jackets. An empty seat caught her eye in the middle of a row. Apologizing, making people stand, she shuffled down to it, discovering that it was George in the seat beside her.

You should thank me, he said. I've been saving it for you.

It's the only one left.

I think we both know why you sat here. He smiled like he knew her. George Clare, he said, reaching for her hand.

Catherine—Cathy Sloan.

Catherine. His hand was sweaty. In just a few seconds an intimacy seemed to infect them like some contagious disease. They talked briefly about mutual classes and professors. He had a very slight French accent and said he'd lived in Paris as a young boy. An apartment like *Floor Scrapers*. Do you know Caillebotte?

She didn't.

We moved to Connecticut when I was five, and my life hasn't been the same since. He smiled, making a joke, but she could tell he was serious.

I've never been to Paris.

Are you in Hager's class?

Next semester.

He gestured at the screen, where the artist's name was spelled out in crimson letters. You know about him, right?

Caravaggio? A little.

One of the most incredible painters in history. He'd hire prostitutes for his models and transform saucy street tarts into rosy-cheeked virgins. There's a certain poignant justice in that, don't you think? Even the Madonna had a cleavage.

Up close, he smelled of tobacco and something else, some musky cologne. In the close room, the high windows fogged with condensation, she had begun to sweat under her wool sweater. He was gazing at her as one gazes at a canvas, she thought, perhaps trying to solve her riddles. Like most Williams boys, he was wearing an oxford shirt and khaki trousers, but there were stylistic anomalies—rawhide bracelets around his wrist, the black canvas slippers (from Chinatown, he later told her), the rain-splattered beret on his lap.

Didn't he kill someone? Over something stupid, right?

A game of tennis. Apparently a very bad loser. Do you play?

Tennis?

We could play some time.

I'm not very good—

Then you won't have to worry.

About what?

That I'll kill you if I lose. He grinned sharply. That was a joke.

I know. She tried to smile. Ha, ha.

I have some friends—we could play doubles. I'd much rather be your partner than your opponent.

I'd be a lot safer that way.

True. But playing it safe can be rather dull, don't you think?

The overhead lights began to dim and George lowered his voice to a whisper: He got away with it, actually. I guess it's not all that surprising when you consider what a genius he was.

Genius or not, nobody should get away with murder.

You'd be amazed what people get away with.

What do you mean?

We *all* do it. It's like a little bonus, a cheesy door prize for all your good behavior. The book you borrow and never return, the tip you never gave. A friend's shirt you forgot to give back. Getting away with something— it's a rush. Come on, you can tell me. I know you've done it. Admit it.

I can't think of anything.

Well, you're more innocent than I thought. I can see you are a Very Good Girl—he enunciated each word as if it were capitalized. I recommend a swift and thorough corrupting.

A little embarrassed, she asked, What about you?

Me? Oh, I'm as corrupted as they come.

I don't believe you. You don't look it.

I've learned to blend in. It's a survival skill. I'm like one of those pick-pockets in Venice. Before you know it, you've got nothing left—no money, no papers, no identity.

Sounds dangerous. I'm not sure I should be talking to you.

Just wanted you to know what you're getting into, he said.

Are you planning to pick my pocket?

I might try to get away with something.

Such as?

The audience erupted with applause as the speaker, a gaunt, white-haired gentleman in a herringbone suit, walked onto the stage.

George put his mouth up against her ear. Such as this, he said, sliding his hand under her skirt as the master's *Triumphant Eros* filled the screen.

* * *

FOR REASONS she didn't entirely understand—for they were opposites, it seemed, with very different priorities—they became inseparable. She was a virgin, he exalted in his reputation as a ladies' man. If she knew his true nature, then she ignored it, misinterpreted his self-absorption as intellect, his vanity as good breeding. He would ride her around on his handlebars, taking her to the coffeehouse on Spring Street or the Purple Pub or sometimes the VFW where the whiskey was only sixty cents a glass and they'd drink too much of it and talk about dead painters. George knew more about painters than anyone she'd ever met. He said he'd wanted to be an artist but his parents had talked him out of it. My father's the furniture king of Connecticut, he told her. They're hardly sentimental about the arts.

They'd wander around the Clark, kissing in the elegant, unmonitored rooms, the walls painted austere Berkshires colors: pewter, leek-white, goldenrod. Side by side they'd gaze dreamily at Corot or Boudin or Monet or Pissarro, her head on his shoulder, taking in his reedy tobacco scent. They'd visit the speedway in West Lebanon, sitting high in the stands in the blinding sun, counting the screaming revolutions of the cars, the metal bleachers vibrating under their legs, the smell of gasoline rising off the tarmac. They walked through woods and grassy meadows, making whistles out of fat strands of grass, kissing under the lazy muzzles of cows.

Though not especially handsome, he reminded her of someone Modigliani might've painted, angular and grim, with thinning hair and rosebud lips and tobacco-stained teeth. His wry intelligence was at once pretentious and intimidating, but he made her feel beautiful, like she was somebody else, somebody better. For a few heady weeks she lost herself in the dream of love. In her mind, he was a version of Jean-Paul Belmondo in *Breathless,* a movie they'd seen together, and she was Jean Seberg in her striped sailor shirts, wistful and fresh and in love. George somehow brought fantasy and spectacle to the world, allowing her to forget the split-level house in Grafton, the tartan walls of her bedroom, the green shag carpet.

They made love for the first time in a motel in Lanesborough with tiny white cottages scattered on a hill. Theirs had a little porch where they sat for a while, drinking bottles of root beer from the machine, and he talked about Mark Rothko, one of those rare painters, he said, who made you feel something that wasn't always so good, something like the truth. She took his hand but he shrugged like it wasn't a big deal, and then they went in and took off their clothes.

Congratulations, he said afterward, lighting their cigarettes. You've been officially indoctrinated into a life of sin and debauchery. He kissed her unhurriedly. I hope it was worth it.

It was, she told him.

But she honestly didn't know. She didn't know much about sex. In high school, there'd been fits of clumsy groping in damp basements; she'd had a few serious make-out sessions with a boy from her English class, but he'd dropped her for another girl. And then she'd met George. Unlike the drawn-out seduction in movies, her deflowering had lasted less than ten minutes. There were no operatic cries of ecstasy, or anything close to the tormented lovers in *Splendor in the Grass*. When she was twelve or so, her mother let her stay up late one night to watch it, and she'd been smitten by Warren Beatty and cried herself to sleep because his romance hadn't worked out and poor Natalie Wood, who'd been so very good, had to go to an asylum, while the love of her life married somebody else, even though everybody knew they belonged together. She wasn't all that sure she belonged with George.

Then why do you look so guilty?

The nuns were very thorough.

You're a big girl now, Catherine, he said. There's more to life than doing what you're told.

The comment made her feel stupid. It made her resent how she'd been raised, her faith. She sat up, holding the sheet over her breasts, and put out the cigarette. I don't even smoke, she said.

He only glanced at her.

She watched him a minute, his cold, brown eyes. We're very different, she said finally.

He nodded. Yes, we are.

Do you even believe in God?

No. Why should I?

She couldn't seem to answer.

Why does it matter so much, anyway?

It just does.

You didn't choose to believe in God. It's something you've been told to do, like putting a napkin on your lap. You're just falling in line.

I don't have to defend myself, she said. I'm not exactly in the minority.

That's for sure, he said arrogantly.

He stood up and pulled on his shirt. When she looked at him now in the dreary room, he seemed anonymous, she thought. He could be anyone. What *do* you believe in, then?

Not a whole lot, he answered. Sorry to disappoint you. He pulled on his jacket. I'll wait outside.

Through the sheer curtain she could see him standing on the porch under the small yellow light, smoking. She stood at the mirror and brushed her hair. She didn't really look any different. In her mind, she reviewed the momentous event: how he'd touched her, held her firmly in place and entered her as she'd lain there, open to him, searching his face. He wasn't looking at her, she recalled, but at the greasy headboard as it knocked against the wall.

2

IN THE FALL, they went their separate ways. He was in graduate school now; he claimed he barely had time for meals. He'd call every Sunday, but she suspected he was dating other girls. She put him out of her mind and focused on her studies and, after Williams, enrolled in a master's program at SUNY Buffalo, to study conservation. She moved into a house with four other students and took a part-time job at a bakery. She had nearly forgotten about George Clare when, out of the blue, he called her. He'd gotten her number from her mother, he told her. He sounded different, she thought, older. He invited her down to the city and, on a rare and uncharacteristic impulse, she decided to make the trip.

They met at a small café uptown where he bought her lunch. You've been on my mind, he told her, taking her hand. They spent the afternoon on a blanket in the park, kissing under the trees. He talked about his work, the thesis he planned to write, his ambition to be a scholar, to teach.

They started seeing each other again. Once a month, they'd meet halfway at a cheap motel in Binghamton and make love till the windows fogged, obscuring the world outside. Lying naked under the stiff Cloroxed sheets, smoking, staring at the stains on the ceiling, they'd dissect their unpromising future together: he came from money, she was working-class; he rejected religion, she was devout; he had no interest in marriage, she wanted a husband and kids and the white picket fence.

Something kept them together, frustration possibly. Like they were two parts of a troubling equation that neither could find the answer to. It was out there somewhere, in infinity, she often thought. Maybe they'd never find it.

Up in Buffalo, she tried dating other boys, but George, like a tedious splinter, was the one in her head. Occasionally, when she could afford the fare, she'd visit him in the city, wearing her signature black turtleneck and wrap-skirt, red lipstick, her hair twisted up in a barrette. He was renting a room in a frat house on 113th Street that resembled sailor's quarters, with a narrow twin bed, just off the common room where the frat boys shot pool and dabbled in disorderly conduct, abrupt disruptions of drunken ceremony that always ended badly. In bed, he was greedy and possessive, provoked, it seemed, by the percussive brutality of the pool table, the smacking collision of balls before they slammed into pockets and the uproarious chorus that followed. When they'd finally emerge from the room, attracting the frat boys' snickering gazes, she felt as if she were on display. They'd go to O'Brien's, a dark, wood-paneled, smoke-filled neighborhood bar that was favored by students from his department, a solemn, cautious group who would drink cheap beer and eat oysters and analyze the tortured geniuses of Western art, the fanatics, the fakes and the drunks, until, at closing, they were herded out into the street.

Toward the end of the spring semester, he called and said he had something important to discuss. Not over the phone, he added, and invited her to come down. On the bus, it occurred to her that he was going to propose. But when she arrived, it soon became clear he had other plans. He took her to a dimly lit bar and told her he was ending the relationship. With the assurance of an undertaker, he gave his reason. His program was demanding, he needed to focus on his work and, more important, they essentially had opposing philosophies. I'm letting you go, he said, as if she were some expendable employee.

She walked to Port Authority alone, inured to the wind, the trash blowing against her ankles, content to inhale the stink of the buses as she wandered up to her gate. She wasn't smart enough for him, she told herself. Or pretty enough. Later, on the trip home, she became ill. Overcome with a sudden nausea, she vomited in the bathroom, tossed from side to side in the tiny compartment. She looked at herself in the grimy mirror and knew, at once, what was wrong. Back in her room, she called George to give him the news.

He was quiet for a moment and then said, I know a place you can go. It's legal now.

I can't do that, she said after a long pause. It's against my religion. You don't have to marry me.

That's very noble of you, Catherine, but I don't do anything because I have to.

She waited for him to say more, but he hung up. Weeks passed and she didn't hear from him. At the bakery, the smells of powdered sugar and vanilla made her sick. Future brides would order their cakes, zealous and determined, their eyes glazed with pride and something else—some deep, unspoken compliance. When she wasn't at work, she took to her bed, incapacitated by the guilty terror of becoming a single mother. She knew her parents would disown her. She'd have to get a job somewhere, go on welfare or food stamps, whatever women in her situation had to do.

Then, two months later, on a rainy August morning, he showed up at her room with a dozen roses and a wedding ring. Pack your things, he said. You're moving to New York.

THEY WERE MARRIED in her hometown church. They held the reception in the grange next door, which was all her parents could afford. George's mother had her nose up; she was French and had black hair like Cleopatra and a smoker's voice. His father was tall and square-shouldered and had the same mud-puddle eyes as George.

After the wedding, George took her to their gray saltbox on the Connecticut shore. His parents were a breezy couple, terribly pleased with themselves in their oxford shirts, whale-dappled trousers and Top-Siders, drinking gin-and-tonics. They were, she thought, like people in a cigarette commercial. Their house was full of breakable things, with not a single object out of place. *She* felt out of place, as if George had brought his parents some ridiculous gift.

From the living-room windows she could see George's boat moored a few yards from shore. He wanted to take her sailing. I don't know, she said, a little afraid. I'm only in my third month.

You'll be fine. You're in very good hands.

They sailed in an inlet, then out to a small island, where they beached the boat and went exploring. Nobody was there, only the sprawling trees, the warm sand, the birds. His mother had packed them a picnic, sandwiches and iced tea and cold beer for George. Later in the afternoon, the wind picked up, the waves rocked the boat—whitecaps, George called them. They swelled up and broke on the deck. The current was strong. He'd have to tack strategically now, he explained, in order to get back. He pulled in the sails and the boat reeled up on a keel.

She gripped the side, terrified. George, she said. Please.

This is fun. This is what sailing's all about.

It's too rough, she said, clinging to the side. I feel sick.

Not in the boat, he shouted, pushing her head down and holding her there, hard. Through the blur of sickness, she became aware that he was right behind her, his hand on her neck, and she sensed in its sudden tentative weight that he was considering something, and then the boat dipped again and she went over, smacking the water and sinking under the surface, her hands floating up, the current sweeping her under the hull, the air squeezing out of her. She could see the boat sliding away, slow as a parade float—until, as if a dark hood had been pulled over her head, she blacked out. A minute later, or maybe seconds, she felt her abrupt transition back into the world as he pulled her up, placed her hands firmly on the side and shouted that she should hold on, for Christ's sake, just hold on.

Somehow, he hauled her onto the deck. It was a kind of birth, she thought.

You're all right, he said, dripping over her. Jesus Christ. Don't ever fucking do that again. You could've drowned.

That night, in his boyhood room, she lay in bed alone, listening to her husband relay the story of the accident to his parents downstairs, conveying the succession of events in a strangely methodical manner, as if he'd thought it all through ahead of time.

She's a lucky girl, his mother said.

When she called the next day, hoping for sympathy, her mother snapped, You had no business going out on a boat in your condition. What kind of a foolish thing was that to do?

3

THEY HAD a daughter, Frances, named for her great-aunt, who'd had some success as an opera singer. Frances had never married and died unexpectedly in her forties. Visiting her aunt in the city had been the highlight of Catherine's childhood, but her mother disavowed her, speaking her name in a grave whisper, as if she were terminally ill. Frances was the only woman in Catherine's family who'd had a career, whose life wasn't determined by the needs and interests of others. So for her, now beginning to understand her own limitations, naming her baby Frances was a private victory.

They bought a crib, and George took hours putting it together. Next time try reading the instructions, she scolded.

Being a mother was hard work, especially when the father was little help. She supposed she was grateful to him, that's what she told herself. She didn't ask for much.

They had a small collection of friends they'd meet at restaurants near the university, mostly people from George's department. As a couple, they projected a sense of domestic ease, their cordiality routine, habitual. But in truth they rarely spoke of anything beyond the superficial. He rarely confided in her, and in turn she neglected to ask any probing questions; perhaps, on some level, she knew he continually deceived her and somehow could not admit to it. Her personal pride wouldn't allow it. Instead, she drew conclusions from the way he looked and moved, the gloom in his eyes and, if they chanced to make love, his aftermath-smile, as if he'd done her a favor.

As the months passed, she concluded that he was living two lives—one with her and Franny, in which he was mildly, distractedly engaged, and another out in the city, where he could pretend to be his old self, going around in a seedy suede coat from the Salvation Army, stinking of cigarettes. Sometimes he'd come in late. Sometimes he'd be drunk. Once, in a frenzy of alcohol, he told her he didn't deserve her. She could have said something to confirm this fact, but that wasn't how she'd been raised. While he slept, she'd lie awake planning her escape, though when she thought of raising Franny on her own, living on half his paltry fellowship, facing the shameful consequences of divorce, she lost her nerve. Women in Catherine's family didn't leave their husbands.

They were like two commuters, randomly paired on a train, their destination undeclared. She felt she hardly knew him.

She called Agnes and begged her to visit, and for a few weeks her sister took up residence on the couch, despite George's obvious dissatisfaction, claiming, after only a few days, that she'd overstayed her welcome. It's having an effect on my work, he told Catherine.

Too bad, she thought.

Happily, for the first time as adults, she and her sister were getting to know each other. Agnes made a fuss over Franny, buying her toys and books, playing with her for hours on end. She'd listen tirelessly to Catherine's worries and complaints.

It could be he's not so interesting, Agnes said. She'd never really liked George. He was, she thought, an elitist. To be fair, she herself had an inferiority complex. She'd always been an average student. I'm not a nerd like you, she complained back in high school whenever they compared report cards. Agnes had excelled at swimming. All through school their mother had forced Catherine to swim with her on the team, but she'd hated it. She could remember driving home after a meet, wet-haired, the windows fogged with winter outside, and Agnes gloating.

Their mother had raised them to be good wives, to make the best of things—a philosophy that had helped the Sloan women through hard times—and Catherine had bought into it with a greedy, childish ease. The women on her side were devoted wives and mothers. They distracted themselves from minor bouts of unhappiness with housecleaning, gardening, children. They tore recipes from magazines and copied them down on index cards. They made Bundt cakes and Jell-O molds and casseroles, cleaned closets, organized drawers, folded laundry, darned socks. They'd mollify their husbands with sex. As Catholics, they had their own deliberate traditions, and denial was one of them.

4

THEY'D SEEN the ad in the real-estate section of the *Times,* with a picture of a white farmhouse captioned *First Time Offered.* It was a blurry shot, as if the photographer had been startled, and a peculiar brightness flourished around the windows. George made an appointment with the realtor, and the following Saturday they drove up to see it, just the two of them, leaving Franny at home with Mrs. Malloy. This was in March, just after he'd accepted his first real job, as Assistant Professor at an upstate college she'd never heard of. They were moving in August.

They took his beloved Fiat for the two-hour drive up the Taconic. He'd bought the car after college and garaged it in Harlem for more than they could afford. It was one of those mornings when the world seemed paralyzed by the anticipation of some unknown calamity, the city silent, cold, windless. The roar of the engine and rattling windows deprived them of small talk, Franny's latest developmental feats being their recent topic, so instead they listened to the jazz station, watching cluttered neighborhoods turn into anonymous suburban yards and then true countryside, like home for her, where icicles as thick as elephant tusks dripped from the great boulders that bordered the parkway, and the bleak landscape unfolded before them. Soon there was nothing to look at except fields and farms.

At last they turned into a town that resembled one of the samplers she had stitched as a child, featuring an old white church and a country store with a sign that advertised *Fresh Pie* in its window. Catherine watched two dogs trot off into a field, one black, the other yellow, following them until they disappeared behind the trees.

That's where we're going, George said, nodding in that direction, and they passed old houses and farms. Fields of sheep and grazing horses. Men on tractors. Pickup trucks full of hay.

At an unmarked road, she considered the map. Turn here, she said.

It was aptly called Old Farm Road, and ran a mile down through open pasture. They passed a small house with a barn, sheets up on the line. *Pratt* was the name on the mailbox. A bit farther along they came to the house they'd seen in the photograph. George parked next to a station wagon with a Rensselaer Polytechnic Institute decal on its back window. Looks like she's here.

They got out. Catherine buttoned her coat and gazed around the perimeter, holding a hand over her eyes in the glare. Brown fields stretched behind the house. Distantly, she could hear the whine of the interstate. The house resembled one of Franny's crayon drawings, with crooked shutters and smoke curling from the chimney. It was badly in need of paint. Catherine wondered what it would be like to raise their daughter here on this old farm. Off to the side were a couple of whitewashed barns, one with the words *Hale Dairy* in brown flaking paint over its doors and a copper rooster weathervane that turned and squealed in the wind. The other had a cupola whose windows flashed with sunlight, disrupting her vision intermittently, like Franny's toy View-Master. Tiny starlings darted in and out of the darkness below.

Used to be a dairy farm, George said, already in love with the place. The house is nice, don't you think?

To her, it seemed dreary and old. She supposed with some paint it could be nice. It has good bones, she said. That's the important thing.

The sky went dark suddenly and snow swept in like confetti. This weather, she said, shuddering.

Let's go in. George took her hand.

As they started up the walk, the door opened and the realtor stepped onto the small porch. She was wearing a bulky leopard-print coat and knee-high boots and bright-orange lipstick. Good morning, she said. I see you found it.

Hello, there.

Mary Lawton, the woman said, stretching out her hand to George, then shaking Catherine's next. It's so good to meet you both. Come on in and have a look around. She held the storm door open, the glass smudged with handprints, and they stepped inside. You'll have to forgive the mess. Houses don't fare well in circumstances like these.

What do you mean? Catherine said.

The woman looked at them blankly. Well, the owners had it rough. Financial troubles, that sort of thing.

Catherine hoped she'd say more, but she didn't.

These are hard times, George said.

Well, it's a buyer's market. That's one consolation.

The house looked sad, Catherine thought. Battered. But the windows were lovely.

Those are original, Lawton remarked, noting Catherine's interest. That's a real bonus. The light here, the views. You just don't find that.

Mary led them through the first floor—a dining room, a living room and a bedroom, what could be a small study—where a gloom languished like a misbehaving guest. The bulbs in the overhead fixtures flickered, and the wind thrummed against the windowpanes like a neglected child having a tantrum. In one spot, she had a feeling that someone was standing right beside her in a cold little pocket of air. She shook her head, folding her arms across her chest. Strange, she said aloud. I thought I . . .

Like conspirers, the Lawton woman and George exchanged a look.

What? George asked.

Nothing. Catherine shook off a chill.

Old houses, the realtor said. They've got aches and pains just like we do.

George nodded. When was it built?

Somewhere around 1790, nobody knows for sure. A long time ago in any case. There's something about this place—a kind of purity, I think. Her eyes went misty, like a poet experiencing a revelation, and she looked at Catherine meaningfully. It's not for everyone.

That's true, George said. You have to have a vision for a place like this.

So much history here. To imagine how long it's been standing. They just don't make houses like this anymore.

The three of them stood there for a moment in silence. Then Lawton broke it by saying, Love goes a long way in a house like this.

Catherine stole a glance at George as he strolled the room's boundaries, then stood at the window and looked out. She wondered what he was thinking. She supposed, with a little work, it could be nice.

You've got three bedrooms upstairs. Shall we go up?

It was a narrow staircase. The banister, unscrewed at the bottom and hanging off the wall, wobbled when she grasped it, the cold wood gritty with dirt. Pictures had been removed from the walls, leaving dark blocks on the faded paint. At the top she paused on the landing to look out the window. She could see a pond in the distance, a weathered canoe tipped over in the mud and an old truck up on blocks, surrounded with tools and rags, as if the person trying to fix it had given up. She followed George and Mary down the hall into the master bedroom. Standing there, she could feel a cold draft coming up through the floors. The realtor explained that the room was over the garage. A not particularly good addition, she said. It can be fixed, of course, and you can factor it into the price. On the positive side, you've got a nice big room here.

In the room across the hall there were three beds. She noticed a forgotten sock underneath one, and for some reason it made her sad.

There's one more bedroom down here, Mary said. Could make a nice nursery, or a sewing room. Do you sew, Catherine?

Yes, I do.

They've got some wonderful patterns these days, don't they?

They went back downstairs and outside, into the yard, to see the outbuildings. The milking barn was full of empty glass bottles. As the wind funneled through them, they seemed to be singing. George said, That's a lot of bottles.

Dairy farming's a tough business, Mary Lawton said.

That's too bad, Catherine said.

There are lots of reasons why things don't work out on a farm. You get a spell of bad luck. Well—some people can handle it, others can't.

She led them out of the barn, into the white, snowy light. Catherine wrapped the scarf around her head under the blowing snow. They walked down a muddy path into the field, then up a hill. Wait till you see this view, Lawton said. You two go on ahead.

They walked up through the wind without talking. At the top they looked down on the farm and stood there respectfully, like a couple in church. The land was like an ocean, she thought, the house a lonesome island in the middle of it.

Two hundred acres, George said. His eyes were bright, a little wild. She felt guilty for not wanting it. I don't know, George, she said gently.

I'll tell you what I do know, he said. We can sure as hell afford it.

5

SOME HOUSES WERE hard to sell. That's how it always was in her trade. People were superstitious, like you could catch someone's bad luck like a common cold. Even divorce made buyers squeamish. But death—suicide? Those houses could sit.

Mary had grown up in the business. Her father was old now, but he'd taught her everything there was to know about real estate. People trusted them both; they had a reputation. Even the city people. Weekenders. Horse people. She had a whole array of clients. Rich and poor, she treated everyone the same.

Chosen had been made by hand, people coming together to raise it up. Main Street had been dug out with shovels, then horses pulled barrels across it to level the dirt. St. James's Church stood in the middle of town, enclosed by an iron fence. In summer the doors were always open, the wind ruffling your hair like the fingers of angels. The bells always rang at noon. If you happened to be driving past, you might see Father Geary out in the courtyard, talking to someone, leaning in and speaking so softly you had to return his attention, concentrating on whatever he was saying, because it would soon be your turn to say something back. Tall maples stretched their limbs over the sidewalks, which were sticky with pods that the kids would peel apart and stick on their noses. You'd find them on the bottom of your shoes when you got home.

Every house had a story. She'd come to know people by how they lived. You saw their nature in unmade beds, haphazard kitchens. Their weaknesses in dark cellars heaped with rusted water heaters, cisterns, defunct boilers, blackened toilets and gunky sinks. You saw their desperation in backyards strewn with busted cars, waiting to be hauled away for scrap. You knew them by what they saved, the things they proudly featured on their shelves. You knew what meant something and what didn't. They'd tell you what they needed, what they feared, what they'd been through. It was much, much more than just selling houses. She was the listener, a keeper of secrets, the purveyor of dreams.

SHE'D BEEN INSIDE every house at least once, at weddings and wakes, baby showers and bridge games. She'd knitted baby booties for the Ladies Auxiliary, baked pies for Election Day, organized potluck suppers and church bazaars and tag sales. She herself had sold changing tables and dressers and scooters and picture books and bicycles and her very first car, a yellow Mustang, with a dent in the fender from the only time in her life that she'd ever hit a deer. She'd grown up here, back when it was just an insular little town, and her parents had sent her to Emma Willard down in Troy with the idea that she might meet an RPI man, and she did. She had married Travis Lawton right out of high school, when he had a gangly, ornery charm that was irresistible. They met at a school dance, where he'd lured her into the music closet and they'd kissed all night to the tiniest accompaniment of cymbals.

That morning in March, the sky was bleary, the wind swift and cold. The pale lawn puckered with crocuses. Mary got there early, as she always did before a showing, to make sure there were no surprises. When houses sat vacant, you tended to find unhappy ones—broken windows, puddles, dead mice. Pulling up to the farm that morning, she couldn't help thinking of her old friend Ella. The house stood plain and white, projecting the dignified symmetry of a simpler time. Using a rusty iron key, she unlocked the door, anticipating the usual dampness, the draft, and went to turn up the heat. The furnace sputtered to life and the radiators began to clang. The thought came to her that it was like an orchestra tuning up before a performance. Pleased with the idea, she went through the house, opening window shades, letting in the light. The trees outside, with their long limbs, caught her attention. It occurred to her that her senses were especially acute. She could hear the jittery windows, the waffling screens, the dry leaves skittering across the porch. For a few moments, it felt as though time had simply stopped, as though she could stand there all day and it would be of no consequence—and then a draft swarmed around her, a door eased open somewhere and slammed shut. For goodness' sakes! It scared her half to death. You couldn't keep the wind out, that was the trouble. It made the brass chandelier sway a little. She watched it for a moment, swirling around, its bulbs flickering. These damn old houses.

She hugged her coat tighter, reproaching herself for that second helping of ice cream last night. Boredom, that's what it was. Having nothing better to do.

She had asked Rainer Luks to clean out the place but he'd refused, saying he hadn't stepped foot in their house when they were alive, so why do it now? They'd had a fight over something back in the day—now he had their kids. The ironies of life never ceased to amaze her. She'd been the one to order the dumpster, not him, another expense she'd have to just chalk up. If it sold, which was unlikely, it would be worth it, and if it didn't, well, no use crying over spilt milk. You couldn't talk Rainer into doing anything he didn't want to, but showing the house in its present condition was, frankly, embarrassing. The first-floor bedroom, where old man Hale had lived out his last days, had an odor she couldn't quite place. Oh, it was urine—and you couldn't get rid of that stink no matter what you did. The room was piled up with junk, the sagging bed's dusty peach quilt heaped with old clothes. The closet door got snagged on the dirty rug, but when she yanked it open another smell came through, human, masculine, the old man's clothes hanging wearily from their hangers. A thick leather belt hung on the hook, moving just a little, like an idle threat. A Hale family tradition, she guessed. Everybody knew Cal beat his wife and their boys, that was no secret. She thought of throwing the belt into the trash where it belonged, but then she heard the car.

She stepped out of the room and closed the door behind her, but it eased right back open, as if mocking her. Unnerved, she shut it again and held her hand against it a moment, as if daring it to refuse.

Oh, Ella, you poor girl! she thought, remembering her dear friend, how they'd sit on the front steps when their kids were little, smoking, how faded and distant Ella sometimes looked, unreachable. Mary had known all along there were problems, but, in her own defense, every time she tried to broach the subject, Ella would leave the room. People talked. Well, in a town like this, there wasn't much else to do for entertainment. Ella was so tenderhearted that she simply couldn't bear it. People looking at her in Hack's. Whispering. After a while, she stopped going to town. She never left the house.

Mary opened the front door and waited while the couple parked. They'd pulled up in a little green convertible, some foreign thing, and the wife got out, wearing a brown wool coat with toggles and a white kerchief over her hair. Behind her dark sunglasses she moved with the fluid grace of a movie actress. Mary wondered if she was somebody important, someone who needed a disguise.

Mary's father had taught her that the first moments with new clients are always revealing. You had to watch their faces, imagine their worst fears. The Clares were city people, with an apartment on Riverside Drive. Mary seldom went down there, but she had a general idea where they lived. It was easy to tell from the way they stood there, looking slightly dumbfounded, that they knew nothing about houses, let alone farms. Yet she suspected they were romantics—they wanted old, they wanted charming. The wife shifted, taking in the fields, her hand shielding her eyes. The land could be off-putting to some, even to most. People wanted space, just not so damn much of it. Mary watched as they stood side by side, squinting up at the place, the wife with her arms wrapped tightly around herself, as if she'd just come out of a swimming pool. The husband draped his arm around her, awkwardly, she thought, more out of possession than love, and as they walked up the front walk, Mary saw in his face that he'd already made up his mind.

This was Mary's cue. She went out onto the porch as they approached.

Good morning. I see you found it. They shook hands and made their introductions. Come on in and have a look around.

They stepped inside and the woman took off her scarf. As she tucked her hair back behind her ears, Mary saw that she was beautiful—a beauty, she ventured, that went largely unacknowledged by her husband, who seemed, in those brief moments, preoccupied with his own. He looked like one of those soap stars, clean-cut and cheerful on the outside, but if you watched the show long enough some dark history would crawl out.

She led them through the rooms on the first floor. The wife seemed to like the Dutch door in the kitchen, and Mary demonstrated how you could open the top half to let in the fresh air. It's the original door, Mary said. This screened porch was added in the forties, when they did the garage.

I've always wanted one, the wife said.

They are nice. We've got a picnic table on ours. It'll keep the flies out of your lemonade, that's for sure.

Upstairs, the wife picked a room for their daughter. How old is she? Mary asked.

She's three.

Three going on thirty, he said.

It's true, she has more pocketbooks than I do.

Mary thought of her own daughter, Alice, and how she'd loved to play dress-up, draping herself in scarves and beads, clattering across the kitchen linoleum in Mary's heels. When she'd turned ten, Mary let her pick out her own wallpaper, a purple paisley that seemed okay in the book but on the wall, with matching twin bedspreads, gave her a headache.

These people didn't know it yet, but they had a whole lot of negotiating in front of them. Mary had learned the hard way that you can't make bargains with your children. Somebody always comes up short.

The wife wouldn't go down into the cellar, usually a bad sign. Mary took him down and he pondered the boiler and the well pump, with its gizmos and attachments, then they all went outside to walk the land. The snow had already melted and the fields were muddy; the cold wind pushed at their backs. Mary pulled her coat around her. Walking behind the couple, she noticed they were a distance apart, their faces wan, thoughtful. The wife had a city body; slim. Clearly ice cream was not yet a priority, or a therapeutic ally in the wee hours of disrupted slumber, as it was for Mary. Catherine's gait was slow, contemplative. She walked with her head down, arms folded on her chest, rings on her long fingers.

The husband took her elbow, a bit roughly, Mary observed, and his wife smiled in that way of hers, the sudden brightening of a child who has been reprimanded and then surprised by consolation, and he looked at her sideways, a fierce, enigmatic grin, and it seemed to signify their fate. Long after they were gone, she would reflect on this single moment; it would keep her up nights.

SHE TOOK THEM to lunch at Jackson's, a dark little tavern she liked in the neighboring hamlet, where they ate steak and potatoes. The husband ordered a bottle of Guinness. Mary told them about the town, its history as an agricultural resource. The richest soil in the state, was how she put it. I know it's hard to tell, she said, but there's real value here. Like I said, a little renovating, a little paint, you'll have yourself a real showplace.

What happened to the family? the wife asked.

They fell on hard times, is all.

He poured off the rest of his beer. Farming is a tough life, isn't it?

Yes, it is, she said, although she didn't want to get into it now—the fact that the Hales had been farming for generations and now all their good land was going to waste. Do you plan to farm? she asked, even though she already knew the answer. He didn't strike her as the type to get his hands dirty.

I'm afraid the only cows I understand are the ones that exist in paintings.

George is an art historian, his wife offered with pride.

Well, that is interesting.

Paintings of cows are very popular, he said. At least, they were in the nineteenth century.

Is that your specialty?

Cows? His wife laughed. Yes, he's very good at cows.

Landscapes, he said, blushing a little. The Hudson River School. That's a rather broad description. And it's part of why we're here.

George is going to be teaching at the college.

What good news, Mary said. We have lots of college folks out this way. I'll have to introduce you. In truth, they were an odd lot; her father had once sold a house in the hamlet to an economics professor with a pet tarantula. I'm told it's a good school.

George Clare nodded. We're looking forward to it.

A week later, Mary called to tell them that, since the house had gone into foreclosure, she was no longer handling it, and referred them to Martin Washburn at the bank. On the morning of the auction, her curiosity got the better of her and she went over to see who all had been lured there by the prospect of legal thievery. Sure enough, George Clare was sitting in the otherwise empty row of chairs, waiting to place his bid. From the looks of it, there wasn't going to be much competition. A few stragglers had come in, more likely to get in out of the cold. There were still a few minutes before the auction started, so she pulled him aside. It wasn't out of any obligation, just decency. He had a right to know. That's how she wanted to be treated herself, and there was no reason she shouldn't give the Clares the same courtesy.

They were good friends of mine, she began. It was an accident, a tragedy. As she told him the rest of the story in broad terms, his expression remained unchanged.

She squeezed his arm, reassuring him that it was none of his concern. You'll be happy there. I know it.

With calculating ease, George considered all she had said and pursed his lips. That does cast a shadow on things, he said. It might have some bearing on what I'm able to bid.

*   *   *

SOMETIMES THE WORK made her weary. People always wanted something they couldn't even name, but expected her to find it anyway. What did they want, *value*? That could be just a code word for a little consideration, to be dealt with fairly, with respect. But some of them wanted more than the usual kindness and solicitation. They wanted to believe they were better than everybody else.

Often, her patience waned as they sat in her car and told her things. Mary wasn't one for indiscretion; it made her squeamish. She didn't need or want to know what kind of medical conditions people had, or how their parents had abused them as children. They cried sometimes. Thinking back, she'd heard just about everything you could imagine, from tonsillitis to sodomy. She was one of those people strangers talked to. On buses, trains and planes, in markets or at the bank, they seemed to come out of nowhere, and the second she gave them a smidgen of attention, they started in with their life stories. Funny, she'd never told anyone hers.

You got good at reading people in her line. Sometimes she was off, but not usually. She got a feeling about someone. Most of the time it was pretty close to the truth.

Mary had a feeling about the Clares and it wasn't a good one.

The thing about houses: they chose their owners, not the other way around. And this house had chosen them.

6

ACCORDING TO a plaque in the town square, the first settlers were Dutch. They established Chosen in 1695. Main Street was a quarter of a mile long, lined with brick row houses that at some point had been converted into shops. It was far from bustling, however. There was a hardware store with a hammer sign, a package store, an army-navy, a café, and a grocery store called Hack's. From where she sat in the café, she saw only a few pedestrians walking down the sidewalk, bundled up against the wind.

The waitress came over, set out a place mat and turned over her cup. Coffee?

She was too pretty to be behind a counter all day, Catherine thought. Please.

You came at the right time. Another half-hour, this place'll be jammed. She filled her cup. Just visiting?

We're moving up from the city. My husband got a job up here.

Where at?

Saginaw?

They're good kids, she said. They come in all the time.

An older man at the end of the counter stood up and laid some money by the register. Take care, now.

See you, Vern, the waitress said as he went out the door, the bells ringing. She bussed his dishes and wiped off the counter, then came back to Catherine's table.

You find a house yet?

I think so. It's a farm. I guess they fell on hard times.

The waitress shook her head. Plenty of farms like that these days.

My husband's at the auction right now, in fact.

Well, I guess I should say good luck. Frowning, the waitress refilled the napkin holder, her hands moving mechanically, as if she could do this in her sleep. People run out of money. They lose everything. She glanced up at the window, clearly a habit, and shook her head. It's happening more and more around here. One day there'll be nobody left.

It's sad.

I've been here my whole life, she said. You got kids?

A little girl.

Just so you know, we make the best pancakes in the state.

I'll be sure to bring her in.

I've got my break now, the waitress said. They don't like us smoking in here. You just holler if you need me.

Catherine nodded and smiled. She sipped her coffee and watched the waitress standing out on the sidewalk, smoking a cigarette, tapping the ashes into a window box full of fake pansies. She dropped the butt to the sidewalk and came back inside. It sure is cold out there.

I don't know what happened to spring, Catherine said to her.

We don't usually get it up here till May. Once it even snowed then.

After a while, Catherine saw George striding up the sidewalk, holding an envelope. There he is now, she said, and paid the check. Thanks so much.

Good luck with your move.

She crossed the street to meet him. He held up the key victoriously and then pulled her close, hugging her hard. We practically stole the place.

Secretly she'd been hoping he'd lose out to a higher bidder. It felt wrong to benefit from someone else's disaster, whoever they were, and there was something strange about that place.

Here, he said, handing her the key, you hold it.

The key was cold and black. She turned it over in her hand and closed her fingers around it. Somebody made this, she said.

It's the only one they had.

The morning sun was now gone. It started to sprinkle, and an odor like bleach stung the air. When the rain began to fall, they ran to the car and sat there waiting for it to let up. She stared straight ahead into the blurred glass. She couldn't say why, but she felt lost, almost bereft. George reached over and took her hand. Let's go home, he said.

He switched on the wipers and pulled out. They passed farm after farm. Horses stood out in the open, their backs glistening. Cows had convened under a tree. Sure is pretty out here, she said.

The house looked abandoned, forsaken. He parked right in front, on the grass. Welcome home, he said, then came around to open the door and help her out, as if she were afflicted with some infirmity.

They walked up on the porch, where she noticed an old bird's nest in the rafters and, inside the porch light, a dense, honeycomb universe. With care and a sense of ritual, she slid the key into the lock, but before she had even turned it the door eased open.

They stood there looking across the threshold. It came to her that it was like an exhibit at a museum, glancing into some historic person's life, except here no rope divided time past from time present. This was their house now, she told herself, and they would make their own history in it—for better or worse.

They must've forgotten to lock it, George said.

Their stuff's still here, George.

That's what you get with a foreclosure. We'll have to go through it.

They stood there, listening.

Should I carry you in?

He didn't wait for her answer and pulled her back outside and lifted her into his arms and carried her over the threshold and up the stairs and she laughed when he brought her into the bedroom and laid her on the dusty coverlet, shoving stacks of old newspapers and *Farmer's Almanac*s to the floor, and they rolled around on the mattress like teenagers who had at last found a place to be alone. He kissed her, pushing up her clothes, and she pulled him into her as the room filled with rain shadows.

For a long while, she rested in his arms and listened to the sounds of the house, the wind pressing up against it, the windows rattling every now and again with the distant passage of a train.

They dressed silently, politely, as if they were being observed, then went downstairs and stepped outside, gazing over their land. The rain had stopped and the sky was clear and black, alight with stars. Breathing the cold air into her lungs, she felt a dizzying sense of freedom. She ran her hands through her unbrushed hair.

They found a pub in town called Blake's and sat at the bar and drank beer and ate lamb chops with mint jelly. The bartender had a round, shiny face, a dish towel draped over his shoulder like a sling. The lights were dim; the place nearly empty. A trio of women dressed in riding outfits shared a small table, two black dogs dozing at their feet. A plumber in his work clothes was drinking at the far end of the bar. They paid, leaving a good tip. 'Night, now, the bartender said. Appreciate it.

They drove the two hours home without saying much, returning to their life in the city, their daughter, their work. But the farm was in her head. The land, the strange house that was now theirs, and the nagging certainty that she'd left something behind.

7

THEY MOVED IN August. The house was waiting for them, the lilies, the wildly overgrown lawn. The net-less basketball hoop on the barn, the old green water pump, the wheelbarrow, the weathervane.

The floorboards seemed to sigh when they entered, conciliatory, resigned. Cut from the trunks of enormous pines, they were honey-colored in the sunlight. They had to use soap to open the windows. The bent wire screens sifted the warm wind and the cloth shades banged against the frames. Left-behind chimes sang in the fragrant trees. They had pears and apples, a quince bush and a pond. Looking out through the wavy glass was like being inside a dream.

The previous owners had left a piano. As a girl, Catherine had been forced to take lessons, and her teacher was severe. You're playing it wrong, she'd shriek with impatience. Catherine sat down on the bench and ran her fingers over the ivory keys; most were dirty, a few had come off. She played "Frère Jacques" and Franny clapped her hands and sang along.

Together, they cleaned. Sorted through junk. Tugged down the old curtains, stiff with dust, and threw them out. They worked together as husband and wife. The first night they all slept in the same bed, Franny tucked in the middle. Hey: what kind of sandwich are you, anyway? George said.

Baloney! Franny declared.

Baloney? He pretended to eat her up. You're full of baloney!

No, I ant, Franny said.

Yes, you are!

They all laughed loud and hard, and Catherine felt a surge of optimism, and while they slept she lay awake listening to the night—the bellowing frogs, the hoot of a cautious owl, the long slow trains. And later, when the rest of the world was silent, the squealing riot of coyotes.

THERE WAS SOMETHING odd about the house. A chill flourished in some rooms and an odor seeped up from the cellar, the rotting carcasses of trapped mice. Even in gentle summer, when the world outside was singing its bright song, an oppressive gloom prevailed, as if the whole house had been covered, like a birdcage, with velvet cloth.

Still, she accepted all this as one accommodates a troubled child. But the house had not accepted her.

She moved cautiously from room to room, as though her status as homeowner had been revoked, downgraded to caretaker. An invisible pair of eyes seemed to be watching, judging her care and management of the household.

One afternoon she found an old radio in the closet and set it up on the dresser and tuned in to NPR's *Reading Aloud*. They were doing *Great Expectations*—with some famous British actor—and she was only half listening, too preoccupied with her tasks to pay much attention. With Franny napping across the hall, she had the volume turned so low she could barely hear it. At half past five she went down to start dinner. She fixed herself a drink, iced vodka with lemon, and sipped it like some prescribed cure. After a moment, it occurred to her that the radio upstairs was very loud. Even if Franny had woken up, it was unlikely she could've reached the top of the dresser. She put down her glass and went out into the hall, her eyes drawn to the landing where she could feel the penetrating gaze of some unseen presence. But, of course, there was nothing up there, just the scuffed floors, the marked-up walls, the dirty fingerprints of strangers.

She told George the story and concluded, I think we have a ghost.

Apparently a Dickens fan, he said.

You don't believe me.

He shrugged. Moving isn't easy. I think you're just tired.

I'm not *tired,* George.

Think of the deal we got. Open your eyes, Catherine. Look at this place.

I know.

He kissed her forehead. And get yourself a new radio.

She considered ghosts the stuff of horror movies. Back in high school she'd seen a movie called *The Haunting* and hadn't slept for a month; just the slightest flutter of curtains in her old room suggested some vicious taunt of evil. Even the work she did now could make her superstitious, some of the churches like hollow caves of reckoning, terminals to another world. But until this house, she'd never thought seriously of ghosts, at all. Yet, as the days passed, their existence wasn't even a question anymore— she just knew.

AS A RULE, George parked in the garage. He didn't like his precious Fiat exposed to the elements. Since Catherine's car was a used station wagon, he argued, it shouldn't make much difference if she parked outside. Truthfully, she didn't care all that much. She'd park under the big maple tree near the screened porch, which gave her easy access to the kitchen. They were using the porch as a mudroom, and it was already cluttered with muddy shoes, tennis rackets, Franny's stroller and little red wagon. One afternoon, returning from the market with her arms full of grocery bags and Franny beginning to fuss, she had trouble opening the door. When she turned the key, the bolt disengaged as usual but the door refused to open. She jiggled the brown porcelain knob—it wouldn't budge. A moment later, she heard a grinding twist of metal—it sounded like the knob on the *inside* was being unscrewed. Through the window, she saw the empty kitchen, just as she had left it. Frustrated, she rattled the knob violently and it came off in her hand. A second later, as if to punctuate her confusion, the knob on the kitchen side dropped to the floor.

What happened, Momma?

I don't know. It's this silly knob.

Silly knob! Franny cried.

Then the door swung open all on its own. For a moment Catherine couldn't seem to move.

It's open, Momma!

Yes, I see.

Franny jumped inside and Catherine followed, dragging in the groceries. Again she was struck with the sense that some invisible *someone* was standing there watching her, and her face went hot with anger. She picked up the knob and inserted its long rusty spindle into the tiny square opening; holding the outside knob securely in place, she screwed one to the other, making the same whining sound she'd heard only moments before—when some *entity,* some poltergeist, had unscrewed it.

That wasn't very nice, she said to the room. You're not making us feel very welcome here.

Who you talking to, Momma?

She picked Franny up and held her tight. Nobody, she said, and realized it was true.

When George came home from work, she told him this new story. Suppressing his obvious irritation, he inspected the door, and swung it open and closed several times. There's nothing wrong with this door, he told her.

Then how do you explain it?

It's an old house, Catherine. These sorts of things happen in old houses.

She listed off the other problems she'd encountered—the weirdly chilly spots, the continual smell of exhaust in their bedroom, the radio—and now this.

You're imagining things, he told her.

I'm not imagining anything, George.

Maybe you need a psychiatrist, then. There's nothing wrong with this house.

But, George . . .

We're not moving, Catherine. I suggest you get used to it.

UNPACKING BOXES in the sweltering heat. The fans going full tilt. She stacked her books on the shelves—art history, philosophy, a rumpled copy of *Ariel*—while Franny played with things around the house—a feather, a brass hook, a jar of marbles—squatting down to turn the object over in her little hands, her nose running, her forehead creased tight with interest, then readily moving on to something else. She'd jump from one sunshine shadow to another, singing, Mary, Mary, quite contrary! how does your garden grow?

The other family had left so much behind that she couldn't help wondering who they were. George said he didn't really know or care. I don't see why it matters, he snapped. It's our house now. It belongs to *us*.

But the closets were full of their stuff. She found hockey skates, deflated basketballs, baseball bats. A shoebox full of baby shoes, three pairs tied together. She held them in her hands, remembering Franny at that size, on the brink of walking. These had been whitewashed with polish, the little heels round and worn. Someone might want them back someday, she thought, storing them in a cupboard. When their rightful owners came looking for them, they'd be right there.

ONE MORNING, when George was out at the hardware store, two boys came to the door. The older one was in his early twenties, the other a teenager. They stood looking through the rain-splattered screen. Faces you couldn't pull away from, with blue eyes and strong bones. It was hot and buggy and they'd gotten caught in the storm. They stood there with their long arms, slapping mosquitoes, the sky warm and dark. She could hear the patter of rain on the maple leaves.

I'm Eddy, the older one said, and this here's Cole. We got another brother, Wade, but he couldn't make it.

We're the Clares, she said, pulling Franny onto her hip. And this is Franny.

Hey, Franny, the other boy said.

Franny blushed and hugged Catherine tight.

We used to—the younger one blurted, but his brother shoved him in the ribs.

Don't mind him. He's a little overexcited. Eddy put a heavy hand on the boy's shoulder. We're looking for work. Lawn work, gardening—hell, he can even babysit. He clutched his brother's shoulder. He don't mind one bit, do you, Cole?

No, ma'am, the boy said, scratching his mosquito bites.

I'll have to check with my husband.

Those barns could use some paint, if you don't mind my saying. He stepped back and looked up at the house. The house, too. We could help you out.

Well, we were planning on painting all that.

Hey, me and my brothers—we're regular Leonardos. And we come cheap.

Where do you live?

In town, the younger one said.

We got references if you want, the other said. You won't find nobody cheaper. Plus, we been doing that work for our uncle.

Thunder rumbled overhead. She could smell the wet grass and something else, gasoline or cigarettes on the boys' clothes. It started to rain again. The younger boy looked up at the sky and then at her, waiting to be invited in. She held open the door. Come on inside.

They walked in, grinning over some private joke. I like what you've done with the place, Eddy said.

We're just moving in, she said, a little embarrassed. They left a lot behind, the old owners.

There's a good reason for that, Eddy said.

Did you know them?

You could say that.

The younger boy looked away, his cheeks flushed and sweaty. He pushed the hair off his forehead.

We might not have bought it, she said, I don't think, if it hadn't been such a good price.

The boys stood there.

What I mean, well, we got it at auction. Nobody else—

It's in the past now. Eddy looked at her uncertainly, like he'd changed his mind about something. Anyway, we better head out. Nice meeting you, ma'am.

You can call me Catherine. She reached out her hand and he took it and she could feel the cold, rough skin. He waited a long moment before he let go.

Catherine. He said her name like it was a thing of beauty. His eyes were dark blue. These boys had history, she thought, too much of it. He took a pen from his pocket and again took her hand. Can I borrow this?

What?

He wrote his phone number on her hand. In case you need us.

Oh, okay, she said, and laughed. Thanks. She noticed the younger one eyeing her cookies. Here, I just made these. She fixed them a bag.

Thank you, Mrs. Clare.

You're welcome, Cole. Their eyes met for a moment, until he glanced away.

Well—see you around, Eddy said.

They went out with their hands in the cookie bag, the older one grabbing one, the younger one punching his arm. They were close, these two. She watched them cross the field and then climb up the steep hill. The clouds were low and dense. Up on the ridge Eddy turned and looked back at the house as if right at her, and he confirmed this with a wave. It was a symbol, she thought, a kind of unspoken agreement—for what, she couldn't guess.

She spent the afternoon cleaning the oven, then roasted a chicken in it. The house smelled good. Like home.

That night, over dinner, she told George she'd found some painters.

Who are they?

Just some boys from town. Looking for work.

She lied and said she'd interviewed other painters who were more expensive, knowing that George could never resist cheap, and he gave his consent. It'll be a big improvement, he said.

I want down, Franny said.

You do, do you? He kissed the top of her head. Are you finished eating, Franny?

All done.

He lifted her out of her high chair. She's too old for this chair.

Franny needs a big-girl chair, Catherine said.

I'm big now, Franny said, jumping, clapping.

Come on, you big monkey, George said. Let's let Mommy clean up.

Obediently, Catherine cleared the plates onto the counter. As hard as she'd worked to make it nice, the kitchen still looked shabby, the cabinets, coated with a thick porridge-colored paint, so warped they wouldn't stay shut. They didn't have a dishwasher yet. George promised to buy her one just as soon as he could, maybe for Christmas. She started the dishes, letting the water get good and hot before rinsing them off; steam rose up as she stacked the clean plates into the rack. The window over the sink was black, animated by the vague outlines of her reflection as she washed the pots. For some reason, she tried to avoid noticing this, as if conscious that another face was superimposed over her own.

I'd put my rings right here, on the windowsill. After doing the dishes I'd put them on again, always thinking what a sham marriage was, how the rings meant nothing. Only that I was off limits to other men. In Cal's hands, I was like some old piece of farm machinery he'd learned how to jury-rig. That's how it was with him, in private. Lift here, insert, push.

Once, I saw the woman. Her name was Hazel Smythe. She was at Windowbox, sitting at a table alone, having a sandwich—egg salad, I think. I stood there, caught by surprise, and she looked up at me, her expression warm, even sad. Apologetic. But I walked out. I didn't want her sympathy.

I guess people in town knew, too. It gave them something to talk about over supper.

Alarmed, Catherine turned around, but confronted only the after-dinner disruption, the worn wooden table and the empty chairs around it, waiting to be filled.

HE'S NOT HERE, a woman said the next morning when Catherine called the number she'd copied off her hand. *No está aquí.* But that afternoon they came back with the other brother. This here's Wade, Eddy said. He can do the mowing.

Hello, Wade. He was bigger than the other two, and moved with the solemn grace of a priest. She shook his sweaty hand.

They walked out to the milking barn.

What am I going to do with all of these bottles?

You could start a dairy, Cole offered. We could help you. We know how to do it.

That's enough, Cole, Eddy said sharply, and the boy looked hurt. Trust me, he added, you don't want to raise cows.

We can cart them bottles off for you, Wade proposed. We got a truck.

That would be great, she said, and registered his proud smile. When can you start?

We'll start in the morning, if that's all right?

They were good workers. They started early, before eight. She'd hear them out there, scraping off the old paint. The hot sun got hotter and hotter but they never complained. By noon their T-shirts were dripping with sweat, though only Eddy took his off. He often had a cigarette in his mouth, squinting against the smoke in his eyes. She found herself studying him, peering out the windows as she did her chores. When she stood beside him she could smell his sweat, the detergent in his clothes. A few times, she caught him looking down her blouse when she leaned over to pick up Franny, holding her necklace, the gold cross, between her teeth.

At noon, she'd bring out lemonade and sandwiches and Franny would hand out the cups. They were sweet with her and watched her squat in the mud puddles, making pies in little tins. Here, Cole, she'd say, offering him one. It's good pie.

Really? Is it chocolate?

Franny nodded. Want more?

Sure, why not make it two?

On their breaks, they played tag with her, running around the field, riling up the butterflies. The transistor radio going. The soft earth under their bare feet. Once, they chased a rabbit, which dove into its burrow. Shh, Cole shushed, crouching down.

He won't come out, Franny said.

We have to keep real quiet, Eddy whispered, and they all crouched in the silence as they waited.

The rabbit came out, twitching its whiskers, and Franny screamed with delight.

Again they chased it and again he outsmarted them, vanishing into the underbrush.

They were unusual boys, she thought. Polite, sincere—broken. There were things she noticed: Cole's halfway smile, like he was sorry for enjoying the work. His brother Wade as stoic as milk, thoughtful, courteous, a little clumsy. And Eddy a shifty poet, an operator, rarely meeting her eyes. When he did, you couldn't look away.

Cole was Franny's favorite. He'd just turned fourteen, still willing to be a boy. Together they made roads and castles and moats in the mud, and sailboats out of rhododendron leaves, with masts out of twigs. He wore a corduroy jacket, a size too big, and frayed at the wrists. She nicknamed him Professor. He was tall and skinny but had big shoulders and square-shaped hands. A born football star, she thought, but too gentle for the sport.

What do you want to be, she asked, when you grow up?

He shrugged like he'd never thought about it. I'm already grown.

She turned to Eddy. What does your father do?

Not a whole lot. He cracked a bitter smile, and she dropped it.

His eyes were like the blue of forgotten soldiers. Without him noticing she would watch him. A strong face like Achilles, she thought, mythical, epic. How patiently he treated Wade when helping him complete simple tasks he should've managed easily, she thought, by himself, or how gently he prodded the kind, thoughtful Cole to take credit for his good work. Somehow, the three of them seemed to come from an older time.

One morning, Wade arrived with a wooden contraption in his arms. It's for Franny, he said. It's a swing we can put up for her.

Wade's good at making things, Eddy told her. It's what he does best.

His brother looked away, but she caught his smile.

Touched by the gift, she said, Thank you, Wade.

That's all right.

The small-seated swing, made all of wood except for the chains, had a bar that would slide down in front of Franny to keep her from falling out, and they hung it out back, in the tree.

I want Cole to push! Franny cried. Push me, Cole!

Swinging back and forth, she dropped her head back to gaze up at the sky. Look up there, Momma? The tree was like a jigsaw, the missing pieces filled with sky.

What kind of tree is that, Eddy?

That's just an ordinary old tree. Oak, I think.

There's a pear tree, too.

Yes, ma'am. Put 'em on your windowsill and they'll get ripe.

The deer love to eat them. Late one night, I saw four of them standing there, eating to their hearts' content.

Yeah, they know what's good.

AT THE END of the day they swam in the pond, stripping down to their undershorts and tossing their clothes in the grass. Leaves on the bottom had turned the water brown. Holding her mother's hand, Franny stepped down to the shore, disrupting whole neighborhoods of frogs, her little feet disappearing in the soft mud.

Cole twisted through the water like a sea lion. Can she swim yet?

Almost. We're working on it—right, Franny?

I can swim, she insisted. Look, Momma, a turtle. She crouched down to watch the creature pushing through the grass, moving slowly under its heavy brown shell, a weary monk.

Have you been in yet? Eddy asked, climbing out.

I'm too afraid. I don't like when I can't see the bottom.

Can't feel it, either. Too deep. It's a mystery. He smiled.

I guess I don't like mysteries.

Gets hot enough, you'll swim.

We joined a club. They have a pool. She regretted this the minute she said it.

I didn't figure you for the type, he said.

My husband plays tennis.

He smirked. Watch out for those people.

What do you mean?

They think they own this town.

Okay. Thanks for the warning.

He looked at her. You don't seem like you really fit.

No?

She waited for him to say more, but instead he sat down beside her and put on his shirt. He took his cigarettes from his pocket and lit one.

You're different, he said. From other girls.

I'm older, she offered. I'm a mother. It changes you.

He glanced at her briefly, with affirmation. You're a good mother.

Thanks, Eddy, that's nice.

I'm not trying to be nice.

No?

He dragged on the cigarette, looking out at the pond. Tell me something, Mrs. Clare. You like it out here on the farm?

You don't have to—

Catherine. His eyes were cold, a little angry. She thought of all of the girls who'd seen that same expression and tried to change it.

Yes, I think so.

Are you happy?

I don't know, she said. What's happy?

He looked away from her, then put his hand down in the grass beside hers. They were almost touching. You're asking the wrong person, he said. I'm no expert on happy.

Someday You'll Be Sorry

I

MAYBE IT STARTED with her. That first time he saw her. Maybe because they'd bought the farm. Or because she'd opened the door that time and he'd stood there like an idiot with his hands in his pockets, saying he could work. Just wanting to be near her, to be close. Her eyes, maybe, because they were gray like his mother's.

I'm Eddy, and this here's Cole. *We used to live here, our mother died in this house.*

This look on her face, thinking it over, then bending down to the little girl, her necklace swinging, and pulling her onto her hip, the white shades moving all at once, the sun flipping through.

She was somewhere in her twenties, not all that much older, and he was taller and bigger anyway. He wanted to hold her.

She looked at him again, with something in her eyes that seemed like hope. And he felt something twist in his gut.

THAT FIRST NIGHT, walking back to Rainer's place, his brother started to cry, and Eddy had to hold him a minute.

She was nice.

Yes, she was, Eddy told him.

I want to go back.

We will.

When, Eddy?

Tomorrow. Okay, buddy?

A state van was parked in front of his uncle's house. The men, fresh out of jail, lurked and spit. One had a lazy eye and a carny smile. Parole like your birthday after fifteen years inside. People called him Paris, like the city. I'm just a roamer, he said, tapping the side of his head. I been all over this world.

There was a horn at his feet, a beat-up trumpet. He looked older than he probably was, with skin like lager, hair all white and curly.

Cole said, My brother plays.

Nah, I'm just fooling with it.

Paris smiled a little and handed him the horn. Let's see what you got.

Eddy held the instrument. It had a story to tell, the old, dull brass warming in his hands. He brought it to his lips and blew a little, played a tune he knew well. She had a nice sound to her.

Yup, you stuck with her. Paris shook his head. That the only kind of love that don't go away. I feel for you, brother. Ain't nothing they can do for you now.

Paris proclaimed himself a man of darkness who'd found the light in prison. He'd been in and out his whole life.

They all find Jesus in prison, his uncle told him. What else they got to do?

He'd go back into the dorm to see him, the cots lined up like in an army barracks. Paris sitting on the edge of his with his elbows on his knees, staring at his hands like they were lumps of clay and he was trying to figure out what to make of them. I couldn't find nothing to do, he told Eddy. Nothing but sit here.

My uncle's putting you to work.

I can work, the man said. I got no problem with that.

He had a small black Bible beside him on the bed, its cover as soft as felt, and he'd marked his place in Revelation with a ribbon from his daughter's hair that he let Eddy handle. The ribbon was pink and shiny and a little frayed. The daughter lived somewhere down south, worked in a truck-stop cafeteria. Paris had eyes like unpolished shoes, scuffed with wear. He played love songs, ballads. The blues. With everything he had he played the blues. You got to live hard, he told Eddy, taking hold of his shoulder. You got to live for her, he said, touching the rim of the horn. I don't see you got much choice.

AT NIGHT he went up to the wires. There was this path through the trees, and wires stretched lazily in every direction. You had all this beautiful country, and then the wires appeared, buzzing, and people got upset. Maybe because they realized they weren't as safe as they thought, tucked away in their little stupid lives. Bottom line: people were afraid of death, most of them were. Not him, though. He wasn't particularly afraid.

Sometimes this mangy old dog came out of the woods to follow him. It had kind of a bashed-in face. But it knew him, Eddy could tell. It would trail him at a distance, just two creatures sharing the night. They probably thought about the same things—the smell of the ground, the hard wet dirt of the trail, the grass thick as his shoelaces and long enough to trip you. Black and wiry-haired, the dog showed his teeth when he went along like he was smiling, his tongue hanging out of his mouth as long as a shoehorn. He'd look at him like: What am I doing here? Eddy shook his head and thought, Don't be asking me philosophical questions. He walked on as far as you could up to a plateau and stood under the trapeze of buzzing wires while the dog went around him a few times making dog noises, and Eddy said, Quit your fussing and sit. The dog ignored him, then lifted his head like he'd heard something, and a moment later Eddy could hear the train.

YOU COULD WALK right up to the house and they never knew. You could look right in the windows. They kept it lit up like a music box. You could hear Franny running around, screaming or laughing, like little kids do, and Eddy thought these were the best sounds ever. He could see Mr. Clare emptying a box of books in his grandfather's old room, taking out each one and examining it like some priceless object before placing it on the shelf as if it were rigged with dynamite. He watched her in the kitchen, doing something at the counter, her hair piled up on her head. She was wearing what had to be one of her husband's cast-off shirts, with a banker's stripes, and cutoffs, and she had a great pair of legs, long and tanned, her elbows pointing as she fixed what he realized was a sandwich. Again, he thought of his mother, whose life was already over and had ended without much consequence. That was the real tragedy.

SHE'D STARTED a garden and was up to her ankles in dirt. Eddy approached slowly, like he wanted to dance, and took the rake. Here, let me help you.

I want flowers, she said. Lots and lots of them.

We'll get you flowers. He turned to his brother. Right, Cole?

Cole nodded.

I love tiger lilies, don't you?

Sure.

What about you, Cole?

Well, I guess daisies.

Their mother had liked daisies. She was always sticking them in water.

Let's plant some daisies, then, Mrs. Clare said.

They were different. They'd come from the city, but they weren't like the other people who came up here. For one thing, they weren't rich. Most of the city people had money. They'd buy summer places. You'd see them in town. They were ornery and undeserving. But the Clares were different. She was.

Anyway, Eddy was working for them now. This was business. She didn't know they'd grown up here on the farm. She hadn't heard any of the stories and he wasn't planning on telling her.

This was work, he thought. Nothing more or less.

If she wanted flowers, he'd make sure she had them. As for the other feelings he had for her—they were not allowed. His mother had taught him right from wrong; he knew his boundaries. There were some lines you just didn't cross.

Now pull out all these weeds, he instructed his brother. I'll give these beds a good raking.

With agile hands, Cole tugged out the weeds. Not one escaped him. Eddy stood watching him. His little brother had things on his mind. Life and all its injustice. You could see it when he frowned at the ground, yanking out some knot under the earth. At first, working here had seemed like a good idea. But now Eddy didn't know. He'd catch Cole gazing up at their mother's window like he was waiting for her to look out and say this whole thing had been a big mistake. He couldn't get past it. Most nights he cried himself to sleep. Everything they knew had changed. All you had left were old memories, pictures in your head, postcards from the person you used to be once. After a while you weren't even sure they were yours.

2

ALL THAT SUMMER it was warm afternoons and her lemonade and the little girl and Catherine's yellow hair in the wind and her bony white feet in the grass. She had exquisite feet. She said he could call her Cathy if he wanted. She said her parents did. She didn't mention her husband. He got a feeling with her. He'd watch her when she sketched. She was always sketching something—the trees, the old tires, Franny's rain boots, the house—and she was good at it. Used a blue pencil for almost everything. She did Cole's face, his pointy chin, his cheekbones, his pretty eyes. She did Wade's hands nestled in his lap like sleeping doves. Let me do you, Eddy, she said.

No, you don't want to draw me.

You've got a good face. She'd already started, her hand moving around the page, parts of him taking shape. We don't look at each other enough, she said. People never do.

That wasn't true; he looked at her all the time, she just didn't know it.

When you really look at someone's face, you see a lot.

Like what?

In you? I see strength.

Then you have a good imagination, he said, and she looked disappointed. If he had strength, he would've figured out how to get out of this town by now.

He lay back on the grass, up on his elbows with his legs stretched out, smoking, watching her. When she moved a certain way he could see the strap of her bra, her long neck.

What do you want to do? With your life, I mean?

I'm a musician. It felt good to say out loud. I play the trumpet.

A musician. She tilted her head, watching him, her hand constantly moving.

Yes, ma'am.

Will you play for me?

Maybe.

Maybe? She smiled, surprised, her eyebrows raised.

I guess I could be convinced.

She looked at him. I'd really like that, Eddy.

She turned the pad of paper around and showed him the drawing. She had gotten his face, his hard eyes. Made him look better than he really did, he thought. Hey, that's pretty good.

I've captured you, she said.

Yes, I believe you have. Now he was sketching her in his mind, her small shoulders, her flat chest, her tiny nipples. She was angular, girlish.

You have a good face, she said. I bet all the girls tell you that.

He shook his head, shaking off a dream; he felt like he knew her.

THE POINT WAS, sometimes you just know someone. That's what he'd come to realize about the thing between them. Something warm and bright was filling him up like his mother's cooking, making him strong again.

Maybe she'd come out to hang the wash. He'd watch her back, her arms reaching up, her elbows as knobby as garden snails.

Across the fields that had been his grandfather's and his great-grandfather's before that, the wind spoke to him. *Wait,* it said.

The old farm, once full of cows, sheep, pigs, even two old quarter horses his pop had gotten cheap. His old man could do horse tricks. He could stand up on their backs and twirl a rope. He was a cowboy; he was a scholar. Smartest man he ever knew and couldn't make a dime. Opera always in the house. And the smell of Mother's cooking. Onions, fried potatoes, bacon.

Now Catherine's daughter was sleeping in his old room. He wouldn't tell her. He wouldn't tell her what had gone on in that house, how his father would come after them, turning over chairs and tables, how his mother would cry up in her room or sometimes sit in one place shaking just a little, like somebody who was scared.

At night, it was too hot at Rainer's to be inside. He'd walk through town. You could see into all the crummy little houses. People out on their stoops, smoking, just passing the time. Living their lives, making mistakes, bad decisions, yelling at each other, or sometimes you saw the joy, the moments of brightness.

It could make you love this world.

The night before she'd left them behind—because that's what she did—she asked Eddy into her room. You're the oldest, she said to him, her voice distant, spare. You look out for your brothers, Edward. Make sure nobody hurts Wade. He's big and strong, but he's too kind. She took his hand briefly. You see to it that Cole goes to college. He can't stay in this town.

Yes, Mother.

I'm counting on you, Eddy.

I know it.

He sat there; he couldn't look at her. You get some sleep, she told him. Good night, now.

He left her there, thinking how his parents' room and everything in it was a place he could never understand. His mother as a woman; his father. How they were together as husband and wife. Whatever they had that kept them there. Their quiet violence. What she took from him. What she endured. The old highboy where she kept her things, a monument to missed chances. Birth certificate, high-school diploma, acceptance letter from a nursing school, a tooth.

HE HAD THIS JOB working nights at the inn as a busboy. That's where he met the girl, Willis. She was younger, maybe twenty, but was the type that had all the answers. She liked getting the goods on people. The first thing she said to him was, You look like an undertaker. To which he replied, They make me wear this. She carried around this book of poems by E. E. Cummings, thick as a dictionary, that she stole back in high school from her school library—she said she wanted to be a poet.

The inn paid pretty good and was a popular place. People came from all over, driving up from the city or down from Saratoga, and everybody wanted to get in, and every weekend the place was jammed. Usually, he could get a plate of food after hours. Lamb was their dish. Sometimes even a cold beer. On breaks, they'd go outside and smoke and she'd tell him a made-up poem. She'd recite, with a nervous tremor in her voice, *The moon is bright above the crazy trees,* or some crap like that.

Willis could be hard to figure. She wasn't exactly beautiful, but something about her drove him a little crazy. Maybe the way she moved, like a Spanish dancer with something on her head, straight-backed, elegant. She had a mole on her face and black-caterpillar eyebrows, eyeliner thick as crayon. She said she was from the city, and whenever she announced this to somebody she jerked her head so her hair flew back out of her face over her shoulder. They'd do shots on their break, out in the parking lot. Once they did flamers. She'd get a little drunk and start crying about her mother, saying she was the worst daughter you could ever have, and she'd get all soggy, with her mascara running all over the place and snot dripping out of her nose and her lips all slippery, and the only thing he could think to do was kiss her. She'd gone to college out west and was in town for a while, working at the inn. Claimed she'd gotten hired on account of her riding skills, for all the rich people in Chosen with expensive horses they couldn't ride. She said she wanted to learn how to farm so one day she could have her own little place and grow stuff. That's all she wanted. They were in the junkyard when she told him this, in the back seat of a limousine that had confetti all over the seats and floor, and kind of a puke smell, and you just knew something had happened in it, something bad.

Life was mysterious, he knew. People never said what they really meant and it always caused more trouble than it was worth. Eddy thought it was a defining characteristic of human beings. You didn't find that kind of thing with animals. Sometimes, late at night, when it was very quiet, he'd imagine that all the words people never said, the true and honest ones, slipped out of their mouths and danced around wickedly over their stupid, sleeping forms.

You couldn't control much in this life. His brothers were counting on him for something—he didn't really know what, none of them did. But something important. That might make them feel better.

It was hard to say what people needed once they'd been hurt. Still, he didn't mind the burden. If anyone should carry it, it was him. He could bear it. His mother had known it. He knew it, too. He hoped he could do some good.

•   •   •

IT WAS a small kitchen at the inn, and even with all the windows open and the fans going the air was blazing. You'd see the blue flames and the sizzling pans. Eddy was only a busboy, but they treated him like someone special. As a townie, he had their respect. Plus, he was fast. He cleared the tables and came back like a ghost; nobody even noticed.

Everybody knew the town was changing. You could spot the New Yorkers a mile away in their expensive clothes, the women with their pocketbooks, their sunglasses, like they were famous, or just better. They had an attitude—what his old high-school teachers would call arrogance before making you stand out in the hall all period. You could feel the world changing. Money pouring in. The rich people getting richer, and everyone else, like him, going nowhere.

One night, the Clares came in for dinner. They'd asked his brother to babysit, so Eddy had dropped him over there before work. Cole complained about it and said babysitting was for girls, but Eddy reminded him of the good money he was making. They're new here. They don't know anybody else. And she likes you.

They were with another couple, some old guy whose wife used a cane. Catherine had on a blue dress that showed off her shoulders and her hair was pulled back kind of fancy, not her usual blond scribble. Mr. Clare wore a starchy white shirt and a bow tie, like he'd been gift-wrapped. Eddy couldn't figure out what a sweet girl like her was doing with an asshole like him. More than once, Eddy had watched her transform into the person who was Clare's wife, when she'd hear his Fiat down the road and start cleaning up the place like she needed to hide something, including her true self. Eddy wondered what it was like to be in his shoes: to have a wife like her in your bed every night, to drive a car like that. He thought it must be pretty good.

Willis was their waitress, and for some reason she seemed pretty upset the whole time, slamming the plates down and acting like a rattling teapot about to blow its lid off. He worried she might spit in their food. At one point he took hold of her arms and made her look at him, and she was all flushed from the heat of the ovens, and her eyes, which were almost black, had tears in them. I made a mistake, she said. I did something awful.

Hey, he said, and kissed her forehead.

She stood there with her cheeks bright red and sweat marks under her arms, putting out the bread plates, the squares of butter, and you could see her tattoo peeking out from under her sleeve, black tears falling down her wrist. They took a break at the same time and went out into the cool air and smoked under the black leaves. The leaves tittered in the wind and you could see this streak of orange in the darkening sky. Willis had a hard little mouth, like the smallest flower. It was the shape your blood took when you got cut. She smoked and shook her head, nodding at the screen door, the buttery light inside the kitchen. Guy's a prick.

Who do you mean?

You know.

He didn't want to know. He didn't press her and that was the end of it.

Later, after they were done, she took him to her room to get high. When you worked in a kitchen you went home greasy, the smell of food on your clothes, your skin. They walked side by side down the empty road. It was a barn fixed up like a dorm and some of the help lived there. These were summer people, mostly, students and the like, who'd go back to their real lives before the first frost. They lay on her bed under the open window and you could smell the sweet stink of the sheep and you could see the moon.

I wish things were different, she said, that people were nicer, you know? I wish people were nicer to each other.

He looked down at her face and saw that she was really just a kid. She let him kiss her a few times. Her mouth was warm, salty, and when he kissed her with his eyes closed it was like being inside a dark little city.

I've done things, she said. Stuff I regret.

Like what?

With men. She looked at him with her big eyes.

You don't have to—

I want to. I want you to know me. I want you to know who I really am.

She turned onto her side and rested her head in the palm of her hand. Her body was like the coastline of some exclusive island, a place only certain people got to see, with white villas perched over the blue sea.

She lit a cigarette and blew the smoke out hard with disgust. I've been having sex since I was thirteen.

Everybody makes mistakes, he said. You have to put that stuff behind you. It was something his mother would say.

I'll try, Eddy. She touched his arm as lightly as a bird landing on a branch, and he somehow felt patronized. Then she said, I don't want to hurt you.

He wondered why she'd say that. You won't, he told her, but he already knew it was a lie. Don't worry about me. I'm a pretty tough customer.

She started kissing him all over, but he pulled her up. He didn't want her doing any favors for him like she did for everybody else. He kissed her tenderly, and she giggled like a kid and hid her face in the crook of his arm. And then they were wrestling and she was like a boy, like one of his brothers, skinny and fierce, and he could be rough with her and it wasn't sex, he didn't even take off her pants—it was something else, something hungry and physical that confirmed that neither one of them would ever really be satisfied. They both knew it and he could see this quiet revelation in her eyes and it got to him and he felt a little sick.

They fell asleep together, and in the morning, before it was even light, they crept down the stairs. He took her to the field of dead cars. They climbed up on the old bus and he played her a slow, somber tune and it came up out of him like something primal. It was the sound of his own yearning heart. She lay back on the cold metal, looking sleepy, wrapped up in his old coat, and he crawled up beside her and they looked up at the sky. She didn't say much about her life except that she'd hitched out here from California, which he suspected was a lie, and that her father was a big-deal lawyer who represented gangsters, criminals. I grew up with pictures of dead people all over the house. There's a lot of interesting ways to kill somebody. Eddy thought this was sad and felt bad for her. Her father wasn't home very much, she said. There's plenty of bad people out there.

Women were mysterious creatures, he thought. She could be nice one day and then ignore him for no good reason. Days would pass and he wouldn't see her. He didn't understand it. He'd see her at work and she'd scarcely say a word to him.

One evening he asked, What's wrong with you?

Nothing. Leave me alone.

Come here.

Get off me.

He had to wonder if she was seeing someone else. She didn't look right. She carried around this big leather sack with books in it. She said she wanted to go back to school. I'm not myself here, she kept saying. Her skin was ashen, a little yellow, smudges of old makeup under her eyes. He'd try to ask her, but she'd just pull away.

It got to him. He tried not to think about it. He'd done something wrong, he guessed. He didn't know what, and her not telling him made him crazy. It made him want her more. Then he'd think: Screw her. Because it became pretty obvious she didn't want him back.

Sometimes he thought about leaving. I'll just pick up and go, he thought.

A COUPLE OF WEEKS LATER, a heat wave pushed through town. When there was no wind, you could smell the dump and the smokestacks on the river. People in town would sit out on their stoops, fanning themselves with newspapers.

With his brothers back in school, it was just him working at the farm, scraping the clapboards. He'd show up early and quit by noon. Sometimes he'd pull up in his father's old truck just as her husband was heading out the door. Eddy would wave. Mr. Clare would nod but always gave the impression that he was in a rush, too busy to stop. Though he was cordial enough, there was something about him that put Eddy off. He was tall and on the thin side but seemed like somebody who could take care of himself in a fight. He could turn on you for no good reason. He was like one of those dogs Mrs. Pratt took in; he could rip you apart.

One morning, Eddy pulled in just as Clare was getting into his car, all spruced up for work. Morning, Eddy said.

Clare smiled like a man paying his toll. Good morning, Ed.

They spoke for a minute about the work, how he'd already gotten the first coat on and how good it looked.

Then he said, You're one of the Hales.

That's right.

She doesn't know you lived here. You might want to keep that to yourself.

Something about the way he said it made Eddy want to punch him in the face.

Scraping paint took time, but he didn't mind. It was almost therapeutic to go over things in his mind. As much as he wanted to move on, he didn't seem able to. He would force himself to dream a little; then everything just came back. His mother. His father's casual abuse. He didn't know why they hadn't tried harder. Why they themselves hadn't thought to paint the house; sure, they didn't want to spend the money, but there had to be some other reason, too. They'd been content to leave everything just like it was, run-down. The place had looked like hell for years. He'd stopped bringing girls around on account of all the junk piled up. Their pride had gone away. He didn't know how that happened to people. He hoped it wouldn't happen to him.

It wouldn't, he decided. He wouldn't let it.

3

SOMETIMES HE'D CATCH her staring. When he took off his shirt. He'd hear her inside with the little girl, then she'd bring her outside to play. He'd take a break and they'd sit in the shade a little while and he'd smoke and tell her his plans. He told her about the time his father ripped up his music-school application, then dragged him out in the yard and beat him with a two-by-four. You think you're better than this, he kept saying. You think you're better? Eddy was hurt so badly that Wade drove him to the hospital when he only had his learner's permit, and they lied to the doctor and said it had been a tractor accident. Heading home, they got pulled over and Wade got a ticket, and when their father found it crumpled in his coat he made him sleep in the barn. That's what it means to be stupid in this world, he told Wade, then glared at Eddy. That barn's about as far as you'll get.

She almost cried, hearing this, then she got mad. He should apply again, she said, and she'd help him with the application and even write the check. You had to submit an essay, and she gave him some paper and told him to write about his life on the farm. So he wrote about how his father had grown up on this farm and his destiny was never a question or a choice, just a fact. How, when Eddy was a boy, they'd lived in a trailer out back, he and his brothers crammed like a litter of puppies on the pull-out bed. How they'd steal their shoes out of the Goodwill bins behind the supermarket. He wrote about waking up before dawn to do chores every single day of the year. How the animals counted on you to survive.

How, when he heard Louis Armstrong play "Someday You'll be Sorry," it seemed like the story of his whole life, because people had wronged him and his family and one day they'd all be very fucking sorry. Then he played it for her and she watched him with her chin resting on her hand and a twinkly look in her eyes, and when he was done she said, Hey, you can really play that thing. I'm impressed.

Thanks. But I got a long ways to go.

I hope you get in, Eddy. You deserve to.

It's kind of just a dream.

It's good to have dreams.

He shrugged like he didn't care, but he did. A lot. It was more than some dream. It kept him alive.

The next day it rained, breaking the heat. He couldn't paint, but for some reason he showed up anyway.

It was almost noon, but she answered the door in her bathrobe.

You okay? he said.

She frowned, refusing to answer.

Your husband here?

She shook her head. At work.

Where's Franny?

Sleeping. She looked at him like a damp flower. It's raining.

I've been waiting for it to stop.

You didn't have to come today.

I know. He didn't really know why he'd shown up.

She smiled a little and held the door open. She looked weak, a little sick. I'll make you something.

He sat at the kitchen table and she gave him a cup of tea and fixed him a ham-and-cheese sandwich, standing there at the counter without saying anything. The quiet house was making him nervous. She brought the plate over and put it in front of him and then sat down, and when she looked at him her eyes were like a distant sky, the sky of another country, a strange and mystical place he might have seen once in a dream.

He chewed, trying not to show his teeth. It's good.

My husband, she said finally. We're—

He waited.

It's just—he's a difficult person.

Eddy nodded because he understood.

We're just having some problems. She wiped her tears angrily. Most people—married people, I mean . . . But she couldn't finish. She looked away and stared out at the rain.

You know, you're even pretty when you cry. It was a line he'd heard in a movie, but she didn't seem to mind it. She smiled.

There was a puzzle on the table of a farm scene—a hay barn, cows, a farmhouse with a porch. With the rain pouring down, she started moving pieces around, and he knew it was to keep from looking at him. He also knew they weren't supposed to look at each other, but it was the only thing he wanted to do. Just to sit there and watch her.

Distractedly, she tried to fit a cardboard piece here and there. I think it goes here, he said, and guided her hand to the obvious spot. Right there.

I'm no good at puzzles.

It's not the shape of the piece that matters, he told her, holding another up. It's these missing parts. You have to fill those. Like that one, see?

They worked together, and when they were done he said, That's pretty good, isn't it? Across the bottom, the puzzle said *Peace and Quiet*. He almost laughed, because a farm was anything but. This picturesque scene didn't have any truth to it. It was just another part of the big fairy tale of America. If you wanted to see a real farm you'd have drunk, broke farmers and hungry animals worried for their lives. You'd have bitter wives and snot-nosed kids and old people broke down from giving their hearts and souls to the land.

You could hear the rain running through the gutters and splattering on the windowsill. She turned in her chair to watch it.

It's sure coming down, he said. Just to say something.

I love the sound of it. I love a good rain, don't you? I sometimes just want to run out into it.

He smiled. Me, too. I've had the same thought.

She suddenly seemed to realize she was still in her robe and got up and took his plate to the sink and stood there scrubbing it. I swear I don't know what's wrong with me.

He watched the bones in her back. The rain can do that. It's just a rainy day.

She shook her head like he didn't understand, he couldn't possibly know what her trouble was.

He went over and took the plate from her hand and set it down gently. You're liable to break this.

She turned around, crying full-out, and he took her in his arms and she held him hard, like a frightened child, and they stood there like that in his mother's old kitchen with the rain pounding down and they didn't move, they didn't move.

All Things Cease to Appear

I

ORIGINALLY ESTABLISHED as a seminary in 1879, the college overlooked the Hudson from six hundred acres on its grassy shore. Most of its buildings had been constructed using pale-gray river stones, but later additions, in the '60s, were in the Brutalist style, long cement structures with rectangular windows, and the overall effect was dissonantly anachronistic. From where George was standing, in a small wooden gazebo on a bluff over the river, he recalled Thomas Cole's *River in the Catskills,* for the view was almost an exact match. In a hundred years or so, this landscape hadn't changed much. But upriver, around Troy and the GE plant in Schenectady, industry edged along the water, monstrous with waste and PCBs. He had to wonder if it was even possible to consider Cole's landscape with innocent, nineteenth-century pleasure, now that the environment had been corrupted—and the viewer's gaze along with it.

His wife criticized him for being too analytical. That's what graduate school did to you, the residual contrariness of the terminal degree. His incarceration had finally come to an end, but, as with most inmates of one kind or another, the experience had changed him. He supposed he'd acquired a few disagreeable habits. As much as he could admire the panorama before him, unlike Thomas Cole, it didn't move him on any spiritual level. But then what did?

The boats of Saginaw's crew team were on the water, gliding swiftly, their oars sweeping in perfect unison. He couldn't help thinking of Eakins's rowers, their broad, muscular backs, the rippling surface of the river. It was early September, a gray hot day, the air tangy with rain. He glanced at his watch and started for Patterson Hall, the building that housed the Art History Department and the domain of its chair, Floyd DeBeers. Students had arrived the day before and now drifted through the quad with fans and lamps, their movements checked, nearly procedural, as they frowned with mock confusion at their sheets of instructions.

Climbing the stairs in his new loafers, he passed two women, one ascending, the other descending, both in longish dresses and clogs, files under their arms. There was an officious air about the place, he thought. He roamed down a hall toward the department office, an octagon-shaped room with tall windows, where he confronted a vacant desk brimming with the sort of autumnal paraphernalia he remembered from grade school—yellow leaves, miniature pumpkins, a Mason jar full of sunflowers—and a nameplate for *Edith Hodge, Department Secretary*. But the secretary was not at her desk.

Is that you, George? DeBeers called from his office, his desk chair honking and squealing.

George poked his head in. Hello, Floyd.

Come on in. Close the door.

DeBeers rose to his feet and extended his hand. He was burly and discombobulated, taller than George, in a wrinkled, ill-fitting brown suit peppered with cigarette ash. His tarnished-silver ponytail, hastily fastened with an elastic band, gave him the look of a dissolute senator.

Nice view, George said, noting the distant river.

One of the perks of being Chair. This office is the only reason to do this miserable job.

He flashed a smile and motioned for George to sit. Your chapter on Swedenborg, it's actually why I hired you. He almost blushed, then admitted, We have a small following here.

George smiled. Though he was grateful, of course, he found it disturbing and a little comical that his chapter on Emanuel Swedenborg, brief as it was, had been the deciding factor. In fact, it was the section of his dissertation that had caused him the most grief. His subject was the painter George Inness, whose landscapes had evolved over time from ornate, meticulous depictions of nature as defined by the Hudson River School to transcendental renderings of an American paradise. Late in his career, Inness had been influenced by Swedenborg, an eighteenth-century Swedish philosopher who claimed, among his varied accomplishments, to be a clairvoyant. *George Inness and the Cult of Nature* had been George's rather clever title, although his adviser hadn't appreciated the irony. While George could credit some of Swedenborg's ideas, his proclamation of being a seer, of having the ability to communicate with angels and spirits, read like the rant of a person with an undiagnosed mental disorder. He'd been dead a hundred years before Inness had discovered him—along with William Blake and William James—but for Inness it went deeper, George thought, to that murky place within. When he was finally baptized in the Swedenborgian Church of the New Jerusalem, Inness was well over forty. To George, this exemplified the classic, obsessive behavior of a man in a midlife crisis. He wasn't about to say this to DeBeers, who for all he knew might be fighting a similar battle.

We even do séances on occasion, DeBeers said, sounding half serious. You'll have to join us sometime.

That could be fun, he lied. But I should warn you—I'm a devoted skeptic.

DeBeers laughed confidently, as if accepting a challenge. I used to be a skeptic myself. You couldn't talk me into anything. You know what I believed in? Conspiracies. I was somehow under the impression that everything that went wrong in my life could be attributed to some devious plot to destroy me. That's how I lived my life, if you can imagine. Waiting. Waiting. Always waiting. With terror! And then something did happen: I lost my wife.

I'm sorry to hear that, George said.

She was, well—we had something special. I don't think I'll ever have that kind of love again. He glanced at George apologetically. I'm on my third wife now, you know.

No, I didn't.

Connie was my second—the love of my life. It was a once-in-a-lifetime connection. I was grateful for it.

Sounds pretty great.

It was. DeBeers nodded, momentarily preoccupied with something on his desk. Anyway, losing her—her death—got me thinking about the big questions: life and death, the afterlife, all the possibilities.

I'm not sure there are any.

You're a realist, yes? One of those people who have to see it to believe it. Am I right?

George nodded. That's probably true.

DeBeers leaned back in his noisy chair, pressing his hands together under his chin. So tell me this. How did a cynical agnostic like you end up with a Swedenborgian like Inness?

He was a great painter. A great *American* painter. I didn't know any of this until I started my research. I'd never even heard of Swedenborg. So, no, that was hardly a factor in my choosing Inness.

Well, then, perhaps he chose you. DeBeers grinned, pleased with himself.

That's one way to look at it.

I take it you're not a person of faith. You're not—he hesitated—open to it?

He looked at DeBeers.

I was living in Boston, DeBeers went on. This was long ago. I was like you. An academic. If you can't prove it, it doesn't exist. And then my wife got sick, and just like that—he snapped his fingers—she was dead. A friend took me to this church, a Swedenborg branch, and I started reading the literature, all the stuff he wrote about heaven. I found it, well . . . comforting. It's actually a very beautiful philosophy. It's about love, more than anything else. The intense love of God.

He glanced at George as if to gauge his response. If George had learned anything from working with Warren Shelby, it was to keep his opinions to himself. He was well rehearsed in maintaining a completely blank expression.

It answered a lot of my questions, DeBeers continued. My life started to have more purpose, more direction. Then, a few months later, she came to me as a spirit.

Your wife?

DeBeers took out a handkerchief and wiped his face and blew his nose, then folded it up and put it back in his pocket, looking at George carefully. She was so real. I reached out as if I could touch her. She was so vivid, so light—so full of love. . . . His voice trailed off as he fumbled for a cigarette.

I know what you're thinking. And believe me, I understand it. Because, before this happened, I was a different man. I was . . . He stopped himself, shaking his head. Very bitter.

George shifted in his chair, more than a little uncomfortable. The conversation was taking an unfortunate direction, but he couldn't just stand up and walk out. This man was his boss. He crossed his arms over his chest.

Are you bitter, George?

Bitter? No, I wouldn't say so. He felt a little offended. He had a beautiful wife, a daughter, a promising academic future. What should he be bitter about?

I was like you back then, DeBeers said. I was bitter, cynical. A person who didn't believe.

Now, *this* sounded like a condemnation.

She came to me, George. I saw her just as plainly as I see you now. He shook his head with renewed amazement. I haven't been the same since.

What could he say to that? In George's mind, the occult—stories about heaven, ghosts, aliens, you name it—fell into the same category as religion, an enduring litany of bullshit concerning the things in life that were not easily explained. Judging from DeBeers's complexion, the vision of his dead wife might have been an alcohol-induced delusion.

George cleared his throat. I guess I believe that an explanation can be found for almost anything.

Yes, yes, I know this. He reached behind him and grabbed a book, a rumpled, sprawling thing, its binding cracked from overuse. Here, this might help. This was Swedenborg's *Heaven and Its Wonders and Hell: From Things Heard and Seen*. Its worn cover, with its faded blue sky and fluffy clouds, was marked with coffee rings and cigarette burns. You can keep that.

Thanks, George said, but he had no intention of reading it.

We can talk about it at some point.

Sure. He could dread nothing more.

The thing about death, DeBeers went on, it scares people. People can't accept the fact that in death we pay for our sins.

I'm not sure we do, actually, George said. Pay, I mean.

Oh, we pay all right.

George shook his head, unwilling to believe it. Dead was dead, and you rotted in the ground. Speculation about the afterlife was the stuff of supermarket newspapers and talk shows. Death was absolute, final, and to someone like him those particular qualities were its greatest attraction. I guess we won't know till we get there.

DeBeers flashed an impatient smile, as if George was too shallow to keep up. It's not surprising about Inness, he said. There's something in the work that goes beyond pure observation. Some spiritual connection.

Beauty depends on the unseen, George quoted the artist, *the visible upon the invisible.*

The soul sees what the eye cannot, DeBeers affirmed.

That's the idea, George said, although he still didn't actually have a firm grasp of it; nevertheless, he elaborated: Inness painted from memory, which is to say that he didn't paint what he saw, but what he remembered. There's a difference. He believed memory was a lens to the soul. It's not the details that matter—the veins on a leaf, say—so much as the *implied* detail, such as the changing light, the wind, the lone peasant in the distance, the sense that something else is going on, some deeper possibility. . . .

God, of course.

Yes, George allowed. God.

They sat for a moment in silence.

He painted not the experience, George explained, but the essence of experience. The nuances of place. Revelation as it exists in a single moment, on a particular afternoon. Ordinary disturbances in nature—the gathering storm, the wind in the grass, a sunrise—take on poetic dimensions. You look at his paintings; in turn, they draw you in. Inevitably, there's an emotional response. That was Inness's genius.

Indeed, DeBeers said, apparently pleased with George's impassioned speech. The essence of experience, that sounds about right. Thoughtfully, he took up his package of tobacco and pinched some of it between his fingers and loaded his pipe and lit it, puffing his cheeks like a trombone player, expelling a rich cloud of smoke.

He lived in Montclair, DeBeers said. I grew up a town over, in East Orange. Of course, by the time I lived there my backyard was a parking lot, and he'd had a field and a stone fence. I lived on a street of row houses. The row houses of East Orange, he said, as if introducing an important new subject. They were the colors of ice cream: pistachio, coffee, chocolate. Again, he shook his head. My mother used to make soup from a can.

Cream of mushroom, of celery—she always liked to serve soup before the main course. I guess she thought it was classy. I'll never forget the taste of that soup, that stringy texture, and when I think of it I instantly see her standing there in her apron, built like a tree trunk, the cigarettes, the Entenmann's cake she'd tell everyone she made from scratch, the plastic on the couch. He thought for a moment. That soup, it's the essence of my childhood. It's no surprise I'm a Warhol fan.

George smiled but couldn't reciprocate a childhood memory of his own. Frankly, the essence of his childhood escaped him. *Loss* was the word that came to mind, though nothing dramatic had ever happened. He remembered only uncertainty, angst. His parents weren't big on communicating and rarely explained anything to George. As a result, as an only child, he'd felt left out. Unwelcome, even. He could recall their door closing, the muffled voices behind it. And often, when he entered a room, interrupting their conversation, they looked at him as if at a stranger, their eyes imploring. What is *he* doing here?

What about you, George?

Sorry?

What's your essence?

George smiled. Hell if I know.

Well, you're in Inness territory now, so no doubt you'll find out. The older man looked at him meaningfully, then stood up. The inauguration was over.

With her heels clacking on the shiny floors, Edith Hodge showed him to his office, at the very end of a remote hallway lined with large plate-glass windows, keeping a few steps ahead of him, her stockinged thighs producing a rustling not dissimilar, for George, to a fingernail on a blackboard. She held a ring of keys in her fist like a jailer. The office had a view of the courtyard and a desk with an IBM Selectric and a small brass lamp with a green glass shade—it suited him just fine. At her request, he fished copies of his syllabi out of his briefcase and handed them to her. She sniffed—officiously, he thought—and considered them with disinterest, clarifying, should there be any doubt, his meager departmental status. These will suffice, she said, and left.

He sat for a moment, looking out at the trees in the courtyard, coming to terms with the fact that he'd already invested a decade in a career that was just now starting. And he found it intensely ironic that a Swedenborgian had gotten hold of his dissertation. He felt a little embarrassed, recalling their discussion, and ultimately their meeting had left him ambivalent, the long pauses, how DeBeers had worn an expression of magnanimity, as if he knew something about George, some damaging truth, but had the grace not to bring it up.

IN THE CITY, keeping his car in a garage in Harlem had cost almost as much as his rent, but he liked the Jamaican attendant, Rupert, who sold him pot. He often went to Rupert's to get high. Catherine didn't know. Rupert's wife was from Louisiana and spoke Creole; he had a hard time following it.

On the day of his scheduled defense, clearly marked on his wife's calendar for months with a big red *X,* he'd gone to Rupert's place. Catherine didn't know, because he hadn't told her, that his reckoning had been postponed. Upon review, his adviser, Warren Shelby, had declared the latest draft of his dissertation insufficient. Admittedly, George had ignored the suggestions he'd given him, particularly to elaborate on how Swedenborg had influenced the painter with his contention that we live at all times in a spiritual realm, that there's a relationship between the spiritual and the corporeal levels of existence, and whether Inness had in fact revealed, through paint—in specific colors that corresponded to celestial characteristics such as wisdom, truth, love—the love of God and the deeper meaning of life.

For George, the discovery that Inness relied on this divine rubric, that God was indeed his muse, was difficult to accept. So he refused to revise the chapter to Shelby's specifications, and just shoved the manuscript into a drawer and tried to forget about it.

Obviously, DeBeers was under the impression that his dissertation had passed scrutiny; George hadn't bothered to illuminate him, or anyone else for that matter. Of course, he had intended to have his doctorate in hand before the start of the semester. This had been his sincere hope, though it had yet to happen.

He hadn't gone home that night. Instead, he hung out with Rupert and his wife and their beautiful neighbor, whom he made love to on the couch, under the bright flash of window light, as cold rain splattered on the fire escape, Lou Rawls barely audible on the turntable. *You'll never find . . . as long as you live . . . someone who loves you tender like I do.* The rain woke him before dawn. The woman had gone. Before leaving the apartment, he looked in on Rupert and his wife, asleep, entwined, and was struck by the true love they had found in each other.

He got soaked walking home on the empty sidewalks. In the windows of dark storefronts he saw a man walking beside him. It was only when he stopped to tie his shoe that he realized the anonymous figure was his own ragged reflection.

At home, his wife cried in his arms. Why didn't you call? I'm stuck here, waiting for you all night. I can't do this myself.

He told her he'd gone out to celebrate with people from the department. She believed him and got up to make him breakfast.

He'd lied. He lied to her all the time. He didn't know why. Maybe he thought she deserved it.

Theirs was such an awful and predictable story that he tried not to think about it. He tried to pretend he actually loved Catherine, and he imagined that she tried, too. They were honorable people. So now they were honorable and miserable, much like their parents.

We're a family of doers, not complainers, her mother had told him when they'd first met. They'd planted him on the sofa in the living room while his pregnant fiancée choreographed a tray of Triscuits and Cheez Whiz. After two apricot sours, her mother took his hand and gave him a tour of the place, trotting ahead like a miniature pony. There was something so tender and humiliating about a middle-aged woman stuffed into a girdle showing off the rooms of her house, the tulip bedspreads and shag carpeting, as if he were a game-show contestant and had to pick. Her husband, Keith, just sat there on the ottoman. A red-faced laborer, he would look at George with a confused expression on his face, as if he required a translator. He was like a can of jiggled soda, George thought: the minute you popped his top he would explode. They were, Mrs. Sloan assured him, of dignified Scottish heritage. A feisty homemaker, loyal, penurious, she clearly kept house like nobody's business. Compensation for her toil was a meal out once a month and a new car every ten years. He could remember wondering if Catherine would eventually transform into a younger version of her, and assumed she would. At the time, this had filled him with a lurid sense of dread. Her sister, Agnes, with her dull state-employed husband and aggressive sisterly rivalry, was their mother's homemaking protégée. They'd even bought a tract house near the parents, in an unfinished development. When George first saw it, standing in the sloppy front yard with water seeping into his shoes, he thought: Put a fucking gun to my head. But he said, Beautiful place, Agnes. Congratulations. I'm sure you'll be very happy here.

To George, happiness was an obscure emotion. True joy, as it was imagined in great books, was more incomprehensible still. He could recall, as a boy, wandering around his father's showrooms, trying out all the different couches and chairs, putting his feet up on the coffee tables. Each living room had a fancy name: French Provincial, Urban Oasis, Classic Country, Rustic Comfort. One day, he asked his mother why they didn't have the same furniture at home. Their store, she told him, didn't carry that sort of furniture. When he asked why not, she said, Our stores cater to ordinary people, not people like us.

If he was a liar, then Catherine was the perfect match. She chose to deny his true nature just as his own mother did, contriving logical excuses for illogical acts, or reasonable grounds for unreasonable behavior, sometimes even blaming themselves for his failures. Poor George! He was overtired, overworked, overpressured—he just needs rest, to be left alone! And George never failed to exploit their misunderstanding.

His wife had married some imaginary version of himself, a better-mannered, more affable fellow, a devoted husband and father. So, too, did their marriage satisfy an unspoken contract with their parents. For Catherine, the pregnancy and subsequent wedding had elevated her from the bottom ranks of the middle class, with its rage and energy, to a status of complacency so often misconstrued as comfort. For him, he'd taken a wife, as all men should, who had the good looks that attracted polite attention, who was smart enough to make dinner conversation, who kept an orderly house.

They had done what was expected. Both of them had.

HE DROVE HOME on desolate back roads. He couldn't resist the exhilaration of speed, the wind in his hair, the sense of freedom—in these parts cops being rare. The usual obstacles were heavy trucks or dawdling pickups, the men easing home slowly from work, tossing empty beer cans out the windows. But just now there wasn't a soul in sight. It was late in the after-

noon, an indecisive hour that painted the road with trickery. Driving reck-
lessly, well over the limit, he stared as if defying his own destiny into the
horizon, where at the moment light and dark and land and sky were perfectly balanced, what Inness would call an ideal composition, a vague and
conniving frontier where all *things* cease to appear.

2

THE FIRST TIME he saw her was at the sheep farm, jumping off the
back of somebody's pickup truck. This was in September. He'd gone out
for a run. His wife had asked him to stop by the farm on his way home
to buy yogurt and cheese, which they sold to neighbors and tourists out
of a cooler in a wood hut, using the honor system and a cigar box where
you were supposed to put your money. The girl apparently worked there.
George watched as they unloaded some sheep and herded them into the
pasture. She was just a girl, really. Dark hair like his mother and pale skin
and a mean grin that curled up out of her like a charmed snake, and he
knew even before she said anything that he would come to know her and
that the knowing would be ruinous.

Hey, she said. I'm Willis.

She lived with the other hands behind the inn in a boardinghouse,
a long, barnlike structure with a plank porch along the front and a line
of windows up top. When the sunlight was full on the yellow window
shades it resembled something Hopper would have painted in his early
career—the setting with an almost nostalgic appeal, a rustic simplicity.
Later that week, out for a run at dusk, he saw her again, crossing the field
from the farm to the house with her colt legs, slump-shouldered, looking
down with intensity, her hands in her pockets, the sun a warm glow as it
began to sink behind the trees. He could hear a radio playing in somebody's window. He watched her disappear inside and moments later saw
curtains sliding across a window on the second floor, a light coming on.
It was getting cool. He walked down the road, great fields spread out on
either side. Dark pines swished in the wind like women in hoop skirts. A
passing pickup had its headlights pulled on.

The house was bright. His wife baking a pie. Yellow apples quartered
in a bowl, browning. Borrowed cookbooks on the table. Catherine in an

apron with her hair up in a knot. No longer a city girl, she'd suddenly become domestic. She rolled out the dough, her arms bare, thin, in a sleeveless white blouse. Looking at her now, he felt warmth, even desire. He wondered why he didn't love her more.

He kissed her and she brushed him off. You're cold.

It smells like fall, he said. I'll make a fire.

He left her alone and went out to the barn to get the ax. Someone had felled a tree and the trunk lay in pieces scattered on the ground. There were wood chips all through the dirt, and he knew that this spot had been used before for the same purpose. He set one of the logs upright and brought the ax down into it, splitting it right in half. Using the ax reinvigorated some primal urge, and he liked the exertion, the weight of the tool in his hands. When he had split enough wood he stacked it against the porch. He could feel the muscles in his arms. He had an awareness of his body, his strength. The air smelled of the earth. It was nearly dark when he was done.

The barn was two hundred years old, full of creatures and relics of the past—toilets and sinks and a broken-down tractor and wobbly metal chairs speckled with bat shit. As he placed the ax on its perch, a disruption in the rafters startled him—a barn owl making its escape.

Inside, he built a fire. The windows in the room had gone black. He stood in the dark, watching the fire, thinking about the girl. Already he wanted her; he sensed a connection.

Behind him, he heard Catherine coming up. She took his hand and they surrendered, briefly, to some fragile notion of harmony as the flames devoured the hundred-year-old wood.

THE NEXT AFTERNOON, he ran into the girl at the library. He and Franny were in the foyer, returning a stack of picture books. She performed this task with great formality, intrigued by the mysterious slot in the wall that accepted the books like some hungry beast.

The girl came over and tugged on Franny's pigtail.

His daughter giggled and said, What's your name? I'm Franny.

Willis, she said, cradling her books under her arm and reaching out for a shake. In case you forgot.

No, I didn't.

Her hand was small and warm. She was wearing an Elvis Costello T-shirt and cutoffs and paddock boots. Her long black hair ran down her back in serpentine ringlets.

I'm a friend of Eddy's. When the name didn't register, she said, Eddy Hale. He works for you.

He was the oldest of the three brothers, George now remembered. When he'd realized that the boys who were painting the house were the same boys who'd grown up in it and suffered the tragic loss of their parents, he told Eddy, She won't want you working here if she knows, and Eddy had squinted at him, arrogantly, and said, That's okay, Mr. Clare. If I'd bought this place, I wouldn't want to know the owners had killed themselves, either.

George had felt they'd reached a necessary if awkward understanding, a kind of fraternal bonding. Once he and his wife were completely settled into a comfortable routine, he'd tell her. Sooner or later she was bound to find out.

Oh, that Eddy.

Yeah, *that* Eddy. Her little snarl of antagonism indicated that she knew George kept things from his wife. He wondered what else Eddy had told her.

Franny pulled on the stringy hem of Willis's shorts. Look what I can do!

Let's see, Franny.

They watched his daughter push another book into the slot.

Wow, you're such a big help to your dad, aren't you?

Franny nodded earnestly. The girl smiled at him.

For some reason his heart was pounding. I've seen you at the inn, he said.

It's just a summer job—I go to UCLA. She pushed the hair out of her face. I'm taking a year off to find myself.

Are you lost?

She smiled blandly. I'm just trying to figure things out.

What things?

How I fit into all this . . .

This?

Life, you idiot.

Well, good luck. I hope you find whatever you're looking for.

Thanks. She paused and seemed to reassemble herself, her stature, then looked him over agreeably. So—you come here often?

Yeah, as a matter of fact. I like the clientele.

Me, too. Most of them are dead. She shifted her books to her other arm. She was reading Keats, Blake.

I see you like the hard stuff. Nothing watered down for you.

That's right. I take it straight.

As long as it doesn't go to your head.

I have a very high tolerance.

They were flirting. It was fun, he thought.

She grinned and held up the Blake. I took a class on him last year. *The Marriage of Heaven and Hell.* Do you know it?

All too well, he said, but his sarcasm was lost on her. He studied her face, her small freckled nose.

Active evil is better than passive good, she quoted Blake.

He makes a very good point, George said. But these days evil can be pretty scary.

I know. She shuddered. There's a lot of it in this world. She slowly raised her eyes and said, Evil is something I know about.

Are you a witch?

She grinned. What if I was?

I'd hope to catch a ride on your broom.

I'm referring to my miserable childhood.

Oh, he said gently. Okay. He waited for her to go on.

When I know you better I'll fill you in.

You've whet my appetite. He smiled and she smiled back, their unspoken arrangement somehow confirmed.

In any case, you can't have one without the other, she said, flipping her hair off her shoulder. Good without evil, I mean.

We'll make a fine pair, then.

Well, I hope you're not too good.

That would be anticlimactic, he agreed.

Tell me about your friends. She nodded at their bag of books. *Goodnight Moon*'s your favorite—right, Franny?

Franny nodded, pushing another book into the slot.

What about you?

Most of what I read isn't available here, he said.

Are you a snob?

No, but I read a lot of nonfiction, journals, books about art. I'm an art historian. I teach at Saginaw.

Oh, she said, then yawned. Is it boring?

Boring? He shrugged, a little insulted. No, it isn't.

I couldn't get past the Jesus paintings. All those virgins and angels. She glanced out the window. Anyway, I should go. I'm meeting someone. Bye, Franny.

She leaned over and shook his daughter's hand, granting him a look down her shirt. See you around, Professor.

Yes, he said. I hope so.

George watched as she went outside, the wind blowing her around. She put her books into the basket of her bicycle and rode off.

Daddy. Franny tugged on his jacket. Daddy! I want books!

You do, do you? Let's go see what we can find.

3

THE TENNIS CLUB, Black Lawn, was an exclusive little haven off County Route 13, down a potted dirt lane overrun with honeysuckle bushes and wild turkeys—he always tried to hit one as he barreled down the lane, scratching up his car. They squabbled into the bushes like fine old ladies, overdressed for the occasion. It was one of the few clubs in the United States that still maintained grass courts, even though the clay were more popular. Tennis whites were required, of course. Alongside the courts were wood huts painted a murky, campsite green, and an unheated pool that overlooked the distant Catskills, its surface littered with pine needles. Nobody swam here except for the Swedish wife of a shipping magnate who spoke no English and traversed the pool prettily in her plug-white bathing cap, and the dogs that ran wild around the property, some four hundred acres. The clubhouse, with its porches and awnings, once the home of genuine aristocrats, was slightly run-down, giving the place a kind of seedy appeal. It had a cozy little bar where they'd drink after a game. The pro, a craggy, sun-bleached guy named Tom Braden, had gotten him into games on the weekends; before noon, the courts were reserved for men. George's partner—Giles Henderson, whom people called Jelly—was heavy and fierce even in his seventies, with cropped white hair and shrewd, relentless eyes, a surprisingly agile player for a man that size. Four years ago, he'd cashed in his Wall Street life and bought the inn down the road with his second wife, Karen (pronounced *Car-in,* naturally). The inn was an historic landmark that overlooked acres of pasture. They'd also started a sheep farm and were known for their lamb dinners. When you drove by at night you'd see candles burning in the outside lights, just as they had been in the 1800s, when this was a stagecoach stop on the Albany route.

George and Jelly played against two challenging opponents: Bram Sokolov, who identified himself as a farmer, and a retired cardiologist named Bob Twitchell whom everybody called Doc. George was a good player. Tennis had, after all, kept him from getting thrown out of Williams; he hadn't been much of a student, but he was skilled on the court and for a while had been nationally ranked. He and Sokolov were around the same age and easily became friends.

One Sunday, just before dusk, an old green Range Rover pulled into their driveway. It was Bram and his wife—Justine, George remembered suddenly. She was an adjunct professor at Saginaw, a weaver, and they'd met on the day he interviewed. Out of his tennis whites, Bram was just shy of disheveled in baggy trousers, a worn T-shirt and old Stan Smiths. Justine was built like a Courbet peasant, with heavy features and the sort of confidence that comes from working with your hands.

They came up onto the porch. Bram was holding two loaves of bread, carrying one long baguette like a rifle, the other football-shaped loaf tucked under his arm.

Well, hello, George said. Welcome.

Good things come in pairs, Bram said. You know Justine.

Of course. He took her warm hand. It's good to see you.

Likewise, she said, smiling. We thought we'd just stop by.

Come in and have a drink. Catherine's just putting Franny down for a nap.

They went inside and followed him into the kitchen, where he found a bottle of gin and some limes. We've got some wine, too.

Wine would be lovely, Justine said.

Bram wanted gin.

George was glad to hear Catherine coming down the stairs.

I thought I heard voices, she said. What a nice surprise.

This is quite a place, Justine told her. I've always wanted to see the inside.

They helped themselves to a tour of the living room and George's study.

Ah, you've got a piano. Do you play?

Not very well, Catherine said.

She's very modest, George offered.

They left it, the people before us.

The Hales, Justine clarified. Poor Ella.

George's wife went a little pale. Did you know her?

Only distantly. She was very beautiful.

Suddenly it was very quiet.

We can go outside if you like, George said.

Catherine then seemed to remember her manners. Yes, there's a terrace. Let me get some food.

Don't bother. We just wanted to say hello.

But Catherine had already disappeared into the kitchen. They sat waiting, out on the terrace, in the late sunlight, until she brought out a tray of cheese and olives and Bram's baguette, which they ripped apart with their hands. This bread is wonderful, Catherine said.

Bram smiled. My own recipe.

He's quite the Renaissance man, Justine said.

Bread making's new to me. I used to be an accountant, then just got to the point where I didn't want to do it anymore.

George met Catherine's eyes for a moment. He knew she didn't approve of people who stopped working when they could afford to. You didn't earn points with his wife for having more money than God.

Now he's writing a novel.

Well, that's ambitious, George said. What's it about?

I have no idea.

Sounds promising.

Justine asked, What do you do, Catherine?

I'm a housewife.

George detected a tone of defiance. When she gazed over at him and smiled, he was momentarily stirred by the gesture.

She's a wonderful mother, he told them.

Oh, that's nice.

Do you have children? Catherine wanted to know.

No, Justine said. I'm a weaver.

There's a shop in town, Bram said, exchanging a smile with her, that sells all her things. They're quite beautiful.

I'll have to stop by, Catherine said.

You don't have to buy anything. Actually, I'd like to make you a scarf. What's your favorite color?

Blue, I think. But I'm happy to buy one.

Don't be silly. She reached out and took Catherine's hand for a moment. We're going to be friends.

His wife blushed, her eyes radiant. I'd like that.

Catherine's also an artist, he said, almost apologetically. He coughed. She's a trained conservator.

Impressive, Bram said.

Well, I didn't finish. Catherine shot him a look. I left before—

You mean you left graduate school? Justine interrupted.

Well, Franny came along. She shook her head, embarrassed. We got married.

Such defeat, he thought.

You can always get back to it, Justine told her.

Catherine restores murals. She's worked with famous architects.

I was mostly cleaning their brushes.

It's become quite a special niche, he added.

Cleaning brushes? Justine said.

No, Catherine said. Painting Jesus. George is right, it's my niche.

She and Justine exchanged glances. It was their secret language, he thought. Their meaningful silence rang in his ears like bells.

Are you terribly religious? Justine asked tentatively, as though Catherine might have some disease.

We're agnostic, Bram explained. Well—she is. I'm a Jew.

Which means, Justine clarified, we eat bagels on Sundays and brisket once a year, during the High Holidays. He makes a very good brisket.

We're Catholic, Catherine said.

In theory, George said. I refuse to align myself with any denomination. She shot him a look. We're raising our daughter Catholic.

That's not official, he said—and how did they get onto this subject? Yes, it was her latest preoccupation. She wanted to take Franny to church; he was against it. He'd outgrown religion like a tight suit. For a moment nobody said anything, but his wife's distaste was apparent. He studied both Justine and Bram, expecting some dispatch of consternation, but they seemed indifferent. I guess I have a general mistrust of anything that has the word *organized* attached to it. Maybe I prefer disorder.

Honey, Catherine said, you know that's not true.

He continued, wanting to say it, wanting her to hear it. Her blind devotion was not only embarrassing, it made her seem common. I guess it all depends what pond you're drinking from.

It's true, Justine said, there's a lot of hocus-pocus. But to each his or her own.

It's a personal choice, Catherine said.

Don't you just love those? Justine looked at George directly, and he felt they shared an understanding.

Who wants another drink? Bram?

The wine isn't cold, his wife complained.

I'll get some ice.

He went inside, happy to have a moment alone. From the kitchen window he could see the three of them out on the terrace. His wife's hair shone in the late sunlight and she pushed it back over her shoulders and tucked it behind her ears, something she'd been doing since he first met her, instantly transforming herself into the awkward girl he'd picked up at Williams. She hadn't changed much. He didn't know why he didn't like her better.

We should play some time, Catherine was saying as he approached the terrace with a bowl of ice and fresh drinks for Bram and himself. Give these guys a run for their money.

On occasions like these George could actually see the benefit of marriage. Four perfectly civilized people spending an afternoon together. His wife sitting there as erect as a violinist. Justine and Bram, having just recently discovered the comforts of civility, impersonating grown-ups.

She plays well, he heard himself say. And it was true: Catherine could hold her own on the court. They'd played in college, and he remembered how she looked in a tennis skirt.

I'd love to, but I'm hopeless out there. Justine smiled up at him as he handed out the drinks. I'm afraid I've been relegated to more creative forms of exercise.

George couldn't resist asking, Such as?

Yoga, of course. Sorry to disappoint you. She turned to Catherine. They have classes in town, if you're interested. In the high-school gym.

That might be a stretch, he said, trying to make a joke.

You'd like it, Justine promised.

Catherine smiled and nodded. I'd like to. Sure.

How about you, George? Justine asked.

He would swear she was flirting. I don't think so. My tendons or whatever you call them are tight as guitar strings. It could be dangerous.

You don't look tight.

Trust me. He raised his drink. Here's to the only thing that loosens me up.

That's too bad. You're missing out.

Justine goes to India every year, Bram offered. She has a guru over there.

Well, George said.

I've always wanted to go, Catherine said.

News to me, he thought.

It's a very spiritual experience.

Catherine glanced at him uneasily and fingered the hem of her skirt. I've heard it's filthy over there. Is that true?

Not where Justine goes it isn't, he thought.

Yes, sure, there's poverty, Justine said. But the people are amazing. And the landscape, the colors, it jumps out at you. Pinks and reds and oranges. It's really something. Whenever I go there, I feel, well . . . She shook her head, as if none of them could possibly understand.

Feel what? George said.

Embraced, she said finally.

Sitting there in the sharp light, he noticed her breasts, the heavy bones of her face, her sandaled feet firmly planted on the ground. She looked like some Roman princess. There was a classicism about her, a strength and intelligence that he found attractive.

Just look at that sunset, his wife said.

That's what you call a cheap thrill, Bram said.

They looked at the sun. It was enormous, brilliant. They sat there, watching it disappear behind the trees. For a long while nobody said any-thing, and soon they were each painted in darkness. The sudden quiet seemed eerie, and they were all glad for the noisy disruption of Franny, thundering through the empty house and calling her mother's name.

4

A FEW WEEKS LATER, Giles Henderson invited George and Bram up to the inn to shoot skeet. It was a glorious fall day, straight out of Inness's *Morning, Catskill Valley,* he thought, the tops of the oak trees aflame with red leaves. George hadn't fired a shotgun in years, but he embraced the bourgeois emphasis on sport and managed to hit a few of the clays as they flew into the air. Afterward, in keeping with the tweedy mood of the afternoon, they sat in the dark, paneled lounge and drank bourbon and smoked cigars. Jelly was a chain-smoker, and his face like a topiary of broken capillaries. To George's surprise, the girl Willis was waitressing there. In the empty dining room she sat alone at a table, wrapping silver-ware in napkins. She was wearing a short gray dress with white piping and an apron, her uniform. Her hair was pulled back with a barrette, a cigarette between her lips. The smoke, coupled with the glaring window light, formed a mysterious aura around her. She turned slightly, as if sens-ing him. In profile, he saw the line of her jaw, the pronounced cheekbone, the curve of her upper lip. She was like the girl in Delacroix's *Orphan Girl in the Cemetery,* with her obvious yet unacknowledged beauty, her black eyes, her fear.

After the three men ordered, she brought their food on a large round tray, balancing it on her shoulder. As she set down plates of oysters and smoked trout with lemon, he noticed her thin fingers, the chipped black polish on her nails. Bending and rushing in her short little dress, she had a tart, wistful arrogance that made him feel useless. They switched to wine, a peppery Cabernet, and watching her open it was like witnessing some-thing sexual, her hands on its green throat as she twisted out the cork, and after a few glasses George was under the impression that her complete avoidance of him held some deep significance. He followed her down the empty hallway toward the bathrooms.

She turned on him, fiercely. What do you want?

He couldn't answer.

I saw you watching me.

So? Is that so unusual?

So what do you want?

You already know what I want.

It just happened, he rationalized. Maybe he'd coaxed her into it. He was older, and he had a certain influence. Maybe she liked his looks, as other women did—his longish hair, his new beard. Catherine used to say he had noble eyes. They were brown, he thought, totally ordinary. He hung around, waiting for her to get off work, and they went to her room, the bed narrow and hard as a coffin. On the small table was a tea tin she used as an ashtray, a miniature Aladdin's lamp that held incense. He sat cautiously on the very edge of the bed and watched her kick off her boots. He was thinking about Catherine, how he shouldn't be here with this girl, up to his old tricks, how he should get up and leave, but she pulled off her socks and he looked at her thin, dirty feet and her small hands and he couldn't move. Her face was pale, her hair dark like a hood, and a sharp light came from her eyes. Stop thinking about her, she said. And then she kissed him and he came back at her and her mouth tasted milky and warm and he couldn't stop.

Afterward, they lay there in the tiny room. It was very quiet. He was conscious of the world outside her window. Of the cold air, the smell of the earth, the dead leaves. It was beginning to get dark.

You look sad, she said.

He nodded, because he knew that everything was suddenly different.

We've done a horrible thing.

Yes.

She appraised him coldly. You need to go.

Walk with me?

They walked into the woods. The air was cool. She shivered in his arms, her mouth warm, salty. He pushed the hair from her forehead and it was damp and he wondered if she was feverish and then he thought if she were he would take the fever from her, he would kiss it out of her. The trees moving overhead, a vigil of mourning. They walked under the trees for miles.

The day had been like a kind of music, a song you hear once and remember imperfectly and never hear again.

Later, at home, he was glad for its comfort and warmth. His wife at the stove, the table set, daisies in a white pitcher. Everything clean and in its place, laundry folded, beds made. His daughter's little boots by the door, scattered pinecones. He had a Scotch, he felt he needed it, and Catherine played the piano. He watched her as she played, the fine muscles in her back, her lovely, expressive shoulders. She was playing Grieg, the music like a river bringing him back to her. He thought about the afternoon with Willis, how she'd smelled of fresh air and earth. She was like some treasure you discover and wipe clean, acknowledging its history, its beautiful tragedies. The music slowly unraveled and he returned to her little room, how she'd suffered beneath him, and he felt a supreme sense of contentment. His life was simple, glorious. The old house full of music, his daughter pretending to be a cat and traipsing across the floor on all fours, then climbing into his lap. Meow, she said, and kissed him.

HE'D BEGUN to see again.

The landscape opened up to him. The brown fields. The pale horizon.

She was too young for him. He knew this. But he trusted her. It was too early to say he knew her, but he did feel they knew each other. Body and soul. It went beyond sex, he thought. It was something else, something deeper. He possessed her. She had given herself to him.

I think I'm in love with you, he told her.

You hardly know me.

He sat and watched her. She was free in her body. Unlike his wife, she moved without choreography.

Naked, she stood at the window, the white curtain brushing her thigh. Sipping from a mug of tea, she looked at him. The room was close, the floor puddled with mustardy light, the smell of horses on her boots.

She rarely spoke of her life, her childhood—anything before they'd come together in this place. She was a girl, just a girl. The only evidence of family was a small framed photograph of Willis and her mother on the nightstand, taken, she told him, on her first day of college. The wind must have been blowing, and it was obvious from their tousled hair and distracted expressions that the photographer had snapped the shot prematurely, before they were ready.

SHE WANTED to be a poet. She was obsessed with Keats. She would sit naked on the only chair and recite poems, "The Human Seasons" her favorite. He'd watch her in the smoky light, her little mouth as the words came out of it, her fingertips on the book, her straight back, her long thighs on the tattered cane seat, her dirty feet on the worn rungs. He could feel the world slipping away and he liked the feeling.

> *He has his lusty Spring, when fancy clear*
> *Takes in all beauty with an easy span. . . .*
> *He has his Winter too of pale misfeature,*
> *Or else he would forego his mortal nature.*

They would go for walks and lie in the grass looking up at the sky. He felt free with her; he felt like himself, even though he didn't know who that man was. He would look at her—her luminous skin, her full dark lips, her black hair—and find himself lost.

They drank wine sometimes at noon, when his wife thought he was at the college. They made love with the shades pulled, horses stomping in their stalls below.

I'll leave my wife, he told her, knowing that he wouldn't.

No, George. This thing we have, it's temporary. It has no true relevance.

For a moment she seemed superior to him. He couldn't look at her. She got off the bed and pulled on her trousers, pushed her feet into her boots. The smell of the barn clung to her and for a very brief instant he despised her.

We have no past, no future. Just now.

Walking back into his life was like waking from a troubling dream. He knew he should end it, never see her again, this sort of thing was beneath him. But there seemed no stopping it now.

How was your run? his wife asked.

I'm up to six miles now.

Impressive. Good for you.

I want to run, too, Daddy, Franny said.

He took his daughter's perfect little hand. Okay, let's chase Mommy around the house.

And so they did. And Catherine laughed to be chased. And her pretty face rose with color. And when they were sweaty and tired he made a fire and they read Franny's books until evening, when the windows filled up with darkness and his wife went in to make supper.

Animal Husbandry

I

THEY'D MET at Hampshire, in an animal-husbandry class. It was a young college that encouraged freethinking and boundless inquiry. On warm spring days they were out on the lawn with their fists in the air. In winter they piled into cars, traveling the interstate to fight corruption wherever it could be found. D.C.; Groton; Harrisburg. They protested Corporate America, apartheid, environmental toxins, negligence, greed. They read Emma Goldman, Kropotkin. They knew how to go limp in the hands of cops. They stood in the cold, shivering, eating a stranger's chili out of Styrofoam cups. They linked arms, making human chains, and sang "We Shall Overcome!" Anarchy, as a concept, was intoxicating. And through its discourse she'd discovered her true self—a feminist, a humanist, an agrarian, a romantic, peeling away the carefully wrought costume designed by her parents to find what glimmered beneath. Gone were the ethical charades promoted in religious school. Gone were the scare tactics that indicted her body as a biological enemy, routine strategies of degradation that made her nearly desperate for a partner, someone who could love even her.

Here was the real Justine: earthy, busty, hairy-legged, fragrant. She had pale skin and dark, somber eyes and wore her hair in a long, thick braid. She had a kind of rare, painterly beauty that seemed old-fashioned. Further, she was not a woman with fragile appetites. Her mouth watered for strong flavors, turnips and onions still dusty with earth, sweet radishes, leafy beets that stained her fingertips, bread as warm as flesh that she made with her own hands.

Her husband, Bram, short for Abraham, had a certain masculine purity, with loose flannel shirts that smelled of sheep and scraggly black hair and brown eyes and the books that fell from his pockets—Rilke and Hamsun and Chekhov. Where would we be without Chekhov? he once said to her. They would make love in his little room at the college, and then she'd sit in the old brown chair he'd found on the street, drinking bourbon and eating tangerines, listening to *All Things Considered*. Mornings, they'd cut through the apple orchard to Atkins, where they ate doughnuts and drank coffee and read the newspaper. They were friends who had become lovers. No, they were lovers who'd become friends. They were married the following summer, after graduation, on a flower farm in Amherst. They had the party at the Lord Jeffrey Inn, under a tent, and went to Provence on their honeymoon. She would never forget all of those sunflowers, fields and fields of them, or the little cinema where they'd watched *Lolita* dubbed in French.

At first, Bram had wanted to be a philosopher. Then a novelist. Now he was a farmer who wanted to be a novelist. The land had been left to him by a distant uncle who'd used it for hunting a few weeks a year. They both came from money but made out like they had little—the renovation of the old farmhouse still unfinished, the scuffed-up floors, the poorly heated, undecorated rooms that contained one or two priceless antiques, the boxy green Range Rover in the dirt yard. Bram was an only child. His father was a famous conductor who had been married to a variety of histrionic women, none of whom particularly fancied music; they saw him every summer at Tanglewood, and the current wife always prepared elaborate picnics in wicker baskets. Bram's mother, an unrecognized painter, had died when he was only a boy, and he once told Justine, in a rare display of vulnerability, that he'd never gotten over it. Justine's mother owned an antiques shop in Savannah, having tired of being a psychologist, and her father was an orthopedic surgeon; she had two prodigious sisters, twins, who lived in Maine and each did everything in threes—three degrees, three houses, three jobs, three kids. Bram and Justine were childless.

Justine made her studio in the borning room, off the kitchen. They raised sheep and alpaca, and she dyed the wool and spun it herself in the farm's old creamery. With all that yarn, the floors swarmed with color and ran through the house like colored rivers. Her loom waited by the window, a patient confidante. Two days a week, she taught weaving and textiles at the college. For a woman, Justine was not especially vain and prided herself on her reliance on the cerebral as opposed to the physical, and on her disdain for ornamentation of any kind. She wore baggy men's jeans, a flannel shirt and work boots, and her beauty regime consisted of soap and water. Her hands were large and thin—the hands of an aristocrat, her father always said—but they were rough and callused and rarely idle. After her work all over the farm and house was done, she wove blankets and scarves, which she sold in a shop in town frequented by the extravagant parents of her Saginaw students.

Justine feasted on the simple blessings around her, the farm table scattered with crumbs and pomegranates and acorns. These images were like lines of poetry, she thought, and she greatly admired poets and people like Bram, who could see beauty in the ordinary. To Justine, happiness was a good soup simmering all day. Wind crossing the field and whistling through the window screens. Burly yarn transforming in her hands. She loved her husband's face and his smell and how his hair dripped over his collar like black paint, but most of all how she felt in his arms—warm, strong, loved.

Besides the alpaca and sheep, they had chickens and rabbits and two big dogs, Rufus and Betty, and far up in the hills there were coyotes and bears and sometimes mountain lions and wolves. She would walk the property and marvel at its splendor. It was almost frightening, and when the wind blew hard at night it could undermine her own small position in the scheme of things. The house itself was cold. That was all right, but in winter the flat and austere light gave back nothing at all. The old pine boards were freezing underfoot. The windows trembled in their frames.

This was where they had come. They had chosen this. It was their life.

THROUGH THE USUAL Saginaw channels, she'd heard about George Clare. He and his wife were the poor suckers who'd bought the Hale farm. Supposedly, he was some kind of wunderkind in art history. On the day he'd interviewed, she pretended not to know who he was when they met standing in line at the cafeteria.

I'm new, actually, he'd said. And they shook hands, shifting their trays and notebooks. I start in the fall.

Clare was the sort of man people called good-looking. Something just slightly off, slightly amiss—but she could be a snob. He was dressed in his interviewing clothes—khaki trousers, a white oxford shirt, a pretentious red bow tie (perhaps a new, defining accessory) and a tweed blazer whose fabric resembled granola. He had the benign, uninteresting beauty of the Disney prince who, out of stupid luck, always got the girl. Challenging his otherwise conservative image, his toast-colored hair was long and shaggy and his wire-rimmed spectacles gave him a kind of John Lennon coolness that was, she realized, a complete fantasy. Within two minutes he'd walked her through his educational pedigree, including a prestigious scholarly prize named for some eccentric millionaire who collected Hudson River School landscapes. Really? she said, already bored. She'd run into people like him all her life. He was the type who'd gone unscathed through adolescence, with no distinguishable marks or scars, no apparent history.

As it turned out, they had a few things in common, tennis for one. George was quick to reveal that he'd been on the team at Williams. Bram was an inelegant player, but powerful and consistent. The men played doubles every Saturday while she and Catherine and the other wives watched from lawn chairs or stretched out on the grassy field behind the courts. Children ran around barefoot. The Clares' little girl, Franny, would sit in the grass, pulling the petals off of daisies, then letting them run through her fingers like flakes of snow. Occasionally, one of the men would bark a curse, much to his wife's dismay; in particular, George was known for his temper on the court. Once, he'd been so incensed when Bram blew an easy point that he threw his racket at him, and Bram needed stitches over his eyebrow. It seemed revealing to her that his partner never bothered to apologize. Still, it was a small town; you had to accept people for who they were. Sometimes, after a game, they'd all have drinks together in the gloomy clubhouse bar, which was famous for its hair-raising Bloody Marys, horseradish as thick as paint chips floating on the surface. Slivers of revelation would emerge as she observed the Clares' practiced charade of love. They weren't country people. They didn't know how to live with all that land. People said the farm they'd bought was cursed. The Hale tragedy was a favorite subject at dinner parties, when people drank too much and made allowances for impolite talk about neighbors and weird fatal accidents. You'd see the boys in town with their uncle. Justine often saw them at Hack's, racing around on the carts, making a ruckus and being generally disruptive, but people felt sorry for them and didn't say anything. Once, a few weeks after their parents had died, she'd caught the youngest boy—Cole was his name—stealing packages of steaks, shoving them down the front of his jacket. Waiting for her to call somebody, he just looked at her, at once surly and vulnerable, and she thought he might break into tears. If you saw those eyes you'd pray he'd get away with it, and she held her breath until he got out of the store.

A lot of townspeople had gone to the memorial service at St. James's Church, where she and Bram went to pay their respects. The boys sat in a front pew, next to their uncle and his girlfriend. Justine had been preoccupied by the boys' faces, each one a derivation of the others', all three with the most remarkable blue eyes she'd ever seen, and it was then that she'd felt, deep inside of herself, the desire to become a mother. She and Bram went home that night and made love like rabbits, and didn't use anything, and she cried in his arms for those boys, and for the child she hoped they'd made. But that spell of maternal longing didn't last, and to her relief her period came the next week.

SHE DIDN'T HAVE to teach. She was doing it, she supposed, as a kind of community service, and to break the assumptions people had about weaving, often considered just an expensive hobby, not an art form. For all the years she'd spent at Saginaw, she felt routinely excluded by the intellectuals in Fine Art, the painters and sculptors who relegated her status to that of a craftsperson, expressing interest in her work only when they wanted to buy scarves at Christmastime. For her and Bram, money was not an issue. They were both accustomed to having it, plenty of it. However, when evaluating herself in relation to others, she thought she could easily live without it. She could still function creatively, and she and Bram were committed to living off the land as much as they could. She spent easily, not frivolously, always in order to procure a good life, a meaningful life. She was selective, too, often traveling some distance for certain items—organic meat, for instance, which they bought from a farmer in Malta, or the wine they favored from a vintner in Amenia. As much as she loved tending the livestock and maintaining the farm, it was all rather demanding work, and she liked having the time alone in the car on the thirty-minute drive to Saginaw, along the river. And she liked her large classroom full of looms, her handful of students working with their nimble, inexperienced fingers in silence, as devoted at harpists.

She didn't want to like George, but she did. They'd have lunch together in the dining hall. At first they'd sort of bump into each other, as if by chance, and Justine would fawn all over him. Not that she found him especially interesting or attractive—somehow he just seemed to require the fuss, like on some level his ego was suffering. Sitting there at a little table over trays of grilled cheese sandwiches and tomato soup, she'd become critically self-conscious, painfully aware of her too-tight waistband, her hips nudging and stretching her corduroy skirt. Even her facial contortions were overanimated, overly enthusiastic and concerned. Soon their lunches together became regular, every Tuesday and Thursday after morning classes, at a table tucked in the far corner, overlooking the sculpture garden with its odd modern pieces, one of them a stone hand the size of a mailbox. George wore his professor's uniform: crisp shirts that were always white, the crunchy granola blazer, khaki trousers and bow ties. Justine found herself puzzling over how long it took his wife to iron the shirts so diligently, since she herself considered ironing a complete waste of time. What was so wrong with wrinkles?

Catherine seemed nice, an unfortunate but fitting adjective. She was a frail specimen of female, too thin for her own good, Justine thought, and somewhat reserved, though George would apologetically explain that his wife was simply shy. Catherine was pretty in a washed-out, underfed sort of way that a lot of the women at the club—the weekenders—went in for. It was some kind of fashion statement, she'd decided, but, again, Justine could be tough on women. In truth, she didn't find most of them all that interesting. Or, to be diplomatic, she just didn't share the same interests. Most of the women her age were busy with their children. It was simply a different mind-set. She'd learned to tell people, her parents included, that she and Bram were trying, even though she wasn't at all sure she wanted a child and he certainly wasn't pushing her. This sort of personal choice was deeply out of fashion, yet Chosen was a place where you could escape the social underpinnings of conventional expectations. For the most part, they hung out with outcasts and nonconformists. Many of the women she knew were older, veterans of broken marriages, poets, feminists, She went to a women's group that met monthly, each member pos a seasoned, ornery particularity that Justine admired, and with thei ..elp she'd made great strides in discovering her own personal strengths.

Blue was a good color for Catherine, she decided. She sat at her loom and began threading the yarn. It was a good French blue, like the chalky blue eye of a peacock feather, and the chunky wool brought to mind the generous sheep who'd made it. Good comfortable warmth, she thought. Just what a woman like Catherine Clare needed, because a town like this could be hard for someone like her. She wasn't like the usual hardscrabble, weather-beaten women you saw walking around the village, showing off the life lines on their faces like circles in a tree trunk. These were country-women, indifferent to frivolity, to style and trends. They were as much a part of the landscape as the grazing livestock, and just as indifferent. In contrast, Catherine was fine-featured, delicate, with eyes the color of bells. Despite how little she thought of herself, her beauty did not go unnoticed.

2

A FLUKE HEAT WAVE came through at the end of the month, provoking brownouts even in Chosen. The news showed people all over the state sleeping on their fire escapes or out on their porches, and temperatures rose to a hundred degrees. The pool at the club became the Clares' refuge.

On the steps in the shallow end, Catherine and Franny were having a tea party when Justine appeared, like one of those old-fashioned Hollywood movie actresses, in a one-piece suit and a terry-cloth robe, with a towel draped around her shoulders like a mink stole. I had a feeling I'd find you here. She joined them on the edge of the pool, and put her feet in.

Just up the hill, Bram and George were playing singles, grunting, cursing, sweating like pigs.

I've got polka dots, Franny told Justine importantly, pointing to her suit.

I love polka dots, Justine said.

Let's sit here in the shade, Catherine said as they climbed out and dried off and spread their towels out in the grass.

You can't get me! Franny challenged.

Oh yes I can, Justine said, clambering up and chasing her around, their ankles crosshatched with grass.

You. *Can't*. Get. *Me!*

Big yellow leaves were dropping, slowly, slowly into the pool. It was nice under the trees with the wind blowing.

Watch this! Franny said, and did a somersault.

Now you can join the circus, Catherine said.

I had a feeling you were a monkey. Justine ruffled her hair, and Franny made chimp sounds and jumped around. Then she went over and plopped down on Justine's lap. Well, hello, Justine said, pleased to have been chosen.

I tired now.

Catherine smiled at her sleepy daughter and said, She likes you, Justine. Do you mind?

Of course not. In less than a minute, Franny was asleep on her ample bosom. It's the padding, she said. She's so adorable.

Especially at moments like these.

Catherine lay back in the grass, cradling her head in her hands and looking up at the sky. They could hear the ball lobbing back and forth across the court and their husbands' muted conversation. They were all becoming friends, she thought. It was good.

Justine. With her strong-coffee voice, her thick brown hair. She was unlike anyone Catherine had ever met. Sashaying around in her bathing suit, the hair on her legs as thick as a man's. Catherine envied her easy pride, the fact that she actually *liked* herself, whereas, in her case, it had been impressed upon her long ago, by assorted freeze-dried mentors, that self-love was conceit. As a result, Catherine was vigilantly critical, fixing and fussing, sucking in her stomach, even resorting to punitive measures such as starving herself and throwing up. Getting her body back after Franny had been a chore. She couldn't even remember the last time she'd walked around naked in front of George. She liked to think of herself as modest, but that, she'd come to realize, was really just another word for insecure. Her beauty was the one thing she depended on to keep George interested. She worried she couldn't maintain it, and worried it wasn't enough.

You and Bram—you don't want kids?

You think we're terrible, don't you?

No—but you'd be a great mother.

Really? She looked at Catherine hopefully but quickly said, I wouldn't know what to do with a baby.

It's one of those things you just *know.*

I've never felt ready, though.

What about now?

Justine glanced down at Franny's sleeping head. Maybe.

I wasn't ready, either, Catherine confided. I didn't want a baby. I didn't even want to marry George. She knew she shouldn't have said it, but the minute the words came out she felt the glee of liberation. I was too afraid to have her on my own.

Justine nodded, though Catherine doubted she would've made the same choice. She imagined that Justine would have terminated the pregnancy and moved on with her life. Catherine hadn't been able to do that. She'd used religion as an excuse, but it wasn't the fear of God that had kept her from doing it. Though she understood all of the arguments, she had her own principles. She valued freedom just as much as the next person—at least she thought she did—but the notion that freedom was a commodity of entitlement still eluded her. She'd been raised to believe there were always limits to freedom, and even now she didn't have the courage to fight them.

For Catherine, religion had become a handy excuse for everything she couldn't deal with, starting with how she really felt about George. Sometimes she wondered what her life would have been like if she'd had different parents, with different values, but you couldn't choose who raised you and taught you what to believe.

How do you feel now? Justine asked.

What do you mean?

About George, obviously.

Sometimes Justine's boldness put her on edge.

The point is, have you grown to love him? You know, like people in arranged marriages.

Yes, of course I love him, she lied without reservation. He's my husband.

They heard the squeal of the door in the chain-link tennis fence, and a moment later their husbands came toward them in their tennis whites, their faces bright red in the heat. They looked happy, well off. As they approached, the men saw that Franny was sleeping and lowered their voices. Catherine watched George register that it was Justine holding their sleeping daughter, not her. The expression on his face, as he gazed down at Justine, was one of tenderness, she thought, maybe even love, and she wondered if Bram had noticed. This brief interlude evaporated when Franny stirred and reached up for her father. Gently, he lifted her out of Justine's arms and she settled onto his shoulder, cuddling up in the crook of his neck as the two couples walked down the lawn to their cars.

Whenever she rode in George's car, especially with Franny, it became clear to her how differently they operated in the world. For one thing, he refused to put a car seat in the back. He claimed the seatbelt was good enough, citing his own childhood, but she knew there was more to it than that. Having a car seat in the back of his convertible would certainly mar his image as the freewheeling young professor. Though it wasn't mandatory, she'd had a car seat in the back of her station wagon since they'd moved out here. George rarely rode in her car. He always made fun of her driving, accusing her of *driving like a woman,* swerving all over the road, which wasn't at all true.

In George's car, she always felt like an intruder. The leather seats, the faint smell of cigarettes were evidence of the things he did when he was away from her, doing whatever he damn well pleased.

He snapped Franny into her seatbelt and climbed in behind the wheel. She could smell his sweaty shirt. He pulled out of the long driveway onto the road, the wind in their hair.

It's windy, Momma, Franny said.

Yes, it is, isn't it? Catherine smiled at her daughter. She noticed a book sticking out of George's briefcase and pulled it out, a tattered antique tome titled *Heaven and Its Wonders and Hell.* What's this?

He frowned. It's Floyd's. He wants me to read it. He's obsessed with that nutcase.

Swedenborg? She turned the book over in her hands, its binding splintered and worn.

You don't have to worry, he told her. You're definitely going to heaven.

Why does that feel like an insult?

It's not an insult, Catherine. You're one of the lucky few.

What about you, George? Where are you going?

Why does that feel like an insult? he mocked.

You know why. She sat there with her arms crossed. You always do whatever you want.

Oh—and you don't? You got exactly what you wanted.

She just looked at him. There was no point in getting into it. He always turned it around, made it about her. It was his strategy for avoiding things he didn't want to talk about. What she wanted? That was a question she herself had never been able to answer.

Good luck with this, then. She put the book between them.

You know I don't believe in that crap.

Yes, I do. You don't believe in anything.

He scowled at her, and she thought he'd come back with something mean, but he didn't. They drove for a while without speaking, the wind hot against their faces.

How was your game?

He makes stupid mistakes. I fucking creamed him.

SHE TRIED to be a good wife. It was her duty; he was out there trying to make a living. When he got home he was tired. He had certain expectations, as if his idea of marriage came with a list of inclusions, like a brand-new car: the peck on the cheek, the gin-and-tonic, plate of cheese and olives, newspaper, the mail.

The rituals of civilized people.

She would lay the tablecloth, pressing it flat with her hand. She would fold the napkins and set out the silverware. She would look over at the window, light still pushing through until it got dark too early.

How was your day? she'd ask.

He told her about his students, his classes. The other professors, he said, were aloof, preoccupied. Yours?

What could she tell him? While their daughter watched *Romper Room* she'd vacuumed, mopped the kitchen floor, cleaned the bathrooms and, when Franny spilled her applesauce, mopped the floor again. Washed the dishes, did the laundry, brought the warm sheets in from the line. They had lunch during a rain shower, then went outside in rain boots and slickers, twirling their umbrellas like geishas, and climbed the grassy hill to the ridge. There were always things to see: the birds, so varied and surprising; the smallest flowers. Catherine took Franny's umbrella and let her run down the hill, her little red slicker vivid across the green grass. They stomped through puddles, splashing their legs with mud. Later, when Franny napped, she had a cigarette out in the field, under the rising moon.

They'd given him three classes, sixty students in all. At night, with stacks of papers to grade, he'd close himself up in his study. When Franny made too much noise, banging her tambourine or rattling her maracas, he'd whip open the door and shout, Stop making noise! How can Daddy get anything done?

Later, lying in the dark, she'd sense something, *someone,* standing there at the foot of the bed. Sometimes she'd wake out of a deep sleep shivering with cold, as if she were sleeping on a bed of snow.

One night she woke to the piano, a single note playing again and again.

She shook George awake. Did you hear that?

Turn off the goddamn light!

She lay awake, waiting, waiting . . . for what she did not know.

Then, around three every night, the drama with Franny started. She'd scamper across the hall, whimpering, and climb into bed on Catherine's side. I scared, Momma.

Catherine didn't mind—in fact, she preferred knowing her little one was safe and sound beside her—but George wouldn't have it. As stern as a drill sergeant, he'd get out of bed, scoop her up in his arms and carry her back to her room, kicking and screaming.

Children don't sleep with their parents, he explained the first time. She needs to learn that.

Heart pounding, Catherine lay there listening as her daughter cried.

Leave her alone, he warned. You'll be sorry if you get up.

Sorry how?

You'll be sorry, he muttered.

What, George? What did you say?

But he didn't answer. Furious, he turned away.

I'm not sleeping in here with you. She whipped off the covers, went into Franny's room and climbed into bed, holding her very tightly. You're safe now, she whispered. Go to sleep.

You're going to spoil her, George said the next morning, from the doorway of Franny's room. That's what's happening here. You're the problem, Catherine, not Franny. It's you.

This went on for weeks. Exhausted and a little desperate, she finally sought the guidance of their pediatrician, who confirmed that nightly disruptions were routine for small children in a new house; it could take them up to a year to adjust. He wrote a prescription for a mild sedative. It's very gentle, he told her. It'll help you get her back on track.

She thanked him and took the prescription, but had no intention of filling it. Aside from Tylenol or antibiotics, she didn't approve of giving drugs to children.

When George came home, she told him what the doctor had said, and they argued about it. He dug through her purse, searching for the prescription, then went to fill it himself. Later that night, he added a dose of the purple syrup to Franny's bottle. Within minutes of drinking it, his daughter was fast asleep.

Even so, Catherine lay awake, awaiting the usual disturbance, but it didn't come.

What do you know, George said the next morning before pushing off to work. The miracles of modern medicine. Designed to help totally incompetent parents like us.

She broke down and called her mother.

What is it, Catherine? You sound upset.

She considered saying something completely irrelevant, keeping the conversation light and happy, like her mother preferred it, but right now she needed her help. I miss New York, she said, which was code for so much more. She missed their old apartment, the little table where she'd drink her coffee and sketch still lifes and watch the slow tugboats on the river. She missed the neighborhood, the Chinese grocer who'd put his palm on the top of Franny's head like he was checking a cantaloupe for ripeness, the Polish woman at the bakery who always gave her a free cookie, the bowlegged shoemaker who'd fix George's worn-down heels. Churches, the smell of incense and melting wax, anguish. I miss my work, she said.

You're making a life with your husband, her mother said. For Franny's sake. Isn't that what matters most?

It was what her mother had done for her and Agnes. Sacrifice. The tradition of compromise had been handed down through the generations like everyday china.

George and I, she said. We're not . . .

You're not what, dear?

Compatible. It was the most diplomatic word she could think of.

Your father and I aren't, either, and look how long we've lasted.

Catherine stood there, twirling the cord around her finger—tighter, tighter. She wanted to say, *He's odd, insensitive, I'm afraid of him,* but only said, We're not getting along.

It's difficult with a small child, her mother told her. I know you don't believe me, but it's the same for everybody. Franny comes first, you know that. Love takes time. And marriage isn't easy. It never has been.

I know, she heard herself say.

And think of yourself alone. Raising Franny. It's not easy to be a single mother, either, you know, with everything on your shoulders, plus the financial strain. I don't know what you could afford—you don't have a steady salary, and your work, well, it doesn't pay much, does it? Remember your poor aunt Frances, look what happened to her. You'll end up being a waitress somewhere, leaving Franny with strangers. Can't you try, Cathy, to just make the best of it? Do it for Franny, she added.

You can stop now, Mother, I'm convinced. She hung up.

The conversation confirmed that the only thing keeping them married was Franny. Their daughter was the mascot of victory, and a prize only one of them could keep.

She took her cigarettes and sat on the screened porch. She could see Wade in the distance on the tractor, mowing the field, going back and forth, back and forth. Faintly, she could hear a Rolling Stones song on his radio.

The day was overcast, the field thick with fog. She stepped outside and walked into the field. The humid air clung to her. She stood there alone in the middle of it. She could feel her outlines blurring, as if she could fade into the opaque landscape and disappear.

Takers

I

IN A SMALL TOWN like theirs, people talked. You couldn't get far without somebody knowing your business. Mary Lawton didn't consider herself a gossip, but you'd still hear things. It spiced up your day. Someone would see something and tell this person or that one, who told somebody else, and all of a sudden it was real. It was news.

The girl worked at the inn, everybody knew that. People had seen them together. Her shiny black hair was hard to miss. Something about her—*bold* was the word. That figure. Those jeans. Mary had overheard some of the men joking about her, what they'd like to do to her if they had the chance. Keep dreaming, she thought.

One afternoon Mary saw her coming out of Hack's with Eddy Hale. They had their arms around each other and were looking plenty intimate. It made her angry, since Eddy had been hurt enough already. The girl had silver bracelets up her arm that looked like a Slinky and jangled when she moved. When Mary said hello, Eddy went a little pink, but his mother had taught him to be polite and he put down his bag and introduced them. This is Willis, he said. Willis, Mary Lawton.

The girl had the tentative beauty of a roadside flower. She smiled at Mary.

Willis is working over at the inn, Eddy explained. That's where we met.

They talked a while longer and he told Mary he'd applied to a music college somewhere in Boston. He asked about her family, careful to avoid the subject of Alice, and she told him nothing was new and then they parted and she stood there a minute, reflecting on what a nice, good boy he was and how that girl, whoever she was, didn't deserve him.

It was after school, and groups of kids were walking through town with their backpacks, the girls with their leather pocketbooks. Two came out of Bell's Five-and-Dime with orange and purple lips; they had a new snow cone machine that was all the rage among middle-schoolers. Walking past the window, she saw Cole Hale and her son, Travis Jr., standing at the counter on either side of Patrice Wilson—Mary knew her parents. She turned on her stool from one boy to the other, giving each the attention he desired, but Mary knew there'd only be one winner in that contest. She considered knocking on the glass, but thought better of it. The last thing Travis needed was his mother catching him in the act of being himself.

THE TOWN WAS changing. You could see it in the cars parked along Main Street. Used to be only pickups and jalopies. One or two new shops had opened, sprucing up filthy storefronts with snappy awnings and brightly painted signs. City people with deep pockets were buying up the old farms that nobody could afford to operate, much less maintain. Honestly, she didn't mind her commissions going up, but it was hard for everybody else. People like the Hales, who'd lost it all. You couldn't blame people for being angry. And it could make things difficult for newcomers like the Clares, forever distinguished as *those people who bought the Hale farm.* They were outsiders, and the fact that he was a professor didn't help. Only a few Chosen High graduates went to college, usually to the community college in Troy for the cheap tuition and a full roster of night classes. Every few years, one or two went to Saginaw, which cost twice as much as the state university. For all of them, travel typically meant they'd enlisted and been stationed in some exotic place. Most of the boys in town had served. Her own Travis would likely want to go, but she intended to talk him out of it.

Still—the Clares didn't exactly try to fit in. They kept to themselves. She'd see the wife in church, always alone, slipping into a back pew and leaving early, before the concluding prayers. More than once, Mary had seen her emerging from the confessional, dabbing at tears with a handkerchief.

As the weeks passed, Mary detected a strain in her eyes, but maybe she was reading too much into it. The cool darkness of the sanctuary did bring out people's emotions, the constant draft over their heads, the smell of candles, the beautiful idea of God. Because you had to wonder if He really was up there. What you did in church—you came to terms with things. You came to terms.

She would pray hard. For her children, her husband. For the world to settle down. She would pray with every ounce of strength. She'd go home, put her feet up and review, not without despair, the consequences of her life. You had to live with the choices you made. You had to live with your mistakes.

ONE AFTERNOON, she drove over to the farm to deliver a church flyer. The door was open and she peered through the screen. She could hear the child pattering around upstairs. The house seemed unusually orderly. Mary remembered how hard it was to keep house with a little one underfoot, but not a single thing was out of place. Even the old wood floors seemed to gleam. No clutter to speak of. No toys, no papers, no shoes. They didn't have a bell—country houses often didn't—and she was about to knock when she heard a muffled cry. Let's not be dramatic, she told herself, and then it came again. It was quiet for another minute, and then the child began to sob, the abrupt result, Mary guessed, of some sudden indignity.

It set her blood boiling. She knocked hard on the screen door and it rattled in its frame. George Clare came down the stairs, holding the little girl on his hip, his expression unfriendly, cold. The vague smell of gin. The child blinked back tears, her eyes wet, her lashes thick. He stood at the door, looking at her.

Is this a bad time?

He didn't answer but was clearly displeased. The child shuddered, wiping her eyes with her little fist.

Is Catherine—

She's indisposed.

Mary had never fully grasped the meaning of that word.

Momma sick, the little girl said.

Well, that's too bad. I was hoping—

Just a headache.

The little girl frowned at Mary.

Your poor mommy has a headache?

The child looked at her father uneasily. Momma *sick*!

Nothing serious, he said pointedly, standing taller, rigid.

Well, if you could just give her this, Mary said, handing him the flyer. We're having a potluck supper. At church? We'd love for you all to come.

George glanced at the blue sheet, then back at her. I'll give it to her, he said, but she suspected he wouldn't. The way he was looking out at her made her nervous. Something about his eyes made her want to leave immediately.

Thanks so much, she said, her singsong as phony as margarine, feeling his gaze piercing her back as she walked to her car and drove away.

TO MARY'S SURPRISE, they came to the potluck. George knew how to make an appearance, something he'd learned at those fancy schools. He was wearing a suit and bow tie and had shaved and combed his hair. She supposed he was attractive; some women would think so. Hello, Mary, he said, in that slippery tone of his.

Welcome to St. James's—

But he'd already turned away.

Catherine and the girl were dressed in mother/daughter dresses, navy blue shifts with thin green sashes. When Mary complimented her, Catherine said, with pride, that she'd made them herself. Look at my party shoes, Franny said, pointing down at her Mary Janes.

Her first pair, Catherine said.

For a tiny, self-indulgent moment Mary had a memory of taking Alice to Browne's for shoes when she was that age—when things were simple and she wasn't shooting drugs into her veins. Mary had tried to do all the right things: Catholic school, music lessons, ballet. She'd been a wonderful little girl, and it was amazing to think that such a heinous transformation was even possible. Almost a year had passed since she'd seen her. Seven months and three days since she'd heard from her. The last time had been a call from a phone booth in San Mateo.

Travis shot her a look now. He could always tell when she was thinking about their daughter—this dark thing they shared, their mistake. On the one hand, it drove them apart; on the other, it bound them together inseparably.

Are you feeling better? she asked Catherine.

Better? She looked confused.

You had a headache. The other day, when I—

Oh, that. She glanced at her husband, who was skirting the periphery of the party, looking bored and talking to no one. I get them sometimes, she said. Her eyes seemed to cloud over.

You okay?

Of course—I'm fine, thank you. Meaning: *It's none of your goddamn business.*

Well—Mary took her hand—you need anything, just let me know, all right?

She met her eyes for a moment and nodded. Thank you, Mary. I will.

THEY'D DRAWN a good crowd and everyone brought something. Father Geary had made his famous chicken fricassee. For a priest, he was an accomplished cook. Catherine Clare had deviled some eggs, neatly arranged on a large plate. Everybody loved Mary's salads, so she made coleslaw and her mother's German potato salad. They put all of the food out on the long table in the courtyard. She had supplied the tablecloths, and there was plenty of iced tea and lemonade to go around. She noticed the Hale boys lurking on the other side of the fence and was glad when Father Geary waved them over. Probably needed something to eat, she figured. They looked up to the priest, although they'd stopped coming to mass. Cole and Travis Jr. used to sit together, acting up all through the service. Not wanting to seem intrusive, she and Travis would sit several pews behind, watching the backs of their heads. What thick hair they had! How tall they were getting! After church, they always went back to her house for supper, and she knew Cole liked her cooking, usually a roast and potatoes, something to warm him up, served on her good china.

And he wasn't shy, good for him. You could see how much the poor thing missed his mother. Sometimes her eyes would tear up in the kitchen. What's the matter now? Travis would bark, and she'd fan her face and say she'd eaten something hot. It's nothing. Nothing.

Her husband could be difficult. Making friends wasn't one of his specialties. But he had good manners; he knew how to behave. With pride and just a sprinkle of impertinence, she watched him introduce himself to George Clare. Unlike Travis, who was built like a grizzly bear and acted like a friendly one, George had a droopy handshake, like he'd rather wash his hands, and wouldn't look him in the eye. Though, to be fair, people could act funny around cops. But still.

A FEW WEEKS LATER, the Clares had a party, what they called "an open house." To Mary's surprise, she and Travis were invited.

Do we have to go? he asked.

Yes.

But we're no good at parties.

Speak for yourself.

But it was true, and they didn't get many invitations. It was something she'd gotten used to as a cop's wife. Cops and priests, Travis would joke. Nobody wants us around.

It was nice of them to include us, Mary said. We're going.

It was a Friday night. Travis was still at work, and Travis Jr. was at a friend's for a sleepover. Wanting to be neighborly, Mary had made a chocolate cake for the occasion. After a long bath, she'd dressed carefully and put on some makeup. She was looking forward to a little excitement.

When Travis finally got home, he ambled up the walk in no particular hurry, twirling the keys in his hand. After eighteen years of marriage, she still liked the look of him, his big football shoulders, his loose gait—a man who knew who he was. As it turned out, that was no small accomplishment these days. Her husband wasn't easily distracted or tempted by what most people considered the finer things in life. It gave her a certain assurance, knowing he'd never cheat on her, but, on the other hand, his imagination was limited when it came to romance. No, he was a man of routine. He'd been driving the same old pickup for years, she the same old station wagon. He favored home cooking to eating out—suspicious of restaurants, especially Chinese—and didn't like surprises of any kind. And she'd learned to keep her thoughts to herself. If I want your opinion, he would say, I'll be sure to ask for it. She did what he asked of her and never questioned it.

When she kissed his damp cheek she smelled the beer he'd just drunk over at Jackson's with Wiley Burke. We have that party, don't you remember?

Half lidded, bored. Aren't you ready?

Let me get my purse.

Oh, so you're not ready?

I'm ready, for God's sakes, she said, thinking: What happened to the gentleman I married?

In the car, she filled the space with words—their son's day at school, his soccer practice, the snack he'd had after, the Swanson's TV dinner she'd made him—fried chicken, his favorite—and then he was off to his friend's house. Travis drove, pretending to listen, which was better than bickering over this party.

He turned into Old Farm Road and the house was all lit up, rock-and-roll music spilling from its windows. A far cry from the old Hale place, and she thought Cal, who'd had little tolerance for disorder, would be rolling in his grave. The barns were freshly painted and the house was in the process, the shutters taken down and leaning up against the side. Cars were parked along the road. Travis pulled their dirty Country Squire up on the grass, behind an old white Volvo with a peeling green Jimmy Carter sticker on its bumper. That's done a whole lot of good, Travis scoffed, pointing. He shoulda stuck to peanuts.

Oh, go on, she said. Don't let's start on that.

They got out and straightened their clothes. It was just getting dark, the sky a pretty blue—cop-blue, she decided. She took his hand and kissed it. What's that for? he said.

Grump. She pulled him close and wrapped his arm around her like a favorite coat. They walked up the dirt road, and it occurred to her that this was all she'd really wanted, just these few moments, walking with her husband's arm around her. Such a small thing, she thought, yet so fine and rare. But it didn't last. She stopped abruptly to shake a pebble out of her shoe. Hold this, she said, handing him the cake plate, then kicked off her shoe.

What you wear them things for?

They're pretty. Admit it.

Yeah, they are. And so are you.

She felt immeasurably touched by this. Thank you, Travis.

He nodded bashfully, like a man who in fact still loved his wife.

She put her shoe back on and took the cake. That's better.

As they neared the house, the music grew louder.

Thinking of her friend Ella, she felt something catch in her throat. Her family and the Hales went way back. Every Sunday night there were bridge games, canasta, even mah-jongg. Mary loved going along, listening to the women talk, sneaking M&M's from the candy dish. The mothers with their scarves and gloves and perfume. Their lives rich with such niceties as cigarette boxes, gold-plated lighters, monogrammed handkerchiefs. These days, you couldn't even count on somebody to hold a door open for you. The courtesies she'd so diligently taught her kids seemed to be vanishing. They were what had defined this country, after all, what defined them as Americans! She was on her soapbox now. Well, she just didn't know, given how some people behaved. Just last week she'd taken around a young couple from Westchester who wanted a summer home. They had a baby—a very disagreeable baby, she might add. Wouldn't you know, a few hours later she detected an odor in her car and found a dirty diaper crammed under the seat! Who would do such a thing? This perfectly nice couple had. Sometimes it got to her, the things she saw in people. How careless they could be.

The air smelled of newly harvested fields, and it was a warm, sultry night. Already she'd begun to sweat. Her sleeveless cotton dress was the perfect choice for an evening like this, but she hated her flabby arms, better to keep the cardigan on. It would cool off soon enough, she hoped. They walked around to the backyard, where guests were standing around under paper lanterns that swung in the trees like hornet nests. There was a long table with food and bottles of wine and empty bottles with candles stuck in them. Chairs of all shapes and sizes grazed in the thick grass, some holding guests, others askew and others still where it looked like Franny had made a fort.

For a moment, she and Travis stood on the outskirts like children waiting to be chosen for a game, she thought, suffering all the emotions that went with it. She saw George across the yard, talking to a woman in a sleeveless blouse and a long skirt. Her arms were mottled like softened butter, but she didn't seem to care, or about the tufts of hair beneath them, and Mary could tell she wasn't wearing a bra. It was Justine Sokolov, she realized. Justine and her husband owned a farm a few miles south. From what she'd heard, money wasn't an issue and her father-in-law was some famous conductor.

That shouldn't be allowed, Travis whispered to her.

Justine's skirt was like a circus tent and a thin chain of gold glimmered around her ankle. Her feet were bare, and she was looking at George with something more than interest. Typically, he was wearing a linen suit and his standard white shirt. He had a girlish habit of brushing his scruffy hair off his forehead. Certain men could get away with longer hair, but not Travis. And men like Travis didn't wear linen, either. Linen belonged in tablecloths and napkins. Her husband didn't even own a suit, not even for funerals, where he wore his uniform instead.

I'll need a beer for this, he said.

Help yourself. I'm going to bring this inside.

The meter's running.

Let me just say hello.

Most of these were Saginaw people, of course, and she knew some of them if not by name, then certainly by sight. She spotted Floyd DeBeers over by the keg. Back in the '60s, she'd sold him a side-hall colonial in Kinderhook, which he'd promptly wallpapered with mirrored hexagons and drawings of naked women, and where over the next decade he proceeded to marry three women in succession. When the second dropped dead of an aneurysm, it had driven him into depression; he'd show up at Hack's in his pajamas and a velvet smoking jacket, chewing on Valium. But now he'd found this new wife, Millicent, who had MS, kind soul, and used a cane. Tonight Floyd was wearing a velour warm-up suit and smoking a clove cigarette, a clear indication to Mary that he was again in the midst of some crisis.

As she moved to the door, George saluted her. Hello, Mary. His tone, she noted, wasn't what you'd call warm. Glad you could make it.

She raised the cake plate and nodded toward the kitchen.

Inside, it was roaring hot, and she found Catherine taking something out of the oven, her hands in mitts, her cheeks flushed. She set a tray of brownies down on a trivet by the sink.

I brought you a cake.

That was so nice. Here, let me get you some wine.

The counters were cluttered with empty bottles, ice trays, ashtrays, platters with remnants of leftover dip, limp vegetables, soggy chips. A metal fan rattled on top of the refrigerator. Catherine found a jug of Soave Bolla and poured them each a glass.

Cheers, she said.

They shared a moment of quiet as they sipped. The house looks wonderful, Mary said. What a change.

Amazing what a little paint will do.

She was about to mention Eddy Hale when his brother Cole came into the kitchen with Catherine's little girl. Mary blinked at him, surprised. Well, hello.

Hey, Mrs. Lawton. He glanced uneasily at Catherine, then added, I'm babysitting Franny.

That's great news, son, she said, a little too loud.

Mary watched them run back outside and thought how good it was to see him here and looking happy. Well—that does my heart good, she said to Catherine.

She looked at her. What do you mean?

You know he grew up here, don't you?

Her expression told Mary that she had no idea.

They live with their uncle now.

Catherine shook her head, confused, clearly wondering, Where are their parents?

Mary waved her off, not wanting to spoil the evening. It's a long story. Another time.

I've got time right now.

She took Mary's hand and led her into the living room. Through the large windows you could see the dark fields, just a whole lot of nothing, and it made her worry for Catherine, because all that emptiness could make you lonesome. They sat down on the sofa and Mary told her the story of the Hales, leaving out the details that still haunted her—the shrill telephone waking her that morning, Cole's wobbly voice on the line, Something's happened to my parents. I think they may be dead. It was six in the morning. She'd shaken Travis awake and he'd raced over here.

It was a terrible accident, she said, even though in her heart she knew it was no accident at all. They were good people. They were friends of mine.

Catherine's face was pale. How sad, she said. Those poor boys.

It was a terrible loss, but we've moved on. All of us have.

Why didn't you tell us? That first day, when we came up here?

I was going to, if you seemed interested enough to make an offer. But then it went to the bank. She reached over and took Catherine's hand and held it tight. George knew, Catherine. I told him before the auction. You all paid a whole lot less because of it.

Well, she said, taking her hand back. That's no bargain.

I know, hon.

He should have told me.

Men don't know anything, do they?

Catherine looked at her with relief, then shook her head. He never tells me anything.

He probably didn't want to upset you, that's all.

George does whatever he wants, she said.

It doesn't really matter now, does it? You're here. You're all settled in. You've brought this place back to life, Catherine.

I sometimes feel so . . .

So what, honey? Mary watched the younger woman's face as she searched for the right word.

Lost.

Mary understood that feeling; she'd had it herself. You call me, all right? When you get those feelings.

I try so hard, she said, her eyes watering. To be a good wife.

I know.

He's like a stranger sometimes, she said softly. I sometimes look at him and think: Who is that man?

It was the wine talking, Mary decided. And now wasn't the time to get personal, not about this. She could hear George's voice in the kitchen, and the pop as another wine cork twisted free.

Moving can be stressful, she said, squeezing her hand. Try to let things settle down a little.

Then Catherine raised her eyes very slowly and said, She's here.

I don't know what you mean.

Their mother. She's in the house.

I don't understand.

These two rings, Catherine said, spreading out her fingers. They're hers.

With a start, Mary recognized them.

I found both right on the windowsill. I'd been washing dishes and saw a reflection of somebody in the glass. And the next morning they were just sitting there.

Mary shook her head, not wanting to believe it. That is so strange. She didn't know what else to say, how to ease Catherine's obvious distress. There might be a simple explanation, she said. It could only be a coincidence. You were too busy to have noticed them before. Maybe they'd been there all along, and Ella and Cal left a lot of stuff behind. But even as she said this, she remembered seeing these rings on her friend's fingers at the wake, and thinking it was strange nobody had bothered to take them off. Somebody must have removed them afterward, she decided, and then the boys just left the rings behind, but that didn't seem likely. Those boys adored their mother and never would've forgotten something like that.

To her relief, little Franny ran into the room, followed by Cole, a welcome interruption. They'd been running around. Cole was flushed and sweaty and his shirt had come untucked. Momma, me and Cole want ice cream!

Catherine put on her motherly face. Cole and I, she corrected her. So you do, do you? Ice cream it is! She took Franny's hand. Come into the kitchen. Cole, what flavor?

Here, let me help, Mary said.

They went into the sweltering kitchen. Music was playing in the yard. George had turned his speakers out the window. *Our house is a very, very fine house with two cats in the yard.* A chorus of singing guests joined in, nearly shouting. *Life used to be so hard!* Through the screen, Mary watched Justine and DeBeers belting out the chorus, their faces full of joy. There was a sassy odor in the air, marijuana.

Time to go, she thought.

She glanced through the screen door and saw Travis standing on the edge of the property, his arms crossed over his chest, looking displeased, impatient. Well, it wouldn't kill him to wait another five minutes.

Catherine fixed them ice-cream cones—Franny wanted chocolate,

Cole a scoop of that and vanilla—and in that moment he was the happy boy Mary remembered from when his mother was alive.

I'm going to put her to bed, Cole. You can probably get going.

Why don't I take you home? Mary said.

My brother said he'd come.

Nonsense. Go and get your things. I want my husband out of here before he arrests somebody!

WITHOUT HIS BROTHERS around, Cole was quieter than usual. He sat in the back seat, impassive, looking out the window. Mary couldn't get those rings out of her head. Unlike her cynical husband, she'd been inside enough creepy houses to believe in the possibility of ghosts or, as the experts called them, entities. Sometimes you just got a feeling. Like stepping into ice water, your whole body went rigid. She'd felt it herself at the farm when she'd gone in to clean up right after the accident. She'd stripped their bed and put the bundle of sheets on the back seat of her car, and, driving home that afternoon, she had the strangest feeling that Ella was sitting back there, too, and she kept looking in her rearview mirror, half expecting to meet her eyes. When she got home she shoved the sheets into the machine, dumping in plenty of soap, as if to prove who was the boss here. Then she fixed herself a stiff drink and stood there watching the sheets churn in the little window. But when she thought about it now, without the hysteria, she decided there might be some truth to it. After all, where does your spirit go when your body dies? It has to go somewhere. If you were happy, maybe you went to heaven. If you were troubled—and Ella Hale certainly had been—maybe you stayed around to sort things out. It seemed to make sense, although it wasn't anything she'd say out loud.

She couldn't help wondering where she'd go herself. She had unfinished business of her own. When she dared to imagine herself inside a coffin, the darkness, the closed-in feeling, she experienced a terror so violent and intimate that she almost couldn't breathe.

How do you feel about biology this year? Travis was asking Cole.

Travis Jr.'s struggling, she added, joining the conversation.

It's not so bad, Cole said. We're dissecting a pig. It's kind of cool.

Then Travis asked, How is it, working for the Clares?

All right, I guess. We painted the barns. Now we're starting on the house, but it's pretty much just Eddy now, 'cause of school.

Good for you, Mary said.

They came out really good.

What's he like, Mary asked, Mr. Clare?

He's all right. Not around all that much.

She knew she shouldn't but went ahead and said, I think he's strange.

I don't know, the boy said, but she could tell he was just being polite.

Now, now, that's not the important thing, Travis said, giving her a look. How's the pay? That's what I want to know.

Pretty good, I guess.

I'll tell you what. I admire a man who saves his money.

Yes, sir.

They drove a few minutes in silence before pulling up in front of Rainer Luks's putty-colored row home, which had once housed mill workers back in the early nineteenth century; now most of those residents worked at the plastics factory over on Route 66, but some were young weekenders who liked the big windows and tall ceilings and narrow backyards.

Say hello to your uncle for us.

He opened the door. Thanks for the ride. Say hi to Travis.

You bet.

They watched him go inside. He'd grown tall like his father and had the same loping walk.

I'm glad we brought him home, Travis said. They were smoking marijuana at that party. I could've had a field day.

Good for you for restraining yourself.

I can't do parties. We ought to know that by now.

She reached across the seat and took his hand. Take me home, Travis. We'll make our own party.

But ten minutes after they got home her husband was asleep. Mary fixed herself a drink and brought out the thick photo album. She flipped through it eagerly and found a snapshot of her and Ella, a little yellow now from the years under plastic. They were out on the steps, smoking, their toddlers, Cole and Travis Jr., playing at their feet. She and Ella were both wearing cardigans and plaid skirts, their lips painted red. They had their hair in rollers. She could remember they'd done each other's hair that day. Those soft rollers were all the rage.

She thought of the Clares living in that house and a feeling went through her. Poor Cole, working for those people, in his own house. Imagine what his mother would think. They'd stolen the place right out from under those poor boys. It just wasn't right. And nobody, not one person, had stepped in to see if they could help. Not even her and Travis. They were as guilty as anybody else.

A sick feeling coursed all through her. Guilt, that's what it was.

And the Clares—well, they'd gotten a hell of a deal.

How sad that we've come to this, she thought. A world of unreliability. A world of takers.

2

AFTER EVERYONE had gone and they were cleaning up, she said to George, Why didn't you tell me about the boys?

Tell you what? His voice was sharp.

Their parents died in this house, George.

So? Does it matter?

Yes, it matters. Did you know?

He just looked at her.

How could you even buy this house, knowing what happened to their parents?

I didn't think it was a big deal.

Not a big deal. She could hardly contain her anger. How could you be so insensitive? Why didn't you tell me?

Because I knew what you'd say.

And you didn't care?

It's a little late to be having this conversation, don't you think?

You're right. We should've had it before we bought it.

As usual, you're overreacting.

She shook her head. I don't like this house, she said. It was a mistake.

You're being ridiculous.

Something about his expression—the flat, cold stare, his flagrant indifference—stirred something wild in her. On impulse, she walked out, shaking, and got into the car and drove. It was very dark, no moon, and the road was empty, as if she were the lone survivor of some global catastrophe. Unwittingly, she glanced at the empty seat beside her, half expecting to see someone there—some vision—but there was nothing, no one. Only the black window, her vague reflection in the glass.

She drove into town, to the house where the boys lived with their uncle, and parked at the curb. The lights were out, but she could see the TV light flashing on the ceiling. She'd planned to knock, explain herself and attempt to distinguish her and George from other people, who had shown their family so little consideration. Instead, she sat there and had a cigarette. Then she thought: I'll just keep driving. A fantasy washed over her, a vivid chronology of her escape, but ended abruptly. Because leaving Franny behind wasn't an option.

She started the engine and drove home.

The next day, when Cole came to the house after school, she said, I didn't know you lived here. I'm sorry. Nobody told me.

She started to cry. She let him hold her. Awkwardly, the way a boy holds a woman. They stood there like that, a strange pair. Here, she said, taking off the rings. These were your mother's.

Cole took the rings and closed his palm around them.

She would have liked you, he said finally. My mother. She'd be glad to know it was you.

Part 2

Hard Alee

FLOYD DEBEERS OWNED a sailboat named *The Love of My Life,* in honor of his second wife. He moored it near the campus dock, by the boathouse and the crew team's weight room. At one time, Saginaw had a sailing team, but then ran out of money, which was often the case. When George mentioned that he was a sailor, Floyd invited him out on the boat, a Valiant 32. It was a sturdy little boat with a canoe stern, rigged as a sloop. One Friday after work, they sailed downriver. It was a beautiful afternoon on the water.

You're an old salt, George said, nodding at the tiller.

I've considered converting it, though a wheel takes all the fun out of it. It's something like being a little deaf—you might get the experience, but you miss things. I bought it for my wife. She loved a good sail. They'd met in boarding school, he explained, at St. George's. His wife had been from Watch Hill.

He let George take the tiller and went down below to retrieve a bottle of bourbon and two glasses with ice. What about your wife? She a sailor, too?

No—she's not a water person.

How'd you meet?

College.

What does she do?

She's busy with our daughter now. Our time's kind of limited.

They say you have to make time.

George nodded. Yes, I know.

Will you have more?

More?

Children.

Fortunately, the subject hadn't come up. She'd turned the small room at the end of the hall into her sewing room in lieu of a nursery. I don't know, he said, and he didn't.

Then again, you have to want all that. Floyd poured them each a drink. Skol.

He held up his glass. The bourbon tasted bitter.

I never did.

Kids?

Floyd shook his head. I regret it now. He looked at George carefully. I think I might have been more fulfilled.

It's great, George said, then realized this might've offended him. But it's a lot of work, too. In truth, Franny was the most important thing in his life. She was the glue that held him and Catherine together. For a moment, he entertained the possibility of leaving her. She would inevitably get custody. The judges, he knew, always sided with the mother. And maybe that's how it should be. Catherine would undoubtedly move in with her parents. He imagined all of them living together in that ghastly house, eating their dinners off of snack-tray tables in front of *The Price Is Right*.

Tacking downriver, they labored against the current. Coming back would be easier. The sun was lower now, almost white in its brightness. The water silver.

What about you?

Me?

Where do you stand on that sort of thing? With your wife, I mean. Your marriage, has it been—has it turned out like you thought? Are you fulfilled?

The question seemed oddly personal. Of course, he said, but it was such a grandiose lie that he coughed.

Well, she's only your first. As I told you, I'm on my third.

It can be . . .

Difficult, I know. He looked at George, assessing him. Let me guess: she was pregnant?

George nodded.

And you did the noble thing?

Tried to.

And now you're—

Stuck?

Your word, not mine. Well? Are you?

It's one way to put it.

Being stuck has its benefits, DeBeers said encouragingly. Raising your daughter, for one. Having a home, stability. Love. He met George's eyes. Not things to take for granted, as it turns out.

George nodded like a chastised schoolboy.

When you come right down to it, there are few things in this world as important.

I'll drink to that.

Not to sound sanctimonious.

No, no, George insisted. You make a good point.

It's hard to see what's good, what's right, when you're in the middle of it.

THE RIVER MOVED like a great conveyor belt, but you couldn't compare it to the ocean. Growing up on the Sound, with its compelling current and trickery, had made George a capable sailor. His cousin, Henri, had taught him on an old Blue Jay, an endearing little wooden boat yet clumsy to launch from the rocky shore. Henri was French, the son of his mother's sister, five years older than George, thin, anxious, philosophical. George tried to read his books, Rimbaud a predictable favorite; even then he'd suspected Henri was gay. George followed him around like a caddy, carrying his easel, watching him paint boats and lobster pots, filling up sketchbooks and journals. In return, Henri gave him cigarettes and talked to him about art. Then, when George was thirteen, Henri drowned in a boating accident. After the funeral, with relatives crowded in the living room of his aunt and uncle's house, George went up to Henri's room and stole his journal. He would read it late at night, after his parents had gone to bed, its pages filled with the torment and chaos of lust. A week or so before leaving for college he destroyed it, ripping it to pieces and shoving it into a trash can outside a McDonald's, amid half-eaten hamburgers and ketchup-splattered napkins.

The theft had stayed with him; he often thought of it during his darkest moments. It seemed to have been a defining moment in his life. Not one he was proud of.

They had another drink as the sun turned red.

Red sky at night, Floyd said.

To our delight, he said, and clinked his glass against Floyd's. Cheers.

They drank without talking. Across the river, the commuter train flashed behind the trees. They sat there watching it. When it had finally gone, Floyd asked if he'd had a chance to read the Swedenborg.

Some of it, he said. I haven't gotten very far yet. To him, Swedenborg's account of heaven and hell read like an awful drugstore novel. As a result, his opinion of DeBeers was rapidly diminishing. I don't know, Floyd. Heaven and hell, angels, that stuff's kind of a stretch for me.

So you thought he was a raving lunatic?

I'm a pretty literal guy, Floyd. It's something to think about, though, he said, wanting to at least sound interested.

We're obsessed in this culture with endings, with results, Floyd said. Grades, scores, awards. Colleges, jobs, cars. Possessions—tangible symbols. Most people are uncomfortable with abstract ideas, he said, finishing his drink. It's almost ironic that so many of us have faith.

People think it keeps them safe, George said. They don't want to die alone.

Death is our collective obsession.

What about sex and money?

Money's overrated. Sex is fear and hope.

Hope? For what?

Love, of course. Redemption. Floyd smiled. Love is light, love is balance. It's a unicycle. Death is easier. Death is absolute. People say death's the great unknown—not so. We know death. We know it when we see it. When we smell it. We court death all our lives. Drugs, alcohol, food. It's all around us. We champion it. At the supermarket; those blazing headlines about overdoses, suicides. Everyday tragedies. The posters of dead people we hang on our walls—Marilyn, James Dean, even Jesus. Floyd shrugged. Swedenborg takes us beyond death. Heaven and hell and, yes, angels, too—what he calls the hidden things of heaven and hell—

He ushered me within the secret things, George said, quoting *The Inferno.*

Obviously, Swedenborg read Dante. I don't know if you've read Frank Sewall's essay on it?

No, George said. But Dante and Giotto were good friends. It's likely Dante saw and reflected on *The Last Judgment*. Have you been to Padua?

Yes, we went one summer, the whole town was strung with lights. It's a miraculous fresco.

This kind of stuff, George said, this pageantry of reckoning—it's been embedded in our unconscious since the beginning of time. And nothing's changed. People are still afraid of going to hell.

But don't you think there's more to it than that? Floyd said. I think it's more about love than fear—the light of the Lord. We're unusual beings because we have a soul that never dies. Swedenborg opens the portal to the spirit world. His account confirms the Lord's promise: Whoever believes in me, though he die, yet shall he live.

And if you don't believe?

You're one of the doomed.

George raised his glass. So be it. I plan to make the most of it.

Telling Floyd that he thought the Bible was the greatest piece of propaganda ever written wouldn't be wise, he realized. As George himself defined life, well, nothing really mattered in the end. You could do whatever you wanted and no bolts of lightning would strike. You have a start date and a finish date. Period. Congratulations, you're dead.

In my mind, he said diplomatically, I guess death is final. They put you in the ground and that's it. The End. Worms and all the rest of it. No gates, no angels. No devil, either. Your guy Swedenborg had a big imagination. If he were living now he'd be making movies. He'd be a rich man.

Perhaps, Floyd said.

George shook the ice around in his glass and finished his drink. He was already a little drunk. He wanted another but thought better of it. Somehow we make the false assumption that, just because we're human, we can make everything better, even death.

Let me ask you this. If you did believe it—that heaven and hell exist, that God is real—would you change?

Would I change? What an absurd question, he thought. You mean would I become a better person?

Yes.

I don't know, George admitted. He looked out at the water, the great expanse of emptiness. Bad things could add up in a life, he thought. They could slowly, slowly disfigure you. Maybe, he said finally. Maybe I would.

Floyd nodded. One has to wonder, do we even deserve heaven, any of us?

The sun was down, the water dark, the wind cool. You could see the moon rising and a scattering of stars. They finished their drinks and came about. That's a nice tailwind, Floyd said. We'll get home quick. Nothing better than an evening sail, don't you think?

Won't be too many more, George said. Getting cold already.

One or two more. You're welcome to join me.

Thanks, I'd like that. She's a solid boat.

IT WAS DARK when he stepped into the house. You're late, Catherine said. Did you forget?

He had. Give me a minute to change.

Are you all right?

Why wouldn't I be?

You're pale.

It was windy on the boat.

Do you want me to cancel?

I'm fine.

She left him alone and went back into the kitchen to tend to Franny, who was sitting with Cole Hale at the table, having supper.

George clumped up the stairs like a man burdened by formalities. Being nice to people all day took it out of you. Now he was tired. He took off his clothes and got into the shower and considered jerking off, then heard her on the stairs. Once she'd caught him in the act—truly weird. He turned off the water and opened the shower curtain. She was standing at the mirror in her bra and panties, doing her face.

He grabbed a towel and dried off, watching her. Without meaning to, he found himself comparing her body to his lover's. You could stand to put on a few pounds, he told her.

She screwed the top of the mascara into the bottom and he wondered if she'd heard him.

In the bedroom, she opened the closet and confronted her wardrobe: seven or eight dresses that were all the same pattern that she'd made herself out of various fabrics. He supposed he should be proud of her for sewing her own clothes. Like her mother, she was penurious to a fault.

He pulled on the same khaki trousers he'd worn that day, a clean tennis jersey and a blue blazer that was getting worn around the cuffs. He didn't think anybody would notice.

She chose a dress, a lavender paisley, and slipped it over her head, shifting her hips from side to side as she pulled it down, then snapped a wide belt around her waist and pushed her feet into sandals.

You look nice, he said once they had started downstairs, conscious that Cole was in earshot. George was aware that he and Catherine had an influence on the boy—representing a different picture of married life than his parents likely had—and he wanted Cole to know that there were certain rules of etiquette, certain customs, that reasonable people needed to perpetuate. He based this presumption on his own childhood, when his parents would emerge from their bedroom dressed for dinner and his father would say something nice to his mother just for his benefit, so George wouldn't think he was a monster.

Thank you, George, she said, then turned to the boy. We shouldn't be too long, Cole.

He glanced at her briefly, as if he were afraid the expression on his face might reveal something—that he desperately missed his mother, perhaps, or that he was in love with Catherine for reasons he couldn't explain. Boys like Cole grew into men who continued to fall in love for reasons that were unknown to them.

Catherine handed him a pair of socks she'd darned. All fixed. She was always doing things for him—for all of them. Sometimes George would come home and find all three Hale kids at the dinner table, eating his food with their dirty hands.

Thanks. Cole looked at George expectantly, his eyes containing a boundless despair, but George refused to feel guilty. None of what had happened to this family had anything to do with him.

He pointed at the backpack hanging from a chair. What's that you got there?

Homework.

You're in ninth?

Yes, sir.

I imagine you're a pretty good student?

Average. But George doubted him. There didn't seem to be anything average about Cole Hale.

Bye, Momma, Franny said.

Catherine leaned over and kissed the top of their daughter's head. You go to bed when you get sleepy, all right?

She should be in bed by nine, George clarified. No later.

As they walked out, he caught Catherine rolling her eyes at the boy. In response, Cole smiled knowingly, their conspiracy intact.

It was Indian summer. The trees were yellow. He put the top down. The moon was out. They drove without talking, the wind in their hair.

Those boys, he said. Maybe we should adopt them.

It was a joke, but she wasn't laughing.

Then she asked, Do you ever once consider my needs?

Your *needs*? he said, wondering where that came from. Suddenly the word was everywhere—in newspapers, on TV, spilling out of the mouths of disgruntled women everywhere, as common as dish soap. Her needs. Hey: who pays the bills? He nodded. You're damn right I consider your needs.

But in truth he'd never really thought about it.

JUSTINE AND BRAM OWNED a hundred-acre farm off County Route 13. It was up a narrow road, behind a bramble of overgrown blackberry bushes, and they had a yellow farmhouse and a couple of barns. When they pulled up that evening, George took in the discreet recompenses of old money—the sprawling house, the Range Rover parked in the drive, the tarped vehicles in the barn (he'd heard one was a 1958 Aston Martin that Bram was restoring). Trust Fund Babies, Jelly Henderson had called them—and they were, unabashedly so. He pulled up and parked and they got out, greeted by two drooling Labradors. Well, hello, Catherine said as one sniffed her crotch; she was never quite so effusive when he got that close.

Come on, guys. Sorry. They're, well, they're pretty friendly. Welcome. Bram was holding the door open, wearing baggy khakis and a faded Lacoste shirt. George was glad he'd worn his old jacket after all. It had, he thought, a certain shabby grace.

Bram shook his hand. Come on in.

They stepped into the warm, good-smelling kitchen. Justine was taking a casserole dish out of the oven and set it down on a battered oak chopping block. She smiled, her face flushed from the heat. I made you my famous lasagna. She was wearing a tea-colored smock made of gauze and a heavy beaded necklace. On her bare feet, black nail polish and a toe ring. Whenever she moved, her bracelets jingled, and she smelled like a wet cat—that damn patchouli oil.

That looks delicious, Catherine said.

Would you like to see the house? Bram swept his arm through the air like a ballet dancer. Come, we'll show you around. He explained that the farm had been in his family for decades, his uncle's old hunting lodge. When we moved in, we had to get rid of all the deer heads. There was even a moose we used to hang our hats on.

I love your antiques, Catherine said, opening the glass cabinet of an old secretary crammed with cookbooks. What a great piece this is.

That was my grandma's, Justine said. These old homes are fascinating, aren't they? I feel as if we're borrowers. We're just their caretakers, don't you think?

Catherine thinks ours is haunted, George said.

All the houses in Chosen are a little haunted, Justine said, but this one has a very good vibe.

As they got the grand tour it became wildly apparent that Justine was not a devoted housekeeper. They lived in chaos. They also had quite the menagerie: dogs, cats, birds, even an iguana that lived in a wood hut the size of a telephone booth. I built it myself, Bram said. We call him Emerson.

George chuckled. Nice.

Their bedroom contained a tall armoire and a large antique bed heaped with a toppling pile of clothes, the status of which—clean or dirty—could not be determined. Towers of books on either side of the bed. A record wobbling on the turntable, the needle skipping around the label. A scattering of birdseed on the floor. A porcelain chamber pot filled with a suspiciously yellow liquid. I meant to clean up in here, Justine stated without apology.

They had drinks on a stone terrace. George was glad to be outside, away from the ruckus of the zoo. Justine brought out a tray of cheese and crackers, figs and olives. She had breasts like his grandmother, practically down to her navel. When the light filtered through her dress, he could see their shape, and her small waist. She had, he thought, the eyes of the

Madonna, at least as Caravaggio had painted her, with a whore's eyes, and long unruly hair that ran down her back. Her naked feet were large, her calves unshaven. Black tufts of hair sprouted from her armpits. As she carried out her hostess duties, replenishing drinks and crackers, he could detect the slightest odor of her sweat. Meanwhile, Bram had the look of a befuddled inventor, a man grappling with large ideas and the mechanisms of change but too isolated to share them, and perhaps he had few friends who understood them. George had known people similarly afflicted by intellect in graduate school, and they'd ended up alone, underachievers to a fault. However, Justine was happy to be his interpreter and Bram was a real sport about it, smiling and nodding with approval as if everything she said was right on the money. In fact, Justine could do the talking for all of them.

What a beautiful night, Catherine said.

Look at that moon, Justine said. You just don't see a moon like that anywhere else.

They all looked up at it.

The moon's brighter here, Catherine said.

I know, Justine said. We lived in the city for years.

Until we absconded, Bram added.

They grinned at each other like accomplices.

We were in one life, she said, and now we're in another.

We didn't want to compromise anymore.

Of course, everybody thought we were crazy for moving out here.

Isn't compromise the status quo these days? George said dryly.

It's certainly unfortunate, Bram said. You have to be willing to be different, to be disliked even by the people you love. Half my family thinks Justine and I are crazy for living out here in the middle of nowhere. They don't like that I married a goy. They don't like that we don't have kids.

You can't let other people's rules define you, Justine added.

Well, George said, for some reason feeling a little insulted. Being defined by others was the story of his life. He glanced at his wife.

Without rules we'd be a reckless society, she said.

We're a reckless *species,* Justine argued. Always have been.

You could argue that it's the rules that make us reckless, Bram said.

Spoken like a true anarchist, his wife confirmed with pride.

It was easy to talk theoretically when you had this much money. From

George's perspective, the Sokolovs had few responsibilities—no kids, they probably didn't even have a mortgage. It's easy to live without rules when you can afford to, he said.

Yes, that's true, Bram said, unoffended. I realize we've been lucky. All this, he said, gesturing at the house, the fields. It's a good life we've fallen into. There's no denying we've been luckier than most.

A good life, George repeated, not knowing exactly what that meant. When he was a kid his parents had pushed him to be on top, to take whatever he could. Even then he'd regarded them as fierce opportunists. You make it sound so simple.

I think it is simple, Bram said. Love. Love is the main thing. Bram took his wife's hand and squeezed it.

The gesture annoyed George. Love is all you need, he said, quoting the Beatles, and finished his drink.

These figs are amazing, he heard his wife announce, tactfully changing the subject.

Aren't they *enormous*? I was just in the city, they're from Zabar's. Then Justine stood up. Come—let me show you your scarf. It's almost done.

It seemed to George that she'd found a new cause in his wife, and as they walked toward the brightly lit house she draped her arm around her like a wing.

Bram refilled their glasses. How are you liking the college? Justine told me about your work. Now you're living it.

I know. I'm reminded of that every time I step outside. Just this—he motioned to the distant mountains, the splattering of stars in the darkening sky, the black trees around the silvery pond—this is classic Hudson River School.

I took art history back in the day. Used to fall asleep. Sorry.

My students—they always nod off during the slide presentations.

Bram smiled. Don't take it personally.

I turn on the lights and it's like: welcome back to the planet. They're blinking and stretching. Yawning.

Seriously, do you grade down for that?

George laughed. I should.

My mother was a painter, though nobody thought much of her work.

That's too bad.

She used to drag me to the Whitney. I used to complain. I didn't realize it at the time, but it had an effect on me. I suppose it made me more perceptive.

How so?

In the way I saw the world. You see the colors. The light. The faces. He lit a cigarette and looked at George. Can you imagine the world without art? Can you imagine the world without Matisse?

No, actually. Especially without Matisse.

It's our cultural sustenance. We'd be completely uncivilized without it. George nodded, and he did agree.

Do you ever notice people in museums? When they look at the paintings? They tilt their heads. They stand back. They get lost in the colors. It doesn't matter what they're looking at—a landscape, a chicken yard, a cathedral. The mind sort of drifts in this state of bliss, detachment. . . .

Transcendence, George said, not without irony.

They leave their bodies, Bram said, and they're *inside* the painting.

Just like we are now, George said, spreading his arms like a chef at the bounty before them.

They sat there pondering it all for a moment. It's pretty fucking cosmic, Bram said.

George refilled their glasses. Here's the pedestrian method, museum not required.

Ah, yes. But there's only one way to achieve true transcendence. Bram nodded toward the women. They were in the kitchen, billowing a cloth over the table.

This is true, George said, but it wasn't his wife he had in mind. He was remembering the swell of Willis's hips, her warm, giving mouth. Just seconds before he'd come he would somehow leave the world, caught in a state of in-between that was neither physical nor spiritual, a freedom of being.

It was, he mused, totally Swedenborgian.

Again they looked at the house. Justine was setting out the plates while Catherine lit the candles.

I'd be lost without Justine, Bram admitted.

Yes, Justine's great. You're a lucky man.

*　　*　　*

THEY HAD DINNER inside at a warped gate-leg table, the wet dogs lying around at their feet, stinking of the pond. The candlelight gave the room a soft, nineteenth-century glow. We make everything ourselves, Bram said, bringing over a salad.

Our garden's fabulous. I don't even go to the market anymore. Well, rarely. Justine served George a plate of lasagna. We even grow our own pot.

He looked at her; she wasn't kidding. Now, that I'd like to try.

George, Catherine protested.

As a matter of fact ... Bram took the top off the cookie jar and retrieved a joint.

Catherine sat there pouting, but kept up the pretense of enjoying herself. Bram lit the joint and passed it to George and he sucked it in, looking straight into Catherine's eyes, relishing her schoolmarm reproach. Feeling the buzz almost immediately, he gasped a laugh. You've got to try this.

No, thank you.

Out of solidarity, perhaps, Justine refrained.

He was suddenly ravenous. This looks delicious.

Please, Justine said, gesturing for him to eat. Catherine picked at her food, wary of the calories, he knew. George made up for it with two helpings. For dessert there was rice pudding and blackberries. Justine, he said, you've outdone yourself. This was incredible.

Justine flushed. He held her, kissed her. She was warm, motherly. He could feel her breasts against his chest. Bram didn't mind, he just sat there with a sleepy grin. Let's go look at the moon again, Justine said.

They went back out onto the patio. Stars like a pincushion. He could feel Catherine watching him. That was her problem; she'd chosen to exclude herself from the evening activity. With purpose, they smoked some more, drank some more. He couldn't say he minded how he felt. Didn't mind it at all. This time Justine took the joint. He was conscious of his outline, a border of energy. He pictured his own sootlike spirit, the black pulp of his soul.

Are you able to drive? his wife asked as they were leaving.

Yes, dear, able as ever.

The road was empty. It was very black and the night was even blacker. The car was loud. Bram had given him another joint. He would smoke it later, he decided. When he was alone.

That's the best thing about living out here, he shouted.

What is?

No cops.

She grunted. None that you can see.

Just for fun, he pushed down the accelerator. They were doing seventy, eighty.

George, please!

Please what? He put his hand on her thigh.

Don't, she said, pushing it away. Slow down.

But he liked the feel of the car, the wind in his hair. Would you relax for once? It's fun.

It's not fun.

God, you're so—

I'm not listening, George.

Dull.

The adjective brought tears to her eyes. Just take me home.

Hey, now, he said, touching her thigh. Hey.

Don't.

What's wrong with you? What's going on?

She glared at him. Nothing. I don't want to be touched.

Oh, like that's a surprise. He left his hand where it was. She tried to push him away, but he was stronger.

Get off, George. Let me out. I want to get out!

Abruptly he pulled over to the side of the road. Fine, get out. You can walk home for all I care.

She opened the door and got out and slammed it shut. A dark road, no lights, no houses. Just empty land, a whole sea of it. He watched her walking along the shoulder like some itinerant Gypsy and pulled ahead, rolling alongside her.

Come on, this is stupid. Get in the car, Catherine.

She kept walking.

Catherine, get in the fucking car.

She ignored him.

God—I'm getting tired of this.

She spun around. Well, I'm pretty damned tired of you.

Oh, that was good. You're finally opening your mouth. Let me show you where to put it.

Two smart people. We should have known better.

Should have known what?

We can't do this, George.

What are you talking about?

We don't belong together. You know we don't.

He sat there shaking his head.

You don't love me. It's so obvious. She had begun to cry. I gave up everything for you.

That makes two of us.

He jerked into gear and drove off, watching her image shrink away in his rearview mirror. Screw her, he thought, and drove fast down the empty road. Yes, they'd had some rotten luck. Yes, he was an asshole. Yes, she was shallow and naïve. But, still, they were doing it—raising Franny together—and it wasn't true he didn't love her; part of him did. She was the mother of his child; of course he did!

He reeled the car around and raced back to her. Get the fuck in.

She kept walking.

Look, I'm sorry, okay? I'm sorry for fucking everything up. It felt good to say it even though it wasn't the truth. It was her fault just as much as his. She'd gotten what she deserved and he had the class not to remind her. Hey, did you hear what I said? Catherine!

You think I'm stupid?

What?

She shook her head. There's no point even talking to you.

You're being ridiculous.

She was crying, mascara running down her cheeks. We've built this spectacular lie, she said.

You're drunk. That's what's going on here. You shouldn't drink—don't you know that?—someone like you.

What? Like what?

So sensitive, so vulnerable, right? So easily tarnished. I've fucking ruined you?

He jerked into park and got out and grabbed her and she fought him and slapped him and he hit her back. She coiled away from him, and he saw blood. I'm sorry, he said. Here, let me— He pulled on her dress and it ripped.

Don't, George. Just leave me alone. You've done enough.

She got into the car. He looked up and down the road. There was nobody around. He scanned the darkness, thick as velvet, and saw a pair of yellow eyes. A lone deer standing in the field their only witness.

THE BOY HAD fallen asleep on the couch. Franny had gone to bed without trouble, he said, watching Catherine hurry upstairs like some glistening animal, holding together her dress, her hand over her eye. George paid him a little extra. There's a lot more of this coming, you play your cards right. Come on, I'll run you home.

The boy folded the bills into his wallet and put it in his pocket. Although his wife criticized him for being callous and insensitive, George could be magnanimous when he wanted to be, and he admired the boy's loyalty, the fact that he always showed up on time, even a little early. Reliable people were hard to come by these days. He knew he could trust Cole to do what he was told. He felt, well, that, in some strange way, Cole Hale was a version of himself.

Nice car, Mr. Clare.

It's Italian.

With the windows down, he drove a little faster than he should. He could tell the boy liked it. On impulse, he took out the joint and lit it. You want some of this?

Cole glanced at the joint, shook his head.

Come on, you don't have to do that. He pushed his hand over. Take it.

I don't know, Mr. Clare.

George decided that the boy was just being polite. Go on.

Hesitantly, Cole took the joint and toked. He coughed.

That wasn't so hard, was it?

Cole allowed a brief smile. It would be the first of many secrets, George thought.

The boy lived with his uncle on Division Street, in a narrow row house. He pulled up to the curb.

The door opened and a man came out, to stand on the porch with his hands on his hips, his expression sharp as a Doberman's.

That's my uncle.

Good night, now.

'Night.

George waved, but the uncle didn't wave back, and once the boy climbed up the stairs his uncle gripped his shoulder and ushered him inside. The door shut and the lights went off.

When he got home George went into his study and opened the bottle of hundred-year-old Scotch, his father's gift for getting his doctorate; of course he'd kept his academic status to himself. He brooded about the university, those assholes in the department. Warren fucking Shelby. Ultimately, they hadn't offered him a position; that was fine with him. George was perfectly happy up here in the boondocks, where nobody second-guessed his expertise. They could take their department and shove it up their ass, that's what they could do. New York could go fuck itself.

He'd had a good time with the Sokolovs. They were different from anybody he knew in the city—grad students who acted like they were in some theater troupe, indulging in a sort of predictable malaise, and his so-called colleagues in Art History, those manipulators. He'd grown tired of all the gossipy eruptions, the leveraging for status. The Saginaw position had saved him from that. He'd lost his faith in the ordinary, in the things that bound them as people, and staggered out of that time warp like an astronaut returning to earth.

His wife was lying on the very edge of the mattress, turned away, her shoulder blades jutting out from the white sheet.

It would be good of you to forgive me, he said to her back. You know I didn't mean it.

George. But that's all she said.

You know I'd never hurt you.

You hurt me all the time.

He stared down at his hands. For some reason he was thinking of how his mother would cry whenever he did something wrong, then beg him to behave himself. At an early age he'd become efficient at misleading them, manipulating their sympathies. I'm sorry you feel that way. I don't think it's accurate.

Are you cheating on me, George?

Of course not.

She studied him carefully. Can I trust you?

Yes. Of course you can trust me.

Why are you always so late?

I'm just starting out over there, he told her. I have to put my time in, pay my dues.

She turned and looked at him, tentatively, as if the consequences of meeting his eyes might be damaging, then turned away again, dissatisfied, and closed her eyes. He wrapped his arms around her, her body tense, unyielding. It made no difference to him. She was upset and he would comfort her.

I'd be lost without you, he told her. Try not to forget that.

The Secret Language of Women

YOU NEVER WANT the ones who are willing to love you. This was some-thing her mother had told her once. And Willis decided it was true. Because she knew that anyone willing to love her had to be pretty fucking desperate.

She knew how to use her body to make him crazy. She used her eyes and her lips, her little-baby pout. She used her long legs, which her mother complained had gone to waste ever since she gave up ballet. She used her knees, which were kind of like upside-down teacups. She used her hips. And her head, when she tossed her hair out of her face like she gave a shit. You could make your body say one thing, while inside your head you were thinking another. That was what she liked best about being female, this ability she had to trick people.

George. He wanted to do things to her. That's what he told her. He had laid her out on the bed, stretching her arms over her head and pulling her legs out straight, and he stood there looking down at her. His hands were even bigger than her thighs, and when he pushed on them she felt caught and her eyes went blurry like she might cry. Then he took his hands off, like she was on fire and he'd gotten burned, and walked out. She hadn't seen him since.

She had called her mother that night, but when she heard her voice and pictured her in the kitchen on East Eighty-Fifth Street, something cooking in the oven, one of her hippie casseroles, and she could imagine her tragic face with every second in her brain a battle between good and evil or fair and unfair or persecuted and privileged, it got so intense and noisy in her own head that she couldn't stand it and hung up.

When she closed her eyes and saw George Clare, Willis felt guilt splashing in her gut, and that was what she wanted, because she was guilty of so much. And she was reckoning with it. With the simple fact of who she was. The alien offspring of Todd B. Howell, the famous criminal defense attorney with his drippy, savage clients. The heavy envelopes he'd leave on his desk, how she'd sneak into his study late at night and unwind the red string round and round and round until its yellow mouth opened and stuck out its tongue, depositions and photographs of the things people had done, very bad things, how she'd spread them out around her on the floor, messy and spectacular as birthday presents. How her father's pudgy face looked when he talked about his clients over dinner, a kind of nauseous pride, bragging about always getting them off—like it was something sexual—because he could find the one detail nobody else would ever think of, that was his special skill. Even this guy who'd put a gun up someone's vagina and pulled the trigger—well, he'd found some loophole, some tiny thing.

Because in this world you could get away with stuff like that. You could get away with being despicable.

That had been it for her, as much as she could take. And she'd walked out onto the terrace, standing there in the crazy wind, so hot it was like you were turned inside out, and the city just waiting, the tall gray buildings, the dark sky, the flash of lightning over the river, and she gave in to it, its routine madness, the countless windows of countless apartments in which terrible things were taking place, and she climbed up on the ledge and held out her arms. Here I am, she'd screamed into the emptiness, do what you want with me.

THEY'D PULLED HER out of school. Her mother didn't want her going back out west in her condition. Her shrink told her it was time to come to terms—stroking his beard, adjusting his bifocals with neurotic regularity. Waiting. Waiting for her to talk about the thing with Ralph.

She'd met him on the subway. It was an ugly name for such a good-looking man—he told her he was a model but wasn't gay. He was tall and big-shouldered, the kind of person who had to watch his weight. He was a little older. She lied and said she was a model, too; he believed her. They lived in the same neighborhood. Like her, he was still living at home with his parents, but he'd found a place, he said, his lease started in a month. After the first times he'd tied her up, she thought about God. She wondered why He'd chosen her for this—why this person, this strange sad boy-man.

There was no one to talk to about it with. People would think she was a freak. And the guilt, because she kind of liked it. Being captured. Held in place. You have no choice but to enjoy it, his eyes seemed to say. They had things in common. His father worked for the FBI, an intelligence analyst. Ralph had a skinny, ugly dog that would roam around anxiously while he fucked her. Then he'd untie her, watching her face, looking for something—some expression or revelation. They'd emerge from the oily arcade of his room into the living room, thick with cigar smoke, his parents watching TV, and she'd put on her nice-girl-from-a-good-family smile and he'd walk her out, standing apart from her in the elevator like they were distant acquaintances and what had just transpired between them was no more than the fulfillment of some clerical agreement of service. She didn't know why, but he stopped calling her. The abrupt dismissal sent her spiraling deeper into isolation—her very own version of exile.

THE NEXT TIME George came to see her, he apologized for acting weird. You're just so beautiful, he said. It's disarming.

She wasn't, though. Not really. Not in the classic sense. I don't know what you're talking about.

He looked down at his hands like a guilty man. You've got me all fucked up. I can't think straight.

Thinking is overrated, she said, and kissed him.

SHE HADN'T LIED about everything, only some things.

She hadn't told him she was rich. Or that she was only nineteen. Or that she wasn't using birth control. Or that her father was one of the most famous attorneys in New York. Or that she'd dropped out of UCLA or—ahem—been asked to leave. The real reason she'd come up here was because Astrid, her mother's girlfriend, who was Dutch and like a Jack

Russell terrier, always wagging her little tail, was moving into the apartment now that her mother had decided she was gay.

Ironically, the only person she wanted was her mother, but she couldn't bring herself to dial the number and utter the words: Mom, it's me, Willis.

She had grown up on horses, and Mr. Henderson had hired her out of the goodness of his heart to ride for all the rich people who pretended they didn't have time but were really just scared. Scared of falling, of breaking something and ending up in a wheelchair shitting themselves. She already knew she wanted to be a poet and would write late at night in her little room, at the table with the little yellow lamp, and the screen a mosaic of gypsy moths, and it was a splendid summer until she met George Clare, because her life changed after that and she didn't even know who she was anymore, the girl down deep whose voice had gone quiet, who'd gone off somewhere to hide like something that needed to die. She had studied psychology and taken classes in criminal behavior and she knew things about George Clare that nobody else did and it scared the shit out of her. He was another one of her many bad mistakes.

Her father had taught her about the system. How it could be manipulated. He said it all came down to perception. When he was defending someone—a creep, usually—he'd hole up in his office for days, reviewing the case and its allegations, the evidence, the photographs, looking for what he called a way in. He told her you had to get into the mind of the defendant. To see things through his eyes. Sometimes it could be some tiny thing, some bogus distraction or implacable truth that shed a fresh uncertainty on the claims against him. Whatever it was, he usually found it.

Unforeseen tragedies were a big business in the city, so her father was loaded. He didn't wait in line for things. They'd open the ropes for him at clubs, where he'd walk right in like some eminence. His clients and their families took care of him. Back when she was little, her parents would entertain them. Thanksgiving, Christmas. They could be nice, too. Some of them gave her presents. They seemed like normal people.

Once, her father caught her in his office, going through his things. Willis, who'd been named after her grandfather, a judge on the federal court, had started to cry. How can you do this? How can you save these people?

Saving people is for God, he'd told her. What I do is uphold the law—nothing more, nothing less.

He had a special mirror, she thought, that made what he was doing look good.

THEY SAID she could work in the barn with the babies. She had to feed some with a bottle. It was so loud in there, you couldn't believe how loud, and the babies wanted all of her attention and looked up at her with sorry furry eyes until she felt her heart breaking. It occurred to Willis that babies needed their mommas, and she thought that for those young sheep life had suddenly become terrible. Their mommas had been taken away from them and the mommas' milk was turning into cheese instead of filling their babies' bellies. She wasn't much interested in farming but liked working with animals and liked being out of doors. Her mother had shipped her off here. Make it work, she'd said, kind of bitchy. Because I'm out of ideas.

Once, she saw her mother and Astrid making love. It was incredibly weird, mostly because it was her mother being sexual, vulnerable, expressing herself. Because Astrid was skinny, inaccessible, even a little grim, and Willis couldn't understand what they saw in each other. She concluded that what connected them was dissatisfaction with how fucked up the world was, how doomed they all were.

HER FAVORITE HORSE was Athena, the biggest mare, black with white socks. They'd ride out together across the field. They'd climb the trails up to the ridge and look down on the old Hale farm. She'd go at dusk, when the lights were coming on. Sometimes she'd tie off Athena and walk down the hill on foot through the tall grass, the sweet lavender. When she got close to the house her legs would quiver a little and her cheeks got hot, the same buzz she'd get when she stole things. You could hear them through the windows, the clatter of dishes, Franny climbing up into her chair and banging on the table with her baby spoon. She was a cute little girl. Patiently waiting for her mother to wake up and give her what she wanted.

Like a panther, she cased the house, just seeing if she would get caught—knowing she wouldn't. Walking past the windows with their wavering shades, the colored bottles on the sideboard turning the dining room into an aquarium, the back-and-forth trilling of the window fan, the wind tousling the crystals on the chandelier. A house that made music. Their footsteps on the creaky floors. The teapot, the thwack of the refrigerator. The little girl making noise.

He had told her things about his wife, personal things. In bed she'd just lie there, like a shovel you used to bury something dead. But she was a good mother. He said he'd hear her crying sometimes when she thought he was asleep. That she was a painter but wasn't very good at it. Painting by numbers, was how he put it. She was Catholic, his wife. They had different ideas. He wasn't attracted to her anymore. My wife is cold, he said. She doesn't like having sex.

THEY'D KISS for hours. Look what you do to me, he'd say.

But it wasn't love. She knew that. It was something else.

WITH EDDY it was love. What they called True Love. She could feel it with him. He was the first person she'd ever said it to, even though she wasn't sure she meant it. And he didn't even touch her. I'm just getting to know you, he told her. We don't have to rush.

She liked just walking around with him. He was taller, bigger. Sometimes he wore this black felt hat. She kind of liked it. He'd pull out a harmonica, play her something. His fingertips were hard and round, like the buds of new flowers. They'd walk down to the creek and pitch rocks. Or he'd come find her at the barn and she'd let him hold a lamb and feed it with the bottle and he was tender with it and she could feel herself giving up inside, because she didn't want to love him so much. He was like a brother. He'd never hurt her. She could trust him. He didn't make her do anything.

But George was altogether different, and it was a dirty, awful love that made her crazy. The mean kind she thought she deserved. Sometimes he'd show up during the day, when everybody was out working. It would be so quiet. She'd hear his footsteps coming up the stairs. Take off your clothes, he'd say, and slowly pull down the shades. Or sometimes it was the middle of the night. What did you tell your wife? she'd ask. She thinks I'm in my study. I'm writing a book. She thinks I'm working. An interloper, he always came on foot, a couple of miles from his house. She'd say no, but he was good at talking her into it. He knew how to convince her. He was smart, eloquent. The things he told her made sense. You and me, we're a lot alike. We require certain things.

They would drink a little bourbon. That fire in her throat. He would talk about art and stuff like that, mostly how people needed beauty in their lives and that's why he needed her. Because you're so beautiful, he'd whisper in a creepy, greeting-card voice, the kind at Christmas with sparkles on them. He'd complain how people were so fake and putting on fronts all the time and how his wife was just a stranger to him and sometimes he'd wake up and look across the pillow and not even know who she was. He said he wanted to go away and maybe even leave the country and live someplace like Italy, in a villa, where nobody knew him.

Show me, he'd say, and she would open her legs and he'd run his fingertips over her like velvety rain and before she knew it he'd be inside her.

She was just trying to get her head clear and stay off her mother's Valium and *grow up*. She'd been doing really well until he came along.

This one day he brought scissors and said, I want to do something. What? she said, a little afraid. He said, Your hair, with a freaky look on his face. She just sat there waiting and you could hear the rain blasting down and rushing through the gutters and she shrugged and laughed and said, What? And he said, Come here. He wanted to hold her down and he touched her a little. He ran his hands through her hair. I want you, he said, like a boy. Then he put his hand between her legs. For me, he whispered.

The scissors made a clicking sound near her ear. Pieces of hair fell onto her naked legs. After, with her shoulders bare, he made her let him and she cried. She could feel herself giving up. And the voice in her head came back. *Jump,* it said.

SHE MET UP with Eddy later. What you do to your hair?

Don't you like it?

No, he said. He seemed mad. What's wrong with you?

I don't know.

I guess I can get used to it.

They walked into town holding hands. She could see her reflection in the dark storefronts. Her hair was flat on her head in all directions. She tried to squeeze the thought of George out of her mind, the awful thing he'd done to her. It was warm there inside her skull, like something sick that could stink and fester.

They went to Blake's and played pinball for a while and she had a rum-and-Coke and watched Eddy's beautiful frown as he gripped the warm machine and tapped the buttons with his long fingers. He was just a farm boy, she knew. He hadn't been anywhere. They were different people.

IT WAS a man on the ground who saw her first. He'd run inside the building to tell Alonzo, their doorman, who'd run out and seen her, and when they looked at each other she knew he was remembering the time they'd stayed up all night in the lobby talking about Buddhism and he'd taught her *namyohorengekyo* and they'd sat there together, chanting and meditating, until it was dawn and she'd gone upstairs to her parents' penthouse and snuck into bed, grateful for everything—so very *grateful*. And his look, even so far down on the sidewalk, was saying, Don't do this. Pretty soon there was a crowd on the street, looking up at her, pointing, and part of her felt like an exotic bird—singular, detached, glorious. She'd climbed onto the head of a gargoyle, perusing the dark geometry of the city, her arms out, feeling the wind flame over her, tasting her fear. Then sirens, trucks. Cops. At the time she was thinking how nice it was to be apart, separate, delivered from evil—an angel. Beyond the periphery of her vision she could see them, her guides to the next world, waiting for her, solemn, parochial, patient. And the wind trying to lift her up. And the wailing sirens, and the men spilling onto the roof in their black uniforms, scattering like she was the enemy, some invader, when really she was just a girl with serious problems, and they froze as if at any moment the world would crack open, the fragile semblance of civility, and they'd all fall into a vortex of darkness, the place God makes to put people like them.

Landscape with Farmhouse

I

HER HUSBAND WAS well liked. He had tennis partners, chess partners. On the weekends, he'd invite people to the house, people from the department. It was never just the two of them. He played the part of the generous host. In front of strangers, he was a convincing husband, a devoted father. People thought they were in love, building a life together. They would beam with admiration.

For her part, she was the image of the scholar's wife in her old kilts from college, somber turtlenecks the color of horses—bay and chestnut, dappled gray. Her skin pale as old bread. She'd pull her hair into a bun and didn't bother with makeup. None of the Saginaw wives did. They were a conservative lot, with their dull fire-sale pumps, wool skirts, frilly high-necked blouses.

Sometimes Justine and Bram would come. They'd bring people along, as if they'd be too bored if they came alone. Artists. Writers. They could be snobs, Catherine thought. Although the parties always got better once they showed up. The air smelling of dead leaves, of fire, they'd sit around on the terrace drinking undiluted Scotch until it got too cold, then jam around the kitchen table, eating whatever they could find—Irish cheddar in its thick wax cape, apricots, walnuts cracked from their shells, black grapes. With their thick hungry hands, the men were savage, common, and reminded her of Van Gogh's *Potato Eaters* with their red faces, red from the new autumn wind. The women grazed off their husbands' plates, smoking incessantly.

Eventually, like some religious cult, the men would disappear into George's study and huddle over books, argue, drink and smoke—she'd find their ashes on the floor the next day like duck droppings. She'd bring them tea, strong coffee, Cognac, cigars, knocking gently, entering the room into an abrupt silence.

ONE NIGHT George invited his department chair, Floyd DeBeers, and his wife, Millicent, for dinner. Catherine fussed all day to make it nice. She cooked a pot roast, only to discover when they arrived that they were vegetarians. Millicent walked with a cane. In private, DeBeers had told George that her condition was worsening. Still, her beauty was dignified, elegant. She wore a long gauze dress, overcast-gray. He had longish sideburns, a distracting mustache and an outlandish taste in clothes—bright blazers with stripes and clashing colors, awful wide ties. She wondered at first if he was color-blind.

While George made a fire, she showed Floyd and Millicent around. She was pleased with how the house looked. The table, the flowers. The good bottle of Bordeaux. Millicent declined going up the stairs, since, she explained, they'd become difficult for her in recent weeks. When Floyd entered their bedroom he stopped abruptly, staring down at the bed.

Is something wrong? she said.

We're not alone.

What do you mean? she asked, even though she already knew the answer.

She doesn't mean any harm. She wants you to know that.

She's watching over her boys, Catherine managed.

So you've seen her?

Catherine nodded. Once. Don't tell George, he already thinks I'm crazy.

DeBeers nodded sympathetically. People like your husband can't accept the abstract. It makes them uneasy. I know that about George. He's afraid.

Afraid?

Yes, he said confidently, as if he were privy to some exclusive truth. But you and I, we're open. Open to life, to all the possibilities.

She looked at his face, his kind eyes. Should I be frightened?

It's nothing to worry about, he said. They're among us. He shrugged as if he were talking about mosquitoes or mice. People don't want to believe it, but we both know better, don't we? He smiled at her and touched the side of her face. It was such a tender gesture she almost cried. I suppose we're special, aren't we, dear?

I don't know, she said, overcome. No one had ever called her special.

Come, now, don't be upset. Let's not spoil such a lovely evening. He pulled her against his chest and hugged her. She can't hurt you. She has her reasons for lingering. If anything, she's grateful.

She held on tight, clutching him like a child. Grateful?

You've been good to her sons.

Tears rolled down her cheeks and she wiped them away. I'm sorry. I don't know why I'm crying.

It's all right. You don't have to explain. Some of us just know things. It's a gift and a curse that some of us have to bear.

He smiled, studied her carefully and asked, How are things with George? Is everything okay?

Of course, she said, embarrassed. Why wouldn't it be?

I know it's hard moving up to a place like this. You're not lonesome, are you?

She shook her head—she wasn't about to tell George's boss everything.

Your husband has his own way of doing things, that's for sure.

She nodded and smiled, but found the comment disturbing. She didn't know how George behaved out in the world. There had been occasions when she'd seen him being discourteous. Once, leaving the mall, he'd barreled through the glass door without holding it open for the woman behind him; the door was heavy and swung back hard enough that the woman was hurt, and she'd called him an asshole while Catherine pretended not to know him. It was a small thing, she knew, but it said a lot about his way of doing things.

An outburst of laughter clattered up the stairs, the result of some silly joke, she guessed. DeBeers took her arm. Let's go join them, shall we?

*   *   *

WASHING THE DISHES, she reflected on the evening. Even without her roast, the meal had been good, the salad and wine to everyone's satisfaction. They were interesting people and she especially liked Floyd. He was warm, kind. More than once she'd caught him contemplating her across the table with a fatherly sort of understanding that she'd never witnessed in her own father's eyes.

She let the water run a minute. She stacked the dishes in the rack, then scoured the big white sink. She wiped down the faded Formica counters stippled with cigarette burns. It saddened her to think how careless people could be. The floor needed sweeping, but it was very late and she wanted to go to bed. It could wait, she decided, and untied her apron and hung it on the hook. When she turned around George was standing in the doorway, watching her. She couldn't tell how long he'd been there. He looked at her dully.

George, she said.

Come over here.

What is it?

Closer.

She stood there waiting. She thought he might be drunk.

He pushed her hair to the side, tilting his head, considering her. He put his hands on her shoulders. You did a good job tonight, he said.

It was fun.

Floyd likes you.

He's a nice man.

You were up there a while.

I was showing him the house.

What did he say?

He liked it. He said it was nice.

About me, I mean.

He didn't say anything about you, George. Why would he?

At length he answered, No reason.

He stood there looking at her. The weight of his hands bore down on her. She realized her heart was beating very fast. She thought he might be planning something, that he might want to hurt her.

Gingerly, she pulled his hands off her and moved away and opened the cupboard and took out a glass and filled it at the sink, just to have something to do. Good night, George, she said without looking at him.

Aren't you coming up?

I want to do the floor. There's something sticky here.

Can't it wait?

I know you don't like a dirty floor.

His eyes shifted to the floor, then back up on her. Suit yourself. He waited another minute. I'm going up, he said finally. And then he did.

She found her cigarettes and shut the light off and went onto the porch and stood there in the cold, smoking. The screens waffled in the wind and dry leaves circled her feet. Her eyes scanned the black fields. Anything could happen out here, she thought. And no one would know.

She stepped inside and closed the door. She could hear the floors creaking overhead, water running through the pipes. The springs of the bed. Then silence.

A glass of vodka made her feel better. She was her own best friend. Her mother had told her that when she was a girl. Whenever you're in trouble, just remember you're your own best friend.

After that night at the Sokolovs', when he'd hit her on the drive home and ripped her dress, she had lain awake all night, struggling over what to do. When she saw her eye the next morning, a bruise like a jellyfish, the answer was obvious. Somehow she got through the day. When he came home he brought flowers and watched as she filled the vase with water, her hands trembling. They were carnations, her least favorite.

She waited for him to pour a drink; she'd already had two. Then she said, I'm leaving you.

Without a word, he backed out of his chair and went upstairs. She could hear him rummaging through the closet, opening drawers. When he came back down he was holding her suitcase.

What's that? she asked him.

You're leaving. That's what you said, isn't it?

She just looked at him.

Obviously, you'll be needing your suitcase.

Franny began to whimper. She reached up for Catherine, her lower lip quivering. Where you going, Momma?

Your mother's going away, George said flatly. She's leaving us, Franny.

The child began to cry.

Catherine could barely speak. She crouched down to her daughter, taking her in her arms. I'm not. It's not true. Momma's not going anywhere.

She grabbed the suitcase and carried it back upstairs and took out her belongings and put them away. Later that night, when he came to bed, he pushed up her nightgown. You can leave anytime you want, he told her, but Franny stays here.

SHE FINISHED the vodka and put her glass in the sink. The house was quiet. She could see the moon through the window.

Then she climbed the stairs, like all the women who had lived in this house before, whose tired feet had worn the treads of the old stairs, solace coming only in the deep of night, when they were at last alone.

Soundlessly, she stripped off her clothes and pulled on her nightgown. She stood there over the bed, the sound of his breathing filling the room.

Taking care not to wake him, she slid beneath the sheets and shut her eyes very tightly. White was the color she saw in her head. Hospital white. White like resurrection, the first color you see when you awake from death, when they unzip your body bag and the world fills again with light.

This in itself was an odd thought. She'd begun to have a lot of them. Whole schools of them swimming in her brain.

She couldn't tell George, he wouldn't understand, but she'd stopped sharing most things with him by now. The only one she could tell was Ella. Whispering into the empty room. Already it seemed to Catherine that she had developed a relationship with the ghost. They were a morbid pair—one dead, one alive. Both stuck.

2

SHE HAD this boyfriend, Eddy Hale. It was starting to get to him. In his rational mind, George understood that she was trying to prove he couldn't hurt her. You don't matter enough, her eyes seemed to say. But Eddy Hale did, he mattered a lot. Jealousy wasn't something George did very well. Sometimes he'd pull up to the house and see Hale's truck, his ladder up against the barn, young Eddy perched up by the cupola with his shirt off and a cigarette hanging out of his mouth, and he'd have to suppress the impulse to knock him down. She would talk about him. This happened usually after sex, when they were lying there naked and sweating, smoking, each of them intent on impressing on the other that this thing they shared was an aberration, an almost clinical disruption in their otherwise respectable routine, the malevolent consequence of some extreme and rare medical condition.

He plays me love songs, she told him.

Is that so?

He's going to be famous. He's very good. We're in love.

Good for you.

She shook her head. You don't even know what that means, do you?

Of course I do.

But she shook her head, disbelieving. No, you don't.

I love my wife, he said.

She laughed. Okay. That's good. That's really good, George, I'm happy for you. She sat up and took a sip of water out of an old soup can. Seeing her sitting there, with her pale skin, her dark hair outlining her face, he could predict the woman she would finally turn into, one of rage and unrequited longing, a woman not unlike his wife.

He reached over and took her hand. How do I make you happy, Willis?

She set down the can and gathered her undergarments, pulling on her panties, her bra.

What is it that you want? Just tell me.

Don't ask me that.

Why not?

Because I don't know, all right? I don't know what I want. She lit a cigarette, dragged deeply and blew out the smoke with contempt. I want to go back to school. I'm getting sick of this place. I can't stay here much longer.

Why not?

I'll go crazy, that's why not. I can't stay here.

I can't stay here with you, was the translation.

I have a life in L.A., George. She glared at him as if it had suddenly become clear to her how stupid he was. I'm a totally different person there.

Oh, really—how do you mean?

I'm nobody's fucking secret.

I see.

I'm not somebody like you, George, she said cruelly. Someone who lies and cheats. I'm better than this.

Well. Good for you, then.

You want to be free, right? She shook her head at this obvious impossibility. You're so full of shit.

Hey, he said.

You know what I think? You're a fucking impostor.

Now, why would you say a thing like that?

Because it's true. It's true and you fucking know it.

She stubbed out her cigarette and stared at him. I don't want to do this anymore.

He sat up next to her and buttoned his shirt. His heart was on fire. He couldn't bear to look at her.

This was the last time, she said.

Okay.

She looked at him, expecting something.

Fuck this, he thought, and walked out. For a day or two he could stand it. But then he went back. He had to.

She stood in the doorway. This was what he liked best, her giving him a hard time. He spoke to her, gently trying to convince her that they had something good, something important. After a while it became a sort of habit, the convincing part, her giving in to it. He'd watch the subtle changes on her face, the flush in her cheeks. She accepted him. She accepted the thing they had. That she needed him as much as he needed her. Why this was so didn't matter. There was no need to explain it. She would stand there, waiting for him to undress her. She had become a source of intense preoccupation. He was infected, he'd become ill. It wouldn't last, he knew. It couldn't.

One afternoon, they lay together on the narrow bed, adrift. It began to rain. They listened to it fall like a symphony, starting out slowly and growing in intensity, splattering violently on the windowsill and spraying their naked arms.

I'm cold, she said, turning her back against his.

He held her tighter. Better?

The feel of her in his arms, her warmth, the smell of her like the sea, like the warm sand at sundown in summertime, the sound of life coursing through her, the blood, the air. He thought of how all his life he'd taken things for granted, the simple beauty of everything he saw. He remembered himself as a boy, standing alone on the beach and looking out at all that water.

She turned to face him and dug into his pants like a gardener pulling out a turnip. He put his hand on hers to stop her.

Don't you want to?

No, I just want to talk.

Talking's boring.

I want to know you.

She turned on her side, leaning on her elbow, her cropped hair sticking up in all directions. He liked her like this, lithe and boyish. What do you want to know?

Ordinary things. Where you grew up.

I told you. The city.

I know—but where? You don't want to talk about it?

She sighed dramatically, as if he was her interrogator and had finally, at long last, broken through. Her eyes were black. Her lips pale. I grew up on the Upper East Side, she said flatly. I went to Brearley. Do you know it?

He shook his head.

A private school for girls, she said in a British accent.

And your parents?

What about them? They're social climbers, like everybody else in that town.

What does your father do?

Suddenly defensive, she asked, Why do you want to know?

I want to know you. Is that so wrong?

Kind of, she said.

Why?

Because. Because it's not part of this. Because you don't deserve to know me.

Why not?

Because you're fucking married, George.

To this he said nothing.

What did you think? That I was an orphan or something? Some kind of Jane Eyre?

He laughed, surprised.

That's what you thought, isn't it?

No, it isn't.

You wanted to cut my hair—do you remember that scene in the book?

I've never read it.

One of the other orphans has beautiful curly hair. This guy cuts it off. It's humiliating.

He ran his hand through her hair. Were you humiliated?

You wanted me to be, didn't you?

He only looked at her.

You wanted me to be some stupid girl, didn't you? That's why you did it.

No, he said, I didn't want that. But in truth, he didn't really know why he'd done it. Even if he did, it wasn't something he'd likely share with her. The things he did to her were kept sequestered in a deep little nasty place he didn't show to anyone. He would do something, and while doing it he was totally consumed in it, and afterward it was forgotten.

You wanted me to have nothing. Isn't that right, George?

Yes, he said. You're my own private orphan.

Seriously. What do you think my father does? Take a wild guess.

I have no idea.

He's a lawyer, she informed him, then added, with what felt like cruel intention, A criminal defense attorney.

Well, he said. That's impressive.

Does that worry you, George?

It did, in fact, but he said, Why should it? He tried to remember what she'd told him. She was twenty-one, on birth-control pills. I'm my own person, she often said. If these things were true, she was here with him of her own volition. He had nothing to worry about.

He defends despicable people, she said accusingly, as if to elucidate *people like you.*

And your mother?

She's a lost cause. I don't want to talk about her. Why are we even talking about this?

He thought of his own parents, how irrelevant they seemed just now. They would never understand his relationship with this girl and would consider it a reckless mistake. You're right. They don't belong in here with us.

She gave him a look, some dark truth smoldering in her eyes, and got out of bed. I need some air, she said. I need to go outside. She pulled on her jeans, her sweatshirt.

Watching her, he lit a cigarette. There was very little light, only dusk showing through the curtains.

Look, George. We need to stop this. We need to stop this right now.

Willis—I've told you my situation. You said it yourself. That thing about Blake. What I have with Catherine, it's not real. It's hypocrisy.

She put her hands over her ears. I can't listen to this bullshit.

With you I feel—he paused a minute, wanting to find the exact word—whole.

Congratulations. She was pulling on her boots. You, George Clare, are exactly the wrong thing for me.

He fished his shirt out from the pile of clothes on the floor, slipped it on and began buttoning it. That's not true and you know it.

You have become the evil in my life.

How can you even say that?

Don't you know how wrong this is? She looked at him, demanding an answer.

Okay, he said. Okay. Maybe it's wrong. He tucked in his shirt and fastened his belt. He was moving slowly, like a drunkard, trying to piece together his thoughts. I don't know why I married her. I wanted to be honorable.

Trust me, not a word in your vocabulary.

You can be so—

So what?

Degrading.

I'm honest, George. I tell the truth.

I know you do. That's something I love about you.

She scoffed. You don't love me.

Hey, he said. Stop trying to sound so mature.

Fuck you, George. This isn't about love and you know it.

Hey. He grabbed her hard.

Let me— She pulled away, angry, and grabbed her coat and opened the door. I need to get out of here.

He grappled with his wallet, his cigarettes, then raced outside after her. The sun almost gone. Cold. You could smell the dead leaves, the dirt.

What's wrong with you? he shouted.

She was walking toward the horses.

He was afraid of them. Why are you so angry?

Because you get whatever you want, George. You do whatever you fucking want. I don't have that, okay? We don't get to do that.

What? That's ridiculous.

She climbed the fence and jumped into the pasture. Willis! he called as she mounted a black one and took off, kneeing its ribs, gripping its mane. He'd never seen anything so dramatic. He froze there, moved by it. A woman on a horse. Beautiful. A little violent. Riding off into the sunset.

WHEN HE WENT to visit her the next day, she apologized. I was in a bad mood. I was getting my period.

They lay there side by side, fully dressed, smoking.

Do you want some whiskey?

He poured them each a drink.

I have cramps, she said.

Are you hungry?

She shook her head. They drank. This is good, she said. Just what I needed.

I'm glad.

You thought I was just some girl, she said.

He waited, watching her.

Just some dumb, ordinary girl that you could do whatever you wanted to.

I never once thought that.

Some girl you could fuck over. That's all men want anyway. To fuck over women.

That's an outrageous statement.

But it's true, isn't it? Admit it.

I wouldn't hold your breath.

Here's the thing, George. I know how you think. That's what you don't get. I grew up with people like you.

What's that supposed to mean?

That there are certain behaviors, she said, certain characteristics. She shook her head, looking at him and not looking, and stopped herself. I know you, George. I know who you are.

An indictment, obviously. For a moment he couldn't speak. I have no idea what you're talking about.

I think you do. She got up off the bed and went to the dresser and found her cigarettes and lit one and stood there before him, declaring his failures. You think you've got it all figured out, but look at you. You're the most screwed-up person I know. You're a fucking psychopath.

He slapped her. They were both surprised.

She turned away, her hand on her cheek. You'd better go.

I'll go when I'm ready.

George. Please.

Put out that cigarette.

She looked afraid.

He snatched it from her hand, took a drag and then ground it out. He wanted to tell her something important—something reassuring, philosophical—but his mind was empty. He was depleted of anything useful. Please, he said. Just let me love you.

I can't. We have to stop this. It's not good for either one of us. It's horrible.

Lie down. Take off your clothes.

At first she resisted. Then she buried her face in his chest and cried. He kissed her hands, her knees. This thing we have, he said. You're like a drug.

Afterward, he said, I can't control the way I feel.

She looked at him, waiting.

I'm not a bad person.

Okay. That's good to know. But guess what? I am. She finished her drink. I'm a very bad person. You need to understand that.

That's not true. I refuse to believe it.

Well, that's your choice, but don't say I didn't warn you. She lit another cigarette. Anyway, I'm in love with somebody else.

He couldn't bear it.

You should go now.

He couldn't move.

George?

He'd never cried in front of a woman and didn't know why he was doing it now. Except that he had an awful feeling inside him.

Get out, she said.

He didn't argue. He went down the narrow staircase that smelled of dirt and sheep shit and sour milk, out into the cold wind. It was five o'clock in the afternoon, nearly dark, and the air smelled of fires. He felt the need to walk. To brace himself for some unknown catastrophe. It would come soon, he knew. There was no doubt.

The Reality of the Unseen

I

IT DIDN'T TAKE long for rumors to circulate about George Clare. Though he had won the favor of students, the older, stuffier faculty members found fault with his showy confidence, his rather cavalier disregard for the mood of austerity that had defined the department for decades. During his office hours, there'd be a little crowd outside his door of students who just wanted to talk. Witnessing such celebrity could be annoying.

Although he was conservative in appearance, Justine imagined that George was the sort of man who entertained unconventional possibilities—what those might include, she didn't dare say. Late one Friday afternoon she ran into him in the corridor. It was just after midterms, students roaming the campus like zombies, professors hiding in their offices with the doors shut, pretending not to exist. TGIF, she said lamely.

How about a drink to celebrate?

She followed him down to his office. To her relief, Edith, the department's drill sergeant, had already gone home. The doors were all locked, the place deserted.

Come in, have a seat. It's good to see you.

It's nice to see you, too.

Like one of his students, she sat across his desk, shifting around on the hard chair. The bookshelves were lined with heavy art books. On an adjacent wall were five small canvases, seascapes. What lovely paintings, she said.

Oh, don't look at those. They're old.

I didn't know you painted.

My wife's the real painter, he said. They're so bad she won't let me hang them in the house.

They are not, George. You have real talent. Are those ospreys?

Yes. They make their nests on those platforms.

Is that where you grew up?

He nodded. I could rig a boat by the time I was five.

Well—they're really good. You should get back to it.

Even as he shook his head, she could tell he was pleased. What's that? she said, nodding at an index card thumbtacked to the wall right above the end of his desk, with something written in blue pen.

Kind of a good-luck charm, he said. It's a quote by George Inness: *Beauty depends on the unseen, the visible upon the invisible.* That's been with me since graduate school.

Are you going to tell me what it means? She smiled, batting her eyelashes.

Literal translation: what we see depends on what we don't see. It's something Inness called the reality of the unseen—a person's spiritual truth. God is hidden, but that doesn't make Him absent. Finding Him isn't necessarily about *seeing* Him. There's a connection between seeing and being blind. Like in the fog, when certain things, certain colors, become important. The possibility of revelation in the ordinary. He sighed, looking at her, his eyes moving slowly as if he were memorizing every inch of her. I'm boring you, aren't I?

Not at all. I think it's fascinating.

Here's my pedestrian version: to know yourself is to forget who you are.

I'll have to think about that.

Let me assist you. He opened a drawer and took out a bottle of whiskey and two glasses.

I see you're prepared.

Always.

Don't let DeBeers know.

Will he fire me?

No, he'll want to join us. And Floyd never has just one.

He's already gone home, George said, pouring her drink, so we're safe. Cheers.

They clinked glasses and she asked, Does anyone *really* know himself?

We're told who to be by our parents, he said.

I'm always telling my students to forget about their parents and do whatever they want.

Like you did?

Yes, actually. But I'm not a good example.

Why's that?

Because, well . . .

Because? A half-smile waited on his lips.

I'm not ambitious. And because life terrifies me. Don't tell anyone.

I happen to be very good at keeping secrets. But what are you so afraid of?

Bad people, she said finally. Deception. Possibility.

Possibility? He tugged loose his tie and unbuttoned the top button of his shirt, then stretched out his legs and crossed one foot over the other. Such an intriguing word. What do you mean by it?

For some reason she now even *felt* like a student. I don't know. I guess I do need this drink. He was still watching her closely. She shifted in her chair, self-conscious, and sat up a little taller. She was wearing a mushroom-colored blazer over a white blouse, a long black skirt, Birkenstocks—an outfit that would make the *Glamour* Don't list. Uncomfortable with the silence, she confessed, I have a small life. Simple. It suits me. I'm content.

He gave her a doubtful look. Nobody's content.

I don't think that's true, George.

Well, I prefer discontent. At least it's honest. He topped off their glasses.

The room had an unpleasant yellowish glow. Through the window, the sky looked dirty. I should probably go, she said.

Me, too, he said, but neither of them moved.

How are your classes going?

I sometimes wonder if they're even listening. They just sit there with these blank faces. I'm convinced I'm boring them. I feel like I should tell a few jokes or something.

Oh, I'm told they like you a lot, she said. Besides, it doesn't matter as long as they can distinguish between a Caravaggio and a Carracci.

It's a challenging course. It can be slightly more demanding than weaving, for instance.

Yes, and it can also be intensely boring.

You don't beat around the bush.

Sorry. One of my many personality flaws. Bram says I have no tact. You know what they say: the truth will set you free.

George shook his head, suddenly gloomy, moving his glass around in small circles on the desk. People don't really want the truth. He looked up at her. They don't want to be free, either.

It's like that Eagles song. You know, we're all just prisoners of our own device.

People might think they're free—unencumbered. But they're not. None of us are.

Bram and I . . . she started to say, but stopped herself. Like most people who were judgmental about their living up here without the accouterments of marital bliss—a house in the suburbs, kids—George would not be easily convinced. But Justine was beyond caring what people thought. She and Bram had achieved it—freedom—they made their own rules. In contrast, George and Catherine were here for the job. They'd fallen into this country life, devoid of the usual constraints, and Justine sensed it wasn't easy for them.

Sorry—you and Bram?

Forget it. It's not important.

Oh, but it is. It's the existential dilemma of our times, freedom is. He finished his drink and practically peered at her. Let's try an experiment.

What?

Close your eyes, he said, and she did. Now put your hands on the desk.

She giggled. Are you going to read my palm?

No, I'm going to demonstrate a point. She could feel him taking her wrists, holding them tightly in each of his hands.

George?

You think you're free until someone comes along and reminds you that you're not. He was holding her very tightly.

Let go, she said.

But he held her there a moment longer.

George, I get it. You've made your point.

She struggled, still in his grip, and it made her burn a little with anger—or something else, a confusing energy. When he finally released her, she opened her eyes; he was looking right at her.

They stood in the buzzing silence, putting on their coats.

For the couple minutes it took them to get down the long corridor, their not speaking was awkward, yet she didn't have a clue what she would say to him. On the front steps they talked briefly of the changing weather. The parking lot was empty, the lamps just coming on. The days were getting much shorter.

He walked her to her car. Are you okay to drive?

Of course. And you?

He nodded. Better than okay.

Say hi to Catherine for me.

I will. Thanks for stopping by.

Such superficiality didn't suit him. Still, she pursued it eagerly. How's the house coming?

She thinks it's haunted.

So the rumors are true, then?

What rumors?

Nothing. She smiled. I'm kidding. You don't believe in ghosts, do you?

He studied her carefully, his eyes on her body as if she were some marble statue. She felt her face brighten with heat. He leaned in closer, as if to smell her, and she rushed with a momentary terror that he was going to kiss her, but he broke the strangely intimate spell by opening her door. Good night, Justine.

Good night.

They each drove out the long driveway and turned in opposite directions at the main road, heading back to their separate lives.

DRIVING HOME, she was distracted. What if he had kissed her? He'd presented that possibility, she thought, but deliberately hadn't followed through. A passive-aggressive gesture that accomplished two things: it let her know he was willing to sleep with her, and also allowed that his supposed interest in doing this was her own creation. Not kissing her when it seemed obvious that he wanted to was his way of demonstrating another point, that gestures of desire were easily misconstrued. Moreover, backing up those few inches had kept him safe from incriminating himself, should she refuse him.

It would be up to her, she realized. He'd made that painfully clear.

Bram was sitting at the kitchen table, eating a bowl of ice cream, when she came inside. Aren't your cheeks rosy, he said.

It's cold. She kissed him and he pulled her onto his lap and held her.

Where were you so late? I've been missing you.

George and I had a drink, she said.

Was that any fun?

I think he's strange, she said, then explained what had happened. I feel violated.

He's an odd fellow, Bram said. I've always thought so.

They went to bed, but she couldn't sleep. She went into the kitchen and made herself a cup of tea. George had upset her even more than she'd thought at the time. Holding her wrists like that—was she wrong to think of it as a kind of assault, a form of intimidation? Even a threat?

THE NEXT MORNING she ran into the Clare girls in town. Catherine was wearing sunglasses and her nose was splotchy red. I have a cold, she said. We're going to get a pumpkin.

I get to pick my own, Franny said.

We're going to make a jack-o'-lantern, aren't we?

She nodded and reached up her hands and Catherine pulled her onto her hip.

Are you coming to Floyd's tonight? Justine asked.

She seemed to be drawing a blank.

He's having a Halloween party.

Oh, I don't think I can get a sitter on short notice, especially on Halloween. George didn't say anything about it.

Through the dark glasses, she couldn't see Catherine's eyes. Well, I doubt we're going anyway. Bram hates faculty parties.

I want my pumpkin, Momma.

Well—we should go. She set Franny down and took her hand as a squall of dead leaves flared around them. My goodness, this wind! She pulled up her daughter's hood and fastened the button under her chin. There you go. Is that better?

It's good to have a hood, isn't it? Justine said.

The child looked up at her and then at her mother, her nose runny.

Well, Catherine said. We're off. See you.

Yes. Soon, I hope.

2

COLE HAD WAITED for Patrice that afternoon, and when she pushed through the heavy green doors of St. Anthony's he noticed the pink cardigan right away, and once he saw the tiny moth hole he knew for sure. That's a nice sweater, he said, reaching out to touch it.

Patrice smiled and blushed. I just bought it at the bazaar. It was on the bottom of this pile and I saw the pink sleeve hanging out. Isn't it pretty?

He didn't want to tell her that it had been his mother's, but he took it as a sign.

He walked her home, a narrow house with painted floors. When they got there her mother was just going to work. She had on a white nurse's uniform and those white hospital shoes. Cole could see her father out on the back porch, sitting in a chair with the newspaper, smoking a cigar. They went up to her room and sat on the floor, playing cards. She won a few hands of gin and then taught him how to knit, showing him how to hold the needles as she moved the yarn around. She was close. He could smell her sugar-cookie skin.

He saw her again later that week, on Halloween, at the fire station. In their town, Halloween was a big deal and all the houses on Main Street had candles in the windows and they strung up ghosts and skeletons in the trees to make everything look creepy; they didn't have to try very hard, since most of the houses were hundreds of years old and plenty creepy even without the decorations. They had a party at the firehouse with doughnuts and cider, and everybody showed off their costumes. Cole was Luke Skywalker and Eugene was Yoda. He thought their costumes had turned out pretty good but they didn't win anything. They ran into Patrice and her friends. She had on heavy makeup and high heels and a short dress and he thought maybe she'd padded her bra. There was a band of skin between her midriff and her waist.

What are you? he asked.

Can't you tell?

He shook his head and her friends all laughed.

I'm a whore, you dope, she said. Kiss me.

3

MOST OF THE STUDENTS in his two o'clock class had dressed up, and it seemed a little silly lecturing to vampires and zombies, ghouls, celestial anomalies, tornadoes. He had to admit, the costumes were good. Catherine had made them pumpkin cookies and they were passing around the tray. She was always doing things like that, and perhaps she thought he needed her help. Between the two of them, she'd been the brighter student. But now he was here and she was home cleaning the house.

He was lecturing about Thomas Cole, his students taking copious notes as they always did. Writing down whatever he said. He saw this more as an attempt to appear engaged rather than to actually learn anything. As you all know, he said, Thomas Cole was well known in these parts. He was the first popular landscape painter in this country, and he loved the Catskills and the Hudson River, and the lakes and streams and the wilderness, and of course these were the subjects of his paintings.

George clicked through several of them on the slide projector. *Falls of the Kaaterskill; View on the Catskill—Early Autumn; Sunny Morning on the Hudson River; The Oxbow.* There were plenty of others, he told them, then explained that Cole emphasized the notion of the sublime in his work, a Platonic ideal of nature—the sense of fear and awe in the divine. He saw this as his mission as an artist, to represent the idea that depictions of an unspoiled paradise were morally uplifting. For Cole, it wasn't about painting leaves; this was spiritual enlightenment and morality. Landscape painting became a means to communicate philosophical ideas and insights. At the same time, it identified the American wilderness—wild and brutal and glorious—as a version of paradise. As Emerson said, true revelation *is always attended by the emotion of the sublime.*

DRIVING BACK to Chosen after work, he reviewed what he'd said to them in class. He doubted that his students grasped any real concept of the sublime, especially as it existed in nature. They saw drugs, not nature, as the conduit for enlightenment.

Perhaps they were too young, he concluded. They didn't know anything yet.

He thought distantly of Burke's theory—that one experienced the sublime in nature only through astonishment, which in turn was a condition of revelation, that only terror gave one access to such elevated experience.

He knew this to be true. He had felt it himself, lately, with that girl—a state of being that made everything else irrelevant. The place that existed between pleasure and pain, without boundaries or light, darkness or gravity, the place where the soul lives. How she looked when he did certain things—her astonishment, her terror—and then the awful pleasure that came at last.

DEBEERS LIVED in a small brick house on Kinderhook Creek. The mulberry tree on the front lawn was strung with ghosts, and when you crossed the threshold you heard the harrowing cries of the dead on a tape. Floyd was wearing a white wig, knickers and a gray vest and waistcoat, and holding a highball glass full of whiskey. Where's Lady Catherine?

She couldn't make it. Not an easy night to find a sitter.

Pity, DeBeers said. Can you guess who I am?

George chuckled at his costume. He'd even fashioned buckles on his shoes. Hmm, he said.

Swedenborg, of course, Floyd announced in operatic singsong. My little gift to you.

Well, that was very nice of you, Floyd.

I thought you'd appreciate it.

Christ, what have you been drinking?

Not drinking, Millicent said, displeased. He's tripping.

Tripping?

Smiling devilishly, DeBeers took his hand and led him into the dining room—low-ceilinged with a raging fire—and snatched a plastic jack-o'-lantern off the table. I've been known to dabble in hallucinogens. It reminds me there's a whole world out there we don't even see. Here, he said, an offering. A little treat from a friend in Berkeley.

You don't have to, Millicent said.

They're fun, a woman piped up, unwinding out of the dark in her costume.

Justine, he said, gaping at her. She was wearing a long blue frock and her face was thick with yellow paint, her eyes blackened, and black lipstick around her mouth. You have me stumped.

I'll give you a hint. She opened her mouth and let out the closest thing to a blood-curdling scream she could muster.

Very convincing, he said. Munch would be impressed.

Thank you. She looked him over. And what are you?

He'd come straight from work. That's a very good question. I've been trying to figure that out for years.

But she didn't laugh.

I'm myself, he said, isn't it obvious?

You're *what*?

Just a humble schoolteacher.

Hardly, she said. In fact, that's one of the scariest costumes I've ever seen.

She was serious.

Ha, ha, he said.

We're doing a séance later, DeBeers interrupted.

Go on, Justine said. Eat your vegetables.

The mushrooms tasted mealy, gritty with dirt. A little anxiously, George chewed and swallowed them, then had a brief, sudden memory of himself as a boy, in the woods behind school, an older kid holding him down and making him eat dirt. It was the same taste, a little foul. He didn't like the memory, which must've been why he'd repressed it. George had learned the deviations of the human spirit at a young age. For reasons that remained mysterious to him, he'd been bullied throughout grade school. For the seventh grade his parents coughed up the money to send him to St. Magnus, where bullying as a spectator sport was not tolerated by the fierce, egalitarian nuns. These were memories he had never shared, not with his parents, not with his wife.

They went out to the backyard and down a hill to the creek, where strangers were toasting marshmallows in a bonfire. He could feel the fire warming his hands and toes. This was nice, he thought. It was something they did in the country, bonfires. He felt the firelight on his face and could see it reflected in Justine's eyes—things were, it occurred to him, getting a little strange. The word *furry* came to mind. The fire cracked and sizzled.

Where's Bram?

Home, she said, staring into the flames, and offering no further explanation. Watching her, he felt a strong bond of love and wondered if she felt it, too.

THE SÉANCE WAS at the round table in the dining room. He tried not to sit too close to the fire. The room smelled damp, and cool air was leaking through the window frames. Candles flickered madly, casting silhouettes of the guests on the walls, a carousel of shadows. The psychic was a dark-haired woman with a high forehead and an accent he couldn't place. Maybe Hungarian or something like it. Her fingernails were painted black. He hadn't been listening to her preamble, preoccupied instead with the faces around the table, yellow and misshapen as ogres.

Let's join hands, she said.

He didn't really want to, but there was no getting around it. He had Justine on one side, DeBeers on the other. Both their palms were sweaty, and Justine's was cold. DeBeers had a big bearish hand, warm, and it occurred to him how seldom he'd held hands with a man, or for that matter with anyone besides Franny. It was something you grew out of naturally, maybe because by taking someone's hand you were admitting to weakness, vulnerability. It was a kind of giving in, he thought, or giving up, he wasn't sure which. He had no recollection of ever holding hands with his mother or father. He sat there thinking about it and then did recall an exception, with his father. They'd taken him to that place. Maybe he was nine or ten. A hospital of some sort, in the city. He could remember the silent drive from their house. Looking out the windows at the skyscrapers. The uncomfortable clothes he had on, an itchy wool coat. He'd talked to a doctor, a square-headed man with thick glasses and enormous hands. They'd left him there overnight. They're just going to observe you, he remembered his father telling him as he walked him down the long blue corridor, holding his hand. Strange, the things you remember. He couldn't remember anything after that. Maybe just the white blocks of light on the slippery tiled floors.

There is someone among us, the psychic said. Name yourself.

The room filled with wind. The sort you get only on water. Papers swirled through the room like white birds. The table shook. Through the shaking cold of the room he saw a familiar face.

It was his cousin Henri, drenched, pale, teeth chattering, lips blue. George could feel the water filling his shoes, rising over his knees, pooling inside his trousers.

Identify yourself, the psychic commanded.

But the apparition only laughed. I thought you loved me, it said to George, and kept on saying it. *I thought you loved me!*

He pushed back from the table and staggered through the rooms of Floyd's house and out the door. He saw the sharp blades of grass spread out under his feet as he crossed the great lawn. He walked to the dark edge of the property and threw up.

Hey, Justine said. You okay?

He felt her hand on his back. He pulled himself up and wiped his mouth.

It's the 'shrooms, she said. Collateral damage.

You sound like an expert.

She was lighting a joint. Here, smoke some of this, you'll feel better.

Sorry, he said, and took the joint. They walked down to the creek and stood there looking at it.

What just happened in there?

Nothing, she said. I think it's bullshit.

Did you see something? Was there a lot of wind?

No, and I didn't see anything. Did you?

I'm tripping my balls off.

Duh.

I don't even know who I am, he said.

They walked into a field and after a while were far from the house. They walked like soldiers, without speaking. Suddenly she dropped to her knees. I have to stop, she said. I need to rest.

Yes, he said. Rest.

They lay there side by side like they'd been shaken out of the sky. The

sky was vast and bright. He closed his eyes, his mind a tomb. The air alive
with sound, a pandemonium of indigenous life that grew loud in his ears.

And then she said, Life.

He looked at her. She was looking up at the stars.

You have to be yourself, she said, finally. In life. Or you might as well
be dead.

What?

Dead, she said. You may as well—

I think you're beautiful, he heard himself say.

No, I'm not. She turned and looked at him.

To me you are.

Which means I'm not actually beautiful, but right now, in this moment,
I am.

Right now, in this moment, he repeated, a confirmation of something
essential. Then he reached out and put his hand on her breast.

She shook her head. That's not—that can't happen, George. Even if I
wanted it to.

Okay, he said.

Do you know why?

He nodded, but he didn't. Not really.

She's my friend.

I'm really high.

We don't have to talk about it. She pulled him up. They were like a
seesaw, he thought. Or the oil rigs in *Giant*. Back and forth, back and
forth.

She stood there looking at him. What are you looking at?

You.

What do you see?

You frighten me, she said. Her makeup had come off, and her skin
glowed in the cold.

I just wanted to kiss you, he said. Nothing more.

Somehow their mouths came together. Hers was warm and sticky, her
tongue thick as fudge. He didn't know how long it lasted. He could feel
her breasts against his chest.

They walked back, she in the lead. Okay, she wanted to be the leader.
That was all right. But he heard someone. Then dogs.

Justine, he called.

But she was gone. He was alone. He was alone in the woods, in a clearing of birches, their white trunks like a cult of surrender. The moon was bright, the ground wild with shadows.

He heard something else.

He saw the long hair first, white, and the long yellow robe. He saw the staff. He saw two black dogs. He saw the face of God.

God, he said.

You are loved, God said.

George stood there, then dropped to his knees and wept.

I HAVE SOMETHING to tell you, he said to his wife. They were lying next to each other in bed as husband and wife. It was not quite morning.

What is it? she said, concerned. She sat up in bed, pulling the covers up across her breasts, and looked at him.

I saw God. Last night, in the woods. He told her the story, excluding the part about the mushrooms and kissing Justine.

You don't believe in God, she said, doubtfully.

I know. He closed his eyes, trying to remember the face. It was at once old and young, familiar. It might not have been Him, he said. It could have been someone's costume.

What did He look like?

Exactly how you would expect God to look.

What do you make of it?

I don't know.

She looped her arms around her knees. I don't know what you expect me to say.

I guess I just wanted you to know.

All right. Now I know.

It kind of freaked me out.

She nodded.

Look: I'm sorry, Catherine. I want you to know that.

What?

I'm just sorry, that's all.

That's not good enough, George.

She got up and went to the bathroom and filled the water glass and brought it back to him with some aspirin. Take these.

He took the pills from her hand.

Now, rest.

She left him alone. He lay there listening to the sound of his wife and daughter clomping down the stairs into the kitchen, taking out pots and pans, opening and closing the refrigerator, making breakfast. They were happy voices. They were singing together, a song he knew. If he tried very hard, he could almost remember the words.

The Mysteries of Nature

I

THEY WERE FRIENDS, good friends. Close.

They'd take long walks together with her dogs, pushing Franny in the stroller. Their farm like something out of a children's book, with dogs and sheep and alpaca and hens. The alpaca would spit. They'd loiter by the fence, aloof as teenagers. She'd lift Franny up to pet their necks.

Justine taught her things: how to needlepoint, how to knit, how to make dahl. Catherine loved her disorganized house, the enormous pillows from India, her menagerie of plants, her good-smelling kitchen. Unlike Catherine's organized closet, Justine's clothes were heaped in a pile. She'd stand there half naked with her Gauguin breasts, in no particular hurry to cover herself, foraging through the mess for something clean to put on, holding it up, smelling it, decisively thrusting her arms through the sleeves.

She'd make coffee in a glass carafe, then set down the cup and say, That'll put hair on your chest. Sugar cubes in a clay bowl. Silver spoons. She served scones that she made herself with thick butter, jam from the cellar in a jar sticky with spiderwebs.

Justine and Bram, they lived differently. They were always touching, kissing. Unlike her and George, always stepping out of each other's way.

In their bathroom, under a stack of magazines—*Vogue, Mother Jones, The Christian Science Monitor*—Catherine discovered a book called *Behind*

Closed Doors. A large coffee-table book, it was full of black-and-white photographs of a couple having sex—a manual of sorts. She flipped through its pages, taking note of the positions—the man and the woman, their ecstasy, their pale, elegant dance of love—and suppressing a familiar apprehension that something dirty was getting on her hands.

JUSTINE BELONGED to a women's club that served the region, and they had meetings once a month in their headquarters in Albany. As a fundraiser, the group was sponsoring a reading by a renowned poet, and she invited Catherine along. Catherine had told George her plans well in advance, but when he came home that afternoon he claimed to have no recollection. Where's this you're going?

I told you, George. The poetry reading?

She was showered and dressed, and had put on a little makeup and had dabbed tea-rose oil behind her ears. That was Justine's idea; she'd given her the bottle as a gift. It suits you, I think, she'd said.

George looked at her, displeased. Oh, that. What about dinner?

It's on the stove. Help yourself.

I'm not eating that, he said.

She just looked at him. Franny already ate. She's playing with her blocks.

Out the door, her cheeks hot, flushed, her heart beating. She could feel him standing there at the screen, watching as she made her escape.

She drove a little wildly onto the interstate, the sun in her eyes. Unblinking, she stared right at it. The club was downtown, on Madison. Blinded by the low sun, she almost missed the entrance to the parking lot, already crowded with cars. It was an old stucco house with a front porch. A plaque stated its vintage, 1895, and that it was on the National Register of Historic Places. Stepping into the large, bustling entrance hall, she realized she was nervous. It had been a long time since she'd done anything on her own, without Franny, and she felt like one of those people with missing limbs who experienced pangs of dislocation. Eager for distraction, she removed her coat and scarf and pushed the scarf into the sleeve of her coat and draped that over her arm. Then she pushed her hair back behind her ears. The air smelled of coffee and perfume. Gazing over the din, she saw a lone hand beckoning her. Justine. She'd saved her a seat.

They kissed hello. I didn't realize it would be so well attended, Catherine said.

I'm glad you could make it.

They settled into their seats. Catherine took in the room, the hundred or so faces of women eager to learn something new, mothers who'd gone to college, grandmothers, students, all ages and all kinds.

The poet was already famous, not only for her poems but also because she'd been a married woman who declared herself a lesbian. Standing there at the lectern, she was a vision of courage, vulnerability, strength. Her voice carried to the far corners of the enormous room. As she listened, Catherine felt something unlock inside of her, a part of her set free.

After the reading, they each bought a copy of her book, and stood in the long line to get them signed. In a tiny, frightened voice Catherine told her she'd liked hearing her poems. What I mean is, I'm grateful, she added.

The poet squeezed her hand and thanked her, giving Catherine the deep pleasure of acknowledgment.

Driving up to the house, she saw the light burning in his study. She'd hoped he would've gone to bed by now, but he stumbled out of his office like a drunk, blinking at her. How was it?

Interesting. She showed him the book.

He flipped through it casually. What does she mean by that title? *The Dream of a Common Language?*

What do you think she means, George?

I don't have a fucking clue.

It's a dream that we all understand each other.

He grimaced.

That women understand men and men understand women. That we share a common language.

What crap. Since when are you interested in poetry?

I'm broadening my horizons.

She's really getting to you, isn't she?

What?

Justine.

We're friends, George.

Do you think she's gay?

Gay? No. Of course not.

What makes you such an expert?

What's that supposed to mean?

You're not the most experienced person on earth.

So?

Something about her strikes me as rather dykish.

Why? Because she doesn't shave her legs?

For starters, yeah.

That's ridiculous.

He shrugged. Put it this way: how well do you really know her?

Well, I think. We're good friends.

He stood there looking at her. It's obvious she's had an influence on you. I'm not convinced it's a good one.

2

IT WASN'T THAT he didn't like Justine. In fact, they were good friends. He'd never been just friends with a female. Usually such relationships were confounded by sex. But he sensed that she was above all that. Plus, she was an ally at the school. George had observed a kind of casual animosity among members of the department, who held him at a distance and treated him with cool indifference. Although his position was billed as tenure-track, he would be reviewed annually and certain things would have to be in place—publications, a book—for it to be granted. His three-year contract stipulated no incremental raises—symbols of appreciation were rare—and yet he was grateful to be employed.

Justine had worked part-time for years. She taught two classes: one on Renaissance Velvet Textiles, and some dubious seminar called Craft Workshop. She was exceptionally popular with students—especially his female students. He gathered that she had a sort of Mother Hen approach, fawning and solicitous. He often saw her traipsing through the halls wrapped like a mummy in multi-textural drapery, ornaments hanging off her like a Christmas tree. More often than not, some remnant of her last meal would be in evidence, a tendril of bean sprout on her bosom after lunch, for instance, or a chocolate parenthesis on either side of her mouth. When they met each week at their usual table, she always had some arbitrary news item racking her conscience. She was the sort of person who demanded your full attention before lecturing you on an array of pressing dilemmas; her manifesto on women's equality or lack thereof seemed to be her personal favorite. In truth, he was a little afraid of her. Lately, when he saw her on the path in front of him, walking with her cadre of forlorn friends, he'd take a circuitous route to avoid her. In their hulking wool sweaters they resembled lumpy farm animals turned out to graze. She'd be wound up in some endless scarf with her hair spilling over her shoulders and those awful baggy pants, a lump of yarn in her pocket, wooden needles sometimes sticking out like a weapon. Come to think of it, he found her a bit repugnant. But his wife thought she was a goddess.

She'd recruited Catherine into the inner circle of her women's group. He imagined a cult of malcontent females, bitching about men and the lousy deals they'd been handed since birth. Catherine would come home from these excursions hardly recognizable, as if someone had slipped amphetamines into her tea. Her vocabulary was now peppered with words and phrases that must've been lifted from some pop-psych book on feminism. *I need you to listen to me,* or *My expectations of us as a couple are not being met* or *We don't seem to be communicating.*

Since the day they'd met, Catherine had always been just slightly prudish, in her wool skirts and cardigans. At first he'd found it sexy, if a tad repressed. Now, under Justine's spell, she dressed like a prairie woman, in peasant blouses and long skirts or bulky Wranglers and flannel shirts from the army-navy store. She wore her hair in a braid, just like Justine, and had the same outdoorsy complexion. Under this free-spirited tutelage she'd abandoned her bra, and her small breasts swam around inside her outsized shirt, flaunting their rebellion.

He found this transformation disturbing. For one thing, his wife was the most superficial person on earth—superficial and gullible, not a great combination in the hands of a mastermind like Justine. Of course, Catherine saw herself as the complete opposite. Oh, she was smart all right—she'd been a very good student—but ask her to come up with her own ideas, well, that's where she ran into trouble. Justine was the antithesis. She couldn't leave things alone, had to keep boring into things like a fucking termite.

He hadn't spoken to her since that night at Floyd's—their tripping extravaganza—and when he recalled their sloppy kiss, his pathetic groping, he was frankly embarrassed. He'd been skulking around campus, trying to steer clear, when she cornered him in the cafeteria, lacquering him with her gaze. You're avoiding me, she said.

Not at all. I've been busy.

They looked at each other. In this context she was the same old Justine, chunky, intuitive, savage.

About that night, he said.

No need to mention it.

He looked at her breasts, her full lips. I'm not that kind of person, Justine.

Neither am I.

Good, he said. That's a relief.

I'm late. She smiled. See you later?

See you.

A few weeks later, he ran into her in the quad. It was raining and he let her under his umbrella. Of course she didn't have one of her own. Not for her, practical solutions. She was too experiential.

Have you gotten my notes? she asked.

They'd piled up in his box. *Need to talk to you,* the first one said. *Kind of important!*

Yes, I'm sorry—I've been busy.

Do you want to grab some lunch?

They went into the dining hall. Their usual table was taken, so they found one near the very back, away from the clusters of students. She took the items off her tray and organized them before her like the ingredients of some elaborate experiment.

I'm a little worried about Catherine, she said.

Worried, why?

She seems depressed.

He watched her take an enormous bite of her sandwich.

You're right to be concerned, he said.

She looked at him, waiting.

She gets depressed a lot. It's an illness. She's on medication.

I see. This news, he was sure, came as a blow. It wasn't something she could pin on him.

She's getting very thin. Have you noticed?

Indeed he had. She has self-destructive tendencies, he said. More than once he'd heard her in the bathroom, making herself throw up, but he didn't mention this now.

She says things at our meetings.

What sort of things?

Things about you.

Well, he said. That's hardly surprising. She has delusions, I think. Paranoia. She has issues with trust.

But Justine wasn't buying it, her expression a mixture of disgust and condemnation. You have an answer for everything, don't you, George?

Look, he said, mustering a benign tolerance. You know what they say about moving. There's an adjustment period. She misses New York, her friends there. As good as you've been to her, it's just not the same for her here.

He could tell she was hurt. After all, there was nobody like her—such brilliance, sophistication, integrity! How could his impressionable wife need anyone else! Don't take this the wrong way, Justine, but you're the one I'm worried about.

She raised her eyes questioningly. Me?

You seem . . .

What? Her tone was indignant.

Forgive me—he lowered his voice, as though admitting a secret no one else could ever know—but you seem a tad obsessed with my wife.

That's ridiculous. We're friends. Friends look out for each other.

He only smiled.

Annoyed, she glanced at her watch. Look, I've got a class. But this feels unresolved.

This? He touched her hand. This?

She pulled away. She looked off a minute. She thinks you're fucking around.

He said nothing; just waited.

Is it true?

Of course it's not! He shook his head as if he were deeply insulted. Catherine is the love of my life, he said, watching her flinch. Why would I do something like that?

Justine looked annoyed and possibly insulted. She stood up and gathered her things. I don't know, George, why would you?

THE FOLLOWING MORNING, as he was standing at the mirror tying his tie, Catherine proposed a marriage counselor. We're obviously not communicating, she said. Maybe it will help. Justine thought it might.

I refuse to speak to some stranger about a problem I don't think we have. He walked over and put his arms around her. We're fine, Catherine. We just need to spend more time together.

She stood there frowning at him. I hardly see you anymore, George.

That's what I'm saying. Look, see if you can get Cole tonight. I'm taking you out.

They went to the Blue Plate, a bustling café famous for its wholesome American cuisine, meatloaf, macaroni and cheese, pot roast, tuna casserole. Not exactly the place for a sexy date, but it was exactly her speed. She ordered the trout, the least fattening dish on the menu, and pushed the almonds off to the side. Using her knife like a scalpel, she deboned the fish, her movements irritatingly self-conscious. It occurred to him, slobbering over his Bolognese, that he despised her.

How to undo what had already been done? he wondered, then answered simply: I'll leave her.

He smiled reassuringly and squeezed her hand. This place is great.

After dinner they walked through town. As they passed the window of Blake's, he happened to glimpse the shiny evil of Willis's hair. She was standing at the bar with Eddy Hale and the son of a bitch had his hand on her ass.

George? Catherine was staring at him.

Let's get a drink.

Now?

Why not? He took her hand. Come on, it'll be fun.

They pushed through the crowd to the other end of the bar, where he could watch Willis without being seen. It was a townie joint and he was grateful that he didn't see anyone from the college. Over his wife's shoulder and through the interstices between bodies, he watched his lover and the boy. Eddy had friends, knew people, and they were all telling jokes, their laughter bouncing off the tin ceiling. While his wife nursed her spritzer, he downed two shots of vodka, and the next time he looked up Willis had disappeared; her boyfriend was still at the bar.

Need to pee, he told his wife. Try not to let anyone pick you up. She laughed, and he felt magnanimous as he walked to the back of the bar. Willis was waiting at the door to the ladies' room, her back toward him, and when the bathroom became free he pushed in behind her and locked the door.

What are you doing? Get off me or I'll scream!

But he pushed her back against the tiles and tugged down her underpants and filled her up right there, wedging her up on the sink, and she bit his hand. You're sick, she said. We're done.

He left her there, fixing her face in the mirror.

What took you so long? his wife asked.

Long line.

We need to go.

He finished his drink and dropped some bills on the bar. He saw Willis weaving back to the boy, her face illegible to him under the dim lights. That would be the last time, he thought.

Out on the street it occurred to him how bright and stark the town was, how empty, and he pulled Catherine close and kissed her, praising her in his mind for her purity, her shame.

3

SHE ENDED UP getting pretty drunk and going back to Eddy's. She was sick and he helped her and then let her sleep on the couch. She woke the next morning with the chills. His uncle was sitting at the table, drinking coffee and reading the newspaper.

I'm a friend of Eddy's.

He nodded. You want coffee?

Okay. Sure.

You look like you need it.

He wore an old hobo robe. Dog tags around his neck. POW bracelets on each wrist. There was only one way to get eyes like that. He'd probably been good-looking once, she thought. She sat down at the table and waited while he shuffled to the counter and poured her some coffee. With a trembling hand, he set the cup down before her, and she thanked him.

Rough night?

She nodded.

Drink that down.

The coffee was thick and bitter. It made her feel even worse, but she finished it.

You're that girl, he said.

What girl is that?

Let's just say I've heard things.

Just then Eddy came down the stairs in his undershirt and undershorts. He kissed her forehead and whistled. That's hot! Maybe you're sick.

That ain't sick, his uncle said.

Eddy drove her home.

He doesn't like me, she said.

He doesn't like anybody at first.

They went up to her room and he put her to bed, pulling off her clothes and laying a wet cloth over her forehead. I'll come back later to see how you're doing.

She nodded. She wanted to cry. She wanted her mother.

Eddy, she said as he was going out the door. She was going to tell him, but when he turned and looked at her, his eyes as blue and open as the sky, she changed her mind. Instead, she said, I need to leave here soon.

He nodded. I know it.

Soon, she said again.

Yes, soon.

It was cold in the little room. She watched the white rectangle of bristling light. She thought maybe she'd hitchhike out west. The important thing was going. Getting away from George. It didn't really matter where.

Back home, her father would talk about his clients, especially the murder cases. Most of the time he believed they were innocent. He claimed he wouldn't take a case otherwise, but sometimes they weren't. You can't get emotionally involved, he told her. It came down to connecting with the jury. With the smarter ones, who could sway the others. There were always one or two.

She had seen him in court a few times. She watched the jury watching him. They didn't want to like him, but they did. They saw in her father the same weaknesses they knew in themselves. How he moved like some burdened, nearly extinct animal—a water buffalo, maybe, humpbacked, disabled by life and its myriad infidelities. Balding, liver-spotted, over-weight, divorced, a shitty father, resigned to excess. That was who he was. And they loved him for it.

The judge would come in; they'd stand. All the seats flapping at once like the galloping of horses. It was quite a show. They tried not to look at the defendant, wondering if it was his own suit or some charity offering. The accused, as ordinary and evil as the best kind of drug. And the pros-ecutor, pushing his generic brand, pointing out the evidence, the souvenirs of menace. Discounting the defendant with queasy detachment. Curating his destiny with blowups of disfigured dead people, bloody sheets, weap-ons of torture you could find around the house, unflattering pictures of girlfriends, wives.

When it was his turn, her father took his time rising from the table, like it was a sacred act. Like he knew something they didn't and he was above this charade, it was all just a show. And here was a life—*this man's life*—hanging in the balance. Then he'd stare the jury down: His fate is in your hands.

In his boxy suit and shined shoes he meandered over to the stand like a man approaching a slutty woman in a bar, but he'd ask his questions with the voice of a priest. It didn't matter what they were thinking now, because he *knew* the defendant was innocent, and eventually the jury would, too.

Her father could make you think he understood you, even if you'd done things that bordered on the surreal. Somehow, he justified it in his mind that, under certain circumstances, you could be driven to do anything.

ONE DAY, soon after they'd met, George took her to Hudson. He'd taught that morning and was still in his preppy work clothes, but he looked sexy in his little green Fiat and they drove with the top down and he put his hand between her legs. Like a bird's nest, he said, clutching her hair.

They went to Olana, touring the rooms and walking the grounds, and he pointed out the glorious vista that Frederic Church had made famous.

For lunch, he brought her to a Mexican restaurant where no one spoke English. They drank sangria and talked about art and she pretended not to know anything. He liked knowing more, being the expert. She didn't mention her mother's collection, which included a Picasso, a Braque and a Chagall, because it would only make things weird. Nor did she tell him about the four-million-dollar penthouse her father had just bought for his new girlfriend, Portia. Or about her own money, and that with a phone call she could basically get anything she wanted. She didn't tell George any of that, because she knew who he was. Her mother had taught her to read people. It was a mechanism of safety, she'd told her. Because you have so much.

George was someone with a limited menu, as her father always put it. Like most people, herself included, he was the product of his upbringing. He wanted to capture her. He didn't know about real money, that getting rich could happen to anyone.

After they ate, they wandered down Warren Street, looking at the antiques. He knew a lot about furniture. They went into a shop with hulking old cupboards and armoires and rooms full of chairs. This is Chippendale, he said, very good quality. And this one's Federal. He explained that a certain chair was diamond-shaped so soldiers could sit down without removing their swords. He told her that he'd worked in his family's furniture stores every summer in high school and his father had made him study antiques, even though the stuff they sold was new and most of it made in factories. His job was to polish the furniture, he said, and he hated it. His father couldn't stand how all the customers touched everything, so they had a special polish to get the fingerprints off.

On the drive back to Chosen he started talking about his wife, the possibility of divorce, the fact that she'd get the kid. *Over my dead body* was the phrase he used—a cliché, she knew, but it made its point. Still, it sounded creepy.

And there were other things. How he talked about the other professors and made fun of his boss. He was competitive. Thought he was smarter than everyone else. You could tell he didn't care. He could be ruthless.

Then they hit something and the Fiat swerved to the side of the road. They got out. It was a deer, still alive. There wasn't any damage to the car, but there was blood on the fender and splattered across the windshield. The deer was making an awful sound.

George stood over it, watching it. The deer kept jerking its head, nervously glancing up at him with its wide, panicked eyes.

What should we do, George? It's suffering.

But he didn't seem to hear her.

George!

He looked at her then, his face drained of emotion. And then he kicked the animal in the head, over and over and over again, and she screamed and screamed for him to stop, to please just stop.

And then it was quiet. His shoe and pant leg were all bloody.

Get in the car, he said.

For a minute they just sat there, watching the wipers clean the glass. Then he pulled onto the road.

After a while they came to a gas station, where he threw his shoes in the trash and pulled a thick wad of paper towels from the dispenser by the pump. Go and wet these down, he told her.

She had to get the key. The room was filthy and stank of urine. Someone had written *Cuntalingus* on the mirror with a Sharpie. She looked beyond the loopy letters at her reflection—pale, anemic, like a girl who'd been depleted of something.

Wipe that off, he told her, pointing at the fender.

She wiped off the blood as he stood over her. It made her think of his father barking out instructions—*Clean this, wipe that!*—and she wondered what it had been like for George.

She put the dirty towels in the garbage, then saw the blood on her hands.

Get in the car, he said.

Just let me wash my—

But he grabbed her arm. I need to get home, he snapped. My family's waiting for me.

4

MIDWAY THROUGH the semester, he chaperoned a student trip to MoMA. When he stepped onto the bus, he was surprised to see Justine. The other chaperone couldn't make it, she told him. Floyd asked me to help out.

To his relief, she was sitting with one of her students; he sat alone. When they hit traffic at the GW, he looked down and studied the people in their cars.

In the museum, he was able to lose her and felt victorious wandering alone through the bright galleries. They stumbled together on the fourth floor, in front of a Cy Twombly.

I think it's brilliant, she said.

He lives in Rome.

The way he uses the pencil, one line can become everything.

She made this sound like something ominous. She vanished for a moment and reappeared in front of Barnett Newman's *The Voice,* a big white square with one of his famous zips along the edge. This is cool, she said. I really like it.

He glanced at it indifferently. It wasn't the sort of painting you liked or didn't like; that wasn't always particularly relevant, especially when it came to things of beauty. The room seemed overly bright, its edges throbbing. The lights were keening. His head began to hurt.

She was standing there with her hands on her hips, tilting her head from side to side. I like how it doesn't ask for anything, she finally said. It just is.

He grunted in response. It's getting late, Justine. We'd better round them up.

Just as they were leaving the museum, pushing through the crowded lobby, somebody tapped him on the shoulder and said his name. It was a familiar voice, bright with accusation. He turned warily and saw his adviser, Warren Shelby.

Warren, he managed.

I got a call from someone about you, Shelby said. About your degree? The letter I wrote on your behalf? He shook his head like someone with a toothache. Then there was an awkward pause when it occurred to each of them that Justine was listening intently.

I don't know where you get your nerve, he said, rubbing his forehead absentmindedly. I just don't.

They watched him wander away.

What was that about? Justine said as they walked to the bus.

I have no idea.

I think you do, she said.

Here's what I think, he said. I think it falls into the category of total unimportance, especially where you're concerned. That was another chapter of my life. It's in the past.

Justine shook her head. That guy seemed pretty pissed off.

They climbed onto the bus and sat down together as the students filed in, taking their seats. A moment later, the driver pulled out into the Midtown traffic.

I get the distinct impression you don't trust me, he said.

Maybe I don't. She waited for him to say something to allay her suspicion, but he found himself at a loss.

I hate myself for that night, she told him, then got up and moved to the only vacant seat, right behind the driver. She turned her head slightly, sending telepathic poison arrows at him, and he made himself look out the window as the bus slogged through the city, and the low sun, so bright and sharp, forced him to shut his eyes.

When he got home, Catherine had dinner ready. The table was set. The kitchen smelled of cumin. She was flushed from the oven. This new Catherine made him nervous. He looked at the food on the table, some strange rice dish, and felt a little sick.

It wouldn't be long now, he thought. That wasn't the last of Warren Shelby.

How was your day? she asked, taking his briefcase.

It smells good. I'll be down in a minute.

Weary, he climbed the stairs, hoping that if he washed his face . . . But then Franny ran out of her room and gripped his leg like a monkey. He wasn't in the mood. He pulled her little paws off and kept going, and she burst into tears.

George?

Ah, Mother to the rescue. For Christ's sake, he muttered.

George, what happened? Franny, come down here to Mommy.

You don't have to come running every goddamn time—you'll fucking spoil her.

Momma! Franny cried, rubbing her eyes with her tiny fists.

Come down, Franny. Right now, please.

For Christ's fucking sake. She's all right, Catherine! Hold the banister, he told his daughter.

Okay, Daddy, Franny said, still sniffling.

George? His wife looked up at him, waiting for an explanation.

I'm tired. I'm going to lie down for a minute.

In their room, he stretched out on the bed, gazed up at the ceiling and then closed his eyes.

You fell asleep, she said. The room was dark.

I'm not feeling well.

What's wrong?

He shook his head. His eyes watery. Maybe a cold.

I noticed you were pale.

I'm fine. He turned away and she went back to the door. He could feel her watching him. Finally, she closed it.

Their voices drifted up through the old boards. Wife and daughter, his only true claim to success, to life. Franny's little feet running through the house. On the TV something about baboons. They were always doing shows about baboons, for some reason. Given those alarming hindquarters, it was a wonder they endured with such dignity.

SOMEHOW HE GOT through the weekend. He put on the storm windows, using the ladder from the barn. He felled a tree that had blight, then split the wood. It would take days to stack it, he thought, wiping his sweaty forehead with the sleeve of his coat.

On Monday morning, at the college, preoccupied with a sense of foreboding, he canceled his afternoon class and went home to an empty house. A complicated pressure filled his head, assuaged only by whiskey and the silence of his study; it occurred to him that he was having a migraine. He lay down on the couch, hearing the wind and the leaves rushing around. He recalled a conversation he'd once had with DeBeers about conspiracies, and that's how he felt now, like the world was out to get him.

DEBEERS WAS AWAY that week at a conference in Chicago and the department was unusually quiet. George preferred the solitude of his office. He stayed late every night, correcting papers. Occasionally, he'd take a break and go downstairs to the pay phone to call Willis, but the phone in the barn would ring and ring. Once, one of the South American stable boys picked up. George waited while he went to find her, hearing the neighing of horses. When he came back on the line he said she was busy, she couldn't come to the phone. One night he drove over there. He sat out in his car in the dark, watching her window. She was in there, he knew. He could see her shadow on the shade, and someone else's—that boy, Eddy Hale.

UPON HIS RETURN, DeBeers asked George to come see him in his office. Before leaving for Chicago, Floyd had mentioned he'd be sailing up to the marina in Albany today, where he stored his boat for the winter, and George assumed Floyd would ask him to go along.

You can go right in, Edith said, as pious as ever. He's expecting you.

Hello, Floyd, he said, reaching out his hand.

DeBeers shook it uneasily and squeezed out a fake smile. Look, George, I'll get right to the point. I ran into Warren Shelby at the conference.

George instantly understood what was about to happen.

DeBeers took up his pipe and gingerly investigated a bag of tobacco with his fingers—somehow, George thought, it was like catching him in an obscene act. He trickled some tobacco into the bowl and lit it. This letter . . . He fished an ecru sheet of stationery out of a file. He claims he didn't write it. He said you'd asked him and he'd told you he couldn't—

In good conscience, George finished.

DeBeers looked at him. You forged it?

I wrote the letter I deserved, he blurted. It felt good to say it because it was true.

The man studied him. I need to think this through, George.

I understand.

But the look on his face told George he'd made up his mind. It wouldn't surprise him if Floyd had already written the letter asking for his resignation.

I'll let you know, DeBeers added in the soft tone you use when talking with someone who's marginally deranged.

His legs felt heavy walking back to his office. He spent a few minutes just sitting at his desk. He imagined they'd check the rest of his credentials, the esoteric awards and grants. It wouldn't be long now.

He went outside and sat in the gazebo. It was unseasonably warm. He looked down at the river. There was a good wind, the water dark.

He had a good view of Patterson Hall from there. When he saw

DeBeers heading toward the dock he walked down after him, keeping a distance behind. Maybe he wasn't thinking clearly, that was possible, but in situations like these you had to trust your instincts. It was Friday, just after five, and everybody was gone. George watched him board the boat, start the motor and prepare to cast off. Stealthily, he stepped onto the deck just as DeBeers tossed his lines.

George, he said, startled.

Mind if I join you?

DeBeers appraised him briefly, seeming to deduce his need for consolation, and nodded. I suppose so. I'm sailing up to Albany. I'm bringing her ashore today.

Yes, I know. You mentioned it before you left.

He nodded. Yes, I remember.

There's no better place to clear the air than out on the water, George said foolishly. I'd like a chance to explain. He looked at the man's red face. We're still friends, I hope?

Friends don't lie to each other, DeBeers said, standing tall and priestly. He gripped the tiller and motored out.

For reasons that are still unknown to me, George said, I was not well liked in the department.

Forgery's a crime, George. I can't have you on my staff. He looked at him fiercely. I'll have to check out your other credentials. Then I'll have to inform HR. That's just part of the job. You're not the only one caught off guard here, George. I rather liked having you around. I felt as if we were getting somewhere.

Getting somewhere?

You and I. You seemed to be opening up.

George nodded that he understood, but these assertions couldn't be further from the truth. If anything, his vision had been siphoned, diluted, misconstrued.

He sat down heavily on the bench. He'd begun to sweat. It shocked him that his career was coming to an end. He could hear the metal doors of his destiny slamming shut on an unemployable and disgraced fraud.

By now they were far from shore, in deep water. DeBeers had put up the sails and cut the motor. Soon it would be dark.

George? he said, alarmed. Are you all right?

I'm not feeling very well, Floyd. Suddenly he vomited onto the deck.

Jesus, man, DeBeers said, and put a comforting hand on his back. Look, I'm sure this can be resolved.

George began to weep, then noticed that Floyd had turned the bow back in the direction of the dock. On impulse, he wrapped his arms around the man's legs, disrupting his balance, and in a matter of seconds, Floyd went overboard. The halyard snaked across the deck, the boom swung and the sails rippled in irons.

George dove into the freezing water and swam hard until he came upon DeBeers flailing about, coughing and spitting. He gripped his shoulder as the man struggled for air. At first Floyd looked grateful—but then he understood, meeting George's eyes with terror just as it occurred to both of them what had to happen next.

5

IT WAS TWO in the morning when she heard him pulling in. She'd fallen asleep with the light on. She got up and put on her robe and found him in the laundry room, naked, starting the washing machine. In the moon-splattered darkness, he had the freakish appearance of an alien.

George, she barely got the word out.

I'm sick, he said.

What happened?

Something I ate.

Are you drunk, George?

A little.

She could smell the gin when he walked past her up the stairs. She knew something was wrong, very wrong. She stood there, hearing him overhead, the springs of their mattress.

Tightening her robe, she slipped on her coat and boots and went into the garage. The car seemed to beckon her. Conscious of every sound, she opened the door and swiftly pulled out the keys. George didn't like her snooping in his business, he'd made that perfectly clear. The interior was odorless and exceptionally clean, no sign of sickness, but the seat was wet. Not just damp—it was soaked.

·   ·   ·

THREE DAYS LATER, sitting next to her husband at Floyd DeBeers's memorial service at St. James's Church, she reflected on that night. They'd found his empty boat in the middle of the river, sails luffing and lines askew, its owner not on board. Several hours later, his body was discovered, washed up on the shore in Selkirk.

There was vomit on the deck, indicating Floyd had suffered some physical event—possibly a stroke—that caused him to fall overboard. Foul play was not suspected, and his wife, who said he'd had a serious heart condition, didn't request an autopsy. The police had concluded it was an accidental death, case closed.

Floyd was buried in the cemetery behind the church. The mourners stood around the open grave as Father Geary said a prayer. It was the first time Catherine had seen her husband cry.

Later, with friends and family filling the DeBeerses' home, Millicent came up to them and said, tearfully, Floyd was so fond of you, George. I want you to have the boat. He would've wanted that.

George stood there. I don't know what to say, Millie.

Don't say anything. I've already made the arrangements. In the spring, all you have to do is pick it up.

We can't accept that, Millie, Catherine told her.

Please, he really would've wanted it. She took Catherine's arm, her eyes filling with fresh tears. I miss him so much.

To everyone's surprise, George was appointed acting chair of Art History, and he seemed immeasurably proud. She hoped, perhaps, that all of his hard work and determination were finally paying off.

6

HE WENT ON with his life. What else could he do? He threw himself into the work routine, now ensconced in Floyd's office. Edith had boxed up every scrap of paper on the desk. It was like evidence collected by a detective, George thought, but instead of scrutinizing this material Edith had stuck the box labeled PROFESSOR DEBEERS in a storage closet and forgotten all about it.

She was nice to him. She even made him coffee.

He would turn his chair toward the window and stare out at the river, making a bridge of his hands, as Floyd always had. A bridge of contemplation, he thought, that might lead him to the other side of himself, if that was possible.

When he walked into his classroom that first morning after the funeral, an Inness painting was already up on the screen, *The Valley of the Shadow of Death,* one of his signature works. But George didn't plan on talking about it in this session and hadn't included it in his lecture notes.

Momentarily besieged by confusion, he surveyed the class like a jury and pointed at the screen. Did someone put this up?

It was up when we came in, one of his seniors said.

He studied them individually, and each looked right back. A girl in the front row asked, Are you all right, sir?

Of course I'm all right, he snapped. Why wouldn't I be?

Tempted to loosen his bow tie, he instead took out a handkerchief and wiped the sweat off his brow. With no small degree of agitation, he rifled through his notes and discovered a statement Inness had made about the painting. Let's get started, shall we? Can someone dim the lights?

This painting, originally part of a commissioned trilogy, was based on a Swedenborgian theme on the Triumph of the Cross, which related to the Last Judgment, as described in the book of Revelation—a spectacle the philosopher, with his skills of clairvoyance, claimed to have witnessed. One can only assume, George said dryly, unable to disguise his cynicism, that God gave Swedenborg exclusive access to these meteoric events. Highly implausible, I know, but Inness bought into it. And so did a lot of other people.

His students, he thought, were buying into it, too.

There's a story about Swedenborg, he said. A woman who'd lost her husband was immediately hounded by a creditor, claiming her husband hadn't paid a bill. She knew it wasn't true; the receipt had merely been mislaid. When Swedenborg heard the story he offered to go into the spirit world and ask her husband where he'd put it. The woman was so desperate she agreed, doubting that anything would come of it, but Swedenborg returned and told her where it was, in a locked cabinet in his office, a place only her husband knew of. And Swedenborg was soon the talk of the town.

An emperor-and-his-new-clothes sort of fairy tale, he said, but you get the idea.

They were listening plaintively, their faces wan, innocent.

Now let's look at the painting.

The painting depicted a cavernous landscape, jaggedly formed around a blue sky lit by a moonlit cross. A lone pilgrim stood on the rocky ledge in silent contemplation.

It looks like an eye, one student volunteered.

Yes—and what might Inness be suggesting?

God, of course, said another.

That's right—an all-seeing God. Inness believed that art was representative of spiritual principles. Although he wasn't a symbolic painter, this one does seem to be an allegory of faith. His intention was to—and I quote—*convey to the mind of the beholder an impression of the state into which the soul comes when it begins to advance toward a spiritual life. . . .*

George surveyed the students, who were listening intently. Death meant something to them, he realized. Its mystery, glory and seduction. The afterlife all lit up in neon, with its tawdry promise of peace.

He read on in the painter's words: *This I have represented by the cross, giving it the place of the moon, which is the natural emblem of faith, reflecting light upon the sun, its source, assuring us that although the origin of life is no longer visible, it still exists; but here, clouds may at any moment obscure even the light of faith, and the soul, left in ignorance of what may be its ultimate condition, can only lift its eyes in despair of Him who alone can save, and lead it out of disorder and confusion.*

Disorder and confusion, he thought. Tell me about it.

Walking to his car, he reviewed the class in his mind. Though unprepared, he supposed he'd pulled it off, and the painting had generated good discussion. How open they were to these ideas! So impressionable. So willing to believe. More than two hundred years had passed since Swedenborg, nearly a hundred since Inness, and they were still eating the wafer, he thought. Nothing had changed. No matter Darwin, science or technology. People still clung to the notion of a savior. The idea that Swedenborg had witnessed the golden glow of heaven, the punitive measures of hell—and lived to tell about it. Well, what could you say to that? It was so extraordinary you almost had to believe it.

Driving home in the dark, he had the sensation that he wasn't alone. In his rearview mirror he saw only the empty back seat and the empty road behind him. In his headlights, only the woods, the spindly bare trees.

For a moment, his route and location bewildered him, until the abrupt reminder of a familiar landmark set him back on course.

He was alone, of course he was, but still couldn't shake the uncanny awareness of another.

He tuned in to the news, hoping to distract himself with the failed escapades of strangers, but the radio suddenly buzzed with static. Seconds later, a classical station came through with alarming clarity—the maudlin reckoning of Mozart's Requiem. Nearly disabled, he found he had to pull over, and he sat there in the darkness, shivering, waiting for it somehow to end.

A Struggle for Existence

HIS BROTHER WADE turned eighteen that Sunday. Vida baked him a cake. His uncle gave him a shot of whiskey. Eddy and Cole chipped in for a radio. It was pretty nice and had a long antenna, so you could get most of the stations.

After supper they all went down to the junkyard to climb around on the smashed-up cars. Eddy brought his horn. They sat on the tin roofs and he played while Willis rolled cigarettes and he and Wade hunted around for stuff. You could sometimes find things. Once, he found a gold lighter with somebody's initials on it. Another time a wallet, empty except for goofy pictures of someone's kids. Eddy had brought some whiskey they passed around and it felt good and warm in his chest. Willis said it made her dizzy and she liked it. She said she wanted to be oblivious. She drew on herself with pen. She drew a horse like it was galloping over her arm. We just go round in circles, she said. That's all we do. And then we die.

Eddy started playing with a jazz group in Troy, at an underground club on Fulton Street called Tony's, and they all went to watch him play, his uncle and Vida and him and Wade. You could hear their music all along the street, and people who couldn't pay were hanging around outside just so they could hear it. A lot of people he knew turned out for it. Even Father Geary came. He sat alone at his own table drinking a glass of red wine, tapping his hand to the beat on the black tablecloth.

After the show, Rainer took Eddy aside and said, Your mother would be real proud, hearing you play like that.

COLE FOUND the note on Monday afternoon, when he got home from school. In his cruddy handwriting Wade said they were sending him to Fort Jackson, South Carolina, and that he'd write again from there. *Tell Eddy not to be mad.*

He sat down on the tightly made bed. The room suddenly seemed emptier. Wade could fill a place up, and things felt complete when he was around. That night, without Wade's snoring, he lay awake thinking about his brother, trying to picture him on the bus on some dark highway. Wade always knew the army was his only way out. He'd told them but nobody listened. They'd figured he was just dreaming. But he'd done it. And now his bed was empty.

As much as he missed him, Cole was proud of his brother. Wade had proved you could do something in this world. And it showed Cole he wouldn't be stuck here forever, either. It was up to him to make his own way. To decide for himself.

HE HAD this class, Communications, with Mr. Delriccio, who had long sideburns and wore a Hot Tuna T-shirt under his blazer. They had to move their chairs into a circle and go around and say how they felt. Cole never said anything except *Fine* and the teacher didn't press him, on account of everybody knowing what had happened to his parents and thinking Cole might do the same thing. Nobody wanted that kind of guilt on their hands. Mr. Delriccio was his favorite teacher. He'd look at them right in the face and wait as long as it took to hear what you were trying to say. You could do no wrong in his class. It got Cole thinking about things. How people were, the way they sometimes acted. It was actually kind of sad. People said Delriccio was divorced and Eugene saw him once on the subway in the city wearing a leather jacket; he got off at Christopher Street and Eugene said it meant he was probably gay. They had to read a book called *Notes to Myself*. When Rainer saw it on the kitchen table he said, What is this garbage?

It's for school.

Their uncle took ill, a virus around his heart. Eddy drove him into Albany to see a specialist, who said he'd be all right if he took his medicine and quit smoking. Vida would catch him sneaking cigarettes and start yelling in Spanish. With Wade gone and Eddy busy with Rainer, Cole was alone a lot of the time. The Clares wanted him most every weekend. He wished he had a real job, even working at Hack's, but you had to be fifteen to get your working papers and his birthday wasn't till August.

Usually they'd want him on Saturday nights. Sometimes they'd have parties. Basically, everyone got drunk and staggered around spilling their drinks and filling clamshells with butts. She'd make exotic food. Hard-boiled eggs cut in half and sprinkled with red powder. Pickles with little toothpicks shaped like pirate swords. She taught him how to make onion dip, emptying a package of dry soup into a bowl of sour cream. Presto, she'd say, tasting it with her fingertip. She'd get dressed up, do her face. Earrings dangling down like key chains. He thought she was beautiful. When they talked about her late at night in their room, Eddy said she was the kind of woman he wanted to marry and have babies with, because she was smarter than most girls and had the kind of beauty you saw in nature that made you stop for a minute, just like you froze in your tracks when you saw a fox or some amazing bird. Eddy said Mr. Clare didn't deserve her and she was only staying married to him because of Franny and she was a good mother who didn't want to mess up her kid.

She drank spritzers. She smoked Larks because she liked the package. A prominent color in Florentine Renaissance paintings, she told him once, pointing out the same red color in a book of saints with red caps. Her cheeks caved in sharp when she took a drag, like the tightly folded wings of an origami bird. She was like some girl in a magazine. Standing in her poncho by the dark pond, her eyes all silvery. One time, he found her out there alone. He took off his jacket and put it around her shoulders. She didn't look at him but told him he was growing up. She said, Life isn't always what you think. Things happen. He could tell she was a little drunk.

I know about things happening, he told her.

She smiled at him, kind of an eerie smile that turned sad halfway through. I know you do, Cole. I guess that's something we have in common.

They'd have people come up from the city. She said they were artists, writers, like they were royalty. They were different. You couldn't predict what they were going to say. They didn't go out of their way to smile and liked to give you the impression they had other, more important things on their minds. The next morning, you'd see them in town at the Windowbox, nursing their hangovers. They'd complain if they didn't get served quickly or if the food wasn't hot enough. Once, he heard one of them ask, Is this margarine or butter? I won't eat it if it's margarine.

Another time, this guy brought a projector and showed a film on their wall. Cole ducked out, but she caught his hand and said, No, I want you to see this. She was always trying to teach him something and it kind of bugged him. She wasn't his teacher. Anyhow, he sat there and watched. First, a block of white light with little hairs in it and people holding their hands up to make shadows. He made a wolf. She did an eagle with its wings spread and got it flying. Somebody else made what looked like an Egyptian lady. Then the movie started and you saw a car go over a bridge, crash right through the guardrail and fall into the river. For eight whole minutes it showed the same thing over and over, with monks chanting in the background. Like a dream, it didn't make any sense, but it was also troubling to him, the same bad thing happening again and again. He decided it was stupid. But they all sat there transfixed, with the light flashing over them like some kind of magic show. The guy who'd made the film had a melodic voice that looped around like fancy handwriting. His film was about chance, he said. How sometimes things can happen for no reason and change your life forever. He looked directly at Cole, like he knew everything that happened and was sorry for him, and Cole figured the others knew, too, because they were studying him like he was some kind of zoo animal. He didn't want their fucking pity. He got up and walked out.

She called out his name but he ignored her. Anyway, she was too drunk to catch up. The door slammed behind him.

What she didn't get: it wasn't even their house, not really. It never would be.

He walked along the road in the cold air. You could smell the earth, the cold smell of winter coming. He didn't want to be thinking what he was thinking, or feeling what he was feeling.

On impulse he stuck out his thumb. It was just after four and beginning to get dark. A few cars passed by, pulling on their headlights. Right when he was about to turn around, a Chevy pickup pulled over to the side of the road. The truck was dirty and splattered with mud, a farmer's truck. The driver put down his window and leaned out a little and Cole recognized him. It was the man from the library who'd given him the stick of gum that time. Two dogs stood in the back with their tails slicing the air like boomerangs. They came over to him and licked his face.

The black guy's Rufus, the gold one's Betty. Where you headed?

Troy.

The man thought for a minute, looking down the road ahead of him. Where at?

River Street.

I guess I could take you. Get in.

Cole thanked him and climbed in. The man hadn't said where he was going. There was a bag of wool on the floor.

Here, put that up here. That's my wife's. We raise alpaca.

We used to raise cows, Cole told him.

The man nodded, commiserating. It's hard, working a farm.

We don't do it anymore.

I don't blame you for that.

It wasn't by choice, Cole said, surprising himself. We got forced into it.

Wow, I hear you. That's too bad, man.

Cole turned away, his eyes burning, and looked back at the dogs. They had their noses pressed up against the window, wagging their tails.

You got a name?

Cole Hale.

People call me Bram.

Is that short for something?

Abraham.

Thanks for that gum you gave me. At the library.

I'm writing a book, he volunteered. Let me rephrase that: I'm trying to write a book. He laughed.

What about?

That's what I've been trying to figure out, he said. It's taking me a while.

How long?

Too long to say out loud.

Sounds hard, Cole said.

It's the hardest thing I've ever done. But, hey, I didn't expect it to be easy. Anyway, it's the hard stuff that makes you stronger, right? You've got to be open to it. You can't be afraid of hard work.

Cole watched him. Here was another adult trying to give him advice. Like he was a radio that just happened to be on. You could take what you wanted or leave it, which was what his uncle told him.

Anyway, he liked this guy. He had kind of a wild look, with messy hair and wild, friendly eyes. The collar on his work shirt was frayed and he had a thermal shirt on underneath that, and around his neck was a loop of rawhide with a colored bead on it.

I'm not afraid of it, Cole said.

Good. That'll carry you far. Man, this truck stinks, doesn't it? I had a load of pigs back there. They sure know how to stink. You can put your window down if you like.

I don't mind it, he said.

Man, they sure do stink, though, don't they?

Yeah, they always do.

They rolled their windows down and let the wind blast through. After a while, Bram turned off the expressway and went over the Green Island Bridge and then turned onto River Street. Cole directed him to the pawnshop.

Here we are, Bram said.

Thanks. I owe you one. It was something his uncle always said.

All right, then. You take care.

He got out of the truck and went into the shop and a little bell rang above the door. The place was empty, but he could hear the sound of a TV coming from the back. He took in the merchandise, the stuff on the shelves and in the warm, brightly lit glass cases. He didn't see his mother's figurines. The same fat guy his mother dealt with came through the beaded curtain and stood behind the counter. Cole could tell he recognized him, but when he asked about his mother's figurines the man pretended not to remember. They're not here, Cole said. I don't see them.

Where's your mother at? the man asked. I don't do business with kids.

Cole put his money out on the counter. She's dead.

The man's expression collapsed. Well, that's a damn shame. Put that away, he said. He opened a small metal box and pulled out a piece of paper, a receipt, then wrote an address on it and held it out to Cole between his fat fingers. I don't usually do this sort of thing, he said, but I got a soft spot for boys like you.

They had a little tug of war over the counter, and when the man let it go Cole stumbled backward. You're a serious fucking kid, aren't you?

When he stepped out of the shop everything was dark up and down the street. It was stupid coming down here on his own, he realized. Eddy would be mad if he knew. A little desperate, he looked out toward the main road and decided to walk up there. After a minute a truck rolled up alongside him.

Hey, kid.

He was relieved to see it was Bram. Don't you have someplace to go?

Not really. I just drive around looking at people. He reached across the seat and opened the door. Come on in.

Cole was happy to climb in again.

You get what you needed?

He nodded, still holding the piece of paper. He glanced at what the man had written down: *Hazel Smythe, 422 Main Street, Chosen.* It was a name he recognized. In fact, he knew it well.

THAT MONDAY, he cut his last class and walked over to Main Street and climbed the stairs to her apartment, just as he'd done when his father was alive. He could smell the wet dirt on the stairs and, coming up from Blake's, the scent of sawdust, alcohol and French fries. He knocked lightly and waited, but didn't hear anything. Just as he was about to leave, the door opened and she stood there looking at him. Her hair was the color of Rainer's van, like pipe rust, and her lipstick matched. She had on jeans and a sweater and seemed younger than his mother had. He could hear a bird going crazy and saw the cage behind her, up on a stand near the window.

Do you want to see him?

What?

She let him in. That's Fred.

Hello, Fred, he said to the parrot.

Hell-o, Fred, the parrot said back.

Cole smiled.

He's from South America. Bolivia.

That's far away.

It sure is. I'm hoping to go sometime myself.

They stared at the bird in the cage.

He likes it here, though, don't you, Fred?

The parrot raised its wings slightly and jumped around on its perch.

My father raised birds, he said.

Yes, I know. Here, sit down. The woman cleared up a little space and Cole sat down on the couch. Can I get you something? When he didn't answer she said, How about some chocolate milk?

All right.

He was glad when she went into the kitchen and started making noise. He looked around the small apartment. He didn't see his mother's figurines. He could remember his father coming here to see this woman, how Cole would wait for him out on the stairs, listening to their stupid laughter. He remembered thinking how the cold stairway was like a terminal to another world, a place where he fit in better than in this one, and he sometimes imagined those stairs stretching out like Rainer's ladders, up and up and out of sight. After his mother died he had the same idea and wondered what it would be like to climb up to the top and see her. He'd climb as far as he could just to see her again.

Once, he went up in their neighbor's little plane. Just him and his father got to go. They took off out of the field and the plane lurched and lollygagged and Cole worried they'd come crashing down backward, but they didn't. His dad took his hand and held it very tight and told him that in cases like these the important thing was to have faith. Sometimes you just have to, he said.

She came back in with the chocolate milk. Here you go.

Thanks.

She sat down in the chair and watched him. You look just like him, she said finally.

I won't make the same mistakes he did.

She nodded, her lips pursed. He could tell she felt bad.

I was real sorry about what happened to your folks.

He didn't want the milk anymore and carefully set it down.

I've thought a lot about it, she went on. You have no idea how much.

Cole watched her. I came for my mother's things. He slid the receipt from the pawnshop across the coffee table. The woman nodded. I can pay you, he said.

She glanced out at the street. He watched the flat sunlight cross her face as she moved in and out of it.

It's the right thing to do, he said. Name your price.

I couldn't possibly, she said. Not for something like this. She got up and went deep inside a closet and came out with a box, then set it down and opened it. She took out one of the figures, wrapped up in newspaper. Cole could see she was crying. I didn't want nobody else to get them, see.

He showed her the money he'd earned at the Clares'.

She shook her head. I don't want that.

Then she carefully wrapped the statue up again and put it back in the box and handed it to him. Your mother was lucky to have you, she said. You're a very special young man.

Cole tried to smile. He didn't feel special. You sure you don't want any money?

Yes, I'm positive. She smiled, but he still wanted very badly to give her some. He didn't want the Clares' money. The whole point of working for them was this moment right now, and it was about to end. Keeping the money felt wrong.

She walked him down the narrow stairs and held the door open. You take good care, all right?

Thank you, ma'am.

Holding the box in front of him, he walked down the street. He knew he'd done something good. He turned around and saw her standing there on the sidewalk with her hand over her eyes in the sunlight, watching him go.

When he got home he took the box upstairs and sat on his bed and took all of the figures out and unwrapped them. Then he set them there on the shelf, where they belonged.

2

IT HAD SEEMED like a good idea at the time. Wanting to write. He didn't know what the novel was going to be about but felt something pushing him to write one, some great inner force. He thought it had something to do with his mother, who from her damp, wormy confines maybe was pushing him to write it. He could almost hear her complaining: *Look at your life, Abraham! A farmer? Who ever heard of a Jewish farmer! Make something of yourself!* For his mother he had suffered through business school and joined a snobby accounting firm in the city. But Justine had saved him from all that. She said breaking the rules was the ultimate turn-on. You need to push yourself, she told him. Just because you're good at something doesn't mean you have to do it for the rest of your life.

On the day he quit they'd driven up to Stockbridge, her bare feet up on the dash, and poked around the Berkshires and made love under a blanket deep on the Tanglewood lawn, to the distant sounds of Mendelssohn.

His father said he had no stick-to-itiveness, but Justine saw things differently. She said he was curious and easily bored, which was true but not of her, never of her. And sometimes, when he'd make love to her with all the finesse he could muster, she called him a Renaissance man. He knew it was just Justine being romantic, but still.

So be it!

He wanted to be a novelist! He wanted to live in the country like John Cheever and sit by a window and write. He wanted to write about, well, something important. An important book that people could discuss at cocktail parties. He would be diligent and *serious*.

Every morning, after chores, he drove to the library to write. It was a fifteen-minute ride and there were plenty of things to notice along the dirt road from the farm, rutted, puddled, clamoring with thickets. In his rearview mirror he watched their farm grow small, the yellow house with its proud front porch and the hen house and the corn crib and the big barn where he kept the sheep and his three Jersey cows. The vegetable garden that Justine had started, around which he'd constructed a high wooden fence to keep out the deer and the foxes and the coyotes and a great many rabbits. Sometimes, he saw his wife rushing to her car with her heavy bag and her hair loose on her shoulders and her lips so pale in the morning light he could only think of turning around to kiss them. She had a warm, full body that made him feel safe. When he'd first introduced them, his father had called her A Heavy Piece of Furniture and said, when Bram asked what the hell he meant, Lots of drawers packed full of stuff. Maybe it was true, but he loved all her drawers and wanted to take his time rummaging through them.

The library was in town, a white clapboard structure across from St. James's Church—for which, back in the early 1800s, it had been the parson's house—and a cemetery enclosed by a creepy black fence. There were two librarians. Dagmar, a tall blonde of German descent, built like a transvestite with a homely, likable face, sat at the front desk, surreptitiously reading some bodice ripper and sneaking gumdrops from a box inside her drawer.

He worked upstairs, at the very back, in a remote carrel near a storage closet that now and again the second librarian, a Mr. Higgins, a white-haired, bespectacled man with a gimpy leg, would stagger into only to appear, minutes later, looking as if he'd been slapped around, trailing the smell of gin.

It wasn't unusual to see the Hale boy at the large table near the window after school was out. Sometimes he had his friend with him. They would do their homework just as distractedly as boys always fulfill tasks, constantly fidgeting, dropping pencils, picking them up, sharpening them, getting a drink from the fountain. His brother would come to collect him just after five and they'd go off together. Bram knew the middle boy had enlisted and now was out of the picture. He'd dropped out of school, apparently, according to local gossip.

One afternoon, driving around on one of his source-material excursions, he saw the boy walking along the road, hitchhiking. He looked distressed, his face pale, his jaw clenched, his thumb like it could poke a hole in the air.

A pawnshop was a peculiar destination for a kid, Bram thought. He let him off there and they said their goodbyes, but the reality of the street, with its lurking addicts, a windblown prostitute on the corner, changed his mind. By then it was dark. He turned around and drove back and found the boy standing there on the curb, looking confused, frightened, his hands jammed in his pockets.

They drove back to Chosen without talking.

You hungry?

The boy shrugged.

That's what I thought, Bram said, and invited him over for supper.

The kitchen was in its usual state of chaos when they walked in, Justine flushed and substantial in her big fisherman's sweater and yoga pants, noisy clogs. A pot of water boiling on the stove, steam rising. Something baking in the oven—one of her raspberry tarts, he surmised. He introduced her to Cole, kind of a gratuitous formality, and Justine smiled and shook his hand. You need to call someone, right? Your uncle, maybe?

There were no secrets in their town and everybody knew it. You were sort of like family whether you wanted to be or not. Accustomed to following directions, Cole telephoned his uncle, turning away as if for privacy and mumbling into the receiver, but Bram suspected there was no one on the other end.

You can't just bring him home like a stray cat, his wife whispered while feeding the dogs, their tails whacking her legs.

He looks hungry, Bram said. And so am I. He kissed her.

Well, he's in luck, I'm making spaghetti.

When the boy hung up, she said, I hope you like spaghetti.

Yes, ma'am. I do.

You don't have to call me ma'am. Please, call me Justine.

All right. Okay. Justine.

It's just about done.

Here, Bram said, grabbing a bunch of junk mail off a chair. You can sit here.

He's so cool. He was standing in front of the iguana's hut. What's his name?

Emerson.

Like that guy?

Bram smiled. Yeah, like that guy.

What does he eat?

Lots of greens like spinach. Basically anything green and leafy.

He's very fond of apples, Justine added.

Cole joined Bram at the table. He was tall for his age, with a kind face and beautiful, deep-blue eyes. He stared at the empty plate.

The kitchen filled with steam as Justine strained the pasta. Do you want sauce on yours, Cole?

Yes, please. He took his napkin and carefully put it in his lap.

What grade are you in, tenth? Bram asked.

Ninth.

What's your favorite subject?

Math, he said.

I was an accountant.

Did you like it?

No. No, I didn't.

The boy smiled for the first time. Not full-out, just a glimmer.

Bram shrugged. What do *you* want to do?

Do?

You know, when you grow up.

Maybe I'll be a farmer, he said finally.

That's a good idea.

Like your dad, Justine said with enthusiasm, as though following in his father's footsteps was a matter of pride. She smiled. That's nice.

But Cole frowned. No. Not like him. I'd do things differently, he said.

Bram looked at him. I believe you would.

Justine brought over the bowl of spaghetti and meatballs and a container of Parmesan cheese. There's salad, too, she said. And bread. And what about a drink?

This water's fine. He took a sip of water and put the glass down. But he didn't take any food. He just sat there.

Justine set down her fork.

The boy's lower lip trembled slightly. Fat, slow tears ran down his cheeks. He crossed his arms over his chest, embarrassed.

Justine stood up and went to him. Hey.

I'm all right.

She put her arm around him and hugged him and said, Watch out, you're going to get me started.

He smiled, blinking, and she sat back down in her chair.

Better?

Yes, ma'am—Justine.

I bet you're super-hungry, aren't you?

I am, thanks.

Allow me. She took up his plate and served him a good helping. You came on a good night, she said, this happens to be my specialty. Help yourself to salad.

I will.

After they'd eaten and Bram was waiting to take him home, Justine took the boy in her arms and said, Whatever's making you sad? It won't last. This isn't going to be your whole life. Things will get better, I promise. Okay?

He looked at her and nodded. Thank you for having me.

Come back anytime.

Once he'd dropped Cole off, Bram worried about what his wife had said. He wasn't sure it was true. There was no guarantee the boy's life would get any better. And Bram thought he probably knew it. He imagined that a boy like Cole knew his limitations.

But women saw things differently. Justine, for example, believed that good people were rewarded regardless of their circumstances. And that bad people paid in the end.

He hoped like hell she was right.

3

A COUPLE DAYS later, when he went back to work for the Clares, it felt like something had changed. Something about her wasn't right. The house wasn't as neat as usual, with piles of laundry, and dishes in the sink. Ashtrays full of butts, Franny's toys all over the floor. An open vodka bottle on the counter. I'm on strike, she told him.

She went out somewhere. When Franny took her nap, he wandered around the house, feeling kind of down. She didn't seem interested in him like she used to. Now it was just work he was there for. He looked in the cupboard for something to eat, but there wasn't much, not even any crackers. After a while, just to feel useful, he went upstairs to check on Franny—she was curled up with her bunny, sleeping—and then lingered in the hall, deliberating, standing there at the door of his parents' old room. For a moment, he tried pretending his mother was downstairs, cooking supper, and his father was out somewhere. But suddenly the memory was gone. And it was just him again, standing there alone in the drafty hall like somebody stuck between two worlds.

The room had a smell that was different. Her perfume, he guessed. And the damp shower smell. Under that was something else, something he couldn't name.

Like his mother, she slept on the side near the door. There was a small jar of pills on the nightstand. He grasped the container and read the label, but didn't know what to make of it. On a cocktail napkin she'd done a drawing of the Virgin Mary where her blue sheath turned into a river. It was pretty neat. On the other side was a list. *Things I Need: leeks, milk, butter, Ajax, shoe polish, call Justine!*

Sweating like a thief, he moved over to the bureau, opened the top drawer and ran his fingers through her underthings, the silk like water. The straps, the cups of her bra. He pushed his hand down his pants. After he finished, he went into the bathroom to wash his hands and dried them on her towel. For some reason he felt justified. Then he sat on the edge of the tub, trying to breathe.

Later, when Franny woke up, he gave her a snack. She said she wanted to color, so he put out her crayons and a fresh sheet of paper on the kitchen table. Then he grabbed his pack and took out his English homework. They worked together without speaking. For her age, she was a pretty good artist. He figured she took after her mother in that. She was drawing a picture of the house, he realized, with black shutters and smoke curling out of the chimney. Then she added a woman with long blond hair. At first he thought it was Catherine. But as the drawing progressed he saw the jumble of pink that looked like a sweater, and the green square that was a skirt. He saw the blue eyes with long rays for lashes. In place of the mouth was a black hole.

Who's that, Franny?

And she wrote out a name in four bold letters: *E L L A*.

When Mrs. Clare came in and saw the picture she stood there a minute with her hands on her hips. Her back was turned and he couldn't see her face. He wondered what she would do. Blinking like she'd eaten something spicy, she held it up. What a beautiful drawing, she said. Then she taped it on the refrigerator and went upstairs.

IT WAS MR. CLARE who drove him home. Cole noticed he hadn't shaved and his skin looked oily, his eyes glassy. He'd loosened his necktie and unbuttoned the top button of his shirt and rolled up his sleeves. There was a joint in the ashtray, and he took a deep drag, coughed a little and then handed it to Cole. He didn't feel like it but could tell Mr. Clare wanted him to, and refusing his boss was hard. The warm smoke rushed through him and he grinned, embarrassed.

Mr. Clare watched him closely, a look of satisfaction on his face. You have a girlfriend?

There's this one girl.

Women, he said. They're frustrating creatures. Don't ever expect to get what you want, let alone what you need.

Cole hadn't given either much thought.

When in doubt, consult the masters. He pulled a book off the back seat and handed it to him. You want to learn about women, take a look at those. That's Courbet. I've marked the page.

Okay.

Take it with you.

The book was heavy on his legs. His fingers traced the edges of the binding, the cloth fabric of the cover. His hands were sweaty. Mr. Clare abruptly lowered the top and they drove in the wind, saying nothing. Cole could see the moon coming up. The sky was a little purple.

His uncle's house was empty, and he remembered that Eddy was taking Rainer back to the doctor's and Vida had gone along. He went up to the attic, opened the book to the marked page and was astonished. It was a painting of a woman—below the waist. Her legs were splayed and you could see right down to her butt, below a black mound of hair and her dark slit. The painting was called *The Origin of the World*. Though he knew the birth canal was around there, he wondered why the artist had called it that. He didn't like the painting and he didn't like that Mr. Clare had given it to him, and he closed the book and shoved it under his bed. He realized he was very stoned and a little out of his mind and he hated Mr. Clare for making him feel like this, and for the weird thing that was suddenly between them.

He didn't go back to the farm for a few days. He couldn't seem to leave his room. Eddy brought soup and toast up on a tray and read him comics and told him dirty jokes. Rainer even hauled himself up the stairs and put his heavy hand on his forehead. You got a fever, boy.

He'll be all right, Eddy said.

The days passed slowly and he was glad to be left alone. He watched the window shades flutter and the sunlight move across the walls. He could feel himself transforming. He was thin and white, his hands were too big, his legs and feet too long. He couldn't control his thoughts and had jags when he cried like a girl.

A few days later Mrs. Clare showed up at his uncle's, standing there on the porch with a plate of cookies when he got downstairs.

Franny misses you.

I've been sick, he said.

Here, I made you these.

He took the cookies and thanked her and watched her drive away, then went back to bed. He figured if he slept some more he'd wake up and everything would be normal again, like it was before his mother had gone, before those strange people had moved into his house.

Part 3

Part 3

Things Heard and Seen

I

THE WEATHER turned grim those last weeks of November, and the sky was an oppressive gray. Snow piled up on the glass table and metal chairs on the patio. The narrow road remained as pristine as cake frosting, save for the intermittent tracks of deer and rabbits, and no lights burned in the great houses of Chosen. Only rugged locals and country folk stayed on. She was one of them now.

They drove to Connecticut for Thanksgiving. Her in-laws had a cocktail party for close friends, the women in bright dresses with matching pumps, the men in plaid pants and blazers. They were heavy smokers; the living room filled with a gauzy haze. Through the large picture window she could see the water, the beach flat and bare. She would have liked to go out there into the fresh air, away from these people, but they'd think it was rude. His parents were intimidating. Under her grosgrain hairband, his mother would look at Catherine like she was nowhere near good enough. This shouldn't surprise her, though; George did the same thing.

Early on, his mother had done the calculations and saw her only child's marriage in a new light. Poor George had done the noble thing, the Christian thing. Once, just after they were married, they'd all gone to church together. She could remember George in the back seat of his father's Mercedes, suddenly a boy again in his too-snug suit, his tie askew, turned away from her, separate, as she tried to keep up conversation with his gardenia-fragranced mother. After mass, standing next to him in the parking lot with his parents' doting friends, she felt self-conscious in her crummy maternity dress, her old scuffed flats; the dress she'd finally settled on at Penney's looked cheap, and she would've been better off saving the money and sewing one herself. Her in-laws' fancy church and strategic do-gooding were relentlessly off-putting. For her, religion was a quiet thing. Her faith was all her own. God was her confidant, her hope. In His eyes, she was her true self, nothing more, nothing less. She was the person George would never see.

Such things were complicated, she'd come to realize. She couldn't discuss her faith with George, because she knew he'd mock her and make her feel stupid, and there was a certain irony to that, because faith was the very thing keeping her married to him.

THEIR LAUGHTER BROUGHT her back into the room. They were telling stories about George when he was young. Making fun of him. It was something his family enjoyed doing, belittling their son for their own amusement. Of course, he couldn't see it. Or at least pretended he didn't. They were talking about how in high school he'd idolized his cousin Henri, who turned out to be a first-class homo, and they didn't know what had been worse for his parents, the fact that he'd drowned or that he was gay. She watched George's face, for once nuanced with shame, and she felt sorry that he'd grown up here with these awful, heartless people.

Henri did these extraordinary little paintings, his mother was saying. He was quite talented.

She described the small canvases he'd done the summer before his death, scenes of the shoreline—the rocky beach, a sailboat with a green hull, the lighthouse on the point, ospreys on the swamp, an abandoned shed with peeling yellow paint. A gallery had wanted to show them at the time, but apparently they'd disappeared. Though his parents had turned the house inside out, they were never found.

The next morning, they had brunch in the dining room. Catherine kept after Franny, making sure she didn't make a mess on her mother-in-law's new chairs. They showered her daughter with attention, but it was abrasive, sardonic, powered by her father-in-law's stiff mimosas. Franny whined and carried on; she rubbed her eyes, pouted. They all complained she was tired—*overstimulated* was the word her mother-in-law used—and Catherine couldn't wait to get into the car.

They left for home in the rain and for the first stretch drove along the shore. The water was gray, the sand ravaged by wind. The empty seascape made her sad.

Sorry about my folks, he said. Even he seemed glum.

It's okay.

They can be difficult, to say the least.

It must've been hard growing up there.

It was, he admitted softly, and it made her regret how she treated him, always judging him, thinking the worst. She reached across the seat and took his hand and held it for a moment, and he glanced at her without emotion before turning his attention back to the road.

When they arrived he went out for a run. It was good for him, she thought, to let off steam. She let Franny watch TV and made herself a cup of tea. She went into the living room and took up her knitting. She'd been working on a sweater for Franny, with two reindeer standing in front of a deep-blue sky lit with stars. She'd found these wonderful wooden buttons. She'd give it to her for Christmas.

THAT MONDAY MORNING began like any other. Franny ran into their room to wake her, climbing up on the bed to cuddle. While George showered, Catherine made the bed and picked up his dirty socks. That's when she saw the book on his nightstand, poems by Keats with a feather holding his place to "The Human Seasons."

Since when are you reading poetry?

What? He stood there with a towel around his waist. The running had made him stronger, lean. It's not for you, his eyes seemed to say. Oh, that, he said. That's just something I picked up from the library.

It's overdue.

He was about to grab it from her but she held on to it.

I'll take it back, she said. Franny and I are going this morning.

After breakfast, she bundled Franny up in the little camel coat and hat from her mother-in-law and tied her shoes and wiped her jelly-sticky fingers. She was glad for the quiet of the car, the certainty that her daughter was, for a few precious minutes, in one place, contentedly gazing out the window. They passed fields of cows, horses and barns, the gunmetal sky shot through with sun.

In town, she turned down School Street and pulled into the lot behind the library, hoping there'd be other children here for Franny. Usually there were, at this hour, and she'd gotten to know a few of the young mothers, mostly the wives of construction workers or men who worked at the plastics factory, though it seemed hard to talk about anything except the kids. Before getting out, she checked her appearance in the rearview mirror, an old habit. The face looking back at her, however, seemed different. She brushed her hair violently, as if to rid herself of the suspicion that something wasn't right, that she was being deceived.

For Franny's sake, she put on her lipstick and her happy-mommy voice, opened the door, then took her from the car seat and held her hand. With the book bag on her shoulder, they crossed the lot and nodded at the smiling women coming out. Once they got inside, she felt a little better.

Can I go, Momma?

Go ahead, sweetheart.

The room devoted to children had a splendid little dollhouse, a replica of a farmhouse not unlike their own, furnished with miniature versions of colonial pieces—four-poster beds, Chippendale dressers, even Windsor chairs. Tiny lights lit the rooms, and the table was set with plates and silverware. It could've occupied Franny for hours, moving the rubber family, totems of domestic bliss, from room to room. Vaguely, Catherine considered what sort of influence she and George had on Franny's imagination. At least they pretended to love each other when their daughter was around. Maybe that was all that mattered.

With Franny transfixed, Catherine went to the circulation desk to return George's book and pay the fine. The librarian pulled her bifocals onto her nose and frowned. There must be some mistake, she said. This book isn't on your husband's card.

Really?

The woman double-checked and nodded and dropped her necklaced glasses to her chest. With the same scrutiny, she studied Catherine's drawn face, the dark smudges under her eyes, the gold band on her finger. Seeming to have decided something, she spun the ledger book around for Catherine to see. There, she said, pointing. Look for yourself.

As she pulled the ledger closer, Catherine realized that the librarian was doing her a favor, that she wanted her to know.

As you can see, she clarified, that's not your husband's name.

The book had been checked out by a Willis Howell. That's odd, Catherine muttered. I wonder who—

It's unisex, the woman said pointedly.

Excuse me?

The name. But in this case it's a *she*. A rather young she, I might add. She works at the Black Sheep Inn. We had her once, as our waitress. She never brought our dessert!

The librarian turned the ledger back around and studied Catherine, then said, perhaps out of pity, I'm sure there's a perfectly reasonable explanation. In any case, you don't have to pay the fine. The cardholder will have to pay.

Her emphasis on the word *pay* made Catherine understand the hazard at hand, but she revealed nothing, wanting to dispel any possibility of scandal, knowing that, like cheap perfume, it could take over a room.

Franny wasn't ready to leave, of course. She pitched a tantrum instead, acting out the maelstrom that was well under way inside her mother, who had to carry her off the premises. Strangers watched as she wrestled the screaming child into the car. With her tires squealing, she pulled out, jerked through traffic and turned onto Shaker Road, barreling past the inn with its strategic landscaping and manicured lawns. Behind it was a long barn that had been reconfigured as some sort of dormitory for the help. She pulled up on the side of the road and sat there for a moment, thinking. She had no proof that anything had happened. It occurred to her that she could very possibly be overreacting. Still, it wouldn't hurt to have a look, she thought. She'd take Franny as her good-luck charm.

The barn was quiet and dark and empty. In the corral, she could see a young man working with a horse, cracking his long whip as it ran around in circles. She pulled Franny onto her hip and climbed the stairs to a hallway of doors, Franny gaping all around in wonder. She opened one of the doors but the room was clearly a man's, with heavy work boots under the bed and a gray wool blanket rolled on its end. Down the hall she came to another door, where looped around its knob was a thin, black ribbon.

She knocked. No answer.

Like the first, this door was unlocked, the room empty. Spare and cell-like, she thought. On the neatly made bed, a riding helmet, a crop, a pair of small leather gloves. On a square table was a spiral notebook in which the girl had doodled various cursive renditions of her name, adding rainbows and hearts that looked like little black tears. Disgusted by this adolescent ephemera, Catherine picked up the small, framed photograph of the girl and her mother, and realized she'd seen her in town.

Daddy's friend, Franny said gaily.

Now a little desperate, she drove to Justine's, and the movement of the car lulled Franny to sleep. She pulled down the dirt lane; it looked like they were home. She gingerly extricated herself from the car and went to the door as an ornery rooster pecked at her heels. She knocked on the glass, but didn't see anyone inside.

Justine? she called as she went in.

Music was coming from the bedroom, something classical, maybe Brahms. One of the cats jumped down off the counter, startling her. The smell of coffee. A pot of soup simmering on the stove.

Like a prowler, she wandered down the hall. As she approached their bedroom she glimpsed them—in bed, naked, making love. Justine was astride Bram's hips, his square hands on her pale, round buttocks, their pleasure apparent, urgent.

Soundlessly, her heart pounding, she hurried out.

Luckily, Franny was still asleep. Catherine started the engine and pulled out to the main road. The sun was bright at midday. Going home suddenly seemed absurd. She drove around for a while through the town, which had nothing at all to do with her. She began to cry, loud sobs rushing up from what felt like the very bottom of her soul. She had to pull over. There was no disguise for real love, she thought, and suddenly understood all that she did not have.

2

IT WASN'T EASY WORK, but it was work she loved. And it was love that made her work. As it was love that woke her each morning, pulled her across the cold floor and dressed her, that time of year, in long johns and trousers, Bram's old duck coat and muddy work boots with broken laces that carried her over the freezing path to the barn. And it was love that made the animals never stop giving. When you worked with wool, love from your quietest place ran through your fingers—love you gave by hand to strangers. Clunky tapestries that hung on their shoulders, verdant, mossy, twisted brown roots, icy black streams. Sunrise. Gentle hills and waterfalls, chicaneries of thickets, winterberries. Because what she made—every scarf, every blanket, every wall hanging—was, for her, an offering of love—in return for what she had, for what she saw all around her, the beauty of the land and sky.

She was known for her work. Important people owned pieces—even the famous sculptor you'd see in town, walking with his lover against the wind, wrapped up in a squall of blue and gray. No two of anything were ever alike. It wasn't just the wool. It was really all about the dye. She used the same techniques that had been around for centuries and it was the dye—and the dissonant assemblage of colors and textures—that distinguished her work.

You always knew a Sokolov scarf, that's what people told her, so when she saw that girl in the Agway parking lot there was no doubt in her mind that she was wearing one of hers. The color was really extraordinary, she thought. Cochineal with an iron mordant had produced the dreamy purple of a twilight sky. It brought out the girl's lovely dark eyes. She was putting a sack of feed in the back of a pickup truck that had *Black Sheep Inn* painted on the doors, and then climbed up into the passenger seat.

It wasn't until much later that Justine remembered that particular scarf and the man who'd bought it as a gift for his new secretary. Considering the somewhat awkward circumstances of his promotion, he'd told her, he wanted to get off on the right foot.

3

ON TUESDAY, George had lunch with Justine at their usual table. She was wearing a shawl around her shoulders whose black threads kept dripping into her soup as she ate; she didn't appear to notice.

How's the commando treating you?

You mean Edith? He smiled. Miss Hodge is remarkably capable.

What did she think of the scarf?

George chewed his sandwich and swallowed. She liked it very much.

A sound came out of Justine as if something had popped and now the air was running out. She shook her head with smiling amazement. I have something to say to you.

What?

Not here, she said, wiping her mouth with the back of her hand. Later. You won't want to miss it.

They agreed to meet in his office at five. He plodded through his afternoon class, his lecture waning into abstraction, and their blank faces made it clear that he'd completely lost them. So be it, he thought. He let them go early to make up for it.

Edith was just leaving when he walked into his office. You got a message, she informed him—someone by the name of Shelby.

George shook his head. Not a name that rings any bells.

Warren, I think. You may want to try him. He said it was a matter of importance.

A matter of importance.

The number's on your desk.

He saw the pink slip sitting there. He listened to Edith's footsteps fade down the hall, then crumpled the paper up and threw it in the trash.

When Justine finally showed up the room was nearly dark. It was five in the afternoon, the last rays of sunlight pushing through the trees. The river was nearly frozen, the color of asphalt.

Hello, Justine.

You've really had us fooled, George.

I don't know what you mean.

What's your deal? Her tone seemed hostile.

He glanced at his watch. I'll need to cut this short.

Do you have plans, George? Do you need to get home to your wife?

Judging from the look on her face, this question was rhetorical. It occurred to him that the only solution with a woman like Justine was to fuck the nerve right out of her. He should have done it when he'd had the chance.

What's this all about, Justine?

She sighed, seemingly flummoxed. Why do people get married?

Children, he proposed amenably, assuming she was getting to the point.

I'm married, but don't have any. Maybe we will someday. I don't know. I'm not sure. But I know I married for love.

You're an optimist, then.

Love is all that matters.

Justine, he said. What's going on?

That girl. I saw her.

I'm afraid I don't—

She was wearing one of my scarves. The one you bought for Edith. There's no use denying it. I took one look at her and I knew.

He sifted through his ready list of excuses, but it was hard to lie to Justine. So?

I'd heard rumors. I assumed you were better than that. It's a small town, George. People are talking.

Let them talk. That's one thing fools are good at.

You're disgusting.

Calm down, Justine. He opened his drawer, and took out the bottle of bourbon and poured them each a drink.

Who is she?

Nobody. Just some girl I met. He took a sip but Justine didn't touch hers.

What's going on?

Nothing.

I find that hard to believe.

You seem unusually interested, Justine.

I care about Catherine. She's a good friend of mine.

Oh, you've made that perfectly clear.

What's that supposed to mean, George?

It means you should mind your own fucking business.

Is that what you want? She stood up. Because I can do that. Gladly.

She started to leave but he grabbed her arm and she winced. He closed the door and pushed her up against it and clutched her hair at the back of her neck, tangling it in his fingers, and ran his hands down her body. Somehow she pulled away, looking morally assaulted.

You're going to be sorry for that, she said, then grabbed her bag and ran out.

He followed her into the empty corridor. Justine!

But she only quickened her gait, intent on escape, noisily galloping down the stairs in her little half-boots.

Justine! What are you running away for?

They were now in the dark parking lot, and it occurred to him that in just a short span of time they had become strangers to each other. Justine, he said.

Leave me alone.

He stood there watching her fumble with the keys and finally slump into the car. Slowly, almost methodically, he walked to his own car and started the engine. She was a cautious driver and he easily caught up. She turned onto the main road, heading home, and he decided to follow. He could see her eyes flashing in her mirror, a look of terror on her face. It angered him; she was getting this all wrong. If she'd just stop for a minute, he could explain everything. He pushed the pedal down, nudging up to her rear, just brushing her bumper. Again her eyes flashed, her nostrils flared, but it was a comical expression that made him smile and it was like they were playing a game. On the empty road she was doing seventy, eighty, probably faster than she'd ever driven, and he was riding her hard, hissing, Justine, you fucking cunt! You glorious fucking cunt!

He'd forgotten about the curve—it came up so quickly—and he hit his brakes and watched her plow into the guardrail, then flip over into the ravine. The car turned over and over, rolling down the slope.

He pulled over and got out and watched its spectacular fall. Headlights crossed his back. Another car had pulled onto the shoulder. A man shouted, What happened?

I don't know, George said. They ran off the road.

Maybe drunk, the man said.

I'll go call someone, George said. There's a gas station down the road. And that's what he did. From the pay phone at the Texaco station he called the police and told them what he'd seen and that they'd better send an ambulance. They told him to wait on the line so they could take down his name and information; he hung up.

THEY GOT THE CALL in the middle of the night. George could hear Bram's voice coming through the phone. Catherine sat on the edge of the bed, turned away from him, like he didn't deserve to hear the news. She hung up the phone and sat there a minute, as if gathering the strength to utter the words. It's Justine.

What? What about her?

She was in an accident. She's in a coma.

In the morning, they went to the hospital. They weren't allowed to see her, but Bram came out and they went down to the coffee shop across the street and had breakfast. For some reason he was hungry and ordered fried eggs, muffins, sausage, even cornflakes.

It wasn't like her to drive fast, Bram said. That's why she loved that old Volvo—it rattled if you went over seventy. He smiled, shaking his head. I was trying to talk her into buying a new car. But she refused, said she loved that old wagon, that god-awful dirty white. It was her mother's car. It saved her life.

Even if she came out of the coma, he explained, she might never walk again. It remains to be seen, he said. They don't know. It's just too early to tell.

God willing she'll be all right, Catherine said. I'm going to pray for her.

You do that, George thought.

He went to the register and took care of the bill. In the lobby, he shook Bram's hand. Anything you need. Just let us know what we can do.

Later that afternoon, he drove into Albany, to the Sears, and bought his wife a dishwasher. He bought the cheapest model on the floor and paid to have it delivered and asked the salesman to make sure to put a red ribbon on it. His wife, he told him, would be getting what she wanted for Christmas.

4

IT RAINED all afternoon. She stayed on the couch, watching cartoons with Franny under a blanket, her body heavy, enervated, like she was sick. When she heard his car she didn't even move. She stayed where she was. It was strange to think that Franny could protect her, but that's how she felt.

George appeared in the doorway, looking slightly deranged. I need to talk to you, he said.

They went into the kitchen. He sat down at the table and took her hand. I made a mistake, he told her. He didn't look sorry.

She sat there waiting.

There's this girl, Willis Howell.

She was conscious of her hand in his, the sweat, the stain of lies. She slowly pulled it away, as though from a loaded gun, and folded her arms across her chest.

It was all just a big misunderstanding, he said. She's young, a college student, impressionable. She kind of fell in love with me. Then he went on and on. It put him in a bad position. He didn't want the girl to be hurt; she had some serious issues. She came from a wealthy New York family. Spoiled, used to getting whatever she wanted. These people think the world owes them something. She'd been in therapy her whole life. She had real problems.

Catherine sat there trying to ascertain his guilt. I don't know what to say, George.

Nothing happened. You need to know that. There's nothing going on.

HE STARTED being nice to her. Brought her flowers, wine. They sat there at the table, drinking it in silence. He gave her a present, a locket. Put our pictures in it, he said. We're a family. We'll always be together, no matter what.

She tried to think. She tried to be patient.

His eyes said, *Forgive me.*

And she did. That's how she'd been raised. That's what the women in her family did. They got through things. They kept going.

She went to confession, because, for some reason, everything wrong in her life seemed like her own fault.

As the days passed they were quiet, separate, vigorously respectful. He didn't touch her. He seemed happier, confident. Like a game they were playing, taking turns with hateful strategy, and him moving ahead.

SHE WENT to the hospital every day. It became part of her routine. The nurses showered Franny with attention. They were very kind. Justine lay there motionless, on all kinds of machines, her brown hair spread out on the pillow. Catherine sat on the bed and held her hand and talked to her. She prayed.

She tried to occupy herself. She cleaned out the oven, reaching her arm into the dark cavern. She reorganized the linen closet, refolding all of the sheets and towels and stacking them neatly on the shelves.

One morning, doing the laundry, she pulled a mysterious lump out of George's pocket. It sat in her hand, brown and jumbled, like a nest. It was somebody's hair.

Days and weeks passed. Christmas decorations appeared in the hospital halls, silver tinsel as long as rain. I'm praying for her every day, she told Bram.

I don't know why this happened to her, he said. She's too good for something like this. It's not fair.

One afternoon, watching George pull up in the Fiat and get out to open the garage doors, she came to fully understand the reach of her predicament. Maybe it was the physics of the moment, the particular angle at which he'd parked, but a shaft of late sunlight glinted off his bumper and exposed a shallow indentation in the metal and a flake of white paint so insignificant it might have fallen with the snow. And then he walked inside, his too-handsome face meeting her eyes, registering what she'd seen and what she knew, which secured for them both the terrible problem of their destiny.

Oh, Come Let Us Adore Him

I

ON CHRISTMAS DAY they gave a party and all the windows in the house fogged up. Both sets of Franny's grandparents had come, and her aunt and uncle, and he and Eddy had also been invited as guests. Mrs. Clare introduced them to everyone and tried to make them feel like family, but it only made Cole feel like more of an outsider.

She had on a shiny red dress. She was like the bow on a present, too pretty to throw out. The heavy beads around her neck like a noose.

She asked Eddy to help make the drinks but he was too slow and careful, like a chemist, and people got impatient and started pouring their own. Eddy slipped Cole something strong with orange juice and started telling jokes. He knew how to make her laugh. She'd show her teeth and lean her head back a little. He had something women liked. They couldn't resist him.

There was a lot of food. Ham and a turkey and mashed potatoes and green beans. But it wasn't as good as his mother's. After they ate, Mrs. Clare clanged her glass with a fork. I have an announcement, she said. We're going to have some music.

Mr. Clare looked surprised and put on a fake smile. Eddy came in with his horn and stood at the far end of the room, and everybody settled down and waited politely with their hands in their laps. He brought the horn to his lips and closed his eyes and began. It was loud, the kind of thing they'd play in some royal pageant, and the guests sat up a little taller. That's Handel, someone said. And Cole was proud of his brother.

About halfway into it, Franny came up and pulled him into the dining room and pointed out the window. Willis was standing in the yard like somebody's loose dog, lurking and smelling. He went through the kitchen door and got her onto the porch. What are you doing here? She was shivering, crying, maybe a little drunk. You don't have a coat.

I'm cold, she said. Hold me.

All right. He held her very tight. She was a small girl, with small little bones.

He doesn't love me, she said.

Yes, he does, he's crazy about you.

She shook her head. He used me up. And now I'm empty.

Here, why don't you come in? At least let me find you a coat.

He thought he might get in trouble, bringing her inside, but it was Christmas, so he didn't think they'd mind. He gave her a glass of water. He hadn't seen her down at the junkyard for weeks, maybe not since October, and she seemed different, scared.

She should know, she said. His wife. She should know who he is.

He must have been looking at her funny, because she clarified: Catherine. She should know.

And then Cole understood this wasn't about Eddy. No, it had nothing to do with him.

I'll get Eddy, he said, but he didn't move. He watched her take a small compact from her pocket and look at herself in the tiny mirror. She licked her finger and rubbed at the dark circles under her eyes. She sniffed loudly and ran her tongue over her teeth.

What are you doing here? It was Mr. Clare coming into the kitchen.

I'm here to see your wife, she said.

That's not happening.

She should know about you. She should know who you are.

By then Mr. Clare realized Cole was standing there. Get out, he said to him, and he did, but he looked back through the doorway and saw Mr. Clare push Willis roughly out the door, and a minute later, from the dining-room window, he watched the car pull out of the garage and swerve down the icy road. He stood there, unable to move until the red taillights vanished.

Back in the living room, Eddy had just finished and everyone was clapping, including Mrs. Clare, who had no idea that her husband had even left the house.

2

GOING UP THERE had been stupid, she knew that now, too much coke making her feel invincible. She'd stood outside, watching him and his wife, with something burning inside her. Not jealousy. An even uglier feeling, remorse. She wanted to hate him, but at the same time she wanted him to come out and hold her and tell her he was sorry. She wanted to disappear inside his big coat. She wanted him to tell her that she meant more to him than his wife and little girl. That she was who he loved, no one else.

It was the drugs, she knew, doing this to her. The tangle of yearning inside her that wasn't about him at all.

She knew some of those people from the inn. A couple of the men had tried to get to her. One pinched her ass when she walked by. It was humiliating. And that woman with the ferocious laugh always gypped her with the tip.

When he saw her there in the kitchen, he gave her this perturbed look, like she was a stranger. Some nuisance. He'd shoved her into the car and slammed the door like she was the criminal. Someone who needed to be put away.

Driving her to the inn, he said he'd reconnected with his wife. They were trying to make things work, for Franny's sake. Only days before, she'd seen the happy couple in town, all dressed up. Even the little girl, in tights and Mary Janes. They were going to church, she saw, as they walked through the gate, soaking up the approval of strangers.

He was over her, rehabilitated; he no longer needed her services.

He pulled up to the barn and they sat there for a minute. You could hear the wind. The clock ticking on the dashboard. She didn't say anything but she felt things—so many things. Mostly she felt sad.

How old are you?

Nineteen. I'm mature for my age.

What's wrong with you? Why aren't you in school?

Because I went a little crazy.

He looked at her. She could still feel the thing between them.

Goodbye, Willis, he said, finally. Take care of yourself.

She saw in his face that he didn't love her. Love had never been part of this. She knew as much, of course she did. She'd known it all along.

She got out and watched him drive away. For a moment she couldn't move. She was shivering, her teeth chattering, and her throat was a little sore. She felt almost like a little girl. Like everything else in her life was just pretending.

She could hear the horses in the field. They knew her sorrow. They understood how he'd tricked her, twisted everything around to make it seem like she was the sick one, a sick girl with problems, and he was doing the right thing in letting her go.

Part 4

Because

BECAUSE SHE KNOWS HIM, she knows what he is, and because she's known it all along, she just couldn't bring herself to admit to it. She even knew about the dissertation, since she'd read it in secret and seen its flaws, and days after his defense, which never actually happened, she'd found Warren Shelby's letter and wishy-washy encouragement that George should revise and resubmit it. But it wasn't until much later, after they'd moved and she'd wasted so much energy telling everyone how smart he was and how great the new job was, that she realized he was an impersonator in his costume of academia, how every morning he inspected the shirts she'd ironed, holding up each on its hanger like a curator, and when he found the slightest wrinkle he'd yank it off and iron it again himself, standing there at the ironing board in his undershorts, making her watch, then lead her around by the wrist and point out all the expectations he had that weren't being met, the dust on the bureau, the fingerprints, it simply wasn't acceptable, this was a small town where people didn't bother to call first, so you always had to be ready. The time she saw him with the girl, he'd told her he was going for a run, and she'd been cooking something, a challenging recipe that called for shallots, and in a happy mood she took the scenic route past the inn and they were standing there by the barn, the girl with black hair that looked like a mistake, something crossed out in ink, waving a cigarette around and blowing out smoke as if to blow him away. They were fighting, that was obvious, and she was crying, and Catherine drove right by, didn't even slow down, just went about her business, gliding through the aisles of Hack's with her purchases, and everything kept going on like that and then came Christmas with all the presents, her new dishwasher, his proud parents beaming at him in the starched white shirts, the perfectly shabby jacket, the wire spectacles—and thinking, *Poor George with such a neurotic, washed-out wife with no fashion sense or sophistication, dried up like an old fig, how good of him to stand by her!* Because his parents never liked her, not from the start, his mother's disdain like poison—and her own parents, timid, provincial, her mother's tag-sale roots and bookkeeper-spread, her father's gravel pit, white dust thick as flour, their ranch house on the cul-de-sac, the sad, unfinished houses, the developer a crook, the empty lots overgrown with weeds, the room she'd shared with Agnes, the green plaid walls, her mother had picked the paper, she'd never liked it. This was nothing like George's house with his mother's pretty things and inviting meanness, her accent exaggerated so their friends would consider her superior, all of them gin drinkers and heavy smokers, listening to his father bragging about his stores, the big signs on the interstate, the discounts, they were the gold standard in furniture, they could be generous, but it felt like charity. And because she knows about George's women, not just the girl at the inn but also the others there'd been all along, and because she has never trusted him, not since the very beginning, and because people knew and never said anything, they didn't want to hurt her, even though this hurt her more—because he'd made a sucker of her. *I want to separate,* she practices saying while making the beds. *We're no longer compatible,* vacuuming the living room. *I no longer love you,* cleaning his study. *I have never loved you,* emptying the ashtrays. *I loathe and abhor you, I want a divorce!*

THE NEW YEAR comes with sunrise, waking her from sleep. Gradually, it registers in her mind that George is not in bed. She sits up, listening intently, but the house is silent. She doesn't like not knowing where he is. A little frightened, she pulls on her robe and hurries into the hall, past the door of her sleeping daughter, and down the stairs, momentarily bewitched by a glimpse of herself in the hallway mirror, the sunlight floating all around her, making rainbows on the ceiling, and in her eyes a dazzling clarity, as if confronting another version of herself, one who is more mature, composed, courageous—who can get her out of this place.

She finds him in his study, his back to the door, an open bottle of bourbon on the desk, a cigarette burning in the ashtray.

George? He doesn't answer. Are you all right?

Why wouldn't I be?

It's then that she sees the blood. Drops splattered on the floor.

You're hurt.

Yes.

What happened to you?

I cut myself.

Doing what?

He turns around in his chair and looks at her. She can see the towel around his hand, soaked through with blood. His eyes are glassy and mean. He stares at her a long minute, deciding something. Go back to bed, he says. No one in their right mind should be up this early.

ON VALENTINE'S DAY it snows all afternoon. She and Franny cut pink hearts out of construction paper, then paste on doilies and candy hearts. It's important to tell people you love them, she advises Franny.

They drop the cards off at the Hale boys' house in town. That's when she asks Eddy and he says, sure, he can take her. He touches her shoulder. You'll be okay.

Read this, she says, handing Cole his card. I mean every word of it.

GEORGE FORGETS Valentine's Day. He comes home empty-handed. She doesn't make an issue of it. He's tired, overworked, complaining about all his administrative responsibilities and how the students want so much.

It's a stupid holiday anyway, she thinks.

But Franny cries and carries on. George goes out and comes back an hour later with candy hearts for Franny and a glittery card. These are for you, he then says, and hands Catherine a heart-shaped box full of chocolates. Happy now?

She looks at his unshaven face, the sheen of sweat on his forehead, the tricky glint in his eye like broken glass.

She doesn't answer and goes upstairs, sits on the edge of the tub and opens the box. The smell whirls up. She begins. One after another, dropping the wrappers on the floor, little brown scraps of ridged paper that remind her of chestnuts. The sticky caramel and chunky nougat coat her throat. After a while she doesn't even taste them.

He finds her later, over the toilet.

What's the matter? What are you doing?

I'm throwing up my marriage, is all she can think to say.

NOW THAT it's here, this day, it's harder than she thought. At quarter to seven, once he's in the shower, she hurries out to her car. As she's pulling out, he trips down the front steps in his bathrobe, shaving cream on his face. I have an appointment, she shouts. You'll have her all day.

But I have to—

She doesn't hang around to hear him complain, her tires skidding on the slippery road.

She drives into town and parks by the café, where Eddy's waiting as they'd planned. When she gets into his truck he says, You okay?

She nods. Thank you for this. I didn't know who else to ask.

They don't talk on the highway to Albany, where they cross the bridge and she can see the buildings, the train yard with its long black trains, the smokestacks near the port. It's a clinic downtown, on Lark Street. The nurse takes her hand and he waits for her outside.

After it's done, they give her Oreos and grape juice and show her how to wear the pad. She feels a deep and unending emptiness. That's expected, they tell her. It's a hard thing. It's not easy for anyone.

There's a diner across the street and she treats him to lunch. She orders tomato soup and grilled cheese and he has a burger. He shares his fries. The soup is more fresh and delicious than anything she's ever tasted before. I just couldn't do it, she says to Eddy. He doesn't deserve me. I couldn't put a baby through all that.

You don't have to say anything, Eddy says, and touches her hand. You're beautiful, Catherine. Try to remember that.

When she gets home she finds George and Franny watching some old movie. She offers no explanation and goes up to bed.

He watches her and doesn't say a word.

In the bathroom, she notices that the wastebasket where she'd left the test is empty. It was right there, hard to miss. She'd left it for him. She'd wanted him to know.

On Wednesday, Bram calls to give them the news that Justine is awake. With amazement bordering on euphoria, she drives to the hospital alone. A little frightened, she follows the nurse down to her room.

Justine, she cries, hugging her. Thank God you're all right. She pulls up a chair and takes her hand.

Justine searches her face like some long-lost relative. I've been in another place, she says.

Catherine nods. You've been sleeping for a long time. Do you remember anything? Do you know what happened?

Justine shakes her head. No, not really. I remember being terrified, but I don't know why. She looks out the window, where you can see the tops of the trees.

I don't know where the sun went, Catherine says.

They said more snow on the news this morning.

Catherine nods. It's snowed a lot since, well, since your accident.

They sit there looking out the window, not talking.

It's such a beautiful world, Justine says. People don't know. They don't realize what they have.

She turns her head back to Catherine and squeezes her hand. You have to live exactly the way you want to, she says. I know it's hard to know what that is. But life—

She stops talking suddenly and shakes her head, as if it's impossible to put her thoughts into words. I saw things, she says finally. Marvelous things.

She leans back against the pillow as if the conversation has exhausted her, and Catherine decides she'd better go. She gets up and starts for the door.

It's a fragile thing, life is, Justine says. That's something I know now. You have to live your own way. Before it's too late.

THE NEXT MORNING, when George is at work, she begins to pack while Franny watches her programs. She thinks of calling her mother. I'm leaving him, she imagines telling her. He's a dangerous man. But the possibility of her mother's clever persuasion worries her and she decides against it. Because her mother doesn't know George, not really. In her mother's eyes, their marriage has the blue-ribbon stamp of authenticity.

She finishes filling the suitcases, packing in as much as she can, then lugs them downstairs and out to the car. There is the sense in her mind that she must leave and leave now, and she is filled with a nearly desperate excitement. But the weather is not cooperating. A storm descends, a harrowing blizzard. Schools are closed, roads unplowed. Still, she dresses Franny in her coat and hat and socks and snow boots, moving slowly, numbly, fumbling with her pocketbook, her keys, the bag of snacks she prepared for the drive. As they walk to the car, the snow whirls up in their faces and Franny starts to cry. She hurries her into her car seat, furious at George for making her park outside, more concerned about his stupid ragtop than his wife and daughter. There have been signs, she thinks. There have been signs all along. She just couldn't see them.

She starts the engine, shifts into reverse, but the car doesn't move and the wheels spin futilely in the snow. She floors the engine and it makes an awful sound like someone screaming. Defeated, she shuts it off.

Why can't we go, Momma?

We're stuck.

Stuck?

In the snow. She sits there, unwilling to move, too angry to even cry as it becomes ominously clear to her that they won't be going anywhere.

Resigned to the weather, she leaves the suitcases in the car and brings Franny inside, shielding her from the falling snow as if from an explosion. She will try again later, she decides, once the roads are cleared.

But with classes canceled, George is home earlier than usual. She hears him coming in, stamping snow off his boots. She doesn't bother getting up. He is looking for her now, searching the rooms downstairs, speaking her name to the darkening emptiness with growing agitation until he finds her there in the bed.

What's wrong?

Be quiet, Franny's sleeping.

Are you ill?

Another headache, she lies.

They closed the interstate, he mutters. I had some time getting home. I wish it would stop.

He stands there in his overcoat. What are those suitcases doing in your car?

I was going to . . .

Going to what?

With difficulty, she pulls herself up, as if there's a great weight upon her, a great force pushing her down, and then the truth falls from her mouth. I tried to leave, she blurts. But I couldn't get out.

Of course you couldn't, he says, his voice unusually soft. He sits down beside her on the bed. She can smell the cold on him and something else, the faintest scent of pine.

I thought I'd go—

Where? He looks at her with confusion.

Home, she says, barely audible, her lips trembling.

Your home is here, Cathy. He puts his hand on her back, heavy, heavy, her old name ringing in her ears, making her cry, and finally nothing seems to matter anymore—who they are—what they are—the ridiculous game they've been playing—and she says what's been on her mind for months: The seat was wet.

What?

That night. In your car.

I don't know what you're talking about.

It was soaked.

What's wrong with you? he says.

You were on that boat, weren't you? The night Floyd drowned.

He shakes his head and looks at her strangely. I think you've really fucking lost it, he says. Abruptly, his face drains of all emotion and he clutches her arm and pulls her up and shuffles her out into the hall, down the stairs. I want that car unpacked. Now. You won't be needing any suitcases, I can promise you that. He shoves her out the door and slams it shut.

Without her coat, her shoes, it's freezing out. Shaking, she gathers the suitcases, cold tears running down her face. She swats them away irritably. She will have to appease him somehow; she will have to convince him she didn't mean it—that she understands, even forgives. A secret she will keep forever, she rehearses telling him.

She brings the suitcases inside. Of course he doesn't help her. He watches her struggle to carry them upstairs. She takes everything out and stuffs it back into the drawers, then shoves the empty suitcases into the closet. In despair, she sits down on the bed and tries to think, to plan. She can hear him in the kitchen, the sound of steak frying on a too-high flame, the fat sizzling in the pan, wafting smoke. She can hear her daughter's voice.

Somehow they get through dinner. He fixes her a plate and sets it down, but she can hardly eat. She cuts the meat in tiny pieces, the limp green beans jumbled in her mouth. There's wine, thick and bitter, and he makes her drink some. For your nerves, he tells her, refilling her glass.

She tries not to look at him. But he won't stop looking at her, chewing slowly, deliberating. They're enemies, she realizes. True, bitter enemies. She can feel his hatred of her. His wanting something—she doesn't know what. Planning something.

She cleans up the kitchen, conscious of his whereabouts. He plays with Franny—such a good daddy. Noisy. Forced. Making her laugh too hard.

Time for bed, she interrupts.

No, Momma.

Come on, sweetie, she says, holding out her hand.

She gives Franny a bath, then puts on her pajamas and reads to her, snuggled up close in her warm little bed, alert to the vicious wind, the whirling snow, the black thoughtless trees. Both grateful and impatient, she watches her daughter fall asleep.

The house is quiet. She's lost track of him. They are like animals in the woods, waiting, waiting. She tiptoes into the hall and looks down through the banister spindles. The rooms are dark, but she can smell the joint he's lit in his study, and hears a glass clunking down on his desk, the rattle of ice.

Suddenly drained, she takes a shower, and lets the water pour over her face, her open mouth. Her whole body aches. It comes to her that she has been through something intense, these months here in this house. They have taken so much from her that she doesn't believe she will ever be the same.

She puts on her nightgown and sits on the bed, brushing out her hair. She thinks maybe she should call someone. She doesn't feel safe. But look at the snow, the falling sleet. She hates its icy indifference, its mindless treachery. She hates that God has trapped her in this house. She hadn't closed the shades, and the windows reflect the perfect symmetry of the room: the bed with its two pillows, two nightstands, two lamps—and two women, one of flesh, the other of air.

Then

AT FIRST there is the awful weight, her head impossibly heavy, her hair coated with something thick as syrup, and a blade jutting out. It is medieval, she thinks, a medieval death, but it is of no consequence to her. She doesn't feel any pain, only amazement. She rises then and looks down at her body, draped in blood, and at the figure waiting for her in a circle of light.

Are you ready to join us?

Yes, she answers. Yes, I'm ready.

You are loved; you have nothing to fear.

A watery light leads her out, shimmering and dancing over the dreaming child. Her cold breath turns the mobile with its tiny fairies the size of thimbles in pointy hats; the music plays. The girl opens her eyes, but only for an instant. She watches the mobile, transfixed by its circular motion, and again sinks into dreams.

The field is white, the sky. The trees—they, too, are white. God's light pouring through. Blinded by it, she disappears into the beautiful oblivion.

Behavioral Science

I

IT'S TOO EARLY to go in, so he stops at a doughnut shop down the road from the college. He sits there a moment, looking through his windshield. A few stragglers go inside. The cold hits him when he gets out. He buttons his coat, but the lining's torn and a draft seeps up his back. A banker's coat, he thinks, either a banker or a gangster, one of his father's hand-me-downs that he's been wearing since graduate school. He meant to have his wife mend it—sewing being one of her many practical talents—but now he decides he should just get rid of it. Like most things, the coat has outlived its usefulness.

The sweet warmth wafts over him when he steps inside. The smell of coffee and powdered sugar. He tells them what he wants and then takes the coffee and doughnut over to a table on a little brown tray. The windows are so bright it hurts to look out. The plastic chair barks when he sits down and takes off his gloves. He has to concentrate on picking up the cup, putting it down. The coffee is too hot. With his hands in his lap, he watches the black woman behind the counter as she takes care of her customers, her smile flashing bright before going flat again as soon as the person turns away. Such dishonesty is a riddle, he thinks. At this hour it's mostly construction workers pulling up in diesel pickups, no women to speak of except the one behind the counter and another mopping the floor, and he smells the restroom every time somebody goes through the door. The doughnut is nice to look at, a pillow of fried dough filled with jelly. It reminds him of sticking his tongue into something. Taking a bite, he knows to be careful not to drop any of it on his clothes. It's the sort of thing that can ruin a shirt.

2

THEY GET OUT early, since it's the start of winter recess. People are going away. Not him, he's not going anywhere. But he is glad to be out of school.

Mr. Clare had asked him. He knew it was a half-day and said he'd pay extra.

The shades are pulled. That's the first thing he notices. But her car's here, parked under the big tree, as usual. Maybe she's sewing, sitting at her machine. But when he goes inside, through the unlocked door, he doesn't hear the hum of the machine or anything else. He stands there a minute, listening. The house is quiet. Only the windows trembling a little. And then he sees the money.

He moves the sugar bowl and counts out the bills. A hundred dollars. More money than he's ever seen in his life. He wonders: Is this for me?

There's a note, too. From him. *My wife is ill, please do not disturb her. Franny should take her usual nap. Her bottle is in the fridge. You can go once she's asleep.*

He shoves the note in his pocket with the money. He can feel the wad of cash on his leg. Hello? Anybody here? Franny?

He hears Franny upstairs in the hall. She comes down the stairs on her bottom, one step at a time. She's still in her PJs. The house smells a little like throw-up and the stuff you use to clean it up with.

Hey, Franny.

Momma sick, she says, dragging her bunny.

I know.

Franny frowns and shakes her head. Momma *sick,* she says again.

Should I go up?

She whines a little and collapses to all fours. With her head jerking she looks like a whinnying horse. I want my momma, she cries.

Cole stands there trying to think. Franny doesn't seem right. Wound up, loopy, maybe a little sick. Want to watch TV?

They curl up on the couch in the living room and watch cartoons.

After a while, Franny says she's hungry. They go into the kitchen to see what there is to eat. There's a plate of sandwiches in the fridge and he brings that out. They sit at the table and Franny eats and he pours her some apple juice. He can tell Mr. Clare made the sandwiches, because the crusts are still on and Mrs. Clare always cuts them off. But Franny eats them anyway, leaving the crusts on the plate. He decides he's hungry, too, and makes a sandwich for himself and pours himself a glass of milk.

I want my bobba, she says, seeing her bottle.

Why are you talking like a baby, Franny?

She stamps her feet and jumps up and down. I want my momma!

Be quiet, she's sleeping.

But I want her, Cole.

I know. But she's sick. Let's go back and watch TV.

They watch for another hour, and he says, Are you ready to take your nap?

She nods. I want my bobba!

Okay, okay.

When he takes the bottle out, something sticky gets on his hands. There's a smell, too, like grape, and he thinks there's something in it.

I thirsty, she says, reaching for it.

You're too old for a bobba.

No I ant! She starts to fuss and cry and jump around again.

So he gives it to her. Be quiet, you're going to wake your mother up.

Momma sick.

I know. Shhhhh!

Franny puts her finger to her lips. Shhhhh!

It's dark in her room, the shades pulled over the windows, the night-light burning. It registers in his mind that no one came in here today. Usually, by the time he gets here, the light's shining in and her bed is made. But now the room's messy and dark. Since she's about to take her nap, he leaves it alone. You sleepy?

Franny nods and climbs up on the bed and he covers her and hands her the bunny and she squeezes it tight. She's just a little girl, he thinks. For some reason it worries him.

Drink your bobba, Franny.

She does. And her eyes flutter closed.

Out in the hall it's quiet. Too quiet, he thinks.

He knocks lightly on the Clares' door. Mrs. Clare?

Nothing.

He puts his hand on the knob. Mrs. Clare? Catherine? No answer. I'm going now, he says, a little louder. She's sleeping, he decides, and leaves, just as Mr. Clare had instructed him to in his note.

Walking up to the ridge, he tries to remember if his mother ever got sick. She caught colds every now and then, jamming her used tissues up her sleeves, but she never took to her bed like this. She was too busy to be sick. There had been times when Cole faked sick. One morning when he didn't get up to milk and his brothers accused him of faking, she sat on the side of his bed and pushed the hair off his forehead and said he felt a little warm, even though they both knew he wasn't sick, just being lazy. He remembers her saying that going to school or not was up to him, it was his business, and that she assumed he had his reasons for not wanting to go and that was all right with her. You need to make up your own mind, she'd said. And then she brought him tea and toast and even bought him comics later, when she went into town.

For some reason he starts running. Something telling him to get far from that house. How weird the trees look, like they're outlined in pencil, the clouds hard and full like their cows' udders. The field is deep, his boots fill with snow and a chill rises up his legs. He almost can't make it. He gets through the woods to the empty lot and then cuts through backyards, hearing people in their houses, mothers calling in their kids, and he's relieved to be back in town.

He finds Eugene at Bell's, playing pinball. Where were you?

Nowhere. He kicks the snow off his boots and drops off his coat.

You can go, Eugene says, and Cole takes a turn, shaking the warm sides of the machine with all his strength. The ball shoots up and he wins a free game. The whole time, he's aware of the money in his pocket. It feels like something dangerous. He tries to forget the absolute silence of Mrs. Clare's room. He knows that silence. He knows, because the house told him.

3

FINALLY, late in the day, the corridor dwindles to silence. George straightens the files on his desk and pulls the beaded gold chain of his desk lamp. In the darkening room he puts on his coat, staring out at the trees, then steps into the empty corridor. He walks a bit aimlessly, in no particular hurry, across the green linoleum. All along the corridor the large plate-glass windows are now painted white with winter sky. It puts him in mind of that painting at the MoMA, the Barnett Newman, a white canvas that asks for nothing, and it fills him with a kind of deluded hope.

The overhead lights are dim, creating the strange, intermittent half-dark of a sinking ship, and his balance is briefly compromised. As he walks through the Art History Department, its stark walls corrupted by posters espousing every variety of life-changing opportunity, it occurs to him what a betrayal life is. How nothing turns out even close to what you thought.

He drives home in silence with the heat vents blasting, the snow built up in heaps along the road. The salt trucks are out, making their rounds. After only half a year here in the country, the winter is already getting to him. Already he's had enough of it.

The house looks dark. He eases the car up the driveway and drives around to the garage, then gets out to open the doors, a routine he has come to hate. He always thought down the road they'd install an electric, overhead door, but there doesn't seem much point in doing that now. He pulls into the darkness, like a cave, he thinks, and sits there a minute, letting the engine idle, pulling on his gloves.

4

TRAVIS'S SECRETARY TAKES the call at 4:57 on a Friday afternoon, just when he's heading out the door. He didn't get lunch and hoped to get home, but now that's not happening. He can already predict the accidents, weekenders from the city with no business driving on unplowed country roads.

It's a friend of yours, Brigid says. A Joe Pratt?

An old college buddy from RPI, now an engineer with GE. He takes the call in his office.

I got my neighbor here, Pratt says. Something happened to his wife. He muffles the phone a minute, then comes back on. I think he may have killed her.

Travis and his undersheriff, Wiley Burke, set out in the unmarked car, the tire-chains grinding through the snow. The snow is falling, thick and fast. They don't have much cause to come this far north, the wealthiest section in their jurisdiction and filled with spoiled New Yorkers buying up the old farms. *Too rich for my blood,* he likes to goad the old-timers down at the Windowbox, people who grew up working these fields and tending the livestock and now can't pay the taxes on their farms. Back in the day, he used to work summers on the Hale farm. Good memories.

Pratt owns a small cape on the outskirts that might have been a share-cropper's cottage at one time, a modest place with a split-rail fence and kennels in the back for the dogs. His wife, June, runs a rescue outfit in the back of the house, something he's always respected her for. Just a little slip of a thing, working with dogs that could rip you to pieces. George Clare is standing in their living room like a man under a low-flying helicopter, looking windblown. The little girl fusses in his arms, wriggling to get down. Clare's dressed in khaki trousers and an oxford shirt, penny loafers. He looks well tended.

George, Travis says.

Hello, Travis.

Let's go take a look, shall we?

They leave the child with the Pratts and walk down the road up to the house. Even with the new paint it looks forlorn. Mary always says houses are like children, they don't forget the bad things that happen to them.

They go in through the porch, just as George had earlier that afternoon.

Somebody did this, George says, pointing out the broken window, the glass scattered on the cement floor.

Inside, like some choreographed procession, they climb the stairs in single file.

I can't go in there, Clare says.

All right. You stay right here.

The last time he was in this room was to clear out Ella and Cal. People say this house is cursed and he's starting to believe it.

Catherine Clare is lying in the bed with an ax in her head.

In all his years of police work it is something he's never seen.

Facing the door, she lies on her side in an elongated fetal position. It comes to him that the flannel nightgown is familiar because it's the same one he's seen on his wife.

They stand there looking at her.

Jesus, Wiley mutters.

Just like Mary, she's on the side closest to the door. Even dead, a mother can get her point across, and with a deal like this you can't ignore the elusive systems of cohabitation, the humdrum accord of married life.

Good and cold, isn't it? Wiley says.

Yup.

They both look at the open window.

Yup, it sure is. She's good and stiff, too.

I'll go radio the unit, Burke says.

Get him in the car.

Out here, they don't have their own forensic team. They have to call on Albany County for help. Eventually, in a case like this, the FBI will step in, but for now it's him in charge. And a long night ahead.

He looks at the woman, the taste of bile in his throat. Getting too old for this nonsense, he thinks. Gone soft, all out of heartless grit. Used to be he'd feel useful, even kind of a hero. Not anymore. Over the years he's seen just about everything—every twisted machination, most ill-conceived or plain stupid—but you get to the point, you get to the fucking point where you don't want to see it anymore. He'd had this Origin of the Species epiphany and from then on he's been a changed man.

Cops. They see things—they *see*.

Mary's the churchgoer in their house. She believes people get their just deserts. But what if they don't?

He stands at the foot of the bed, just looking at her. It's an ordinary ax. Nearly everybody in town owns one just like it. Every hardware store has one in stock.

He studies the bed. On her side the sheets are down near her ankles, but on his they're undisturbed, the blanket and sheets still tucked in.

We got company, Travis.

He glances out at the lights as the parade starts—the crime-scene truck, three staties, a handful of pickups with cherry tops and volunteer firefighters, an ambulance they won't be needing. The thing about rural towns, anybody with a pair of hands shows up to use them and help out. Travis can't imagine what the world would be like without their good service. These people know how to work.

He steps into the small master bathroom and a chemical smell hits his nostrils, bleach maybe. He notes the gleaming sink. None of the usual hairs and toothpaste globs, a hell of a lot cleaner than his own bathroom, in fact, and the toilet seat's down to boot. Clare has better manners than he thought.

When he gets home Mary's up waiting, her eyes rimmed in red. I saw the news, she says. Who would do such a thing?

God, I don't know.

It's just awful, isn't it?

Yeah. It is.

Do you want your supper?

I guess I will.

She takes a plate of meatloaf out of the oven and sets it in front of him and gets a fork and knife from the drawer and a beer and ketchup bottle out of the fridge and brings it all to the table. Then she sits in the chair across from him and opens the beer and pours it into two glasses. She drinks some of it, and they look at each other across the old oilcloth, her hair pulled back in a barrette, her skin scrubbed clean, the tiny cross at her throat. Looking exactly like the schoolgirl he married.

How's Travis? he says.

Sleeping. She lights a Marlboro, blows out the smoke. They had a game today. Lost.

Nothing wrong with being underdogs. It's good training.

I don't know what for, she says.

This is good, he says.

It was better a couple hours ago. Poor thing—she didn't deserve that.

Nobody does.

I just don't know who would do such a thing.

We'll find out, won't we?

I pray you do, Travis.

They look at each other again, a bargain of doubt.

Where's the husband now?

At a hotel with his folks.

I never liked that man. Not one bit.

It don't make him a murderer, Mary. You know that.

Yeah. She stamps out her cigarette. Well, I'm no detective.

Under the yellow circle of light her face looks worn. He reaches over and takes her hand. I want this solved just as much as you do.

I know it.

Been a long day, he says. Got another coming tomorrow. He swallows the rest of his beer, then gets up and sets his plate in the sink.

I'll tell you one thing, she says. That house—it makes its own plans.

Yes, I guess it does.

He watches her light another cigarette. I'm going up. You?

Not just yet.

He leaves her there to finish her beer. He knows she wants something from him, some kind of comfort, but just now he's all out of tenderness. Come morning, he figures, he'll find her on the couch, blanketed in newspaper, the ashtray full of butts. Marriage is a curious arrangement, he thinks, climbing the stairs. Even after all these years there are things about his wife that he will never understand. The mystery, he guesses, is what keeps it interesting.

5

EUGENE'S GRANDMOTHER LETS him stay for dinner and they have fried chicken and mashed potatoes and she's the best cook around, hands down. After they eat they watch *The Dukes of Hazzard* and he says good night. Walking by Blake's, going home, he sees her face on the ten o'clock news. People crowding around the bar to watch.

Where you been? Eddy says when he walks in.

Eugene's.

They're watching it on TV, him and Rainer and Vida. Sitting there, glued.

At the commercial, Rainer asks, Were you over there today?

Some instinct tells him to lie. He shakes his head.

I didn't get that, his uncle says.

No, sir.

Cole tries to think if anybody saw him. He doesn't think so. Only Franny.

Something happened to that woman.

What?

Come over here, Eddy says, reminding him of his father. How he'd question him every time he did something stupid. You just couldn't lie to him. For some reason his legs go weak and he sinks down into the couch.

Catherine, Eddy says. She's dead. Murdered.

Cole feels the money against his leg. He concentrates on his hands like he does at school when somebody pisses him off and he has to control himself. The afternoon feels like a dream he can't remember.

You don't look right. Did you eat?

At Eugene's. Call his grandmother if you don't believe me!

Quiet, now. It's coming on. They're doing a report.

They show the coroner's truck, the same one that took his parents away. They show the yellow streamer pulled across the front door. They show a picture of Catherine with her twinkly eyes and white teeth, then one of Mr. Clare. They show the house, an old picture from before, when it was still a poor people's house. They watch the flashing pictures one after the other, and their uncle says, Well, I'll be fucking damned.

They sit there in silence.

What a horror, his uncle says, taking Vida's hand.

Eddy looks mad. He sits there with his arms crossed over his chest.

Cole can't look at him. He stares down at his hands again. For some reason he feels guilty, not just because he lied but also he maybe did something wrong, like he was part of it.

He should have opened that door, he thinks. He should've done something.

I'd put money on it, Eddy says. That son of a bitch killed her.

AT DAWN, Eddy shakes him awake. Get up, he says.

They tiptoe downstairs and put on their coats, their boots.

The whole world is white with snow.

Eddy has his trumpet. They walk through the neighborhood, behind the sleeping houses, through the empty lot and into the woods. The woods are still. The trees stand there like people waiting to be told the news. All the animals seem to be hiding. They come to the ridge and stand there looking down at their old house. There's nobody there now. The place looks desolate. You can see the thick tracks their trucks made in the snow.

This is for her, Eddy says, and brings the horn to his lips. It's a song most people know, the only song to play at a time like this. Taps.

6

THE NEXT MORNING, George Clare doesn't show up and Travis isn't sur-prised. He probably knows he doesn't have to—there's no law. Plus, he has an alibi. Another conversation would have been helpful, though. For one thing, he was the last person who saw his wife alive. That fact alone makes him more than interesting.

Maybe he's just too broken up to talk, Travis thinks. It's not every day your wife gets bludgeoned to death with an ax.

And yet after the interview—granted, it was late—Travis overheard him remark to his father that he didn't see the point in going over it again. He'd given his side and that was all there was to it.

Not quite, Travis thinks now. No, sir, not quite.

He spends the morning fielding telephone calls, mostly townspeople calling to goad him. He tracks down Wiley at the coffeemaker and asks him to load the tape of the interview on the VCR in his office. Compared with Clare's unmarked face, Travis looks old and bothered. He has to wonder what Mary sees in him. Across the table sits the professor, his arms crossed, as ornery as a street hood. Like a foreigner unscrambling sentences, he takes his time answering questions, offering only brief, ele-mentary statements, as if he lacks the vocabulary to explain himself fully.

Something about this guy rubs me the wrong way, Burke says.

Travis backs up the tape and again watches Clare's mannerisms. At one point Burke asks him about the Hale boys. Now, which one painted your house—was it Eddy?

Clare nods, his jaw noticeably tight.

He's a good kid but he's had it awful rough, Travis says. They all have. It's made them hard around the edges.

I wouldn't know.

People say Eddy's got an attitude—a chip on his shoulder over losing the farm. You notice that?

He shakes his head.

What about your wife? She ever say anything?

About him? No.

He's got that girlfriend, Burke says. The one from the inn. He gives Clare a knowing smile. You ever seen her? Man, what I wouldn't do for some of that.

For a minute George says nothing. You can see his jaw tensing up again, like he's clenching his teeth. I don't think I know her, he says.

Oh, you'd know if you'd seen her. Black hair, a body like—

What does this have to do with my wife? Clare shouts.

For a minute nobody says anything and the air turns thick as old lard.

Let's rewind that a minute, Travis says. That part right there, about the girl.

They watch it again. The look that crosses Clare's face when Burke mentions the girl, an expression, Travis thinks, that distinguishes him as a person with the capacity to go beyond the limits of civility. But maybe he's got it wrong. Maybe killing comes naturally to people, an instinct nobody likes to admit, a survival reflex inherited from our Neanderthal cousins. So maybe it's the other stuff, the good manners that supposedly make us human, that are the real aberrations.

Good-looking is a fair description of Clare, he decides. On the surface, this man doesn't look like he has it in him, but Travis has learned all too often not to draw conclusions based on physical attributes. Ordinary people have demons inside them.

And in that singular moment, Travis Lawton sees the demon inside George Clare.

7

EDDY'S GETTING THE PAPER off the front porch when he sees her. She wanders up like a nomad, pale and nervous. Says she's leaving town, has her stuff all packed. She has to go, she tells him. She has to go now.

What's the big hurry?

I'm done here, she says.

She stands there on his uncle's porch with her bony shoulders and boy's haircut, gnawing her swollen lip. I wanted you to know, she says. I wanted to say goodbye.

He wants her to come inside, to take her up to his bed, but he can see her mind's made up. Where you going?

California.

He watches her nervous little dance and how her eyes shift around, her pupils big as peas.

You coming?

Is that an invitation?

She smiles, a jagged little grin that leaks so much sadness. Yes, she says. I want you to.

He touches her cheek and her eyes get watery and when he kisses her he can taste the sad story on her tongue.

All right. I guess I could go.

Her eyes go as bright as a little kid's.

Just give me a second to get my stuff.

He goes upstairs, taking care not to wake his brother. Cole rustles under the covers and Eddy stands still, waiting for his sleeping face to go calm again, the new little hairs cropping up on his chin, a boy deep in dreams. He pushes his things into a knapsack he once used on a camping trip. In the doorway he looks once more at his brother, deciding in that instant that he's grown up enough to leave behind and knowing, too, it'll be a good while before he sees him again.

THEY TAKE Rainer's hearse, just walk right in there and take it. He leaves his uncle a note: *Going out west to find my fame and fortune. Borrowing your car. Promise to return it.*

It's a decent set of wheels, if a little creepy. While he drives, she holds his free hand. Hers is sweaty and cold and he can feel her trembling. It's like they have some kind of secret, one she hasn't told him yet. She leans up against the window, looking out, not talking, pale and trembling like she's sick. What's wrong with you?

Nothing.

He has a painful love inside of him. Don't worry so much, okay?

She nods and pulls up the hood of her sweatshirt. Her eyes, rimmed in black, remind him of their old cows, how they sometimes looked after they were milked, like they'd given so much.

After a couple hours he pulls into a motel. They're somewhere in Pennsylvania, out in the country, just this roadside place with a sign that says *Vacancy* and a small café where you can maybe get a beer. They hurry through the sleet into the little office, where this old lady comes out and hands them a key.

They lose two days getting drunk and eating onion rings from the café and she shows him her thin naked body, her tiny wrists, her hungry sad eyes, her toes like mushrooms. I knew him, she says. I knew George Clare.

How? What happened?

I just did, that's all.

You were friends?

No. Not friends.

Well, then, what?

You don't want to know.

The way she says it, he thinks she might be right.

What, did he try to pick you up?

Yeah. He tried kind of hard.

He waits for her to say more, but she won't and he's not so sure he wants her to.

I'm afraid of him, she tells him later, after they make love. I just want to get as far away as I can.

He does all the driving. She's a city girl, there's no point trusting her behind the wheel. He has a little money, not much. All across the country they stay in one cruddy motel after another. They sleep on a blanket under the stars in South Dakota and wake the next morning to a stampede of cattle. They see some of the sights, the Black Hills, Mount Rushmore. Bryce Canyon. Near the Utah border one morning, an old gray coyote crosses the interstate right in front of their car. There's nobody else on the road but them, and Eddy sees it as a sign. The wild dog grinning. On his way into the hills.

She says she knows someone in San Francisco who's in a band. So that's where they go. He ends up selling the hearse for cash to an outfit that does haunted cemetery rides; he figures his uncle will understand. For a while they stay in this old motel near the bus station, cats crying all night in the dumpsters, and he comes to know her way. She is a quiet girl, mysterious. Sometimes she murmurs in her sleep. He'll watch her when they are sitting around doing nothing, just the way she looks in the sorry gray light through the window, the curtains billowing. How the shadows always find her.

He likes it there, the city on water. The wind funneling through the streets. The wharf with its noise and fish smells and stragglers with lazy eyes. It makes him want to play his horn, to play for her. When he does, her eyes slow down like the fog in this city, how it comes in sneaky and wet and like magic can make you disappear.

THEY FIND a place to rent on Hyde Street, over a Chinese restaurant. The apartment, if you can call it that, is the size of an eighteen-wheeler, with a little porch off the back that overlooks the parking lot of a church. You see brides in their netting and lace, their cars trailing soda cans, or sometimes big white limos or black ones and hearses and now and again the spooky gleam of a coffin, its pallbearers holding it like a battering ram to break open the gates of heaven. You see them adjusting their corsages or tugging at their sleeves.

Willis finds work as a waitress at a fish place on the wharf. Her friend Carlo introduces him to somebody affiliated with a marching band. It's for funerals, he explains. This fat Chinaman listens to him play and gives him the job. It's called the Green Street Band and they're pretty famous. When somebody dies, usually a Chinese person, they march through the streets of Chinatown playing a dreary repertoire. It's all about the horns, so it's good practice for him and he likes the other players and they sometimes play cards. They're mostly older, red-faced men beat up by too much of one thing or another. They give him a suit. He washes the shirt out every night.

Rainer sends him articles about the murder, cut with surgical precision from the *Times Union*. Eddy opens the envelopes with trepidation and pulls out scraps of newsprint, never with an actual letter, like his uncle thinks he had something to do with it. Like he knows something and that's why he left.

Every time he pictures holding her that one time in her kitchen, he is overcome with pure despair. He should have done something. Saved her.

How she cried that day after he took her to the clinic, how he held her hand for a long time till she stopped trembling.

He lays the articles out for Willis to see. She chooses one picture of George Clare and studies it carefully, like it was some telling artifact.

Do you think he did it?

A look of fear crosses her face. Don't think, she says. Know.

8

YOU HAVE to let them come to you. The dead. Eventually, they tell you. He had learned that in Troy, on the few homicide cases he'd worked before coming out here. But you have to be open to it. It's not just the body that matters. It's all the other stuff around it, the stuff nobody bothers to notice.

The house is all taped off. You can see the white barns, the fields flooded with moonlight. It's a bright, beautiful night. He gets out, letting the cold inside his jacket, wanting to feel it, and goes in through the porch the same as before, retracing the steps of the killer. The house is dark, but moonlight shines through it and lights up the stairs. He climbs slowly, carefully placing each step on the treads, the wood creaking under his feet, producing a noise bothersome enough, he thinks, to wake a sleeping woman. He finds it hard to believe she was still asleep when the intruder finally got to her room with his ax.

Travis stands there, looking down at the bed. *What happened to you, Catherine?*

In a few days they'll have the autopsy report and the lab work back from serology. But his instincts tell him that whoever did this already anticipated those things.

He sits down on her side of the bed and turns on the light. A few books on her nightstand attract his attention, thin volumes of poetry, the wire spirals of a sketchbook. He fishes the sketchbook out and flips through the pages, seeing various drawings of the Hale boys, mostly, working around the farm. She'd done a good job getting a likeness, one face a variation of the other. Brothers, he thinks. They'd sure had a full share. They'd gone through something and come out the other side.

When he starts down the stairs the windows begin to tremble. Momentarily disarmed, he freezes, discerning the distant clatter of the train and its mournful wail, a mile of freight rolling through the night.

The next afternoon, he and Wiley drive over to Division Street. They find Rainer snoring on the couch, something rattling around in his chest like an old muffler. Burke shakes him awake. What do you want now? he says, displeased.

Hello, Rainer.

We got nothing to do with it, so don't even ask, I might get insulted. I got a real nice clientele right now, we don't want no trouble.

We got no quarrel with your men.

Rainer looks as if someone's cracked an egg on his head that's starting to run down and he doesn't like the feeling. What do you want, then?

We know your nephews did some work over there, Travis says.

Yeah?

We just want to talk to them.

Well, Eddy's gone.

Gone?

Ran off with some girl.

Any idea where they went?

California. He's in some kind of a band out there. The other boy enlisted—but you already knew that.

Travis nodded. Good for him. He'll make a fine soldier.

Collecting himself, Rainer sits up and scratches his head groggily.

What's ailing you, Rainer?

I got emphysema. They tell me I'm dying.

I wouldn't count on it. Your kind don't die easy.

I'm telling you. I ain't long for this world. To cheer himself up, he puts a cigarette in his mouth.

Might help if you quit those things.

What for? Gonna die anyway, so it don't make no difference now. He lights the cigarette and spits out the smoke. Here comes the boy now. He could know something.

With his backpack over his shoulder, Cole Hale climbs onto the porch and steps through the door. He has the same gaunt slouch as his father, the same sharp blue eyes.

Say hello to the sheriff, Cole, Rainer says.

But the boy only nods, the pallor of surprise washing across his face.

Where's your milk and cookies, Rainer? This boy looks hungry. Travis reaches out his hand. Hello, Cole.

Sir.

The boy knows what to do. His mother raised him right. He shakes Lawton's hand first, then Burke's. Something tells Travis he's been expecting them. He has a fleeting memory of Ella Hale roaming the aisles of Hack's with her boys, gripping them at the neck when they misbehaved like stray kittens.

Am I in trouble?

No, son. We just want to ask you some questions about those people who bought your mother and daddy's farm.

Travis gives him a minute, letting this statement and all it implies sink in a bit. You worked for them, isn't that right? You and your brothers?

Cole wipes his face on the back of his sleeve like he's broken a sweat. We painted the barns.

You did a real fine job.

Those folks got a hell of a deal, too, Rainer says.

I wonder what your impressions are of the Clares.

The boy gives him a blank stare.

They want to know what you think of the husband, his uncle says.

He was okay, I guess.

Did you notice anything unusual? Any strange habits? Anything at all?

No, sir. None that I can think of.

What about Mrs. Clare?

The boy flushes, embarrassed. She was nice.

Oh, she was nice all right, his uncle says. She liked you. Used to make him cookies. Fix his socks. She was a real nice lady. Wasn't she, boy?

I just worked there.

I bet you miss her, Travis says gently. I know I would.

For the first time, Cole meets his eyes man to man. But says nothing. Reveals nothing. Travis knows he's not the type to share his feelings.

I think he might have hit her once, he says finally, and describes an evening after a party where the wife came home in a ripped dress. She had her hand over her eye like this. The boy demonstrates, putting his hand over his eye.

Do you remember whose house they went to?

Cole shakes his head. Somebody from the college, I think.

When was the last time you were there?

I can't remember.

Travis stands there waiting.

Last week, the boy adds uncertainly.

You didn't happen to be there that day, did you?

What?

I think their daughter might've mentioned you were there.

No, sir. I had school.

As I recall, it was a half-day, isn't that right?

The boy's eyes go watery. I wasn't there, he says.

Take it easy, son, Rainer says, putting his hand on the boy's shoulder. He ain't accusing you of nothing.

Can I go now?

Yeah. Sure. Thanks, buddy. You done real good.

Rainer walks Travis out and they stand on the porch for a minute under the yellow light that's always on no matter what time of day. Them boys had nothing to do with this, Rainer says. You know that just as much as I do.

Travis looks into the old man's rheumy eyes. What about this girl that Eddy's with?

I couldn't say. I don't know where she come from. She worked for Henderson over at the inn. That's where they met. The boy was pretty taken with her. Anyhow, they took off together. I guess she was in some kind of hurry.

On the drive home, after dropping Wiley off, he stops by at the inn, but Henderson's off somewhere in Mexico. One of the stable hands shows him the girl's room. There's not much to look at, just a cot and a rolled-up mattress. The young man doesn't speak much English. *Ella regresó a la escuela en California.*

It's a big state, Travis says. Where'bouts in California?

UCLA, *creo.*

According to Clare's secretary, on the morning of February 23 he'd shown up as usual at seven-thirty and left around half past four. No, he didn't seem any different. He was just his usual self, she tells him. Had he ever raised his voice to her? No, he had not. She shows him into Clare's office and explains that it had been Floyd DeBeers's office before his death and that he'd been the real chair of the department, not George. He's just a stand-in, she says with a twinge of relish, until they decide on someone else. She leaves Travis alone for a minute and he sits in the swivel chair and takes in the room, the river view, the exceptionally orderly desk, the surface of which gleams as though it were freshly polished.

EVEN CLARE'S ALIBI doesn't convince Travis of his innocence. In domestic cases, nine times out of ten it's the spouse. And that's a percentage Travis never ignores. The coroner's report could change that, but he doubts it.

He starts toward home through town but then cuts out onto Route 17, where the empty road might help him collect his thoughts. He pulls over at Winterberry Farm and gets out to look at the horses, a whole cavalry standing in the field as if awaiting instructions. He has to work at forgetting all the times he brought Alice out here to see them, how she'd climb up on the fence and reach out her little hand to pet one. It all just goes so fast, doesn't it? Well, it sure does, goddamn it. Neither he nor Mary had succeeded in keeping her safe, and that's what hurts more than anything.

This sets him to thinking about the little girl being alone in that house all day with her dead mother. That's the part that's hardest to digest. As much as he distrusts Clare, it's hard to believe he'd contrive a plan to murder his wife and deliberately leave his daughter behind with her corpse. If that's true, it puts him into a whole other category of criminal, because it means he figured his daughter into his plan and was willing to endanger her to save his own ass. Maybe Clare was banking that reasonable people would assume an upstanding family man like him could never do something like that.

Time of death is what they're waiting on, but even the coroner's report will only be able to narrow it down to within a few hours, and here the margin of error really works against them. George would have you believe that his wife was killed in her sleep *after* he left for work, but Travis doubts this account for at least two practical reasons.

She was pretty stiff when they found her, suggesting she'd been killed a good twelve hours earlier, around 5:00 a.m., *before* he'd left for work. Someone had left the window cracked and the thermostat turned down—the temperature in the room was fifty-six degrees. This would have slowed rigor mortis, feasibly confusing the time of death and supporting what Clare had said in his interview.

But a young woman like Catherine, with a small child across the hall, would be attuned to the sounds of the house. In Travis's mind, it's likely that her husband's alarm clock would have woken her up. Even if she fell back asleep, it's likely the child would come in shortly to wake her. This didn't leave a random psychopath much time to get in there with his ax.

So, too, is Travis confident in his assumption that a woman of her age would've woken up when someone came up those creaky old stairs. Further, if she had woken she might have looked up and seen the assailant's face as he lifted the ax. If that's what happened, the blade would have come in at a slightly different angle and possibly made a wider wedge in her skull. There would have been much more blood. As it was, her blood had congealed at the base of her head in a neat puddle on the pillow, and there wasn't the splattering you'd expect.

Travis concludes that when the intruder entered her room the victim was in fact in a sleeping state, as George had suggested, but she sure as hell wasn't dreaming. Because when the ax went into her skull she was already dead.

An ax killing is no ordinary homicide. It's a crime of the spectacular, a performance. Staged, deliberate. Whoever killed Catherine Clare wanted to give the impression that the crime was an aberration committed by some roving psychotic, a fluke tragedy that defies understanding. But here this scenario is unlikely. In cases like these, the blood, the spectacle, is always a terrifying distraction. Whoever did this had a strategy that was anything but random; every single move had been carefully planned and enacted.

BURKE RAPS on the office door, then comes in and sits down heavily in the chair. So far it's looking like a robbery. We found a hatchet in the yard used to break the window.

A hatchet? What the hell would anybody need that for? You don't need a hatchet to break that old glass. You could do that with your knuckles.

Yup.

Any footprints outside?

Ground was too hard. Plus, it snowed. Nothing on the floors, either.

What got taken?

Nothing.

Then it wasn't a robbery. Travis watches a plow clear the street. Any prints on the ax?

'Course not. Not a single print in the entire house, either. Not on the walls, doors, doorknobs. Like no one even lived there.

That's more than a little strange.

Yeah, it is.

I'll tell you what, Travis says. In all my years, that's the cleanest goddamn crime scene I've ever seen.

We need someone to interview the kid. She could've seen something.

We'll need his consent first.

Yeah. Good luck with that.

You'd think he'd want to know.

He's worried she'll get traumatized.

Well, that's a very good reason, isn't it? But I got a hunch she's not the one he's protecting.

Wiley nods. I'll start building a life history, he says as he leaves.

Travis sits there listening to the phones ringing outside his office. Everybody calling with questions, concerns, fears. No tips yet. They've already taken hundreds of calls, but not a single one from any member of the family—on either side. He understands they're grieving. Plans need to be made, the funeral parlor, the church, the graveyard. But where in hell are her parents, or sister? And his people, where are they? With the tables turned, if it were his wife, he'd be camped out here, demanding answers.

Travis's secretary pokes her head in. You got fans. She jerks her chin at the window, the local-news trucks parked along the curb. Reporters standing around in heavy coats, smoking, drinking coffee out of paper cups.

I got nothing, he says. Still, he has to give them something. He takes his time putting on his coat. Then steps out into the firing range.

Was it a robbery? one of them asks.

We haven't ruled anything out, he says.

People are saying you have a suspect in custody.

No, we have no suspect at this time.

Are you planning to interview the little girl?

Not at this time.

Can you describe what sort of evidence was found?

I'm not at liberty to share that information just now. We're hoping someone will come forward. At this point we're looking for some help.

What about the husband?

Travis coughs into his glove. It's not easy coming home to something like this, he says. He's very distraught.

Later, back in his office, the phone rings. He looks through the glass window at his secretary's desk, its neat surface, the pushed-in chair.

He picks it up. Lawton.

What he hears is the sound of air. Just air, that's all. Coming from someplace far away, into his ear and back out again.

LATER, when he's going through the victim's car, the thought comes to him that there's something going around in ordinary American households, a virus of the soul. Marriage, with its all-you-can-eat menu of disenchantment. It's a Ford Country Squire, a name too fancy for a station wagon with fake wood siding. He still remembers the ad campaign when it first came out: seven or eight school-aged kids sitting on the roof of the car with their backs to the camera, watching other kids on swings at a playground. It sent a message to young women that this was the car to drive if you wanted to bring up happy, well-adjusted children. Well, who doesn't want that?

His own wife has been driving hers for at least seven years now, but she doesn't like the green vinyl seats or that, the first week they owned it, their daughter threw up in the back after a sweet-sixteen party where she'd injected enough dope into her bloodstream to opiate a small suburb. He can remember that night in the hospital, watching over his Alice in the emergency room, how pale she looked, and coming to terms with the fact that she was doing things that scared him, things he had no control over. When the doctor pulled him and Mary outside he told them she'd almost died.

Every parent is guilty of something. You try everything you can to make things right. Sometimes it works. Other times, well, you just have to let go. When he thinks about the situation with Alice he has a hard time coming up with a reason for it. At first, when they were just getting into it, he took the blame. Maybe he'd been too strict, or maybe she couldn't handle his being a cop and it embarrassed her. But now he sees that just enabled her even more. It gave her the excuse to keep doing it.

It took him a long time to stop thinking it was about him or what he'd done. It was all on her—her problem, her weakness, her bad choices. You can't take the blame for other people's mistakes even when you want to, even when you think you should.

The victim's car is spick-and-span. No surprise there. The only thing he finds, crushed under her seat, is a grocery list: eggs, oranges, pork chops, lettuce, furniture polish, Rexall.

Later that afternoon, he stops at the Rexall on Chatham Avenue, whose pharmacist, Dennis Healy, he's known for thirty years. How's the family?

Just fine. What can I do for you, Sheriff?

Just following up on something for work. Would you see if a Catherine Clare picked up anything last week?

Give me just a moment.

While he goes back to check, Travis stands there getting looks from some of the customers, who recognize him from the news and are none too pleased with his performance so far. He's relieved when Dennis comes back to the counter.

Nothing for her, but the husband filled a prescription for a drug called niaprazine.

What is it?

A mild sedative. It's used for sleep disorders in children.

Mind if I get a copy of that prescription?

Sure thing.

People can't be saved, he thinks, walking out of the store. That's just the goddamn truth. They make their own problems. It's not a one-way street—no, sir. Not ever.

The thing about dead people, it's too late to save them. And no matter how convinced you are of someone's guilt, you still have to prove it. The people of this town are waiting for him to do just that.

9

MARY DOESN'T SEE her husband much those first weeks. Like most women in town, she can't sleep right, thinking there's some psychotic ax murderer on the loose. That first morning, the hardware store sells out of locks. People on the street seem hunched with suspicion, fearing they'll be the next to get hacked to death in their sleep. The idea that something like this can happen in Chosen—it makes ordinary things seem strange. You look at cars and faces and wonder: Could it be him in there? Or maybe *that's* him.

Everybody's talking about the Clare woman, her status in town turning her into a saint. The Windowbox is a hive of nervous chatter. Most people think it's the husband. They give Mary dirty looks in Hack's or come up to her in the street. Why hasn't Travis arrested him yet? one woman remarked. You don't have to be a genius to know he did it.

The law isn't some gossip magazine, Mary shot back.

She and Travis Jr. watch him on TV, microphones jammed in his face. He's a nice-looking man, she thinks, even when he's beleaguered by all this drama. We're building a life history of the couple, he explains to the reporters. Hopefully, something useful will turn up.

Now, that ticks me off, he tells her later that night, watching himself on the late news. That's the biggest goddamn disappointment in this whole case, that the family hasn't banged on my doorway wanting answers. If this happened to you or one of the kids, I don't think I'd sleep a night till I got something. Hell, I'd scour the earth till I found your killer.

She takes his hand and squeezes it. I'd do the same for you, honey.

Even *her* side. Where are *her* parents? He shakes his head in amazement. I just don't get it.

Maybe there's a reason they're not asking, Travis.

What do you mean?

Parents—they know their children. Just like we know ours.

I'm not following you, Mary.

Maybe they're not asking questions because they don't have any. Maybe they're not asking because they already know.

Travis gives this a thought. I can see what you're suggesting, Mary, and it makes sense on his side but not on hers. If her parents thought George had done this, wouldn't they try to bring charges against him?

People are funny, Travis, you know that. First, they have no evidence to make such a claim. You've said it yourself that there's not much here to go on. And second, if they did press charges it would obviously destroy their relationship with him and his parents. Maybe they think if they accuse him they'll never see that little girl again.

EVERY DAY there's a little more news and the papers sell out. Travis is late every night, and when he finally makes it home he looks worn out. She sits with him while he eats, drinking a little bourbon, watching him turn the pages of the file as delicately as some surgeon changing the dressing on a wound. Even on weekends, with Travis Jr. practicing his clarinet or shooting baskets outside, he keeps on digging, hoping to turn something up. Somewhere inside those brown flaps is the answer he needs.

They rule out the robbery scenario. First, there hasn't been a robbery in Chosen in almost ten years, and that was just school kids stealing liquor. Catherine's wallet was sitting out in plain sight with not a dime missing. And if it was a robbery, why the ax? Why make the special trip into the barn? Take what you want and go—the lady's asleep upstairs. Why kill a sleeping woman? Why, even if she was awake? Scare her if you want, even knock her out. Then do what you came to do and get out. Even a thief has his standards and common sense. Say you get caught robbing a house, you do some time and then you're out. But murder? That's for life.

Unfortunately, the autopsy report doesn't advance the case, only confirms what is already known: it was a single blow that killed her; there were no usable prints on the ax or in the house; there were none of the usual hairs or flakes of skin on his side of the bed; the drains contained no evidence of blood or chemicals. Forensics determined that the time of death was somewhere between 2:30 and 9:30 a.m., allowing the possibility that some roving madman got in there after Clare had left the house.

It's a pretty big window, Travis says. It's possible, I guess, if you believe his story.

But Mary bristles when she hears this. You know as well as I do, Travis, that a woman with a small child is up at the crack of dawn. She was long dead by 9:30, I can tell you that much. I would bet she'd been dead a good while before her daughter even woke up. He did this in the deep of night. Maybe by accident, all right, but he did it all the same. And then he wiped down that house and went to work

Travis nods with approval. She isn't saying anything he doesn't know. She's just saying it out loud.

HE MAKES HER go with him to the funeral. You and Catherine were friends, he says. It's only right. But Mary knows her husband better than that.

You don't have a suit, she says. And you can't wear your uniform.

You better find me something.

She drives to Macy's out at the mall and buys him a suit off the sale rack, and the next morning he tries it on. About time, she says, smoothing his shoulders like a mother, tugging on the back of the jacket. You look nice.

They drive down to Connecticut, a little town on the shore. The church is on a hill overlooking Long Island Sound, the water glittering silver in the distance. They sit in the last pew and Travis takes her hand. His is big and warm and it brings her back to him. At times, over the course of their marriage, she has imagined her own mortality, anticipated the ravages of age. She has pictured herself in varying states of infirmity, wondering what Travis would do if she lost some vital piece of herself—her mind, for instance. Would he honor her, would he stay? The big questions you're too afraid to ask. You wait till something happens, then deal with it.

It's an old cemetery of crooked stones. A cold wind comes in off the shore. Her shoes sink into the wet earth as they walk out to the grave. She and Travis keep to themselves, hunkering behind the other mourners, observing both families from a distance. Catherine's seems cautious, reserved, like strangers. The Clares more like royalty, stiff and formal. Their son's expression is passive, self-conscious, as the little girl wriggles in his arms.

They're walking back to the car when a woman comes up to Travis. You've got some nerve showing up here, she says. She looks something like Catherine, only shorter and stout, with darker hair. The sister, Mary realizes.

We're just paying our respects, is all. The deceased was a friend of my wife's.

But she isn't having it. We know what you're trying to do, she says in an unfriendly tone. And I'll tell you right now we don't appreciate it.

I'm not following you.

With George. Trying to pin it on him.

Travis takes his time answering. That may be your perception.

You're damned right it is. I think I'm speaking for my family when I say we're behind George a hundred percent. What happened to my sister has nothing to do with him. There was no reason for it. She didn't have any enemies. There was no reason for anybody to kill her.

10

Motive is an elusive word, Travis thinks, because you can never be certain what lies beneath the misguided things people do to one another.

At this time of the year, a month shy of spring, the land looks barren. Brown fields. The ever-present gray sky. Travis pulls down the long dirt road to the Sokolov farm, scratching up his cruiser on the overgrowth of pricker bushes. The car rocks and shimmies over mud puddles. He parks near the house and gets out and looks around. The place looks desolate, but then two dogs roam over to say hello, sniffing his trousers, their tails whacking his legs. You smelling Ernie and Herman? he says, petting one and then the other. They run off when a tractor pulls into the barn. A minute later, Bram Sokolov emerges from the dark bay, a tall man in work clothes and muddy boots, not the genteel farmer he was expecting. Hello, there, Sheriff Lawton.

Mr. Sokolov. Travis shakes the hand of a farmer. Thanks for meeting with me.

Call me Bram.

Over coffee in the kitchen, Bram tells him about his wife's accident. She's in a rehab facility in Albany, he explains. Learning how to walk again.

You all were friends of the Clares, isn't that right?

Bram winces like he's burned his tongue. For a while we were. My wife worked with him. I always got the feeling he had a thing for her. He's sort of an arrogant guy, to tell you the truth. Thinks he can have anything he wants. One night—it was Halloween—there was a faculty party and he tried to seduce her. According to Justine, he was pretty persuasive.

Meaning?

She said he held her down. They were out in this field. She showed me the marks on her wrists. I never spoke to him after that. But he came to the hospital after the accident. My wife was in a coma. He stood there over her bed and I swear—Bram looks at him, his eyes watering—I swear he was smiling.

THEY WERE OUTSIDERS, I guess, June Pratt says, slicing into an angel-food cake she'd made earlier that afternoon. With her small hands she serves him cake and tea and then helps herself. It's a funny name for a cake, isn't it?

Yes, it is.

Do you believe in angels, Travis?

No, ma'am. I don't.

Well, if they ate cake, and I'm sure they do, this is what they'd have.

It's very good.

It's nice to have a little cake in the afternoon, isn't it?

Yes, it sure is.

He asks her again about the night George Clare knocked on her door. My heart was pounding, she says. I just knew he had something to do with it. You just know, don't you? We're no different than animals. We have a built-in instinct for sensing danger, don't you think?

Yes, I believe that's true. Only we don't always act on it. And that's when we get in trouble.

She nods, considering. I always thought there was something odd about them. We weren't the best of neighbors, I'll admit that. I didn't go out of my way. But after what happened to the Hales I had a hard time even walking down there. Plus, it rubbed me wrong that they'd gotten the place so cheap. But that's life, isn't it? You just never know.

Yes, ma'am. That's the truth.

Travis gazes across the checkered tablecloth at the woman he'd been in love with when they were high-school kids. She'd been in the cheerleading circle and much more popular than he was. Anyway, he'd met Mary soon after. It had all worked out just like it was supposed to, he guessed.

They seemed friendly enough. June sips her tea and sets the cup down soundlessly on her saucer. That little girl, she was always dressed up so cute. I feel so awful for that little girl, don't you?

Yes, I do.

More tea, Travis?

No, thanks.

She came by once, the wife. Said she was in the middle of cooking something and didn't have enough sugar and could I loan her some, so of course I asked her in and after a little while, as I was measuring out the sugar, she said there was a stink in her house she couldn't get rid of. I asked what it smelled like and she said it was kind of like urine and she couldn't get it out no matter what, and so I told her to wash down her floors with vinegar and she said she'd try that and then she started crying. I asked what was wrong, but she just shook her head and said it was nothing, she was just having a bad day. I've had a few myself, I told her, and then she took the sugar and left. I don't know what else you can say to someone like that, do you?

HE HAS his secretary call down to the Clare household in Connecticut to request an interview with George, but the call isn't returned. He gets through to Catherine's mother, who cries for a good ten minutes, until her husband grabs the receiver and tells him to let them mourn their daughter in peace. He sends some men down to Connecticut in hopes of getting inside the Clares' home, but they're turned away and the door is closed in their faces.

Two weeks into the investigation, a criminal defense attorney named Todd Howell contacts Travis on behalf of George Clare and lays out a list of requirements that they'll have to agree to if they want to talk to his client, one of which stipulates that Howell himself must be present at any interview with the police. Which basically means that any question asked of Clare would be met with the same reply: I don't recall. After a little research, Travis gets the goods on Howell—a partner at some splashy New York City firm famous for high-profile cases and getting people off.

During a televised press conference, when asked if George Clare will be issued a subpoena to testify before a grand jury, Perry Roscoe, head of the district attorney's homicide bureau, announces that they have no such plans. In New York State, he explains, a subpoena would grant Clare immunity from prosecution unless he waived that right, which would be unlikely.

We've decided not to do that, Roscoe says, then spells it out: We're not prepared to give Mr. Clare immunity in this case.

II

HE SAID he could be himself with her. He didn't have to pretend. That was hard for him, pretending all the time. He'd lean back on the pillow and smoke with this distant, melancholy look on his face, lying there in his bigness, all length and angles, with his legs open and his penis sleeping. The last time they had sex, she cried a little and told him it was over, that they couldn't go on like this, it was destroying her, and he just shook his head and smiled and said, I don't know why you insist on stopping. You seem to enjoy what we do.

Well, I don't.

That's not the impression I get. You just won't admit it.

I just said I don't, and I mean it.

She turned away to grab her clothes but he pulled her back, hard.

You pulling away like this just makes me want you more.

He held her down; he was a cannibal, eating her, biting and prodding, consuming her.

He told her she'd conjured the monster inside him. This is your doing, he said. He made it all her fault.

HIS WIFE WORE Chanel N° 5, same as her dad's girlfriend, but Portia was racy and wore high boots and short skirts and had this curly red hair she'd tie up in scarves. Portia was a real New Yorker and Catherine Clare was a hick from upstate. My wife is from modest circumstances, was how George put it. Her getting a full scholarship to college was a big deal. She'd done better than him in school. That doesn't mean smarter, he was quick to point out, then admitted, as if being generous, that his wife could have done much more with her life if he hadn't gotten her pregnant. *Things sort of changed when we got married.*

Weirdly, Willis admired her for sticking it out with him for the sake of their kid. Her parents hadn't done that. You had to admire a person who could make a decision even if it was for somebody else's benefit, unlike her own mother, who couldn't make decisions about anything and would stew over certain choices, only to change her mind at the last minute, even if it was something dumb like taking a pottery class.

Back home, when her parents were still together, her father usually slept in his study when he was working on a case. Often, very late at night, she'd hear the sound of the cassette player, her father listening to his clients' statements as he prepared his arguments. They were her strange little bedtime stories. The voices of the bad people, she often thought, putting her to sleep at night.

There were things she noticed about these statements, how they spoke and the stories they told. There were certain consistencies. Phrases repeated. Particular manners of speech.

Her father had told her that a true sociopath has the ability to convince himself that he's innocent. So everything that comes out of his mouth rings true to him, and usually to everyone else. They separate themselves from the event. Like they'd never been there. Like it never even happened.

They get so good at it they can pass a lie-detector test, her father had said.

Although those results weren't admissible in their state anyway, it still made the prosecutors uneasy—a soft spot in an otherwise muscular case.

These people—people like George—were predatory. They had skills of perception that regular people lacked. Maybe because, unlike most people, they knew what they needed and weren't afraid to admit it. Survival skills. So they could go out and do it again.

THESE MORNINGS IN San Francisco, she goes to the library to keep up with the case, to know where he is, to work on feeling safe. She reads the articles on microfiche and every day there's something new. Not just details of the investigation, but things about George and Franny. They were living with his parents. He was working for his father in one of the furniture stores. There was a quote of him saying, *Parenting was kind of my wife's job before and now it's mine. It's something I think I owe her.*

She wonders bitterly what Catherine would think of his assertion that mothering had been *kind of* her job and that he *thinks* he owes her, as if he's not really sure. And why does he owe her in the first place? What does he owe her *for*?

His tentative sentiment gives her the chills.

Sickened, she almost doesn't finish the article, but then something at the bottom catches her eye, a surname she recognizes. Hers.

On impulse, she goes outside and finds a newsstand and gets some quarters to make the call from a phone booth on the corner. She knows her father's office number by heart and dials it now, determined to warn him about George Clare and tell him what she knows. Taking his case was a mistake—a travesty. But when the switchboard picks up she's promptly put on hold and kept waiting and waiting, and in these moments of concentrated anticipation she is gripped with a sense of terror as a realization takes shape in her mind.

Good afternoon, Todd Howell's office, a woman says. Hello? Is anyone on the line?

She hangs up.

Tears fill her eyes with such force that she's momentarily blinded as the full picture of what George has done finally sinks in.

She was just some girl, she imagines him telling her father. Some girl from the inn. For him it was a regrettable fling—but the girl became obsessed and wanted him to leave his wife, his child. A real mess. A girl with problems, serious issues. She'd flunked out of school. Once, she even tried to jump off a building. He'd tried to end it but she simply wouldn't let go. Her father would only have to establish that this unstable, pathetic wreck of a girl might have, in a jealous rage, done this awful thing to poor innocent Catherine. Worse, once her father discovered it was *her,* should that regrettable disclosure come to pass, he'd be obligated to hand the case over to one of his partners. Even if she revealed all the sick and fucked-up things about George, they could, based on her psychiatric history, easily persuade a jury that she was making it up. They'd call in her shrink as an expert witness, who'd expose her mother's gayness, her father's girlfriend—it would be downright ugly. Even with no real evidence against her, their job would be done and George would seem as guileless as a choirboy.

A week later, she's wiping down the counter when a man comes into the restaurant. He sits down and drinks a cup of coffee and orders a piece of pie with a slice of cheese on top. She's seen his type before, hanging around her father's office, only this guy's even sleazier. Thank you, Willis, he says pointedly, and walks out. She's thrown a minute until she remembers her name tag. He's left his money on the counter, no tip but something else, a manila envelope bound with a red string. It's slow, so she asks for a break and goes outside, lights a cigarette, sits down on the old metal chair, opens the envelope and slides out the photographs. They're of her and George having sex, and show a lot. There's a note attached in George's twiggy handwriting: *Don't make me send these to Daddy,* is all it says.

12

SHE GETS MOODY, distracted. Burns her poetry in the kitchen sink. Works from noon to closing at the restaurant and comes home stinking of fried fish and grease, slippery with sweat. He has to do everything, play in the band, fix the meals, haul their dirty clothes down to the Laundromat. She hardly talks to him, just skulks around the apartment holding a drink and pushes him away in bed.

What's wrong with you?

Nothing.

Then, lying in bed one night under the fluid shadows of passing trolleys, she tells him about George Clare. I got caught up in something, she says. I couldn't get out of it. He had this power over me.

He tries to listen carefully, to be open to her, but her confession only makes him angry. He turns away from her.

She presses her naked body against his back and cries. I'm better now, she tells him. I'm over it.

You lied, he says in the darkness.

I know, I'm sorry. I was afraid. I hated myself.

That's not why.

I don't know why, she says. I honestly don't.

He turns to look at her, her wet, dark eyes, her lips, and suddenly feels nothing.

I'm moving back to L.A., she tells him. I'm going back to school. They said I can come back if I do an extra semester.

That's good. You should.

What about you?

I'm sure I'll think of something.

When will you hear from Berklee?

Soon, he says. May, I think.

Will you go? If you get in, I mean.

He nods. I have to see.

Boston's nice. I want to go to law school there. I want to study law, she blurts. To put people like him away.

You'll make a good lawyer, he says, and means it.

You're going to be famous.

I don't care about that. I just want to play.

He sits up on the side of the bed and lights a cigarette. He doesn't want her to see his face.

She puts her hand on his back. I'm sorry, Eddy. I never meant to hurt you.

People always say that.

But I really mean it.

You broke my heart. Just so you know.

It's not broken, she says. It's broken in.

He looks at her and she smiles in that crooked way of hers and suddenly being mad seems pointless. She's just a girl trying to grow up, he thinks. He still loves her, always will. He holds her in his arms and they lie awake all night long, listening to the songs of the city, the walls alive with shadows, knowing that, come morning, she'll be gone.

A Scholarly Temperament

AT FIRST there's the continual assault of cameras, the abrupt contortions on strangers' faces when they realize who he is. He rarely leaves the house. He spends whole days up in his room, staring out at the Sound. He feels trapped inside the wrong life, where even escape offers no peace, no deliverance.

In May, he gets the interview. The woman's name is Sara Arnell. They have lunch in the student union, in an area with white tablecloths designated for faculty. She seems young to run the department, he thinks, and refreshingly unassuming. She tells him she's an ex-nun. He can see this history in her wan, hermetic face, her muscular calves, her peasant hands. A genuine do-gooder, she'd been a missionary for years in Africa.

I went where I was needed. I did what I could. I suppose, when it comes to people in trouble, I'm too easily persuaded to help.

He only looks at her.

Charitable acts, she clarifies. They're my weakness.

A kindred spirit, he thinks.

After lunch she looks again at his CV, as if to remind herself of his credentials. You're clearly overqualified. Compared with Saginaw, our students are, well, let's say, variously equipped. We get people of all ages here, all backgrounds.

Tell me, she says gently. What made you leave Saginaw?

My wife, he says. He looks off toward the busy street, the blur of afternoon traffic. She died unexpectedly. It was a tragedy. He meets her hazel eyes; she has the face of St. Thérèse.

She frowns with compassion. I'm sorry for your loss.

I appreciate that, Sara.

She watches him, considering, then seems to decide something. We have an opening for a visiting lecturer in the fall. But I'll warn you, we don't pay much. This is a community college. Things are a bit different around here.

As I said, I'm eager to get back to work.

Well, then, consider yourself hired.

They shake hands and she says she'll be in touch. As he is leaving the student union, it occurs to him how good it is to be back on a campus, with its structure and energy. The bright, earnest faces of the students. Their faith in the possibility of a better world. He has truly missed it.

Heading back to his car, walking the long black path to the acre-sized parking lot, he is stirred by a bitter nostalgia and almost weeps.

LATER, at dinner, he tells his parents the news. They are old now, burdened. This thing with him has taken its toll. Perhaps it is inevitable that they should feel such guilt. Now it is death they fear most. Everything has changed—even the food on the table lacks flavor. They chew for the sake of swallowing and are glad for their cigarettes at the end of the meal. The taste of death, at least, is honest.

When do you start? his father says.

Right after they'd moved in, his father had put him to work at the store. It was, George knew, a gesture of good faith, his father showing George—and the rest of the community—that he trusted him. Mornings, they rode in together. George knew it was somewhat embarrassing for him—the other employees' awkwardness, the slight elevation of their voices, their patronizing appeals for his favor. *You can have this seat,* or *No, it's all yours, I was just leaving!*

Of course, he and his father didn't discuss it. They tried to pretend everything was the same.

His mother looked after Franny, which was less than ideal. She had the patience of a mosquito, her reactions often startling Franny into tears. With him it's her suspicion, her disdain. She lurks in his presence, following him around the house. She goes through his things when he's out. Searches his pockets when she does his wash, laying out the coins, matchbooks, toothpicks she finds like evidence, souvenirs of deception.

Working summers back in high school, overseeing the showroom floor, he'd wander through the designer rooms when it was slow. Urban Oasis was his favorite: two black leather couches, a glass coffee table, a hifi stereo cabinet. He would sit there dreaming up a life in that scenario, the music he'd play, the women writhing on the leather cushions in G-strings.

As it turned out, retail did not come naturally to George. His father would just look at him: *Can you possibly be this stupid?* They'd been bowled over when he got into Williams. It was the tennis, they all knew—not his intelligence. As an undergraduate, he was reclusive and unexceptional. With the deliberate finesse of a cardsharp, his art-history professor told him that he lacked a scholarly temperament and should consider another career. In defiance, perhaps, he went on to graduate school and suffered through his dissertation, attempting to disprove another devoted critic, the notorious asshole Warren Shelby. None of it had actually made a difference. He'd ended up teaching at a second-rate college.

Life is full of surprises, that's for sure, his mother concluded one night, sitting at the kitchen table with her drink and cigarette, ruminating over her spoiled life. Who would've guessed we'd have come to this?

He is not to be trusted, that's what people think. Even the checker at the market, how she avoids his eyes. The librarian. The frigging gas-station attendant. After a few months at the store, his father had to sit him down. People don't want you showing them around, he told him. It's just not working out, son.

He understood, of course he did.

You know how people are, his father said. Suspicion is more than enough for them. They don't need to know for sure.

The Free Wind

NOTHING STAYED the same in this town after they left.

The house just sat there. Year after year, the paint Eddy Hale had so carefully applied peeled away. The clapboards went wobbly, the porch floor buckled. Lilacs pressed up against the windows, gangly and fragrant as streetwalkers. The lawn sprawled with weeds. Occasionally, she'd drive over just to see the place, and would gaze up at those awful black windows, imagining that poor woman looking down at her.

The people of this town were hard on Travis. Never forgave him. But he stayed with it, waiting for George Clare to slip up and tracking his whereabouts from a telescopic distance, as though he was a calamitous weather system whose onslaught no one could survive. He was living in Branford, Connecticut, in an apartment complex near the water, and working at a community college. Travis even knew about the women he found, and there were always women. Mostly of a certain type, coaxed out of bars and into cheap motels.

As convinced as Travis was of Clare's guilt, there was never enough hard evidence to indict him. Her husband's certainty was frustrated by the powerful protections of the law and it flat wore him out. You can't convince a jury without evidence, he would say, shaking his head. I got nothing but hearsay.

She watched his face shut down like the circuits were being pulled one by one by one—the bad things he saw in people, the bad things they did, the criminals he couldn't stop, the people he hadn't saved. He thought of

Catherine Clare daily, and at night he'd lie awake thinking about her, too. Every February, on the anniversary of the murder, he'd pull out that old file and go through it all over again. There must be something here, he'd say. Something I missed.

It doesn't matter anymore.

It does to me. I guess I'm the only one.

It's not your fault.

Oh, but it is. I take full responsibility.

Always the same conversation. The same flat-footed defeat. His presumed failure had built a prison around him. Nobody could come in. Not even her.

Eventually, he stopped trying. Years went by and she witnessed his dedicated transformation, a self-induced oblivion of saturated fats, cigarettes and Wild Turkey. He'd come home from work and plow into bed. His cigarette would wake her in the morning. Their relationship got whittled down to perfunctory remarks in passing, things like who was going to pick up the milk. Weekends, he'd spend all his time at the firing range, practicing, then come home and start drinking and pass out on the couch, watching reruns of *All in the Family*.

FIVE YEARS AFTER the murder, on a warm summer evening, Mary got a call at her office. The voice on the other end sounded familiar, but at first she couldn't place it. Hello, Mary, he said. And then it came to her. It was George Clare.

Her taking the listing had been the last straw for Travis—the thing that did them in.

I don't see how you can do anything for that man, he said.

I'm not doing it for him. I'm doing it for Franny.

She probably doesn't even remember her.

You don't forget your own mother, I don't care what you say.

The argument escalated into an emasculating treatise on money and the lack thereof and how much good the commission, any commission, would do them.

It's just another house, she told him.

No, it is *not* just another house. That's when he left the room.

Despite her considerable efforts, the house never sold. Every time she showed it she got the same feeling in her bones, a deep, rattling chill, as if someone had opened up her head and poured in a pitcher of ice water. Each year, around Thanksgiving, inspired by a bitter nostalgia, she'd advertise the place in *Antique Homes*. Shouldered by all those pretty autumn leaves, with mums and pumpkins on the front porch, the house almost looked inviting. There were the sugar-white barns, the sun glinting off the windows of the cupola, the old copper weathervane. The ad always brought in calls. At first her clients always seemed interested, taking in the land and the pond and the barns, just as the Clares had done, but once they wandered through the suffocating gloom of the darkened rooms they'd hurry back outside.

The day after they took their son to college, Travis came into the kitchen before work with a sheepish, grave smile. I have something to say to you.

She stood at the stove, making his breakfast. Just a moment, she said. He liked his eggs runny, but something about his tone made her stay at the stove a little longer. He sat down at the table with his coffee and unfolded the newspaper. He was in no hurry. I'm showing the Hale house today, she told him.

Travis grunted. You're wasting your time.

You never know. I've got a feeling about this one.

He grunted again. You and your feelings.

Spurned by the comment, her eyes went prickly. She shuffled his eggs onto a plate and brought them to the table. You had something to tell me?

You cooked these too long. He ate them anyway, then pushed the plate away, finished his coffee and set the cup down.

Travis?

He looked at her dispassionately. I want a divorce.

She was angry with him, but more out of surprise than anything else. Why leave her now? They hadn't been unhappy. She hadn't been discontented. She was a good wife, a good mother. She had done it all—mothered, tended, protected, washed and cooked and administered medicine and read to them and nurtured their minds, bodies and souls—because she loved him. It was the kind of love only women had, an idea that had sprouted the moment they were born, when their mothers, and occasionally their fathers, held them in their arms. When they'd met, he was there to complete her; it was his duty, his assignment. He, Travis

Lawton, in his RPI jacket, represented the rest of her life. A *real* man. Strong, handsome, educated, an amalgamation of all the right adjectives. The rugged, courageous, even heroic sort they used in the cigarette ads. He was a cop. Her mother, Irish, poor, a round-shouldered woman in a crocheted shawl, making soups, boiled sausage and black pudding in her row house in Troy—she'd married for her. Suddenly, she finally understood that. Her whole life a blur, and now, all at once, she was old. She had suffered—oh, yes, she certainly had. And now she was suffering the consequences.

Here was the reckoning. First at church, whispering to Jesus. Whom she adored, even though He had not been fair or faithful to her. He hadn't. What peace had *He* returned?

She had swallowed his body, whispered Hail Marys, and *Forgive me, Father, for I have sinned,* a million times, and what had she done? How had she sinned?

She hadn't sinned. She'd been good.

In actual truth, she'd been grateful to Travis for marrying her—a gratitude her mother had instilled—and for staying with her all these years, always feeling, or perhaps being reminded, that she was the weaker end of the bargain. Well, she had her good points, built durably, unafraid of using her hands, an admirable cook, a patient, nurturing mother, but she admitted she had her issues, her weight, shaped like a goblet with pretty legs, top-heavy, the first place people's eyes always went, even the women, and then her moods, the persistent tease of depression, not that she'd ever called it that. Disoriented by menopause—yet not defeated. Somewhere down the line she'd lost sight of her old self. Her old self had deserted her. Routine was her friend, her reliable mate. There was the early walk up the hill in the half-sunlight with Ernie and Herman, then the walk back down again with the sun on her back. The black pond. The wet field. The pudding-thick earth sucking at the boots she'd kick off and leave on the stone. The old bell knocking in the wind. The silent house. Then breakfast, two eggs, dry toast, a cup of tea. Time and again she'd started Weight Watchers. The quiet of the small kitchen, the window. The pasture in early spring.

She had started out as one thing, a cop's wife, and had turned into another, a cop's ex-wife.

People didn't know her. Not the real her. Just the lady who sold houses.

She was like some billboard they recognized and thought about in terms of what she could do for them, but nobody really *knew* her. She wondered if she did herself.

You got comfortable the way you were. Good, bad or ugly. And the years went by.

She goes to the market in her heavy coat. Like a big walrus. Or maybe a sea lion. With a few spiky hairs under her chin. She tugs on them when she's nervous, sometimes in church, when Father Geary cajoles the good out of her.

Lately, some festering internal confusion, like her brain's been marinating in Vaseline. You know things are bad when a trip to the supermarket's your day's main outing. Meandering under the relentless yellow lights of Hack's, wandering the aisles without really needing anything, just lured along by the music: *Ventura Highway in the sunshine* . . .

She tries not to look at anyone. They don't look at her, either. Sometimes one or two do. Burnouts. Crusty guys in plaid farm coats, their pockets jammed with cigarette packs. She's let her hair go, maybe in defiance. It's a wild silver now. Used to be she was careful. Not anymore. So what if she doesn't brush it. Who's looking? The weight like monkeys on her hips, her blousy fat-lady arms, all of her rocking through life like an old tugboat. She keeps her coat zipped, her hood up, burrowing inside it like a little mole.

Late fall, she finally sells the place. A couple from the city, drunk on Wall Street. Their daughter rides horses, shows. The wife fell in love with the land. The husband only so-so, but it's a second marriage; he wants her to be happy, though he would rather be out in the Hamptons.

She doesn't tell them about the murder. Something she could be sued for, she knows, if they find out, but she doesn't care.

Over tea one afternoon in Father Geary's office in the rectory, she confesses to this omission. He only listens, offers no comment, and she imagines that he secretly is pleased. In any case, he doesn't seem to judge her for it. She wonders how he manages celibacy. She would like to ask him, but of course she can't. She would like to ask why it's even necessary to require it of people of the cloth. She, too, is celibate, though for different, more pathetic reasons.

You never get used to living alone. That's a fact. It's become who she is, that woman you'll see every now and then, walking alone down the road or through the woods. She is known for her solitude. Maybe even admired for it.

Now, let's talk about something important, Father Geary says, pouring more tea. Why don't you tell me about Alice.

TRAVIS HAD BEEN gone almost a year when she was awakened one winter night by the sound of a car, the scary thumping bass of its stereo.

She lay there in the dark, rigid, just listening, then heard those unmistakable footsteps. The same feet that wore Mary Janes to church, to birthday parties with all the children from St. Anthony's. And then knocking on the door. Stealing herself, she put on her robe and went downstairs, shaking. Looked out the window and saw the yellow strands of her daughter's hair. No coat, short sleeves, Alice shivering on the doorstep, her skinny, child's body—even at twenty-six—bouncing around like she used to when she had to use the bathroom. It wasn't difficult to assume she was on something. It had snowed earlier, and the whole world sparkled under the moon.

Mary opened the door. Who's that in the car?

Just a friend.

What do you want?

Can I come in? Her face broke a little, the same child's face, a girl who'd ridden horses and taken spelling tests and indulged in daydreams.

Mary let her in. What about him?

He can wait.

Who is he?

No one special.

She stood there trembling and it occurred to Mary how small she looked, how pale. Where's your coat?

Alice jutted her head toward the car.

Do you want to eat?

I need to go pee.

In a hurried skip she darted into the powder room, and Mary just waited, shaking, wanting to let go, to cry. Afraid that maybe she was dreaming this. Terrified she'd wake up.

Her bare feet were cold. She pulled on a pair of old socks and stood there in her bathrobe, conscious of the pulsating beat coming from the car.

She went to the window and looked out. It was a big car—a sedan—and she could see the glow of a cigarette and the black exhaust dirtying the snow.

It came to Mary that Alice was not aware that Travis had left her, that she was alone in the house. She knocked on the bathroom door. Are you all right in there?

No answer.

A mother never loses her right to intrude on her child, she thought, even when they're fully grown and infested with poison, and opened the door, bracing herself for whatever she might find. Hon?

Alice heaved over the toilet. I'm sick.

I can see that, Mary said harshly.

Just let me be. I'll be all right.

What about him?

Get rid of him. Alice looked up, on her knees on the bathroom floor, her eyes brimming with tears. Can you do that for me?

Mary studied her daughter and could see the years on her. I'll try.

Get Dad.

He's not here.

Alice shook her head, too sick to talk, and waved her off.

Mary went up to the bedroom and opened the closet and found the shoebox in which she stored the gun, a small pistol. Travis had given it to her for her fortieth birthday and she hadn't taken it out since. It was loaded.

She went back downstairs and put on her boots, feeling a thrumming in her chest, a quiet rage coming up her throat. She pulled on her coat and hat and opened the door and walked down the brick pavers and pounded on the front window with her gloved hand. The windows were as fogged up as if the car was full of clouds.

The window came down and the driver, a black man in his forties, leaned over to see who she was.

You can go now, Mary said. Alice is staying home.

That right?

Yes. Go away.

The man chuckled. He turned off the engine, then got out. His body stretched up tall and he moved with the same showy bravado as the bears that occasionally played with her trash cans.

She's sick.

Oh, yeah, she's sick all right.

My husband, she blurted, he's a cop.

The man stood there. You know what? You can have her. She ain't worth it.

Mary shook her head. Is she on drugs?

Naw, she just high on life.

He got back into the car and turned up the radio so loud that she could feel the sound throttling her legs, her back, her fingertips. He waited a long while, maybe five or six minutes, two whole songs' worth, then finally pulled away.

Aware of the gun in her pocket, she watched the car creep to the end of the road. Slowly, it turned onto the paved road and disappeared into the night.

Mary waited for a moment. She almost didn't want to go inside, fearing she couldn't deal with it. But she pushed herself, climbed the steps and opened the door, smelling the potato she'd baked for supper—and her life, her stupid little life. The bathroom door was ajar, the light off. Kind of afraid, she ventured into the kitchen.

Her daughter was sitting at the table, eating a bowl of cereal.

You might as well know, she said, I'm pregnant.

Where've you been all these years?

Around, she said. New Jersey. Newark.

Why didn't you ever call me?

Alice sighed and shoved away her bowl. I don't know. Because I thought you'd hang up.

That's not true and you know it.

I know I screwed up. Alice gazed at her tenderly. I can't erase all that.

Mary swallowed. Look, she said. Your father's gone. He left me. I don't have much.

What happened?

I don't want to talk about it.

Alice nodded and looked down at her hands. Just for a little while, okay?

I imagine you could use some sleep.

She nodded.

Are you on something?

She shook her head.

How long?

She doesn't answer. Please, she says.

All right, then.

Alice stood up, giving Mary a glimpse of her small belly, and came over to her. Thanks, Mommy, she said, and kissed her on the cheek. Then she climbed the stairs to her old room and closed the door.

Mary stood in the kitchen, hearing the dripping faucet, the electricity running through the refrigerator. Her daughter's bowl was on the table, empty now. At least she'd eaten a little something. Mary took the dish and washed it unhurriedly, remembering everything, then set it in the rack and went up to bed.

Part 5

Invasive Procedures

Syracuse, New York, 2004

I

FRANNY CLARE IS in the third year of her surgical residency when it occurs to her that the work has become unbearable. She experiences this revelation during a lung resection, assisting the surgeon with the procedure, her movements fastidious, precise. It's a city hospital, a cumbersome mecca of suffering. There are wings and corridors, countless beds, endless days and nights when she surrenders to a kind of terminal abeyance. Sometimes, moving from one bedside to another under the eerie, otherworldly fluorescence, she feels an inexplicable sense of loss. What had first attracted her to medicine—biology, physiology, healing the sick— now quite distinctly fills her with dread. Unlike the other residents, who glide through the corridors like white-coated warriors, sucking up to the attendings, Franny feels unhinged, disconnected, bereft. Like someone who has been banished, she thinks. Like some Kafkaesque nightmare. The hospital with its annexes and ramps. Strategically placed crucifixes. Billowing smokestacks. The city cold and gray under hovering clouds.

She walks home on sidewalks, swaddled in wool, her satchel swinging, the same faces coming and going. Nurses, young doctors, orderlies. They pass one another without acknowledgment. Her life is only this: work and after work.

She lives in a yellow brick tenement built in the 1940s, with slow elevators and narrow, odorous hallways, in an efficiency apartment with leaky faucets and mice, rusty crank windows. In the courtyard, old Russians in overcoats feed pigeons or play checkers. Young mothers on cell phones, indifferent to their children's histrionics. As in the countless dorm rooms of her youth, the walls are bare. There is nothing distinct or revealing. She tolerates the hours, eager for disruptions—the vodka in her freezer, the reeling scandal of a passing ambulance, the drunken busboys shooting craps in the alley, her bickering neighbors, the babies always crying.

Her lover visits occasionally, a married vascular surgeon with three kids, his wife a cellist with the local symphony. Like most surgeons, he is arrogant, temperamental, surprisingly sensitive. Aside from a shopworn sort of comfort when she lies in his arms, she resents their strange closeness. Like most of the attendings, he lives a good distance from the hospital. Once, last summer, when his wife had taken the kids to their cottage on Canandaigua Lake, they drove to his house, an English Tudor in the suburbs, in his black Saab, the back seat cluttered with picture books. They pulled into the driveway and she watched the garage door rise like the curtain at a play. They walked through the garage—the servants' entrance, he'd joked, cluttered with sleds and bicycles and monogrammed golf bags—and had sex on his kitchen floor, near the cat bowls, while his children, pinned under magnets on the refrigerator door, grinned down at them with the glee of spectators.

Her pager wakes her and it's a number she doesn't recognize, an outside area code. Disoriented, she looks at the clock: four in the afternoon. The sky a crumpled white, like an idea that can't be rescued. She pulls a blanket around her and looks in the refrigerator. A limp carrot, a bottle of tomato juice. Again her pager vibrates. When she calls the number, a woman identifies herself as Mary Lawton, a name Franny vaguely remembers, someone from her father's past. I knew you when you were little, she says.

I don't remember.

Of course you don't. The woman explains that she's a realtor from Chosen, the strange little town where her parents once lived. We've finally sold the farm, she says. It only took me a quarter century. I believe I've earned my commission.

Franny laughs abruptly and a pair of pigeons on her window ledge drop down like torpedoes into the courtyard. That's funny, she says. That's a long time.

In the beginning, after the murder, her father had hired a special cleaning service and decorators, but except for some random renters, the house has been empty for all these years, since the day he took her away from there. Fragments of that morning sometimes come back to her like the insult of a disrupted dream: the grieving house as they pulled away, the terrible darkness of her mother's room.

Congratulations, Franny says dully. She doesn't really want to hear about the place. Not my problem, she thinks.

Here's the reason I'm calling, Mary says quickly, as if detecting her lack of interest. Somebody needs to go in there and clean it out. From what I've heard, I don't imagine your father is up to it?

No, Franny says. I don't think he could manage that. Her father, a diabetic with severely diminished vision, no longer can drive. The last time she saw him—Christmas—he'd moved into an assisted-living facility in Hartford, and she'd gone down to help him unpack. They sat in his room, listening to opera on the radio—*Tosca,* she remembers now—while the snow drifted down. They're teaching me Braille, he told her. Preparing me for total darkness. It won't be long now.

Then he took her hand, alarming her, and ran her fingertips over the Braille pages of his book. It felt strange, sitting there with their hands together. For an instant she closed her eyes, feeling words under her fingertips like grains of sand. Everything's different now, he said. I'm trying to get used to it.

I could hire somebody, but I thought you might want to go through your mother's things. Mary Lawton pauses meaningfully. I just wanted to check with you first.

Of course her father hadn't called. It doesn't surprise her; they'd never spoken about the house in Chosen. My father's going blind, she tells Mary, almost protectively.

Yes, I know. That's why I . . .

She goes on but Franny isn't listening. In her head she sees the old place, shapes of bright white and agony, the cold, watery rush of an open window. A place that is waiting.

I'll come, she interrupts the woman. I'd like to do that.

They talk for a few minutes more, making their plans. Hanging up, Franny feels strangely excited, almost grateful for the excuse to return—as if nothing of importance ever happened there, as if that awful house isn't the root of all her unhappiness.

I NEED SOME TIME, she tells Dr. Patel, head of the surgery program. I need to take a leave of absence.

A surgeon from Pakistan with grim, impatient eyes, he folds his arms across his chest and shakes his head. I'm afraid that's impossible.

She suddenly begins to cry. She doesn't know why, whether it's for her long-dead mother or because she's decided she can't live like this anymore. He watches for a moment, then hands her a box of tissues and waits for her to collect herself.

It's a family problem. I'm sorry, it can't be ignored.

How long will this problem persist?

A few weeks, she says.

You are a fine doctor, he says, studying her carefully, stroking his goatee. A contender for chief resident when the time comes.

She looks at him, confused by this impossible truth.

You will be missed. He flashes a quick smile and stands up. Go, then. He flaps his hand, as if he can't stand the sight of her, then adds, wryly, You have my blessing.

She finds her guilty lover in the green corridor outside the OR. He has just come from surgery, his hair matted with sweat. It's how he looks after sex, his face damp and flushed. I'm leaving, she says, relishing his surprise. Something's come up, a family problem. I don't want to go into it.

Always so mysterious. He smiles, amused. Can I see you later?

I don't know.

I understand, he says, taking her hand and kissing it.

She looks at him, at his sharp little mouth. Probably not a good idea.

But he comes anyway, to say goodbye. It is early evening, the sky soot-gray, drizzling. As they embrace, she imagines his trim, ponytailed wife doing homework with the kids in the kitchen. She thinks of his dinner going cold.

Wickedly, she has dressed for the occasion in old scrubs and a T-shirt, her hair twisted into a messy knot. She wants to look as ugly as possible so he won't want to make love to her. But he doesn't seem to notice. Their work, their tolerance for unpleasantness, what they see every day, the transformation of the body in the grip of disease. Afterward, they lie on her futon in the half-dark, listening to the rain.

What are you thinking? he says. He always asks her this, as if she's withholding something, or he regrets he can't see inside her head. A surgeon's mentality, she figures, wanting to examine every part of her, every anguished organ.

She sits up and glances at the window, the wet black sky. What am I thinking?

How do you feel? He puts his hand on her back so tenderly that she wants to smack it off.

I don't know how I feel. I feel like shit, she wants to say. I feel ugly, miserable. I hate this life, this work. I feel uncertain, she tells him.

Uncertain?

Yes. I feel—she hesitates—tentative.

What?

Like I'm not really here.

He shakes his head. I don't know what that means.

Vacant, she mutters.

She has been sleeping with him for months. That's long enough. It isn't a smart thing to be doing. I don't like this anymore. I don't like you anymore.

What?

This. You.

Franny.

But she turns away and looks again at the window, at the rising moon.

I have feelings for you, he says.

Keep them to yourself. She gets up and pulls on her sweatshirt, her scrubs. It's cruel, perhaps, she knows, but it's what he likes best about her, her cruelty. You need to go, she says.

She watches him get dressed. Doctor, husband, father. He says nothing. Then walks out the door. Back to his wife and children in the house they share. She imagines him pulling into the garage, entering the kitchen, washing his hands at the sink, his eyes going bright when he sees the woman he really loves. The kids might come down in their pajamas. He'd pick up his daughter and hug her, have a conversation with her teddy bear. It's not that he's a bad man, she thinks. But she's the detour he shouldn't have taken. Now he can't get back.

The small TV blinks with poor reception. In the apartment next door, the husband and wife are celebrating. Perhaps it is someone's birthday. The husband is playing his accordion. Franny lies there listening to it, music suited to a place of simple pleasures and modest extravagances.

In the morning she wakes early, as usual, but instead of putting on her scrubs she wears jeans and a sweatshirt—civilian clothes, she thinks. She packs a small bag and looks around the nearly empty apartment. A strange existence, she realizes, a rented life. She locks the door and takes the slow elevator down in lieu of the stairs. Outside, it is gray and cool, early March. The day hasn't decided what it wants to do yet, the sky pale, colorless, a fog just lifting off the interstate.

She leaves it all behind. Soon the cluttered neighborhoods on either side of the expressway give way to brown fields. She doesn't mind the pretty drive. It is just after noon when she finally exits the interstate and winds into Columbia County, driving through one red brick town after another with their dark storefronts. Chosen is the smallest of them all, and she feels a strange elation as she drives down Main Street, past the country store, the white church, the grassy cemetery with its sprawling trees. She crosses an old metal bridge over the creek—pronounced *krik*, she remembers—and rolls her window down so she can hear the rushing water, the thrumming of the bridge. The clay roads don't exist on any map. There are horses in the fields. The air smells of manure and turned earth and it does something to her insides, something physical, because she remembers it. I'm almost home, she thinks.

She turns into Old Farm Road, a dirt lane cutting through fields. The house waits at the end of it. It's just a white farmhouse, but really there's nothing *just* about it. A house that wants you to look, she thinks. A house that has suffered. She can compare it to some of her patients. Sometimes, even before examining people, she can estimate their status. Everything you need to know written on their faces, in the brightness of their eyes or the tension around their mouths. Not just the body but also the mind and soul, whatever that is. The idea that everyone has one and that one day it goes up to heaven or someplace. She is not preoccupied with death, though occasionally, rarely, she and the other residents discuss it. In their line of work, witnessing death is not uncommon. There is a moment during a code when you just know, even before the equipment confirms it. A kind of warmth in the room—and then it's gone. But the soul, your essence, the thing that defines you, it's not really anything she likes to think about. At some point she'd decided that nurturing this supposedly deep aspect of herself was pure indulgence.

She parks in the driveway and sits a moment, looking at the old place, the long barns off to the side of it. Maybe they're not as big as she remembers. The land seems to cradle the house. The woods behind it, all along the high ridge. The trees look black in the wind. Clouds the color of pearls. You can see history here, she thinks, everywhere you look. You can forget you're living in the present.

The wind thumps against her window as if urging her to move. She gets out, stiff from the drive. The paint is chipped, flakes all around. Some of the clapboards have rotted. Window shades pulled over the glass, torn and bleached with age. The few times her father succeeded in renting it, the tenants always broke the lease and moved out. It isn't something her father discusses with her. He never talks about this place. But Franny has thought about it, trying to travel back inside her brain to that single morning. What comes to her is vague, a smear of yellowed images: a hand in a black glove taking her stuffed bunny, the pleasing grinding of its silver key, the music starting—was it "Clair de Lune"? She's never told anyone.

Years ago she'd considered hiring her own investigator, but then thought better of it. There seemed little point in pursuing it. When she was a child her questions were ignored, and even now, as an adult, they've never been answered. Nobody on her father's side talks about her mother. When she was little, she'd visit her mother's parents, and sometimes her grandmother would cry at meals and have to leave the table. She'd get to sleep in her mother's old room with all of her stuffed animals. There were pictures of her from high school, one or two from college, but none after that. Her grandmother ended up in a nursing home with Alzheimer's, and the few times she'd visited her, her grandmother didn't even know who she was. When she got into med school her grandfather sent her a card with a billfold that held a hundred-dollar bill. She'd put the money in her bank account and saved the card in a scrapbook; it just didn't seem right to throw it out.

The wind comes in gusts. The trees move and go still and move again. The shadows of the trees flash on the windows. One window in particular draws her attention, her parents' old room, and all of a sudden she's consumed with a sadness so deep and bottomless that she can hardly breathe.

A GRAY STATION WAGON COMES up the road, spitting gravel, and pulls up and parks. Hey, there, I'm Mary Lawton. She gets out of the car, wearing an outsized raincoat and mud-splattered boots, wheezing slightly. Unlike Franny, who is agile and slender and has little patience for adornment, this woman is a big woman in body and spirit, with a plate-sized face, coils of necklaces and noisy, jangling bracelets.

Franny Clare, she says, holding out her arms for a hug. It is so good to see you, honey.

Franny tries to relax, unaccustomed to being hugged by strangers—or anyone, for that matter. They break apart and stand there looking at each other.

Lord our God, you are the image of your mother.

I am?

Right here—in the eyes.

Franny has to repress an impulse to touch her face, as if to discover it anew. My father, he never told me that. He never liked talking about her much.

She was a lovely girl, Mary says with an edge to her voice, like she needed to set the record straight. Here, I've got a picture somewhere. She digs around in her bag, retrieves a Polaroid and hands it to her. Here it is, she says.

Franny tries not to seem too eager; there are so few pictures of her mother.

That was the day you all moved in. A beautiful day in August, as I recall.

It's of the three of them, leaning up against an old station wagon. Her parents are standing together, their arms entwined, her father long-haired and professorial in a shabby corduroy jacket and wire-rimmed glasses, her mother in a white shift and kerchief. Beautiful, she thinks, too beautiful for him. She's holding Franny on her hip at age three, in a little red dress, barefoot, squinting at the camera.

You keep that. It's for you.

Carefully, she slides it into her bag. Just now she isn't able to thank her, to say how much it means to her. She knows that if she did she'd begin to cry, which isn't something she wants to do right now, in front of this woman. Later, maybe, when she's alone. Sorry if I seem . . .

Seem what?

It's just—I spend all my time in hospitals.

Wouldn't your mother be proud.

I didn't know her very well.

Of course you didn't. You were little.

It's hard being back. Harder than I thought.

Mary nods. I never had a chance to tell you how sorry I was. I was very fond of your mother. It was a terrible thing that happened—a real tragedy, for all of us. This town hasn't been the same since.

The comment surprises her. It has never once occurred to her that anyone else, much less these strangers, might have been affected by what happened to her mother. Even in Connecticut, nobody ever talks about it.

Coming back here was a mistake, she decides. Not something she really needs, all of a sudden. Not having thought about her mother so very much over the years, she doesn't see the point in doing it now. She entertains the idea of driving straight back to Syracuse, of never coming back to this awful house that took her mother from her, but her cheerless apartment, the bare walls, the empty refrigerator, offers no comfort on the other end.

I don't remember anything, she finally says, and it comes out sounding like an apology.

Of course you don't. It doesn't matter now anyway.

She knows this woman's only trying to make her feel better, but she doesn't agree. Because it does matter, it matters a lot. They never found my mother's killer, she says.

Yes, I know. That's a big disappointment for all of us.

Who did you think it was?

Mary looks away, uncomfortable. I wish I knew, honey.

Somebody does.

Yes. That's true. There's at least one person out there who knows.

It's not fair, she says.

No, you're right. It's not. There's not much that's fair in this life, is there?

They start up the walkway, flat stones overgrown with grass. Franny gazes up at the house. The thought of going inside is suddenly terrifying.

Mary looks at her. Are you sure you want to do this?

Yes. I'm okay. Really. I want to.

All right, then.

They climb the steps onto the front porch and Mary takes out an old-fashioned key.

Who's buying it?

Weekenders. From the city. Horse people.

Do they know?

No, she says. No, they do not. And I don't plan to tell them. I think it's about time we cut this old place a break.

Isn't there some kind of a law?

You know something, honey? I've been following the rules my whole life. I'll tell you what: it hasn't gotten me far. Mary pats her arm. You got to trust me, please. I'm doing this for you. For your mother, too. Can you do that? Can you trust me?

Franny nods.

Good. That's my girl.

They step into the foyer and stand there a moment, taking it in. It's not so bad, she thinks, relieved. The floors are pretty. The light.

They want to redo the whole place, of course. Nobody's ever satisfied, but don't get me started. Anyway, they've got real money, so we're not complaining and they got a very good deal. It's fair and square all the way around.

Franny shudders. It's cold in here.

That dampness is to be expected. We'll get the oil company in. There's this woodstove, which helps. And the fireplace. I'll have some wood delivered this afternoon.

All right. Thank you.

She follows Mary into the living room, which fills with sunlight like it's saying hello.

I never could understand why your father didn't take this piano.

Franny runs her hand over the keys. I think my mother played.

Yes, she did. Sometimes I'd pull up and hear it, Chopin, I think. It happens to be a very nice piano.

It is nice. Franny decides to keep it, but have it moved where? Not her apartment, obviously. She looks around the room. The air is damp and smells of woodsmoke and ash. There's an old couch with a busted cushion that's become home to some mice. With difficulty, she opens a closet, the door stuttering on the uneven floor, and a marble rolls out and comes to a stop at her feet. She picks it up and holds it out for Mary to see, a glass marble with swirls of yellow and copper running through it. It's pretty, isn't it?

Finders, keepers, Mary says.

She puts it in her pocket. Somehow she knows it's hers. She remembers a boy, crouching on the floor and shooting marbles across the room. She remembers his legs mostly, and other sets, too—all boys' legs. She almost recalls they'd made her laugh and wonders if she has ever laughed at all since. Of course she has, she tells herself. She had a perfectly happy childhood.

As you can see, you've got your work cut out for you. I was going to suggest a dumpster.

Okay, she says, suddenly angry that her father never bothered to do it himself. Good idea.

Mary takes a small pad of paper out of her bag and starts making a list. If I don't write it down, it's gone.

No kidding, Franny says, but in fact it was her exacting memory that got her through medical school. And it's why not remembering that day, here with her mother, is all the more frustrating. She and the killer were both *right in this house.*

Her brain must have registered at least an image. It's in there, she knows, it's in her head, she just can't get to it. In college, a girl she'd confided in suggested a hypnotist. Franny refused and, for reasons she couldn't articulate at the time, never spoke to the girl again.

Your mother had great parties in here, Mary says. This room would be jammed with people. They had all kinds of interesting friends. And in that room there—it was your father's study—people would be up all night, talking art, politics, solving the problems of the world, until they staggered out in the morning. Mary shakes her head. People knew how to drink in those days.

The walls of her father's study are a chalky green, lined with empty bookshelves that once, she knew, would've been full of art books. He was teaching then, and writing a book on the Hudson River painters that he never finished.

Once, when she was about five, he took her to the city, to an exhibit at the MoMA. He stood in front of a Rothko for what seemed like forever while she tried to amuse herself. She remembers tugging on his jacket, and when he looked down at her his face was wet with tears.

She doesn't want to think about her father. And certainly not about the room just overhead, where her mother was killed with an ax. She isn't the type to psychoanalyze herself—even during her psych rotation in medical school she'd stuck to the hard evidence rather than succumb to the culture's obsession with subtext—but for the first time it seems obvious that her decision to study medicine and choose the most grueling, alienating specialty was a direct reaction to the fact that she hadn't been able to save her mother, and that the most powerful motivating factor in making those choices was guilt.

You okay? Mary asks softly. Shall we go upstairs?

Yes, let's go.

The stairs are narrow, steep. She remembers her small hand moving up the banister. Breathing heavily, Mary labors up the stairs behind her. On another occasion Franny might suggest a cardiologist, but not today.

You get to be my age, Mary says, stopping to rest on the landing, it's awful. She glances out the window. But I never get tired of these views.

When she was a child here the window had been too high for Franny even on tippy toes, so it's with some degree of accomplishment that she looks out now and helps herself to the expansive view of the barns, the ridge, the distant woods.

Beautiful, isn't it?

Yes, it is, she says, a little sad that she hadn't grown up here. It could have been a good life. Instead of one suburban street after another, each house a version of the others, with rooms that were suitable yet uninspired, anonymous as those in a motel.

They head down the narrow hall. Here the house seems smaller, modest, with just three rooms upstairs: her parents' on the right, the largest room in the house, and hers and another small room on the left. Mary says it was her mother's sewing room, but it might've been a nursery down the road if she'd lived. Franny had been a little kid who'd hoped so much for a sister. Later, her father had remarried, but the new wife didn't want a child of her own. She was an ex-nun, a kind yet elusive woman who insisted that Franny should attend Catholic schools. While other kids were riding bikes or hanging out at the mall, Franny was working in a soup kitchen. Her stepmother, she thinks now, was probably the reason she'd been an A student. Looking back, she understands the marriage was strained; it only lasted a few years.

This was your room, Mary says.

It's smaller than the one in her vague memories, with little pink ponies stenciled on the walls. There was a tenant who had a daughter, Mary explains. There's a twin bed, a small white dresser; otherwise the room is bare. The window, she thinks, the bright light—that's the first thing she recalls. And the enormous white expanse of the door across the hall, pounding on it with her little fists. Had she woken from a nap?

We don't have to go in if you're not ready.

I'm fine, she says. *It's about time.*

The room is dark; the shades pulled. Mary hurries to open them, as if Franny's just another prospective buyer. Even with the daylight it seems dark, she thinks. They stand there taking it in. This is weird, she admits. Hard.

I'm sure it is. Do you remember it any?

Not very well, she says, but that's not entirely true. There was the Persian carpet, the rickety antique headboard that smacked against the wall whenever she jumped on the bed, the bookshelves where her mother kept her books—all poetry, still here, amazingly. She has a hazy memory of taking the books off the shelves and scattering them across the floor like stones on a river. The bed is made up with a spread. There's a dresser and an armoire, both antiques. The wallpaper is faded, and an old wing chair sits by the window, covered in sun-bleached toile.

They stand there looking at the bed. The last time Franny saw her mother, she was right there. She closes her eyes, refusing to picture it. Is that the same—

Heavens, no, Mary says. That's a brand-new bed. The quilt, too—I bought it at Walmart. She wouldn't have approved. Your mother was a purist.

Really?

She liked things that were real, authentic.

Authentic, Franny repeats, intrigued by the idea. Something she's never actually thought about.

After another couple moments Mary says, Why don't we get some fresh air? As if out of habit, she pulls the shades back down, and everything goes soft. The room is like a tomb and they're both glad to leave it, the door closing behind them.

When they're back outside, Mary gets something out of her car, a basket of cookies. I almost forgot. These are for you. Made them this morning.

That was so nice, Mary. Thank you. She gives her a hug.

You look like you could use a cookie or two. I imagine you doctors don't get much time to eat?

We don't have time for much of anything.

You call me, Mary tells her. Anything you need, understand? I'm going to be checking up on you.

I'll be fine, she says, a little embarrassed, not used to people fussing over her.

It's time to put this place behind you, Franny. You're not the only one. We both need to. We'll do it together, all right?

Franny hugs her again, more for Mary's sake than her own, and when they break apart she sees Mary's tears.

Mary shakes her head, flustered. Don't mind me. She blows her nose into a handkerchief and wipes her eyes, annoyed with herself.

Hey, it's okay. I'm used to this kind of thing.

Mary digs around in her purse and takes out a compact and inspects her face in the mirror, wiping the creases around her eyes where her mascara has smeared. For God's sake, look at me.

You look fine.

I used to be somewhat presentable, she says. If you can believe that.

Of course I do. You're presentable now. More than presentable.

I just wish things weren't always so difficult. Don't you?

Franny nods. I don't know why they are.

Maybe God's trying to tell us something. I wish He'd stop sometimes.

He might've given up on us by now, Franny says.

I sure hope not. We need all the help we can get. She walks back to her car and opens the door. Life's hard, that's all there is to it. And this place, this old farm, is a testament to that.

She gets in, starts the engine and rolls down the window. I'll go ahead and order that dumpster and get the Hale boys over here to help you. I guess you don't recognize that name, do you?

Franny shakes her head.

This was the Hale farm back before your folks bought it. Those boys used to look after you. Cole and Eddy? 'Course, Eddy's off in Los Angeles. A trumpet player. I hear he's pretty famous. It's just Cole and poor Wade now.

Huh, I don't remember them, Franny says, though they've been there, inside her head, all this time. Dark, blurry shapes. The sound of that horn.

They've sure had their share. We all have. But Cole, he's done well for himself. Almost every house in this town has his mark on it. It's his eyes, I think, because they're so blue. Women take one look at him and pull out their checkbooks. His little girl has the same blue eyes, just like all the Hales. She and my granddaughter are good friends. It's something, isn't it? Like that expression—what goes around?

Comes around, Franny says, and smiles.

Well, I'll get going. Don't forget, I'm just a phone call away. Even for something small.

Franny watches Mary's car until it disappears down the road. She holds herself tight against the chill in the air. She looks across the empty fields, the barns, the black trees. A mood of isolation.

Then she turns, as though someone has called her name from that window on the second floor, her mother's room.

The shades are up now. The room brimming with light.

SHE DRIVES into town to buy some beer. Not that she likes to drink, it's merely medicinal. She will have to get drunk in order to sleep. On second thought, maybe vodka, her old standby. Given the chance, she might have succumbed to alcohol. There'd been a brief unraveling in boarding school, when she'd been made to see a shrink. In college she figured out how to drink and get A's, but medical school put an end to it. You had to be on every minute. You had to be ready, clear.

The town has a strange, frozen-in-time quality. Driving past the church, she sees a priest opening the gate, a white-haired man in a thick wool scarf who's pulling on his overcoat and talking—consolingly, she imagines—to an old woman in a plastic kerchief there on the sidewalk. It's windy, the treetops moving wildly, battering the sunlight around. There's a small movie theater, a doughnut shop, a café.

The liquor store is at the end of the block. The place is empty, unlit, streaming with dusty sunlight. As she peruses the shelves, a mackerel-colored cat circles her ankles. The large window in front, covered with a see-through yellow shade, makes the street beyond look like an old-fashioned sepia-toned photograph. The man behind the counter coughs and says, Let me know if you need anything, then goes back to scribbling in his ledger. When checking out, she is surprised to see that he's writing a poem, an abacus of words that add up to something. She sees the words *beguile, thrush;* she studies his face as he rings her up.

Next door, at the market, she buys a sandwich and a bag of chips that she eats in the car, stuffing her face, looking through the windshield at the sky. Anonymous, she thinks, a stranger in a strange town. The sky is different here. Something about the clouds, how the sun pushes through.

BACK IN THE KITCHEN, she searches the cabinets, but there are no glasses, only jars. You'll do, she says to an old pickle jar, then fills it halfway and dumps in some ice. The vodka gives her strength to begin the closet, a whole dark world unto itself. A city of toppling boxes. Mostly junk—tattered clothes, round-soled shoes, broken appliances, a prehistoric vacuum. Like treasure, she finds a shoebox full of photographs. As much as this delights her, it's disturbing that they're here. A history left behind, she thinks, partially her own. Her mother's last few months in the world.

How cruel that her father hadn't bothered to take them, had never understood their importance. She deals them out like tarot cards, snapping them down, thinking: This is your past, it can't be helped; this is your future, the only way into the rest of your life.

Brittle, yellow with age, the snapshots are quiltlike patches of a larger story. Most of the pictures are of her, a busy toddler in a sunny house. Playing with wooden spoons, pots and pans, naked save for underpants in the summer grass, a garden of black-eyed Susans behind. Sitting on a baby chair blowing bubbles. Chasing a kitty. Pulling a wooden dog on a string. It does her good to see that she was happy here, loved. She'd never known how to envision this part of her childhood, because her father hadn't bothered to enlighten her.

Who *were* they, she wonders, her parents? Who was Catherine Clare? There are just a few pictures to choose from. Here she is in the garden, in a white sleeveless dress. Here by the fire. Here on the front porch, smoking, a look of knowing in her eyes—of what, exactly, Franny can't be sure. There are pictures of parties, with strangers holding drinks, poised with their cigarettes and dark countenances like writers on book jackets. And here is her father, young and thin in his professor duds, a tweed jacket, argyle socks, penny loafers. Something about him—aloof, indifferent, the expression on his face more like arrogant. The dark eyes, the unsmiling mouth. An ambiguity, she thinks.

Was he really so unhappy?

Maybe she's reading this into it. Or possibly that's her own story about her father, the one she's been making up all along.

LATE IN THE AFTERNOON, a truck with *Hale Brothers* on the doors stops out front. She steps onto the porch, shielding her eyes from the sun.

I got a cord of wood here, the driver calls. Where do you want it?

Around back. I think I saw a shed.

He nods and turns the truck around, then pulls down alongside the house and parks. Another man's in the passenger seat, squinting, motionless. Back inside, she stands at the window and watches the driver go about his business, his plaid coat shifting as he moves back and forth to the shed, tossing armfuls of logs onto the pile. The other guy doesn't get out to help, just sits there looking straight through the windshield.

After an hour, at sundown, the driver comes to the back door, cradling wood in his arms like a baby. I was told to light the stove.

Yes, please, come in.

He walks past in his big coat and she can smell his day: horses, woodsmoke, cigarettes, sweat. He takes off his wool hat, stuffs it in his pocket, wipes his forehead with his sleeve and shakes out his flattened hair. She's already noticed his good looks, and when his blue eyes roam over her she realizes she's still dressed in the old scrubs and her favorite T-shirt from college, her hair in a ratty ponytail. His glance pauses on the vodka bottle next to the pickle jar. Having fun?

Sort of.

Cold in here, ain't it? Let's see if we can't do something about that. He crouches before the stove—pushing in the wood, crumpled newspaper, the match—and it immediately flashes to life, warm and yellow. He closes the door and secures the crank. That should hold you.

Well, thanks.

You bet.

Do I owe you?

She took care of it.

Okay.

He takes her in again. You okay?

She shrugs.

You don't look it.

It's just kind of hard being here, that's all.

Somebody should've burned this place down a long time ago, he says. I grew up in this house. I'm Cole Hale. You don't remember me, do you? I used to babysit you. Back when we were kids. I knew your folks. Your mother was really nice to me.

Slivers of memory come back, a boy in a plaid coat, dirty boots, socks with holes.

He pushes the hair out of his face, more out of habit than necessity. I see you're all grown up now.

So are you.

Yes, ma'am. Only I'm old.

How old's old?

You don't need the gory details.

She did the math in her head. Maybe thirty-nine?

Just about.

That's not old.

It's a whole lot of years, though. They sure go quick. He smiles at her and everything stops.

The jar's got an inch of vodka left and she holds it up. You wouldn't want one of these, would you?

I gotta get him home. He nods toward the truck outside. That's my brother Wade.

Is he okay?

He's been over in Iraq since the invasion. It didn't go too well for him.

That must be hard.

It's worse than that, but he'll be all right. You gonna be okay out here on your own?

I'll be fine.

Fine ain't much good, is it, Franny?

She shakes her head. I think I remember you, she says.

Well, that's good news. I remember you, too.

She stands there waiting for him to hug her, and when he does his arms feel good, strong. For a minute, they hold on to each other, then he puts his hat back on and heads out the door.

2

I've been waiting for you my whole life, he wanted to tell her. But you can't tell anybody that. Anyway, she's probably got someone. Christ, she might even be married, though he hadn't noticed a ring. And her beauty just complicates things. What he knows about beautiful women: they always seem to know it. His ex-wife used to wield her beauty like an AK-47 and never didn't get what she wanted. For a long time he thought that was enough in a marriage, him trying to make her happy. Turned out it wasn't.

Predictably, his brother asks, Was she nice?

Yeah. She was nice, all right.

Pretty?

That, too. Very.

You gonna call her?

Now, why would I do that?

'Cause she's pretty. That's usually a good enough reason.

She's just up here for a couple days.

It don't take long.

Okay, Romeo, I'll keep that in mind.

He pulls into the driveway and gets out and goes around to the other side to roll Wade out of the truck. The new chair is better, worth every penny, but they're both still getting the hang of it. He pushes him up the ramp and gets him in the house. You okay there, Captain?

Oh yeah, I'm right as rain. He shakes his head like it's the dumbest fucking question he's ever been asked.

You want something to eat?

A beer.

What else?

I'm not hungry. Though a beer might taste good.

We've been over this, Wade, you gotta eat.

I sure wish I was, but it ain't likely.

He brings his brother a beer. What's on?

Thanks. Oh, just the usual shit.

I gotta get Lottie. It's my night.

You go on ahead. I'll be fine. Give that sweet little niece of mine a kiss.

There's that leftover chicken, you get hungry.

Already preoccupied with the show, he waves Cole off.

THE LAST TIME he was in that house it was with Patrice, back when they were seventeen.

After the murder, his old house had become a town landmark, and a popular destination on Halloween. Kids would drive down the road past it and sometimes they got out to look in the windows, later claiming they'd seen ghosts and no end of weird stuff.

It was raining that night. He didn't want to take her to Rainer's, and at her place her mother made them leave the door open. They couldn't get up to much on her noisy canopy bed. They drove around a while and ended up at the farm.

There's nobody here, he explained, we can be—

Alone, she said.

By then it was all overgrown. Lilacs were climbing up the clapboards and you could get dizzy from the smell of them.

She looked at him. Do you think he did it?

I'm not sure.

Travis thinks so. So does his father.

You spend too much time with him.

We're just friends. Are you jealous?

Yes.

He remembers how much that admission pleased her.

She was standing there in the foyer, listening attentively, and he pulled her close and kissed her, already ahead of himself and wanting to get her clothes off, but she said, No, wait. I want to go up first. I want to see.

He couldn't stop her. Halfway up she paused, listening to the rain and wind gusting in off the fields. These sounds were familiar to him.

With her delicate fingertips she traced along the wall in the hallway. A minute later she said, It's pink.

It was the daughter's room. They changed everything.

She stepped across the hall and stood at the door of the cursed room.

Don't, he said.

Why not?

I don't want you to.

She nodded. How could somebody—

Nobody knows. Nobody has the answer for that.

People are strange, she said. Scary.

Not everybody. Most people are pretty good, don't you think? He took her hand, watching the shadows on her face.

I know why we're here, she said.

We don't have to.

But she took his hand and led him downstairs, to the room where he'd watched his granddad die. There was a couch in here now, instead of the old man's bed. Slowly, he undressed her. Kiss me, she said, and he eased her back on the cushions and they kissed for a while and then she said, Come on, do it.

Are you sure you want to?

Hurry up, before I change my mind.

They were just getting going when he heard someone upstairs, pacing back and forth across the floor.

Do you hear that? she whispered.

They lay there frozen, clutching each other. Now whoever it was started down the stairs.

He'd never gotten dressed so fast in his life. They ran outside, jumped in his truck and drove off.

And he hadn't been back since.

3

IT'S HER SUSPICIOUS NATURE, she thinks, digging through the closet, that keeps her from getting close to people. Something she picked up from her father, maybe because they'd moved so much. He was overly cautious and critical, nothing ever good enough for his daughter. He'd buy them a house in some new town, rip out the old kitchen and hack up the cabinets, doing everything with the ferocity of a crazy person, only to be dissatisfied with the outcome. Deciding it was hopeless. She'd come home from school and see the sign.

He tried hard, but she knew he wasn't like the other dads. Detached from the regular world. Their quiet dinners, watching *The Cosby Show* while they ate. Hours of homework afterward. Luckily, in the eighth grade, a concerned teacher suggested boarding school and even helped Franny with the application. It's for the best, she told her father once she got in. For both of us.

Drunk, suddenly weary after the long day, she climbs the stairs, half expecting some zombie to wander out. As she passes her mother's door, she does exactly the wrong thing and opens it. Like an actress on a stage, she stands there in a wedge of light, awaiting some dramatic turn. But the room is quiet and dark. Defiant, she flicks the light switch and an ugly overhead fixture floods the room. I just want something to read, she says into the emptiness, crossing the worn Persian rug to the bookcase, where a dozen or so volumes lean and wait. And something else. A large, heart-shaped box like the ones you get on Valentine's Day.

She opens it warily, expecting to find long-decayed chocolates—but instead there are envelopes, five or six of them, stuffed with letters. She closes it back up and brings it with her.

From the doorway she surveys the room once more. A room where a murder occurred, she thinks.

Leaving on the light, she gently closes the door, as if her mother is in bed with a cold, resting.

It's too late to take a shower and the bathroom's too cold anyway. Mary has laid out a towel and a bar of soap, and Franny's touched by the courtesy. She washes quickly, avoiding her reflection, her persistent beauty, and hurries into bed, pulling the covers up to her neck. She props herself up on pillows and angles the lamp. Then she opens the box.

The letters aren't addressed, the envelopes blank, so she assumes they were never read by anyone but their author, who'd written them on lined paper torn sloppily from a spiral notebook.

Exile

Dear Mother—

Greetings from Siberia.

I know I have written to you about this before, but you'll forgive my redundancy. I have no one I can confide in. Remarkably, to no one's surprise but my own, I have no true friends, no trustworthy allies. It has become undeniably clear to me that, in marrying George, I have made a severe error in judgment. I am tired of making excuses for him. I used to think he was maybe overworked or worried about his career. That glum face he puts on. Now I just think he's strange.

I know you have told me to hang on for Franny's benefit, that money will be difficult—that it will be nearly impossible to find anyone to love me with a three-year-old. But I must confess that my emotions outweigh practical reason. I understand your argument, Mother, and know that you have made many compromises in your own marriage, but I am not as strong as you—

October 9, 1978

Dear Mother: A Thank-You Note

Thank you for helping me to keep on my toes about my weight. It is always so good to know where one stands in life. I have tried to cut down my intake of calories. Sometimes I even

feel a little light-headed and have to remind myself to eat something. But it is, of course, all for the best. I know my husband
prefers me this way.

Thank you for teaching me such self-control, such persuasive
endurance.

On another note. I have come to the conclusion that you are
right after all, it's better to be married than divorced. There is still
such a stigma attached, I think, even now. There is one divorced
woman in this little town. I have seen her eating in the café, picking at her salad. It's sad.

Therefore, I must thank you for encouraging me to stay married to George even though he:

   a) has no clue who I am
   b) has no true interest in understanding my needs
   c) has not even an inkling of what I think about or dream
      about
   d) secretly finds me repulsive
   e) hates me even more than I hate myself.

October 21, 1978

Mother,

I made that recipe you sent for the chicken piccata. It came out
rather well. George even mustered a compliment; he is so picky
about my cooking.

October 25, 1978

Dear Mother,

I have been walking a lot. The landscape is at once consum-
ingly bleak and somehow uplifting. I suppose one has a kind of
religious experience when looking at the sky.

October 30, 1978

Dear God,

I'm writing to ask your opinion of ghosts. I believe this house
of ours is haunted—I feel that she is trying to warn me, to tell
me something. Why else would she be hanging around? Is it true
about ghosts? Are they real? If I died, would I

As a Catholic, I do believe there is a place called Heaven ~~and that good people go there to exist somehow in peace.~~

November 1, 1978

Dear Agnes,

I have been reading *Rosemary's Baby*.

In the book—you really must read it—the devil makes love to poor Rosemary and she ends up having his baby. It's fabulously creepy.

For some reason it makes me think of the Virgin Mary.

Anyway, I am really enjoying it.

Mother tells me you are trying to get pregnant. On second thought, you probably shouldn't read the book!

November 4, 1978

Dear Mother,

Thank you for the consoling words the other night. I know these issues are mainly my problem and have little to do with George.

November 9, 1978

Dear Mother,

I have discovered poetry. Last night Justine took me to a poetry reading by Miss Adrienne Rich. She had been married, you see, and then, over time, discovered that she didn't want to be married anymore, and that she was in fact a lesbian. I don't think it is fair to assume that being a lesbian caused the failure of her marriage—obviously it had a great deal to do with it, but I don't think it was the only reason (I can practically hear your thoughts!!). Now, Mother, don't worry about this being my confession of homosexuality—I proclaim I am not a lesbian! But what Miss Rich says in her poetry about women coming into their own lives, their own imperfect bodies, their experiences as free women of strength, about pursuing their own pleasure (can you imagine!)—this is what I want to convey to you. This sense of liberation! There is more to life than a clean kitchen and a well-darned pair of socks. I am throwing out my sewing machine! I am going to dedicate myself to just being myself, not the person I am now, going through the motions, reciting my lines. I am going to wander through my house naked—that's right, naked—without worrying about what George will think of my bumps and swirls, my broad motherly hips, my stretch marks—even the mole on my thigh, a witch's tattoo, you used to call it. No more! I am throwing out my razor. I am simply letting my body do what is natural. I want to stink, Mother; I want to glow with sweat; I want to set my breasts free, enjoy their weight, their swagger. I want to masturbate—that's right, you heard me! I want to touch myself without putting on a show to satisfy my husband's tender ego. I want to push his head between my legs, feel his tongue wedge inside me, tasting my bitter, lovely poison.

November 17, 1978

Dear Mother,

How many times have I wondered what keeps George so late at the college? I have even thought of hiring a private detective. I must tell you, I feel he is betraying me. Today, with Franny in the car, I drove over to the campus. I circled the faculty lot. I didn't see George's car parked anywhere. I must've driven around that campus for an hour looking for his car.

Sometimes I notice the way he smells, a cheap jasmine scent on his clothes.

November 25, 1978

Dear Mother,

As you know we went to his parents' for Thanksgiving. Of course, just having us wasn't enough for them. Some of their friends came over for cocktails. Everything looked very nice—you've seen their house—and she filled her fireplace with poinsettias. She made a pretty good turkey and a ham, too, and it was very beautiful sitting there and looking at the Sound. And Franny was dressed up so cute. That new dress I made for her from the McCall's catalog. Her little Mary Janes.

Anyway, yesterday, when we got back, he went for a run. I was making dinner and discovered I needed some things, so I put Franny in the car and started for town. I had the strangest feeling, ~~like all time was suspended.~~ Then I was driving along the small streets where the townies live—there's a trailer park nearby, and several bars, a neighborhood that you, Mother, would not approve of. And I happened to notice one of those statues of the Virgin Mary—you know how rural people like to put them on their front lawns inside old claw-foot tubs (a tradition I will never quite understand)—and something made me stop, and I got out and went up to one and her paint was all chipping off her blue cloak, but her eyes, there was something about her eyes, and I touched her and I felt something go right through me like a jolt of electricity. . . .

Then, when I was driving by the inn, the long barn where they put their help, I saw him. Standing there with a girl. What? I thought. Is that George? I took my foot off the pedal and slowed down. I could see they were fighting; that was obvious. They stood apart. There was something about her sharp outline that seemed familiar, and she was crying. George was standing there with his arms crossed, the way he does when he's angry, unyielding, defiant. I have seen that look, that punitive stance, and found my sympathy going to the woman, whoever she was. In my case, I would be a fool to think there wasn't something between them. It was unmistakably a lovers' quarrel. My heart buzzed inside my chest, and my legs, my whole body went flimsy, weak. I could hardly hold the wheel. It was all I could do to keep driving.

December 3, 1978

Mother,

I am gearing up to confront him. It is not easy for me, because as you know I'm not a confrontational person. Plus, something happened to my friend Justine, a car accident. We went to visit her and she was just lying there and her husband, well, I've never seen him in such a state. I just couldn't believe it. Then, when it couldn't possibly get any worse, George told me about the girl.

She was just some girl he'd met at the library. Some girl with problems. She got obsessed with him. Nothing happened, he said.

There was nothing going on. She had latched on to him. She was a girl with serious issues.

I suppose these problems occur in most marriages. I am trying to deal with it. Everything seems so much harder without Justine to talk to. She just lies there. I don't know, it's really upsetting.

December 17, 1978

Dear Mrs. Clare,

Please accept this tardy thank you for your lovely Thanksgiving. ~~Unfortunately, the sweet potato marshmallow casserole didn't agree with me, but I'm all right now. I have been fairly consumed with the fact that~~

December 17, 1978

Dear Mrs. Clare,

I am actually writing to give you some good news. It's about those paintings your poor nephew had done before his death. They've been found. Yes, it's true. I happened to attend the Christmas party at your son's place of employment. They had put out a nice spread and plenty of booze and it was fun seeing all the little decorations the secretary had displayed, angels made of Styrofoam, that sort of thing, and glitter everywhere.

I'm sure you don't know, because George is so very modest, that he has a very nice office. While he was busy socializing and drinking too much gin, I went into his office to poke around, and that's when I noticed the paintings. Compelled by their subject matter, I found myself walking toward them, getting up good and close. There were five in all. Five lovely scenes of the seaside on which your son, George Clare, had signed his name.

Your devoted daughter-in-law,
Catherine

January 4, 1979

Dearest Mother,

Happy New Year. I took your suggestion and spoke to the priest. He told me that forgiveness is always the best recourse in a marriage. But I have begun to doubt this solution. I am thinking that the priest has no real knowledge of my personal life, and that it is unjust to generalize. I have begun to suspect that my husband is deeply troubled and quite possibly psychotic.

You see, the person we know as George Clare is just a shell—likable, yes, intelligent, charming. But it's just an illusion, a chimera. Because he keeps his real persona to himself, locked up in some dark, awful place, cut off from the world. I have seen glimpses of that other person when I catch him alone, involved in some menial task—polishing shoes, for instance, one hand thrust inside the shoe, the other tenderly rubbing the leather, preoc-cupied, wistful—dare I say sexual. Or sharpening knives, the intensity in his eyes, checking the blade with his fingertips, that same expression of faraway tenderness.

You see, Mother, we are animals. We know when we are in danger. It isn't something that can be argued or discounted. We know what fear is. We know what it means. It's instinctual. It's real. There is no faking it.

February 2, 1979

Dear Mother,

I had some time to myself and walked alone out into the field. It was cold but sunny. I walked and walked and thought about God and tried to feel Him all around me, watching over me. I felt loved. By Him. Only Him. Not even by you and Father. Certainly not by George. He's my adversary. I can't trust anyone.

Except God. I should have become a nun.

February 16, 1979

Dear Mother,

What good news about Agnes.

If you want the truth about such things I will tell you a story of my own discovery. How I began to feel sick. Sick all the time. And that peculiar heaviness in my belly, prickling around the edges, as if I were stuffed with horsehairs. I went to the doctor and he told me what the problem was. It brought back memories of George in the beginning. How we got stuck with each other in the first place. Why had we? I was weak, insecure. I didn't believe I could do anything. I didn't believe I was good enough. Maybe I believed God had a plan for me. But I see now that's just cowardice. That's just making excuses for wasted time. I don't blame you, Mother. You have always done what you thought was right. But it wasn't right, was it? Not really.

The truth is, it has taken me this long to understand that I am in charge of my own destiny. Not you or Father. Not George. Not Franny. Not even God.

My body is my own. I am making my own plans.

February 22, 1979

Dear Mother,

I have decided to leave him. It is for my own safety. For I have recently made a terrible discovery. One night—the same night our friend Floyd drowned—George came home sopping wet. It was very late, and I heard him in the laundry room. He was standing there naked, holding his shirt, his trousers, his socks, and I could see they were wet, not just a little but dripping wet, drenched, like somebody who had just climbed out of the water. After he went upstairs I went out to look at his car. The seat was soaked through. When I pushed on the cushion, water ran out.

Other strange things have happened, but the worst thing is his distance, his cool dismissal of me. As though he can't stand the sight of me.

I will close this letter with the following advice: if something should happen to me, don't assume it was an accident.

Homeward

I

FIRST THING, he drives over there. He likes this hour best. The sky opening, the early sun.

She stands there with her bloodshot eyes, wearing the same hospital outfit she had on the night before, wrapped in a blanket. What are you doing here? she says.

I gotta fix that overhang.

What?

On the porch.

She shakes her head. Now?

Is it too early?

Uh, yeah—it's, what, seven?

Quarter till. Contractor's hours. He holds up his thermos. I come bearing gifts.

Is that actually coffee? she says a little desperately.

Yes, ma'am. With milk and sugar.

She lets him in and they wander into the kitchen. The house smells damp, dirty. It's the same old kitchen. The same buzzing refrigerator. The same crummy cabinets that never stayed shut. He is stirred by a fresh hatred for this place. If she wasn't here, he might just put a match to it once and for all.

How'd that woodstove do? Still burning?

He checks and sees it burned out. Let me get this going again. He sets down the thermos and opens the stove and tosses in some wood and lights it up. There, he says. That ought to do it.

She's standing there shivering, pale, very beautiful, it's almost too hard to look. He takes off his coat and then his sweater and hands it to her. Put that on. She drops the blanket from her shoulders and pulls the sweater over her head and pushes her scrawny arms into the sleeves. It looks good on you, he says. Then he unscrews the thermos and pours some coffee into the little cup. Drink this.

She does.

He rinses out her old pickle jar and pours himself some coffee. Long night?

Yes, very long.

I had a feeling it might be.

She drinks the coffee. This is good. Thanks.

Should we find a place to sit down?

Let's go in here.

They bring their coffee into the living room and sit on the old busted-up couch and she asks about Wade and he tells her about his brother's injury, IEDs, the VA, the whole story.

It's a terrible war, she says. I wish they'd just end it. I've seen some of these guys. It's really sad.

You work there? University Hospital? I noticed that on your scrubs.

I'm training to be a surgeon there.

You mean you're actually a doctor? Already?

She nods.

Man, that's incredible. You turned out all right, didn't you?

For someone whose mother got murdered?

Yeah, he says, and means it. You were so good at serving tea I was sure you'd be a waitress. You used to make me tea.

Did I? Was it any good?

Kind of watery, to be honest.

What was I like?

Little. And happy, he says, because he knows she needs to hear it.

That's good to know. What about you?

Me? I'm not sure. Me and my brothers, we had it kind of rough. I lost my mother in this house, too. He gives her a short version of the story. We were just trying to get by.

That's so sad. That must have been so hard.

It was. But working for your mom kind of helped me out.

They never found out who killed her, she says. It's still an open case.

He doesn't tell her what a creep her father was. How he'd been tricked into helping with Franny that goddamn day. He'd never spent the money Clare had left for him. For some reason it seemed tainted. He'd dug a hole behind his uncle's house and buried it. It's probably still there. She doesn't know they'd never had enough evidence to charge her father, but not for lack of trying. If they had, he'd still be in jail and he guessed her grandparents would have raised her. It just hadn't worked out like that. He wonders what being raised by Clare must've been like. It couldn't have been good.

Well, sometimes it's better not to know, he says.

She looks at him doubtfully. Oh, it's always best to know, she says. The truth—it's all we have.

THEY DECIDE TO take a walk. Together, silently, as the sun rises full and bright, they go through the field and climb up to the ridge. This was all ours, he tells her, waving his hand like a magician over the land, now cluttered with tract houses lined up around a cul-de-sac. Commuters, he says. Used to be cows.

They walk through the woods under the whining old trees. An old coyote used to live up here, he tells her. I've been here my whole life.

Back in the house he hands her his scrapbook. I dug this thing out for you from the darkest corners of my closet. A small history of an ordinary American boy.

There's nothing ordinary about you, Cole.

He watches her turn the pages, the colors of her past starting to fill in. Is this you?

That's me and my buddy Eugene. We went to Union College together. That there is his grandma. And here's Wade in his uniform. And this is Eddy, my big brother.

Where is he now?

Out in L.A. Plays the trumpet. He's a studio musician. Does movies and stuff. He's done real well for himself.

Is he married?

No. He was in love with this girl once. Back then. I don't think he ever got over it. He's had plenty of girlfriends, but no one like her.

Maybe one day they'll get back together.

Could be. I hope so but wouldn't bet on it.

You never know, do you?

No, you sure don't. He smiles and she smiles back and his whole body goes warm. Is this weird for you?

Sort of. But it's kind of good, too.

I'm glad, he says. I'm glad it's good.

She turns the page and gets quiet and he can see she's found her mother. In the picture, Catherine is lying in the grass in Bermuda shorts, her blouse tied at the waist. She's smiling, looking up at the photographer as if daring him to shoot.

Eddy took that, he says. They had eyes for each other, I think. She was older, though, and married, of course. We all loved your mother. You should know that. She was good to us.

She's beautiful, she says softly. He can hear the longing in her voice.

And so are you. He kisses her then. I couldn't wait anymore.

I wanted you to. She starts to cry.

What's wrong?

I don't know. This is hard, that's all. And I'm just so lonesome.

Hey, now. Let's just put an end to that. He takes her in his arms and holds her close. I'm right here. You don't have to be lonesome anymore.

2

HE DRIVES HER into town for more coffee and tells her about his life in this town, his marriage to a girl he'd grown up with, their daughter. She watches his blue eyes as he talks about his ex-wife and what they had together and she can see the love he still has for the mother of his daughter and it makes her feel a little jealous, a little worried, but she smiles and doesn't show it. Somewhere in the back of her mind she is thinking about love, what it is, its unyielding patience—and the fact that she'd never come so close to finding it.

In his truck he drives her around Chosen, showing her his private landmarks—his uncle's place on Division Street; his old school, where his daughter now goes to kindergarten; the little house where he lived with Patrice.

Finally, he takes her home. That's what he calls it, even though he doesn't live there. At first she sees only acres of pasture, battered fields of corn. He shuts the engine and gets out and comes around to open her door and takes her hand and they walk through the field to where an old house waits.

It's not finished yet, obviously, he says. About a year ago, after Patrice and I called it quits, I moved back into my uncle's place. I bought this piece of land out here a couple years ago, before anybody ever noticed it; it was just too pretty to pass up. The house is kind of small, it's just an old farmhouse, but I'm working on this addition. It should turn out pretty good.

He turns and looks at her with those blue eyes, with a faint expression playing over a face that seems both familiar and new. She can see the boy he was, the man he is now.

It's beautiful here, Cole, she says as the wind blows her hair around. This wind's crazy.

It sweeps right down, doesn't it?

They stand there in the middle of it.

I'm sorry, you're just so beautiful I can't take my eyes off you.

Really?

Yeah, really.

He kisses her long and slow and she smiles, laughs, and they linger there a while, laughing over nothing in the crazy wind.

3

EVEN AT A DISTANCE and without her glasses, Justine knows it's her. She'd heard the farm had sold. Over here, she shouts from the studio doorway.

The girl waves. So uncanny, the resemblance. Watching her solemn approach, her long blue-jeaned legs, the gritty blond hair.

I'm looking for Justine?

You found her. Hello, Franny.

The girl won't smile. She's on a mission and it's not a happy one.

She didn't have many friends, she says.

Well, she had me. I'm so sorry about your mother, honey.

Justine convinces her to come inside her studio for some tea. While the kettle warms, she shows her around. I've been working on these wall hangings. Sort of inspired by Louise Bourgeois. Do you know her?

Of course. My father made me take art history.

I've been experimenting with new dyes.

The girl runs her hand over the soft tapestry. They're beautiful.

The kettle whistles and Justine goes to make the tea. Franny's looking at a photograph of the twins.

They're all grown up now, Justine says, handing her a cup of tea.

Thank you. Where do they live?

They're both in the city. John's a sculptor, and Jesse's a writer like his dad.

I read his book, she says. It was good.

I'll let him know. You could tell him yourself, but he's down in town. He works at the library.

They sit on the couch by the window. It's a windy, bright day and the room's full of sunshine. Justine is glad they're sitting here together. They both need this, she realizes. They both need to talk about Catherine.

You know I taught her how to knit. She was making you a sweater and was so proud of it. We used to take these long walks. She was very beautiful, very kind. You two were rarely apart. She adored you. She took you everywhere.

I don't remember her, she says.

She was a fine person.

The girl shakes her head, angry. Then why is she dead?

I don't know. I can't answer that. Sometimes things just happen.

But the girl can tell she doesn't really believe this. I can't accept that, she says.

No, I can see that. And you shouldn't. Nobody should.

I need to know, she says. I need to know what really happened.

Perhaps it's cruel but she can't resist asking, What did your father tell you?

He never talks about my mother.

Why do you think that is?

She shrugs. They didn't love each other.

Maybe so. But that's not what killed her.

What did, then?

Justine shakes her head. I wish I knew. She doesn't mention the accident, or how she suspected—without ever knowing—that it was Franny's father who'd driven her off the road. She doesn't mention the three surgeries it took to get her legs right. She doesn't ask how George is or how his life turned out, because she simply doesn't care. And she wonders if Franny thinks that's strange, impolite. But Franny doesn't bring him up, either. And perhaps their tacit avoidance of the subject is all she needs to know.

I live up in Syracuse, Franny says when Justine asks. Basically, I've been in school my whole life. And now I'm studying to be a surgeon. She talks about how hard her residency is. How the whole time, all through her training, she's been trying to prove something.

That you're smart? Justine asks.

No. I always knew I was. She looks at her with her big eyes as she struggles to get the words out. It's to prove I'm not guilty.

Because you were there?

She nods. And now the tears come.

He wouldn't let me talk about it. And I wanted to so bad. She cries full-out and Justine feels a renewed hatred for George. I wanted that so bad.

Justine takes her into her arms. It's all right, she says. It's all right. You've got nothing to feel guilty about. She holds her for a long time.

When they finally break apart, Justine tells her, Your mother adored you, Franny. She'd be so proud of you now, of what you're doing.

Thank you for saying that, she says, and clearly wants to believe it.

They both lean back into the cushions, exhausted, resolved.

You know, Justine says, she's probably looking down on us right now, happy that we're here together.

They both crank their necks, looking up at the ceiling.

Should we wave?

Franny smiles for the first time.

Hi, Catherine! I'm sitting here with your beautiful daughter.

Hi, Mom, how are things up there in heaven?

They stay like that, with their heads bent back, looking up for something; looking for nothing. Suddenly the wind seems to whirl through the room. The chandelier tinkles and the dry, leftover leaves outside smack against the windows like the hands of somebody trying to get in.

The Shadow of Death

SHE CALLS UP out of the blue. For a few minutes they talk about the house, the progress she's made cleaning it out.

The closing's in two days, she tells him. We'll be ready.

That's good news, Franny. In fact, it's a great relief.

I found some letters of Mom's, she says.

Did you? He wasn't aware of any.

They weren't very nice. She said things about you.

Well, that hardly surprises me. Franny, you know your mother had issues with depression.

Yes, so you've told me.

He sighs. Look, let's not do this.

Dad, I want to know.

Let's not talk about this over the phone.

She hated it there.

I know, he admits.

In Siberia, she says. That's what she called it.

Yes, I suppose it was. Being so isolated was hard. It was hard for us both.

She wasn't happy, she blurts. She was miserable with you, Dad.

He doesn't respond; he can't seem to. Then he says, I tried to make her happy, Franny. I tried very hard.

Well.

What, you don't believe me? I tried everything for that woman.

You never talked about her. Why is that?

I don't know. I was afraid.

Afraid?

I thought it might make you miss her even more.

That's not why, she says.

Well, then, I guess I don't have an answer for you.

Look, she says. I need you to know something. I won't be calling again.

What's that?

I can't forgive you. I don't forgive you.

Franny, let's not—

I don't forgive you, Dad! Do you understand that?

He can't answer. He just can't. He waits, listening. Vaguely, he can hear the room she's in, the chirp of birds.

I'm sorry. I have to go now.

Franny—

Goodbye, Dad.

He holds the receiver in his hand as the dial tone sounds. There are other sounds, too—the squeaking wheels of the mail cart as it approaches, the residents in the main room laughing at something on TV, then someone knocking on his door.

Come in, he says.

It's Rodney, the attendant who brings the mail.

Hey, Mr. Clare, you got something here. Must be important.

What is it?

It's a certified letter. You have to sign for it.

Who's it from?

Says here it's the Albany County District Attorney.

Give it here, he says, grabbing the large envelope and running his fingertips all along the edges. He can faintly make out its brown color. Rodney gives him the pen and he signs the slip, unable to control his shaking hand.

You sure you don't want me to read it to you?

For Christ's sake, Rodney, I'm not a fucking invalid!

All right, Mr. Clare. Just tryin' to be helpful.

Well, I don't need any help. Thank you.

He waits for the attendant to leave the room and push his noisy cart down the corridor, then opens the envelope and slides the letter out.

It's just a blur of print. He fishes his magnifying glass out of the drawer and moves it around over the letter, ascertaining only bits and pieces—*to make you aware . . . dramatic new evidence . . . new investigation . . . the murder of Catherine Clare.*

At the bottom there's a salutation.

Yours truly,

Willis B. Howell, District Attorney

Willis, he thinks with genuine pity, touched that after all these years he's still on her mind.

ON THE FIRST of November they predict freezing rain, high winds. He calls the front desk for a cab and tells the operator he's seeing his endocrinologist.

An hour later, they come to get him. Your cab's here, Mr. Clare.

Diabetic retinopathy is the official name, but to him it's just dirty sight. Reading is very difficult and he will soon be blind, the result of abnormal blood vessels, like jellyfish, swarming his eyes. No matter, he thinks, he has his cane, his reliable mate. Despite the weather, he's wearing summer-weight clothes under an unlined raincoat. His old Top-Siders. On the arm of his nurse, he walks out into the large lobby. He's been here for almost a year—too long for any sane person to endure. In the beginning his daughter had visited him, but she has her own life to worry about now. She doesn't need her old man burdening her.

It hurt that she didn't call to give him the news, that he had to learn about his daughter's wedding from the *Hartford Courant.* It seems incredibly ironic to him, and not a little disturbing, that her name is now Frances Hale. But the truth is, he'd always liked Cole. For the better part of a week he'd sat in his chair trying to think of what to send to her. Something nice, something useful. He went through the catalogues they put out in the main room, pictures of appliances and monogrammed towels and plates and so forth. But it all just felt wrong. In the end, he sent nothing.

She'd have plenty of money once he's gone, he figured. She could buy whatever she wanted. The thought brings him a little comfort. They'd tried to be close; they had tried very hard. Ultimately, he'd failed in that department. He had failed miserably.

The cab is waiting for him in the circle. Lisa, his favorite nurse, helps

him out to the car. She's a pretty girl, engaged to one of the doctors, a ger-
ontologist, and he often thinks of his daughter, the surgeon, involved in
such a life—his pride is almost too much to bear.

'Morning, he says to the driver, getting into the back. The cab smells
of pineapple and some sort of hair oil. All the cabbies are Jamaican these
days.

Medical Arts? he asks in his thick accent.

George takes the cash he has set aside from his pocket, bundled in a
rubber band, and drops it over the seat.

The man holds it up. What this about?

Change of plans, he says, and gives him the address. That is, if you're
not too busy. It's kind of a long drive.

No, I take you. No problem.

The driver heads down Farmington Avenue and gets onto the highway, heading south. George doesn't mind the forty-minute drive to the
shore. The towns they pass are familiar to him, Middletown, Killing-
worth, Clinton. The towns of his youth, he thinks solemnly, with all their
pathetic drama. They ride along the water and he puts his window down,
letting in the cold sea air.

They arrive at the marina in Westbrook, at the Singing Bridge. With
the season over and done with, the place is desolate. He has the cabbie
pull down to the docks. DeBeers's boat is waiting for him. His old friend.

Whatchu doing here, man? the driver asks, staring at the closed-up
office, the empty parking lot. You shouldn't be out here on a day like today.

I'm all right.

You want me to wait?

No, I've made other arrangements, he says. I'm meeting someone, a
fellow named Swedenborg.

The driver shakes his head. You crazy, man. Well—you take care.

He waits for the cab to pull away.

Using his cane, he shuffles slowly down to his slip at the very end. For
years now he's maintained this boat, paying to have it stored for winter
and launched in the spring, and he told them to pull it out next week.
Well, that won't be necessary now.

It's been a long time, he says to the boat as he carefully steps on board.
He doesn't waste any time getting sentimental and gets busy rigging the
sails, mostly by feel. Something he could do in his sleep. He starts the

motor and sets out into the channel. He has just enough vision to decipher shapes, the banners of gritty light along the shore. At this time of year there's no one out here. The tide is high, the wind cold, fast. The clouds dense and low, promising rain. He can smell it on the wind, the torrent that will come. It pulls the ocean in all directions, like an anxious woman.

He motors along until, in deep water, he cuts the engine and raises his sails, the wind now roaring in his ears. The wind is various, wild. It makes him want to shout. He knows he should reef the main, but there doesn't seem much point.

He sets off, pulls in the sails. The line is taut in his hand, blisters forming on his palm.

After a while it is dark. On the empty ocean, he is alone. You don't need a plan for this sort of thing, he reflects. No maps, no compass. He doesn't even need his sight. He opens the good bottle of whiskey he's been saving for the occasion and takes a long drink. He drinks and drinks, wanting to lose himself, wanting to be very lost indeed.

He stands with his arms stretched out as if he's waiting for God. Water swells under the hull, levitating him for the briefest of moments. The bow slams down like a whale, smashing against the rolling surface. He drops his line and staggers to retrieve it, but now the boom smacks him on the head and he falls. What he feels is love. Love like a warm flood.

It begins to rain. Cold, fat drops on his face.

It won't be long now, he thinks. He hopes it will at least be brutal. And then it will end, somehow. It will end.

Acknowledgments

It was a lucky day indeed—and I mean *really* lucky—when the stars lined up just right as Gary Fisketjon was reading the manuscript of this book, and every single day since I have thanked the writer-Gods above for this stroke of wizardry. I am deeply grateful to him for his extraordinary editing of this book and for helping to renew my faith in my own work. Enormous thanks also to the outstanding team at Knopf who had a hand in bringing this book to fruition, including Ruthie Reisner, Lydia Buechler, Anne Zaroff-Evans, Cassandra Pappas, and Claire Bradley Ong.

Another stroke of luck brought me to the Clark Art Institute one afternoon where, just by chance, a woman named Adrienne Baxter Bell happened to be lecturing on none other than George Inness. Of course I had already bought and read her marvelous book, *George Inness and the Visionary Landscape,* but hearing her speak about the artist and his rather unique obsession with Emanuel Swedenborg helped me to better understand the direction of the novel.

Other excellent and indispensable references I depended on include: *George Inness and the Science of Landscape,* by Rachael Ziady DeLue; *Different Views in Hudson River School Painting,* by Judith Hansen O'Toole; *American Paradise: The World of the Hudson River School,* from the Metropolitan Museum of Art; *Conserving the Painted Past: Developing Approaches to Wall Painting Conservation,* edited by Robert Gowing and Adrian Heritage; *Kant on Swedenborg: Dreams of a Spirit-Seer and Other Writings,* edited by Gregory R. Johnson; *Journal of Dreams,* by Emanuel Swedenborg; *Heaven and Hell*, by Emanuel Swedenborg; *The Varieties of Religious Experience: A Study in Human Nature*, by William James; and *Emanuel Swedenborg: The Universal Human and Soul-Body Interaction*, edited by John Farina.

I want to thank my agent, Linda Chester, for staying the course with me these past twenty years and for always being there as a friend and advocate—for getting back to me in record speed, especially when it's about new pages, and for always knowing just what to say to inspire me to make them better. I could not do this work without her. I want to thank Gary Jaffe for just about everything he does and how brilliantly he does it.

My good friends who are also realtors were of great help in so many ways and include: Don Moore, Beth Pine, Nancy Roth and especially Sue Baum, for taking me to a very special farm that she knew I had no intention of buying and which provided me with just the right insight and family history to get started, and to the great cows of Cook Farm in Hadley, Massachusetts, who were always outspoken about their lives and contributed greatly to my necessary, source-material-getting ice-cream breaks, and to the milk guys at Meadowbrook Farm in Clarksville, New York, for answering my questions as they hustled to deliver our milk.

I want to thank our neighbors Jake and Arlene Herzog, Jake Herzog, Jr., Angelo and Claire Dounoucos, Kurt and Joyce Anderson, Janet Breeze, and John Breeze for their wonderful stories about our little town and the residents who have occupied our house for two centuries, many of whom, in spirit, helped to shape this book. Many thanks, too, to Jill Silverstein, sailor Mike Donovan and coyote expert Joseph Cea.

Finally, I want to thank my family: my husband, Scott, for his inexhaustible work ethic and inspiring determination that keeps everyone else going; our kids, Hannah, Sophie and Sam, for their original ideas, creativity and astoundingly practical advice; and Daisy, for insisting on long walks that always lead to some unpredictable discovery. And to my amazing parents for their devotion, encouragement and unrelenting support. I couldn't have done this without you.